Hidden Faces

ANNE E THOMPSON

The Cobweb Press

Published by The Cobweb Press
www.thecobwebpress.com
thecobwebpress@gmail.com

A CIP catalogue record for this book is available
from the British Library

ISBN 978-0-9954632-0-2

Cover design and typeset by Geoff Fisher
geoff.fisher@yahoo.co.uk

Printed and bound in Great Britain by CPI Group (UK) CR0 4YY

For Bob Beffins

The face that I present to the world,
Differs
From the face the world doth see, which
Differs
From the face I feel within myself, which
Differs
From the face that's truly me.

Chapter One

CYNTHIA Mott was late. She slotted her key into the solid front door and pushed it open, stepped into the front room, brushed her feet on the mat and hurried under the low beam into her kitchen. She dumped her bag in the corner, keys on top of the fridge and bent to retrieve her forgotten lunch.

There was a thump. She froze, all her attention focused on listening. It came again. A dull, low thump. Wood on wood. It came from the cottage garden, which should have been empty.

She glanced at the clock, irritable, there was no time for this, had not really been time to even collect her sandwiches. Another thump. That decided her. She dropped the lunch box into her bag, kicked off her shoes, struggled into the wellingtons by the back door and marched across the lawn.

The grass was still frozen, glistening from the hard frost which had hardened the sprinkling of snow into icy tufts. She crunched as she walked, hurrying towards the shed. The door should have been fastened but a slight breeze was blowing, stirring it. It swung open, paused for a moment as though holding its breath, then thumped shut. As she approached, Cynthia could see the outline of a man through the cobwebbed window. She frowned, began composing caustic sentences, flung open the shed door. She too paused, held her breath.

He was dead. There could be no doubt about that. His face, already tinged with blue, had one eye open, gazing sightlessly at the ceiling. He sat on her abandoned rocking chair in the corner, trousers stained and mouth drooping. His grey hair poked thinly from beneath a brown cap and his feet, strangely angled, were clad in muddy boots. There was a newspaper on the floor, she supposed it had fallen when he drifted from consciousness.

Suddenly suffused with anger, Cynthia glanced once more at her watch. 12:40. The tension rose within her like an icy bubble, overwhelming her ability to think.

'I do not have time for this,' she announced, 'not today.'

Decisively she reached out, shut the door, fastened it with a large bolt. She turned and hurried back to the cottage, slipped back into her sensible low heeled shoes, retrieved her bag and slammed the front door behind her.

***

The road was slippery as Cynthia joined the long line of cars edging their way into town. It was a week before Christmas and lights hung from trees that swayed tiredly in the breeze. The lights did not appear to have any shape at all and one felt they had been sneezed across the branches rather than designed. Shoppers hurried from rare parking spaces, ever aware of the nearing deadline, carrying immense lists, failing to look jolly. Chewing her lunch as she drove, Cynthia avoided careless pedestrians as she navigated the High Street. Marksbridge was a small market town built alongside the river. It had a collection of small shops clustered along a single road with facades dating back to the 1800s. One of the large supermarket chains had recently arrived on former scrub land at the bottom of the High Street but other than that it seemed that the outside world had failed to notice the town.

The school was on a car lined side road leading from the top of the High Street. As she navigated the parked vehicles, she hoped her parking space would be free. It was not, of course, it was that kind of a day. A large black Land Rover now filled the space she had vacated less than an hour earlier. She supposed it belonged to dinner staff and she reversed back onto the crowded lane.

By the time Cynthia had parked and hurried back to the school, the bell was ringing for the end of playtime. She entered the school via a side door in an attempt to not be seen by Mr Carter, the caretaker. She had neither time nor energy for a conversation. Hoping there had been no changes to the afternoon's schedule, she rushed to her classroom and struggled out of her coat before the first child appeared at the door.

Everything about Miss Mott was round. The autumn months had not been good for her figure and were she the kind of woman who paid attention to such things she would have been disappointed by its size. Instead, when dressing that morning she had pulled her cardigan down as far as it would go in the hope of disguise and thought no more about it. She now sat solidly on her chair and opened the register.

The children crowded into the classroom in an excited rush. Their pink faces looked expectantly at her as they jostled for space on the worn carpet. Some sidled as close to her legs as they dared and one put out a tentative finger to touch her shoe. She waited until they were still and then began to read their names, marking who was present. It was an unnecessary activity in her eyes, as no one would have left since the morning registration but it did provide a chance for the children to settle after screaming around the playground and she valued calm very highly. The boys' names were always printed first in the register but Miss Mott read the girls' names first. It seemed illogical to her to reinforce the boys' natural inclination towards dominance.

When two children had been dispatched to the office with the completed register, Miss Mott explained the afternoon's activities. Her voice, low, calm, slow, gave directions clearly. She explained that the children would change into their costumes, wait quietly with a book until they were called to the hall. Everything would be calm, sensible, controlled. Her tone and manner did not allow for anything else. The children watched, listening carefully, keen to please. June Fuller, the classroom assistant hovered near the back, sorting costumes, waiting for her instructions to begin.

Miss Mott looked at the children's faces. They were full of barely contained excitement, all eyes watching her attentively. She felt suddenly tired. She had seen so many Christmases now, they all seemed the same. She knew that each parent would only really watch their own child, the only thing that mattered was that their precious son or daughter was given the opportunity to shine, even if only for a minute. They had been practising the songs since September and Miss Mott was thoroughly sick of them. Their cheerful tunes grated on her nerves and the easily sung but rather puerile words made her slightly nauseated.

The children began to change into their nativity costumes. Miss Mott moved around the classroom fastening hooks, positioning headdresses. Her thoughts wandered back to her shed.

'That wretched man,' she thought, 'why did he have to die today?' His name was Clarence James and he had worked in her garden since she had moved into the property ten years ago. She had told him repeatedly that he should retire but he had stubbornly refused and now this had happened. She knelt to help Tommy tie his shoe lace. She could hear June asking Mandy which outfit belonged to her. Much as she disliked the annual nativity performance, it demanded her full attention and she would think about the Mr James problem later.

***

The children were all ready and seated quietly when the message arrived that they could walk to the hall. Miss Mott led her class slowly to the space allocated to them and indicated that they should sit. She found her reserved seat behind them. She lifted her glasses from their chain around her neck and looked around. The parents were all seated on blue plastic seats which had been designed for infants. They were much too small to be comfortable and had been squashed together in an attempt to fit as many parents as possible into the school hall. Now they sat, perched uncomfortably, touching shoulders with people on either side. Some of them looked rather red faced and sweaty as they wore winter coats and the hall was hot.

'They were told,' thought Miss Mott, 'to kindly leave their coats in their cars.' She sighed, they never listened.

Andrew Smyth and Cherry Class had not yet arrived. This was intensely irritating. There was a lot about Mr Smyth that Cynthia found irritating. He was the newly qualified teacher and she was his mentor. It was not a role she enjoyed. He didn't seem to value neatness or record keeping. Nor did he seem capable of keeping his classes calm and disciplined, which surely was the most important role for a teacher.

Cynthia had known it was going to be difficult when he first showed her his plans for his history lessons. He had decided they were going to focus on the burnings of martyrs during the reign of Henry VIII. He had enthusiastic plans for a large wall display with tissue paper flames and showers of gold stars, showing how packets of gun powder, tied to the martyr's necks, had exploded their heads. It would have been a visual feast and would no doubt have scarred Cherry Class for life.

Now he was late for the nativity performance. It had been agreed that her class would arrive last, so that the youngest children would have less time to sit before the play began. Mr Smyth taught Year One, so he should have been waiting. Cynthia heard a noise at the door and turned. Cherry Class stumbled into the hall. Some were not properly dressed and had their costumes draped across their shoulders where they had neglected to fasten the back. Behind them was Mr Smyth. He entered the hall smiling widely, with his shirt untucked at the back. He led his shambolic class to their assigned seating area, tripping over a mother's legs on his way to his own chair.

Esther Pritchard raised both her hands and eyebrows, then began to play the opening notes on the piano while the children scrambled to their feet. They were mostly all standing in time for the first word. The nativity play had begun.

Miss Mott faced the children, mouthing the words with an exaggerated smile in the hope they would copy her expression. Most of them were looking at the floor of course, or scouring the audience for their parents. Nigel Stott stopped singing to nudge the child next to him, pointing out his mother, who waved back at him.

'Silly woman,' thought Miss Mott. She glared at Nigel, who turned red under her gaze, straightened his back and tried to sing with the rest of his class. He joined in loudly but singing the wrong verse. The boy next to him giggled until he too caught Miss Mott's eye.

She looked at the children.

Angel Gabriel was being glared at by Mary, who had a red mark on one arm. Cynthia guessed there had been an argument. It looked as if Mary had been crying and she kept rubbing her arm as though to make a point. Angel Gabriel was grinning triumphantly.

Joseph's headdress was too large and kept slipping over his eyes. Rather than push it back, he was tilting his head backwards and peering at the audience from under its rim.

One of the shepherds had a cold and no handkerchief. Every time his nose ran, he surreptitiously picked up the fluffy toy lamb, wiped his nose on it, lowered it again. The fluff tickled his nose and nearly made him sneeze. Miss Mott frowned her disapproval and he slowly, slowly, inch by inch, placed the lamb back on the floor.

One of the kings had been ill all week but had returned to school so he didn't miss the play. He looked decidedly green. Cynthia wondered at the logic behind sending an obviously ill child into school. He was sadly uncomfortable. Her only hope was that all the other children would catch it during the holidays and not have to miss school. It was always tiresome to have children absent when you were attempting to teach.

Unbidden, a thought occurred to Cynthia. She had fastened the bolt on the garden shed. From the outside. Should anyone find the unfortunate gardener, it would be obvious that he had been found previously. She felt dread, like cold fingers through her stomach.

Was ignoring a body a criminal act? Could she be put in prison? Would there be a court case? It now was hard to concentrate on the play. The song was finished and the children were shuffling to sit back in their places. The Year Two narrators were standing to attention, waiting for Esther Pritchard to nod and signal they should start reading. Cynthia was feeling sick. She was unsure of her options. She could not leave the school hall before the end of the play, that would cause untold fuss. Neither could she escape before the end of the school day, she needed to oversee the changing of the children and the safe stowing of the costumes.

A small girl crawled towards her and tugged her skirt.

'I need to go to the toilet,' she whispered loudly.

'Can you wait? We did all go to the toilet before we came in,' she reminded her. The child nodded uncertainly and crawled back to her place, stepping on fingers as she went, receiving scowls and dark sighs. The children glanced at Miss Mott to ensure that she had noticed.

Cynthia decided there was nothing she could do at that moment and forced herself to focus on the play. She looked around the hall. Esther Pritchard was avidly following the script from her piano seat. Everything about Esther Pritchard was avid. Her fair hair refused to sit neatly and sprung around her face like a wiry bird's nest. Her eyes bulged slightly and her mouth was always smiling. She was one of those nice people who Miss Mott found thoroughly irritating. She never swore, never gossiped and always spoke softly. She was married to the minister of the local chapel and this also irritated Cynthia. She should not be earning money and having a separate career. Cynthia was well qualified in this area as her own father had been a vicar.

Next she looked at Jane Lancaster. She was the head teacher and had worn a suit for the occasion. She had not introduced the play, such a shame. Cynthia hoped she would give a short speech at the end. Standards needed to be upheld. Jane Lancaster was a naturally shy person and whilst she was competent when making policy decisions and organising the curriculum, she did tend to avoid confrontation and disliked public speaking. Cynthia considered this to be a failing.

The children were again struggling to stand as the piano played the introduction to the donkey song. They were sitting in much too small a space and it was almost impossible for them to avoid stepping on each other. The donkey set off for his walk around the audience, followed by Mary and Joseph. Mary had thankfully stopped rubbing her arm and was now concentrating on not stepping on her long blue gown.

The chairs for the parents had been arranged with small aisles along each side and along the back, so the children could walk around the entire audience. This was a new idea, introduced for the first time this year. Cynthia was not at all sure that it was a good one.

She noticed that the donkey was walking much too fast, the threesome were meant to walk for the entirety of the song, they would be finished before the end of the first verse. Parents sitting next to the aisle shuffled even closer together to make room for them, their chairs scraping on the wooden floor.

Without warning, Mary stopped. She had seen her mother. Triumphantly she rolled up her sleeve to reveal red fingermarks.

'Timmy Beal slapped me,' she stated in a loud voice. 'It's because I told him that angels are really girls. They are, aren't they?'

The piano continued playing but very few children were singing. They were straining to see what would happen next. This was interesting, not something they had rehearsed in their daily practice. Parents sitting at the front of the hall turned around to watch, some of the children stood on tip toe to try and see what was happening.

Miss Mott rose from her seat and turned towards the indignant Mary.

'Carry on, Belinda,' she said, in a voice that expected to be obeyed, 'we can discuss this later.'

The child obediently continued walking, Joseph trailing behind, the donkey giggling uncontrollably in the lead. The rest of the school continued singing, some of them giggling to copy the donkey, some looking upset because they knew their play had been spoilt. Jane Lancaster looked ready to burst with anger; Esther Pritchard continued to look peaceful. Andrew Smyth was clearly having trouble containing his own laughter and was pretending to blow his nose.

There was some whispering when the children sat again and Miss Mott raised her eyebrows in warning. They settled down and the play continued.

Joseph knocked on brightly coloured doors which wobbled alarmingly. They had been made from large cardboard boxes which had been flattened and painted. No one knew what doors looked like in the New Testament era, so they closely resembled the children's own front doors, complete with numbers and letter boxes. Excited innkeepers informed them there was no room, prompted by their wives, who knew the script and wanted to share the lines. The last one obligingly offered the couple his stable and they followed him to a different corner of the hall where a manger stood waiting. The school shuffled round to see.

All the angels clustered around the couple, hiding them from view and singing the angel song. It was meant to be sung by only the angels but some of the school forgot and joined in. There was then lots of nudging and loud shushing as they were reminded to be quiet.

As the angels moved away, the parents glimpsed Joseph throwing a doll, head first, into the manger. Some of them sniggered, which Cynthia thought was rather rude of them. Then the angels walked across to the area that was meant to be a hillside. They walked slowly in their unfamiliar clothing, keeping their heads upright so their halos remained steady.

As Gabriel approached, Mary saw her chance for revenge. Waiting until he was level with her, she stuck out a black plimsolled foot. It caught his leg and he tripped, sprawling on the floor, pink legs sticking out from his tunic. He banged his head on the manger, a loud crack, everyone heard it. Blood gushed from his forehead. He lay very still.

'You've killed him,' stated Joseph, impressed.

Jimmy Brown started to cry.

After a second, Tommy Beale aka Gabriel opened his mouth and roared. He sat up, blood on his hands and costume, running down his face and dripping onto the floor. His mother rushed forwards and scooped him into her arms. Belinda's mother also stood, ready to do battle if necessary.

Jane Lancaster rose to her feet. She smoothed down the skirt of her suit and cleared her throat, uncertain as to what she should say. Miss Mott stood and took control.

'Mrs Beale, if you could please escort Tommy to the office we can ascertain if he needs medical attention. Perhaps you could apply some pressure to the wound, do you have a handkerchief?'

Mrs Beale looked about to argue, then changed her mind when she met Miss Mott's gaze.

'Could the remaining angels please stand in your place ready to sing to the shepherds,' she continued. The children obeyed, happy that someone was taking charge. 'Lucy, do you remember Gabriel's words? You do? Well done. Could you be very sensible please and say them, then we can carry on with the play.'

The play continued. All went smoothly until the last song. The entire school was standing, the hall was very hot and Cynthia noticed Sally Marks swaying in the second row. She was very pale and looked rather unsteady. Silently, Cynthia rushed forwards and caught her as she fell. Without stopping, she whisked her past the parents and out into the fresh air. She laid her on her side on a bench and within seconds the child had stirred and was trying to sit. Her anxious mother appeared at Cynthia's side.

'One of them always faints,' said Cynthia, 'make her lie down for a little while then take her home to rest. Please inform the office on your way out.'

She turned towards the hall. The doors were open and the first class was emerging. There had not been time for any sort of speech, Mrs Lancaster had said nothing. Cynthia sighed and went to collect her class from behind the wriggling mass that was Cherry Class.

***

Andrew Smyth followed his class to their classroom. The children were almost running and began pushing to be first through the door. He entered the room, amazed at how quickly they could fill a space with noise and mess.

'Quiet!' he shouted. For a moment there was silence, then gradually the noise began again, quietly at first, quickly growing to the same level as when he had entered the room.

His teaching assistant was already there, helping the children to change. She was called Maddy Brown. 'Mad Brown Cow' is what Andrew called her in private, in the pub with his mates. She was a nice enough woman, old enough to be his mother and sometimes she treated him more like a forgetful child than the teacher, not that he minded.

He flung himself into the chair beside his desk and slumped against the armrests. He was tall, with a mass of sandy hair and eyes that twinkled when he smiled. He was slightly too thin, but with good shoulders and a confidence that girls seemed to like.

'Well,' he said, 'I think that went pretty well. We certainly gave them a show.'

Maddy Brown came across to ask him where he wanted the costumes to be put.

'Let's just heap them on that table,' he said. 'We can sort them out later, when the kids have gone.'

'Do you think it might be better to put them straight onto their hangers?' suggested his assistant. 'It will be difficult to remember who wore what, and when we put them away in the costumes cupboard they all need to be labelled and back on their hangers, ready for next year.'

'Oh, okay,' he smiled. He did not really care. He was hoping that he wouldn't be there next year.

Andrew Smyth was a teacher by default. His passion at school had been history. He was good at remembering dates, could argue causes and evidence and had loved the stories that explained why and how things had developed. Unfortunately he had loved socialising and having a laugh even more. His exam results were nowhere near good enough to read history at university and he looked destined to join his father in the corner shop, stacking cans all day and being polite to people who dropped litter and tried to steal bars of chocolate.

A careers teacher at school had taken him to one side and suggested he try to get a place on a teacher training course. Andrew had regularly helped out with the boys' local football club and that would help his application and one of the minor universities, one that formerly had been a polytechnic, was sure to take him. They would take into account his working class background and the school would give him a good reference. He just had to perform well in the interview and that would not be a problem, he was an excellent public speaker and enjoyed an audience. His father was keen to have 'someone in the family who went to university' and Andrew decided it would be a good way to avoid shop work, so he applied. He had hoped to teach history but was told that he stood a better chance in primary education. The government was trying to encourage more men to teach the younger years, he was more likely to get a place.

That had been four short years ago. He had attended university, made friends with the sports teachers and endured regular teaching practices in a variety of schools. His grades were not great but they were good enough to graduate with a middling degree and, as promised, being male was definitely a bonus when it came to applying for jobs. He had survived one term at the school and was very much hoping to leave in September. He found Miss Mott, his mentor, to be a stressed and pernickety woman. She gave a whole new meaning to the word 'pedantic'. Nothing that he did was right, from his wall displays to how his class sat in assembly.

The trouble was, he just did not care. He liked the children, enjoyed chatting to them and making them laugh. He liked being a mini celebrity in their eyes, the centre of attention in the playground. He just couldn't bring himself to care if they ran in the corridor or knelt up on the carpet or (worse sin of all) played around in the toilets when they should have been outside on a freezing playground.

He watched them now as they struggled out of their costumes.

They were all talking loudly, laughing about 'the fight' and saying whether or not their parents had been there. Maddy approached him with a stack of reading books.

'Do you want to hear readers while I help them change?'

He took the books and read the name from the first card. Billy came across, wearing vest and pants and sat on the small chair next to him. Maddy draped a grey sweatshirt around his shoulders to keep him warm as he opened his reading book and started to read. He knew the story by heart and could say the words without looking. Andrew was not looking either, so sometimes what the child said did not match the words on the page, but neither of them noticed. He got to the last page and paused.

'Can I have a new book now?' he asked hopefully.

'Not today,' said Andrew. 'I think we need to read it once more, to be sure you really know those words.' The new books were stored in a cupboard in the corridor. He didn't want to have to spend time looking for the next book. Not today. Today had been enough work already. He just wanted to get them all dressed and hand them back to their parents so he could leave for the day.

He called the next name and sent the disappointed Billy back to continue getting dressed. The boy meandered back to his place. He stepped over newspaper that was spilling from a bin in the corner, trailed his fingers through a tub of Lego bricks and walked past a display board where paintings drooped from their pins. They had all painted Christmas gifts and cut them out, and they had been stapled under a large paper tree. The paper had started to curl in the warm classroom, some of the shiny stars they used were now on the floor. Billy could see his picture, where it was pinned, near to the corner of the board. Mr Smyth had written 'Lots of Christmas Presents' in large paper letters and Billy's painting was partially under the last 's'. He thought they would probably be allowed to take them home on Friday. Usually the walls were cleared before the holidays. He hoped someone had told Mr Smyth. Sometimes he forgot things like that.

Maddy Brown carried six laden hangers to the rack in the corner. She noticed a heap of props, the treasures carried by the kings, abandoned on the painting rack. They belonged in Miss Mott's classroom, so Maddy scooped them up and went over to Andrew.

'I think I'll take these over to Oak Class now,' she told him. 'It's not worth risking them being spoiled or lost. It would be annoying if at home time someone put one in their bag "by mistake". Can you manage for a minute?'

Andrew nodded, lost in a daydream while Lucy stammered over words in her book. Maddy watched them for a moment then decided not to comment and walked to Oak Class.

As she walked along the corridor she could hear various levels of noise drifting from the open classroom doors. Cherry Class was by far the loudest. Had she not just departed, she would have assumed the children had been left unsupervised. The volume of Pear Class was audible but subdued. Esther Pritchard allowed Year Two some freedom but kept the noise below a certain level.

Maddy nearly collided with a small boy solemnly carrying a book in both hands as he left his classroom.

'I finished my book,' he said proudly, walking towards the book cupboard to collect the next one.

Maddy watched him walk. One plimsoll was only partially on and he was squashing the back as he lopped along the corridor. He gazed at the walls as he walked, absorbing the nativity scene collages and the paper chains that had been strewn across the ceiling.

She turned back to the open door of Oak Class and knocked politely as she entered the quiet room, looking for Cynthia Mott, cautiously, as though she might be told off like a child. She respected Miss Mott's teaching experience but she was not an individual who was easy to like.

The class was in near silence. Most children were already dressed in their grey sweatshirts and navy trousers or skirts. June Fuller was kneeling in one corner, helping a girl with her tights. She was trying not to grimace as her hand made contact with the clammy foot speckled with grains of sand. She hastily pulled up the sweaty tights and smiled at Maddy.

The class sat at their tables, costumes heaped in mounds in front of them, books in hands, mouths closed. Cynthia was carefully hanging the costumes one at a time, while her gaze constantly swept the room, ready to pounce should she spy the beginnings of an illicit conversation. Outwardly calm, only a small frown belied the tension within. She nodded at Maddy.

'Ah, Mrs Brown, are those the kings' treasures? Lovely, I was hoping that someone responsible would take care of them. Could you kindly place them on my desk and I will put them away later. Thank you.

'Uh, Judith, I do not believe anyone asked you to move from your seat. Sit down and read your book. When you have finished you can put up your hand.

'Tommy, stop wriggling. If you need to go to the toilet go at once.' The nervous Tommy sighed with relief and pushed past Mrs Brown on his urgent visit to the toilets.

'And do not run!' he heard as he rushed full speed along the corridor, unsure if he would get there in time.

Maddy followed his departing back along the corridor. She smiled at his panic and wondered why boys always left toilet trips to the very last minute.

Cynthia Mott continued sorting the costumes, hanging them tidily. Her mind was a whirl of thoughts.

'If he died yesterday, I might not have noticed. Maybe he was in my shed all night. In which case, his family will report his absence and begin to look for him. If they find him bolted in my shed they will know he was discovered previously.' A new thought came to her, striking her already taut nerves and causing bile to rise in her throat.

'What if they think I locked him in while he was still alive? What if the police arrive and accuse me of causing his death? What if they are there now? They could arrive at the school at any moment. I will be publicly humiliated. I might even be arrested.'

Footsteps could be heard approaching the classroom and Cynthia dropped the costume she was holding in alarm. A form appeared in the doorway. It was Jane Lancaster.

'Ah, Miss Mott. Sorry to disturb you but I think we need to have a staff meeting when the children have left. We can discuss this morning's play and write down our thoughts for next year, while it's still fresh in our minds.'

'No.' Cynthia snapped. 'That will not be possible.'

Jane Lancaster looked rather taken aback.

'It won't be for long,' she said, 'I do feel it would be of huge benefit. I realise you are all tired but ten minutes in the staffroom seems a sensible plan.'

'No,' Cynthia repeated, 'that will not be possible.' She hesitated, searching for a legitimate excuse to give to the irritating woman. It seemed a ridiculous idea, even if she were not embroiled in impending disaster.

'I am afraid I am suffering from a terrible headache and need to return home promptly.'

Jane Lancaster looked at her. She certainly did look extremely pale. It would be inconvenient if she were absent for the last few days of term. She decided to relent.

'Of course, I am sorry to hear that,' she sympathised. 'Are you okay to carry on or do you want June to see the children out? There's only ten minutes until home time.'

Cynthia leaped at the unexpected reprieve.

'That would be most appreciated,' she replied, looking at June for confirmation. June surveyed the classroom, strewn with costumes waiting to be hung, and the children, who would explode into gleeful noise as soon as Miss Mott left. She had her own children to collect from the junior school but she supposed they would just have to wait a bit longer. She knew they would greet her with resentful eyes at having been left until all the other children had gone. They would be standing in the school office, looking abandoned and uncared for, and she would feel like a negligent parent. Again. She wondered why it should be her and not Jane Lancaster who had to cover for Miss Mott. She thought, yet again, about how little she was paid in relation to what was expected of her. As usual, she seemed to have no choice. She sighed in acquiescence.

Cynthia Mott hurriedly gathered her bag and struggled into her coat. As she flew from her classroom she spied Mr Carter, bucket in hand, as he prepared to start cleaning the floors when the children had left.

'Do phone me nice and early if you are too ill to work tomorrow,' she heard, as she rushed along the corridor, scrabbling for her car keys even as she walked. She needed to get home and sort out this ghastly mess before it was too late.

Chapter Two

JANE Lancaster returned to her office and sat at her desk. It was nicely solid, bought as a congratulatory gift by her husband when she first received the headship. She sighed. Life was sometimes so complicated. She felt the burden of her news like a physical weight within her and she had wanted to start preparing the staff. She realised that they would be tired after the nativity play, but that would have worked to her advantage. None of them would have wanted to linger today. She could have discussed the play, let them all vent their feelings and then at the end, just before they left, she could have told them the news and suggested they arrange a special meeting before the beginning of next term in order to fully discuss it. They would be shocked. Of course they would, that went without saying. But she had so little information to give them that she hoped to avoid too much discussion initially. She just wanted to warn them, let the idea sink in during the Christmas break and then try to confront it properly when they were all accustomed to the idea. Now that wretched woman had scuppered her plans. Whilst she could not help having a headache, Jane felt that Miss Mott would have been more accommodating had she respected Jane's position. Had she, in fact, respected Jane. She reached for her pen and a sheaf of letters that needed signing and with another sigh began to read.

Cynthia reached her car feeling highly agitated. She fumbled with her keys and dropped them twice before she was able to fit them into the lock. She was feeling very sick and slightly light headed as she steered the car back into the High Street and began to drive home. A gaggle of teenaged boys saw her approaching and purposefully stepped out in front of the car, staring belligerently at her car as they strolled slowly across the road.

'Oh, they need to learn a lesson in manners,' thought Cynthia, pressing on the accelerator rather than the brake. She was surprised by the speed at which the car lurched forward, having intended to only rev the engine before braking to give them a warning. The boys leaped onto the kerb, the car narrowly missing them. They turned and Cynthia saw real fear in their eyes as she passed them. She glanced in her rear view mirror and watched as one spat his contempt at the departing car and then she was gone, driving around the slight bend at the end of the street, pausing at the roundabout. She felt a laugh rise in her stomach and giggled.

'Goodness, I might have killed one of them. That really would give the police cause for suspicion. Two bodies in one day. I would be positively notorious.' She indicated and turned slowly into her own lane. The giggles had subsided now and she felt very close to crying. What was she about to encounter? In her mind she could already see flashing lights and police tape cordoning off her house. She could imagine the solemn faced constable approaching her car, could hear him cautioning her and telling her she needed to accompany him to the station. She could almost see her neighbours' faces peering from behind their curtains, hear the mutterings of judgement and her respectability crumbling. She rounded the last corner.

***

Esther Pritchard had also been keen to leave school promptly, so was delighted to hear that the impromptu staff meeting had been postponed. As soon as the last child was safely handed over to his parents, she collected her coat from behind the door of her tidy classroom and left. She rarely stayed for long at the end of a school day as both her boys walked home from their school and although Rob was often there, he certainly could not be relied on.

She parked in the driveway of the modern semi that served as the Baptist Manse and hurried inside. She was greeted by a trail of shoes and bags and coats, leading from the front door to the kitchen. She walked along the hall, tidying as she went. She was hoping to chat to Rob, tell him about the nativity play and maybe have a tea together.

'Hi Mum,' called Joseph as she entered the kitchen. 'What can I eat? I'm starving.'

'You're always starving,' she reminded him, removing the open box of cereal from his hand. She reached for the kettle and began filling it. 'There's some cold pizza in the fridge from yesterday,' she suggested. 'Do you want a drink?'

'I'll have a hot chocolate,' said Samuel through a mouthful of toast, spraying crumbs over his pullover. He brushed them off absently and stuck out a foot to kick his brother as he passed. Joseph ignored him and pulled the pizza from the fridge.

'You need a plate for that,' said Esther as he took a mouthful, 'and where's Dad?'

'Study,' stated Joseph, moving out of reach of Samuel, who was endeavouring to steal some of the pizza.

'Honestly, you two,' said Esther fondly, leaving the kitchen to find her husband. She was approaching the study door when the telephone shrilled. She stopped and listened, hoping it would be nothing important. She really wanted to share her day and laugh about it.

'Hello? Rob Pritchard,' she heard her husband's rich voice answering. 'Oh, hello Roselyn, how are you today?' Esther made a face. The telephone rang a million times a day, usually at meal times. At least half the times it seemed to be Roselyn. She was somewhat needy, which Esther understood. Her husband was always willing to listen to her problems, even the imagined ones, for many hours at a time. This Esther did not understand. She pushed open the door. Rob smiled when he saw her and blew a kiss. She moved her hand in a drinking gesture and received an upraised thumb in response. Wishing she could sometimes disable all telephones she returned to the kitchen. The boys had disappeared, leaving crumbs and dirty knives strewn across the work surface. She could hear the television blaring in the lounge so took the hot chocolate in there.

The lounge was fairly large, though when filled with chairs for prayer meetings and Bible studies often felt too small. A worn blue carpet covered the floor and curtains from a previous house, which did not quite match, hung forlornly at the large bay window, partially hidden now by the Christmas tree. The tree was much too big for the room and Esther wondered why she always allowed Rob and the boys to persuade her that big was essential when it came to trees. It was covered in an eclectic array of ornaments, some collected over the years, some teacher gifts from classes she had taught and some made by the boys when they were younger. All looked rather tatty this year but there was no money to replace them. Esther felt that she was the only person who noticed. There was a computer on a small table in one corner which was for family use. The boys were not allowed computers or televisions in their bedrooms. It was the cause of frequent arguments as one invariably wanted to play something noisy while the other was attempting to watch a programme. Of course, neither boy could enjoy either when the church held a meeting there. Esther wished the church had invested in a house that had a study large enough for meetings, but there was nothing she could do to change it. Ministers were supposed to feel led by God to a church congregation, they were meant to have no opinion about the house which that church then provided. Except for gratitude of course.

Both her sons were lying on sofas, socks off, cushions behind heads, elongated limbs draped randomly across the chairs. She smiled, proud of their size and jealous of the relaxed abandon they portrayed.

'Ooh, thanks Mum,' said Samuel as she came in, struggling to sit up so he could receive his drink.

'Do you two have any homework?' asked Esther, knowing they would say no whether they did or not.

'Nope,' they both confirmed, settling back to watch a cartoon family that seemed to be firmly entrenched in all the stereotypes that society claimed to abhor. Samuel's drink dripped onto the sofa and he moved his arm to cover it, hoping his mother wouldn't notice and make a fuss about cleaning it up. School was finished; they were turning off for the day. Esther noticed that the Christmas tree needed watering and returned to the kitchen to begin preparing dinner.

***

Andrew Smyth was one of the last teachers to leave the school and it was dark before he closed his classroom door. Maddy Brown had stayed to help him hang the rest of the costumes and pick up the discarded plimsolls and socks that always seemed to litter the floor after the class had changed clothes. She told him that on Friday the children usually took home all their paintings from the term, so perhaps she could spend tomorrow clearing the display boards and sorting artwork. He planned to let the children mainly play for the last two days while he heard readers, so that seemed a good plan. They were too excited to learn anything he felt, why bother trying?

He returned to his lodgings and was pleased to find the house was empty. He had found the room in a newspaper ad when he was first appointed and it seemed ideal. The house was owned by a divorced woman, who hadn't wanted to sell the family home when her children moved out, and she now rented out two of the bedrooms to paying guests. He shared the bathroom and a tiny sitting room with the other guest, an IT specialist who never seemed to be there, and they all shared the kitchen and garden. Best of all, his landlady also smoked, so he had no restrictions when he wanted to relax.

He lifted his satchel strap over his head with one hand, dumping it on the stairs before making his way to the kitchen. He pulled a beer from his designated shelf in the fridge and took it upstairs. He threw his navy jacket over the back of his desk chair and loosened his tie. He had a nice room, right at the top of the cottage. It was well furnished, with a sturdy oak bed and matching desk and chair that suited the solidness of the walls and the sloping ceiling.

Sprawling on the bed, he downed half the beer before reaching for his laptop to check his email and Facebook accounts. He had enjoyed the day for once. The children had all been so excited and it was fun to provide a show for the parents. On days like today he quite enjoyed the job.

'Maybe I'm just bored,' he thought. 'Maybe it wouldn't be so bad staying there if I had something a bit more interesting to think about too. I need a hobby. Something that entails meeting some interesting adults who don't have children. Maybe something a bit artistic too, I'm good at that.' He finished his beer and threw the can towards his waste paper basket. It nearly went in. He ran his fingers through his hair. It was getting rather long at the front and flopped over his eye. He had better get it cut before he went home or his mother would nag him.

He began an email to his mother, sending her some dates when he could visit during the holiday. Definitely Christmas Day itself, he would not be missing out on her turkey dinner. He had mixed feelings about going home. It was nice enough seeing his parents and sister again. The food was much better too. But he did feel that he was going back in time. His dad would ask him to help stack shelves in the shop and want advice about his banking and his mother would start tidying his bedroom if he left things on the floor. He seemed to revert back to being a child the moment he stepped inside their house and he was not entirely sure his parents had noticed that he was now an adult. It was strange to be telling a whole class of children what to do all day, and then to go home and be told by his mother and sister what he should be doing himself. They even monitored what he was eating and how much he was smoking. That was partly why he had been so keen to find a job not too near his parents' home. It was always nice to see them, he just did not want to live there any more. He was his own person now.

***

When Cynthia reached her cottage, there was nothing. No police cars, no restricted areas, no line of predatory journalists. The lane was as quiet as one would expect on a wintery afternoon. Cynthia slowed and parked in front of her cottage. She bent her head over the steering wheel and allowed a deep shudder to escape. She breathed deeply, afraid she might actually be sick. After a few minutes, she opened her door and rose stiffly from the seat. Perhaps she could now sort this out, put her life back on track and begin to forget all about this most grim day.

Leaving her bags in the car, Cynthia entered the cottage and walked straight through to the kitchen, pausing only to pull on her boots before hurrying across the lawn. All was as she had left it. The bolt was still in place and she hastily removed it, though decided against actually opening the door. She had no desire to revisit that particular scene. She hurried inside and lifted the telephone.

'Hello, is this the Marksbridge police station? Splendid. I am afraid I need to report a death. It seems my gardener may have passed away whilst in my garden shed. Is it you people who deal with such matters or do I need to telephone the doctor's surgery? My name? Certainly. Miss Cynthia Mott, of 5 Railway Cottages.'

***

It was several hours before peace descended once more on Cynthia's cottage. A blue flashing car had arrived within a few minutes of her telephone call, containing two extremely young policemen. Cynthia was fairly sure she had taught one of them when he was aged five but he clearly did not recognise her so she declined to mention it. Once they had ascertained that the body actually was dead, for which they had required the services of an ill dressed harried looking man, they had sat on her floral chairs, in their big black shoes and asked her lots of questions. Those shoes still carried mud from her garden but she did not quite dare to request they removed them before walking on her carpets. Instead she gave them frequent glances, though the men seemed impervious to her disapproval.

Thankfully, they did not seem to think it at all strange that she should go to her shed when returning from work and she gave no indication she had discovered the body earlier. They left their radios on and every so often they squawked a message. Cynthia found this extremely irritating and rather rude. It was in her eyes akin to those people who held a conversation while simultaneously checking their mobile phones. However, when she suggested that they silence them they merely raised their eyebrows at each other and told her they were working.

Before the young policemen had finished taking details of Mr James's address and employment history, another van arrived, this time to remove the body. They asked if there was an easy way to access the garden without going through the cottage. There was not. The only outside access to the back was along a winding footpath at the end of all the gardens in the terrace, which was entered at the end of the row of houses through a tall gate. It was both narrow and overgrown. The policeman who appeared to be in charge suggested that Cynthia might like to vacate the downstairs while they carried it (she could not think of a corpse as a 'him') through to the road. They were concerned she might be upset by seeing the body removed. She declined. In her opinion, young men were not so very different to young children and she wanted to be sure that none of her possessions were damaged when they carried their load through the house. She was then extremely surprised at the difficulty they seemed to have, to manoeuvre the black encased burden through the narrow doorways of the cottage. It was clearly heavy, and seemed an unwieldy shape. She stood to one side, pressed against the little wooden door that led to her stairs and watched in alarm as her standard lamp wobbled when they passed, her occasional table hauled roughly to one side.

Finally, everyone left. Cynthia sunk into her chair and allowed her eyes to close for the briefest moment. She felt drained. Unexpectedly, there was another knock on the door, rather tentative this time. She hauled herself to her feet and crossed the small sitting room to open it, expecting to see a nosey neighbour.

Instead, Mr Carter stood awkwardly on her step. He stared at her face when she opened the door, checking her expression.

'Goodness. Whatever brings you to my door?' Cynthia asked in surprise.

'I saw the police here earlier when I was passing. I thought I had better wait until they had gone and then check that you were alright.'

She paused a moment, then decided he was genuinely concerned for her wellbeing and not merely a spectator so decided to answer openly.

'Yes, it was rather unnecessary. My gardener decided to die in my shed. The police came and removed the body. They have gone now.'

Suddenly, tiredness overwhelmed her. Her body leaned slackly against the doorframe and she felt the very core of herself weaken. Much to her surprise, she felt tears prickle her eyes and she began to blink rapidly. This was terribly embarrassing, to appear in such a state in the presence of the school caretaker.

David Carter stepped towards Miss Mott, placed a large hand firmly on her elbow and led her inside.

'Come along Miss Mott, I think you need a sit down and something to drink,' he suggested with authority. Somewhat to the surprise of both of them, she allowed herself to be led to a chair where she sat, perched uncomfortably on the edge. Mr Carter turned and shut her front door, asking, 'What do you want to drink? I can get it for you before I go. Is the kitchen through here?' He turned in the doorway to the kitchen and waited for her answer. There was no question of refusing. Cynthia recalled that prior to being the caretaker, he had worked in the police himself. She supposed that his authority came from that. If she was honest, she felt terrible. The thought of someone taking care of her for a moment was rather nice. She felt tears threaten to fall again and sniffed loudly.

'Tea. Tea would be lovely. If you are sure it is no inconvenience.'

He smiled and disappeared into her kitchen. She edged back on her chair, listening to doors banging in the kitchen as he searched for crockery and tea bags. The gas hob popped as it caught light and the kettle sang as it came to the boil.

'I should really use an electric kettle,' she told herself, knowing she never would because she loved the historic romance of a kettle that whistled.

When he emerged a few minutes later he carried two mugs of dark tea. Mugs, not cups and saucers. Cynthia wondered however he had found them, as they had been stored at the rear of a high cupboard. They were useful when her nephews visited. She took a sip and grimaced. It contained sugar.

'You need something sweet,' asserted Mr Carter, watching her. 'You've had a shock and the sugar will be good for you. You don't have to drink it all but do your best, you'll feel better if you do. Can I sit down?'

'Yes, of course,' she replied, indicating an armchair next to the fireplace. He sat, looking very large in her room of floral patterns and neat ornaments. She felt herself redden under his gaze, unaccustomed to adult scrutiny.

'Now, do you want to tell me about it or have you had enough for one day? You don't need to talk if you don't want to,' he added kindly. 'I shall stay until you have had a hot drink and then if you are well enough I shall leave you in peace.'

'It has all been an unnecessary fuss,' began Cynthia, then stopped as she saw his quizzical expression. Perhaps this was not the way to describe the death of someone, even an inconvenient someone. 'I mean, the police coming seems unnecessary,' she explained lamely.

'They have to attend an unexpected death,' explained Mr Carter.

'Did you discover him yourself?' he continued, 'That must have been a nasty shock. Especially after such a busy day. How are you feeling now? I can stay longer if you'd rather not be alone.'

Cynthia was astonished by his kindness. They had worked at the same school for several years and she had found him to be a pleasant character with surprisingly good conversation for a caretaker. However, the difference in their status ensured they were not friends, barely colleagues in fact. He was someone to whom she would go to request help with structural matters at school, when something needed replacing or moving. He was helpful and discreet, would talk to her about the news or weather or other inconsequential matters. She knew nothing about him other than what the staff had been told when he joined the school, that he had taken the job due to the police compulsory retirement age being younger than when he wished to stop working and he enjoyed working with children.

'Thank you for your concern, but I am absolutely fine,' she replied, her words in contrast to her voice which seemed to be shaking as much as her hands. 'It was something of a shock,' she explained, 'but Mr James was very elderly. I have suggested to him many times that it might be appropriate for him to stop gardening and stay at home. I believe he lives with his daughter. Lived,' she corrected. Yet again her emotions threatened to overwhelm her and she wished he would leave. She realised that her body was reacting to the release of the day's stress and she disliked to be seen in such disarray. 'And I have seen a dead body on a previous occasion,' she went on, eager to illustrate that she was not a weak, fainting kind of a woman. 'My father. It was I who was with him when the cancer finally won.'

Without warning, unbidden memories swamped her. Her mind whirled back to that terrible day, felt again that surge of helpless emotion, the overwhelming loneliness, and there was nothing she could now do to stem the flow of tears that filled her eyes and trickled wetly down her cheeks. Mr Carter moved to her side and placed a large white handkerchief into her hand. She checked it was clean then wiped her face and blew her nose loudly. She was terribly embarrassed but he seemed perfectly at ease and simply patted her arm gently.

'There, there,' he soothed, as though comforting a child, 'you cry if you need to. Don't you worry about me. I know about death and it always catches us unawares. Can't fight those feelings, better to just go with them for a minute.'

As he stood at her side he looked around the room, wishing to avert his gaze and allow her some privacy while she fought to control her emotions. It was a cosy room. The door from the road opened onto a small mat for brushing shoes and then there was a dark green carpet, which contrasted with the woven red curtains. On one wall was the original fireplace, with a small oil painting of something pastoral hanging above it. There were three armchairs arranged facing the fire, with an empty vase standing on a lace mat on the window sill that looked towards the back garden. The ceiling sloped over the kitchen door, he supposed where the stairs went. The mantelpiece was strewn with a few ornaments, a small clock, a candle and a photograph of two boys who looked to be in their mid-teens. It smelled of wood smoke and was, as he would expect, scrupulously clean. A shelf above a tiny television was laden with books and more were hidden in a neat stack in one corner. It was a very feminine room, with lace throws and delicate crocheted head rests on the sofas, but not an uncomfortable one.

He felt sorry for Miss Mott, knowing that she would hate to be seen as showing any weakness. He found her an interesting character, often rudely brusque but with a fighting spirit which he admired. She reminded him of an animal that was defensively aggressive but he felt there was warmth there, underneath all her insecure blustering.

He turned back when he heard her give a small cough. She looked rather endearing with her hair all tousled and her red nose and damp cheeks. He smiled and placed his hand on the shoulder of her pink cardigan. He felt her stiffen under his touch and moved back to his own chair.

'I am exceedingly sorry,' she began. He raised a hand to stop her.

'Don't be. You are only human. We can't always be in control of everything. Now, will you be alright or do you want me to stay?' He did not offer to telephone for someone else to come, guessing correctly that she lived an emotionally independent life.

Cynthia reached forward and placed her empty mug on the china coaster on the table to her left.

'I will be completely well,' she said, 'it has obviously been more of a shock than I realised but I am composed again now. Thank you for your consideration.'

He smiled, wondering why she always spoke so awkwardly. He assumed she had been wounded somewhere along the way and even her words were formally structured, as if any form of spontaneity would be wrong and criticised.

'Well, if you're sure.' He stood and reached towards his empty mug.

'Oh, please leave those,' said Cynthia, 'I can clear them up on my way to the kitchen.' She was eager for him to leave now, to start preparing some supper and to relax with a book before going to bed. She walked to the front door and opened it, standing to one side as he passed.

'Thank you once more for being so kind,' she said. She paused. She wanted to ask him to not mention this encounter at school, to not tell anyone else that he had seen her in such a state but was unsure how to continue. He stood on the pavement and lifted a hand in a half wave.

'You take care now,' he instructed kindly, 'I'll see you tomorrow I expect.' Then he turned and went towards his car.

Cynthia quietly closed the door and drew the bolt across. Her eyes shut and she allowed herself to sigh before collecting the mugs and going to the kitchen. She looked at the mud strewn doormat and considered whether she should go and check the state of her shed. Then decided she had coped with quite sufficient for one day and instead began to wash the mugs. It was a long time since she had entertained a man in her home. As her embarrassment began to fade she pondered Mr Carter's visit. It had undoubtedly been kind of him. She recalled the feel of his hand on her arm. It was rare indeed for her to have physical contact with a man. She could still feel the warmth where he had touched her arm and shoulder. Not unpleasant, she admitted before blushing at her foolishness. He was after all, just a caretaker.

'I must be more overwrought than I first thought,' she told herself. 'Now start to scrub a potato for supper and then bath and bed and no more silly ideas. Let us assume tomorrow will be a better day. It could hardly be worse.'

Outside, David Carter started his car and glanced at his watch.

'Well,' he thought, 'that was certainly an unexpected end to the day.' He decided the fish and chip shop would probably have started frying so turned back towards town. His cold house did not seem enticing but at least he could arrive with his tea sorted. He still was not completely accustomed to eating alone. Thankfully all the drama seemed to be over and finished with in one day. He liked things normal, he had known enough hard times in his life already, was old enough to know that 'ordinary' was something precious. Tomorrow would be better, he thought, just two more days until the end of term and there was nothing that could happen in such a short time, was there? He touched the CD button and Dvořák's cello concerto filled the car, relaxing him as he drove away from the red brick terrace.

***

In the stylish kitchen of her modern detached house, Jane Lancaster pulled open the freezer door and thought about what she wanted to eat. Really, she just wanted to drink, to blunt the worries that were battling for space in her head.

'Chicken pie from Cook,' she decided. Her daughter had not yet returned from university, so she only needed to prepare food for herself and Bill. Bill was the better cook and enjoyed throwing together a selection of fresh ingredients to produce something enticing, but today he had a meeting after work, so the task fell to Jane. Even on good days she was a lazy cook, preferring to prepare something cleaned and trimmed by the supermarket, maybe opening a few packets but never a recipe book.

She eased the pie onto a suitable tin, turned on the oven to preheat, then reached into the fridge for wine and poured a large glass. She carried it through to the conservatory, hoping the large pot plants and the musty smell of soil would somehow calm her nerves. Instead, the glass ceilinged room was just cold and slightly damp. She perched on a wicker chair and swallowed rather than sipped, wanting to absorb the alcohol quickly. The blue Chinese urn and pots of orange saplings with their dark green leaves did little to change her mood. The urns were dusty and the young trees had grown ferociously long thorns which threatened to snag anything which passed too close.

'The play was a fiasco,' she declared to the empty room, 'but there is always going to be an unpredictable element when dealing with infants.' She had endured some rather stilted conversations with the school governors over coffee following the performance, but no one had actually criticised her outright. They had mumbled about it being 'such a shame' and 'unfortunate' but no blame had been placed.

'But then, they knew what was coming next,' thought Jane. 'They knew what little bombshell they were about to drop into my lap. Maybe they thought they should hold back a bit, not be too harsh in case I completely went to pieces when they told me their plans.'

No, there was nothing to be done about the play. She would ask the staff for some feedback tomorrow; highlight any 'action points' that might be useful next year. Then she would draw a line under it and move on.

It was the moving on that worried her. In a small school, staff interacted continually. It was essential for morale and motivation that this was harmonious. All the theories she had read suggested a mix of ages and gender made this easier, so Jane had been careful when making new appointments and so far the theory had proven right in practice. Whilst Andrew Smyth clearly had not aroused any latent maternal feelings in Cynthia Mott, she most certainly did not see him as a threat. Esther Pritchard seemed to positively enjoy the freshness he brought to staff meetings. Any friction between staff had been minimal.

However, this was unlikely to continue. The governors had wanted her to keep it quiet but she had staunchly refused. She was now worried she was about to destroy any unity they had managed to achieve. She was not entirely sure just how nasty things might become.

With a sigh she rose, carried her empty glass into the kitchen and slid the pie into the oven. The timer was set and all she had to do was wait.

Chapter Three

THURSDAY brought drizzle. The world resembled a depressing Monet painting, all fuzzy edges and blurred dimness. It mirrored Jane Lancaster's feelings to perfection. She arrived at school before the staff and after a brief hello to Mr Carter, she began to organise the day.

Jane first went into the staffroom and updated the day's timetable. It hung on the brown cork board behind the sagging armchairs where the staff had their coffee at playtime. Each morning, on their way to their classrooms they were supposed to check the boards for any changes. She was aware that only Cynthia actually did so, the others relying on their assistants or waiting until playtime before they checked.

Using a red marker pen, Jane boldly wrote 'Staff Meeting' under the activities. Adding '3:25 prompt', as an afterthought. She knew it was extremely unlikely that all the children would be with their parents by this time, but it gave the meeting an element of importance and she did not intend to be thwarted a second time. She made herself a cup of instant coffee and carried it through to her office to begin trawling through emails.

Cynthia Mott was the next staff member to arrive at the school.

She walked quickly, her heels tapping rhythmically on the hardwood floor as she made her way to the staffroom. Pushing open the door, she noted the recently boiled kettle and a mound of chocolates on the small coffee table. Crossing the stained carpet she checked the timetable and hissed her disappointment when she spied the staff meeting.

'Three twenty-five? That's optimistic to the point of lunacy,' she declared to the empty room as she went to turn on the computer.

At the end of each half term, the staff entered grades and comments into a computer record for each of their pupils. Cynthia had added her own grades and comments the previous day. She now needed to check those for Cherry Class. She called them up onto the screen, pleased to note that Mr Smyth had added them as requested. She read the grades and comments, and frowned. Most of the children had been awarded an A or B grade for both attainment and effort. The only exception was Tommy Beale. He had received an E for effort. The comments were also unsatisfactory, being single words rather than a short sentence. Her eyes skimmed the list of adjectives, 'Good. Good. Fair. Okay. Lazy. Okay.'

'This is not acceptable,' she said. 'It is not professional. What, one wonders, does "okay" mean when relating to a child's termly progress? Really, this is much too sloppy. I shall need to discuss his evaluations at the earliest opportunity.' She shut down the computer and hurried to her room.

On her desk was her TA book. Each morning she wrote the tasks for her teaching assistant. June Fuller thought the book a complete waste of time and energy as the moment she arrived Miss Mott would tell her in great detail what the day was to entail.

This morning the children were to make little books about their nativity play. It would not occupy most of them for long, so she also decided which games they could play when they had finished. She was still heaving boxes into a stack in a corner of the room when the first children began to appear.

The first half of the morning passed in a whirl of activity. The children made their books; the adults helped, and listened to a handful of children read while the rest of the class played. Every few minutes Miss Mott would raise her head and scan the room, choosing one child to ask to work more quietly, thus keeping the general noise level to the minimum. At the appointed hour, they walked to the hall and sat for Assembly, uncomfortable on the cold floor and too excited to pay attention to Miss Lancaster's quiet voice. The staff sat stiffly, facing the front, their thoughts elsewhere. It ended much too quickly.

Glad to be free from the confines of the hall the children walked eagerly to their cloakroom. Miss Mott and Mrs Fuller helped them into their coats and outdoor shoes. One child put their coat on completely upside down, another put their mittens on first and then found it impossible to use their hands for the tricky manipulations necessary for fastening buttons. Several children put shoes on the wrong feet and had to be told to swap them over. Finally, they were ready and Miss Mott led them onto the playground before going to the staffroom.

Cynthia mindlessly made herself a drink. She slumped on a chair and briefly closed her eyes. The winter term always seemed to last forever and they ground to the end wearily. The nativity play and parties, plus records and reports, all had to fit around the pretence of continued education. She was tired. Yesterday's drama had certainly not helped and now she just wanted the day to be finished. Andrew Smyth was on the rota for playground duty, so only Esther Pritchard was in the staffroom. The two women largely ignored each other as they drank their coffee, tired, thinking about what they needed to prepare for their next lesson. When the child arrived from the playground to announce the end of playtime, they both heaved themselves to their feet and went to collect their classes from the damp playground. Three rows of pink-cheeked children stood waiting. It was cold; Cynthia pulled her cardigan tightly across her chest, waiting for the children to stand calmly.

Andrew Smyth led his class into the school and told them to collect their gym kits. Maddy Brown was busy emptying boards and the mound of paintings to be distributed that afternoon had grown. The children changed noisily, pulling shorts and tee shirts from their cloth bags, scattering clothes on tables, chairs and floor as they changed. They chattered freely, giving scant attention to how they were dressing or where their discarded clothes were falling.

When most children were dressed in their sports shorts and tee shirts, Andrew Smyth called for them to line up at the door. They stood in a straggled snake, many facing the wrong way. The floor and tables were strewn with clothes and shoes. Asking Mrs Brown to send the last children to the hall when they were changed, he led his merry class from the room. As they walked the length of the corridor, Andrew had an urge to shout 'Charge', to rush forwards with the class following. He didn't.

They arrived in the hall, Andrew Smyth slotted the movement CD into the stereo and pressed 'play'. The children stood listening as the authoritative voice rang out.

'Hello children, are you standing in a big space? Let's begin. Let's warm up our arms. Can you stretch them out to the side? Now reach up as high as you can. Can you touch the ceiling?' Some children lifted their arms apathetically in the general direction of the ceiling, others strained with effort as they stretched as far as they could, jumping to add height.

Andrew settled himself on a chair in the corner. He found 'musical movement' to be a fairly boring activity but it enabled him to tick the 'physical education' box in his planning schedule and allowed the children some relaxation away from the classroom. His role, as he saw it, was to watch and check no one was silly and injured themselves. He was quite happy to let the disconnected voice do the teaching for him. After all, he reasoned, they were obviously the experts, so why interfere? His mind drifted away as the class began to gallop around the perimeter of the hall.

When the CD finished, Andrew checked his watch and was pleased to see that it was nearly lunchtime. He led the class back to their room, some of them still 'galloping like horses along a beach', others chatting as they walked. He did not turn round, so did not see.

'Right,' he informed them, 'you have five minutes until lunchtime so get dressed quickly. And hang your bags back on your pegs before you sit down.' He moved to his desk and slumped in his chair. This was such a boring job sometimes. He looked in dismay at the mountain of work Maddy had removed from the walls. That would take ages to distribute. He wondered if anyone would notice if he put some of it into the recycling bin. Jimmy came up to him, wearing his shirt, shoes and socks but no trousers. His skinny legs protruded from his baggy underwear, pink from cold and speckled with dirt from the hall floor.

'My trousers are gone,' he stated.

'Gone where?' asked Mr Smyth, 'They must be here somewhere, have you looked under the table?'

Jimmy nodded, looking forlorn.

'I checked everywhere. They're gone. Someone has stolen them.'

Andrew got up and followed Jimmy to his table. 'No one will have stolen them,' he said, 'they must have fallen somewhere.' He began to search the table and chairs. The trousers were not to be seen. Maddy came over and started to check the children's bags, folding clothes as she replaced them. There were no trousers. Most children were dressed now and sitting on the carpet, holding books and talking loudly. Andrew and Maddy began to search other tables, going into the cloakroom to check the bags that were hanging. Jimmy stood miserably watching, sure he had been targeted by a trouser thief and was doomed to wear pants for the rest of the day. There was no sign of the trousers. Andrew and Maddy looked at each other in bewilderment. Where could they have gone? They began to check cupboards and drawers but to no avail. Finally, Andrew told Jimmy to put his shorts back on.

'You'll just have to wear shorts until they turn up,' he said. 'It's time for lunch now, line up at the door everyone.' The class scrambled to their feet and waited by the door until their 'dinner lady' – old fashioned term but it refused to fade – arrived to lead them away. Jimmy thrust his feet through the legs of his shorts. It was hard to fit his shoes through the hole, but he managed it with a bit of force and hurried to the back of the line. Full of misery he followed the class to lunch.

Miss Mott's class were also ready to leave and they followed Cherry Class along the corridor, in one long snake of writhing children, lunch boxes bumping against legs and faces shining. Cynthia tidied the last few items in her room before collecting her bag. It would be a short afternoon, she thought, barely time to give out all the old paintings before they went to sing carols. She remembered she needed to discuss his grades with Andrew Smyth and thought grimly that it was lucky he was not being graded himself. He was not showing much diligence in his first term. As she crossed the playground, a movement caught her eye.

Andrew Smyth and David Carter were standing close to the school wall, partly concealed by a bush and clearly hoping not to be seen. Wisps of smoke furled skywards. Cynthia strode towards them, intent on confrontation. As she neared, snatches of conversation and male laughter drifted towards her carried by the damp breeze.

She paused. There was something intangibly male about the scene and for a beat she wondered if she dared interrupt.

'Doesn't it get to you? Working with all these clucking women? Like being in a hen house.'

'Sometimes.'

'Not sure I can hack it for long. You ever think about retiring?'

'Only when I'm awake.'

'Ha. I don't know how you've kept sane mate. I don't know who's worse, the staff or the parents. All those mothers who think their little Sammy is an undiscovered genius when really he's just a pain in the arse. And not a yummy mummy to be found.

'Mind you, it's hard to find a proper bloke in a Primary school. When I go on my training courses there's two other blokes, but they both look like they belong in the sandals and guitar set. Know what I mean?'

Andrew paused, taking a lung warming pull on his cigarette. He felt the nicotine surge through him, relaxing him, calming some of the tension that he always felt in school. He pushed his fingers through his fair hair, wondering if it still contained flecks of blue from where the powder paint tin had exploded on him that morning.

David Carter nodded and smiled. He liked Andrew, liked his honesty and enthusiasm. He hoped the women would not drive him out with their emphasis on tidiness and their suspicious judgements about anything new. It was good for the children to be around a man, he thought, good for them to not be cocooned all the time. Nice for him too, to have some male company for once.

'What's the score with our Miss Mott then?' Andrew continued. 'She never marry?'

Cynthia froze. She had not anticipated that she might be discussed. Now she did not know what to do. To confront them would be embarrassing, it might appear that she had been watching them, eavesdropping. However, to retreat would make her feel reduced, as though guilty in some way. She leaned closer to the fence, behind the laurel. Then she realised that in fact this was worse. Now it looked like she was hiding, concealed in a bush in order to overhear their conversation.

David Carter shuffled, trying to decide how much to reveal. Cynthia prayed he would not discuss the events of yesterday.

'She's not so bad really,' he began, 'you just have to understand her a bit.'

Andrew made a sound somewhere between a snort and a cough.

'Understand her? That's a fine one. She's out to get me I reckon. She's hoping I'll give it all up and get a job in a bank or something. All that bollock talk about handwriting and wall displays. Like that's going to teach them to read and write.'

David stretched his back and grinned.

'She's been teaching these kids for years,' he placated, 'they're her whole life. Maybe she has got herself in bit of a rut but she means well. She's her own worst enemy really. She's kinder than she wants to appear.' He flicked some ash, watched it fall to the ground, decided what to say.

'Do you know, we had a kid here a few years back who was almost completely neglected. No dad, mum too young to know which way was up, no grandparents on the scene. The boy used to arrive filthy dirty some mornings, poor little beggar. Always early, because mum would drop him on her way to work, used the school as a child minding service. The other kids started to bully him, he smelled so bad. No one wanted to sit next to him on the carpet or let him join in their games.

'Well, your Miss Mott knew it wasn't worth talking to the mother, she was incapable of doing anything else. And no one wants to involve the Social, all that fuss and paperwork and you never know what the outcome will be. No, she took matters into her own hands. She started bringing in breakfasts for him, kept a flannel in school and a toothbrush so he could clean up when he arrived. She found clothes out of lost property for him so he had something to change into and every evening took home his uniform to wash. Never said a word to anyone. I only know because I spotted her sometimes, hanging up the clean clothes for him in the morning when she thought no one could see, or giving him a sandwich to eat in the playground.

'So you see, she's alright inside. She likes to seem hard but there's a kindness there too.' He took a last drag of cigarette, stubbed it out on the wall, watching the sparks turn grey.

Cynthia backed away. There was no way she could interrupt now. She was mortified. She had had no idea that anyone knew she had helped that child.

'Well, she sure isn't kind to me,' she heard as she rounded the corner and scuttled towards the staffroom.

It was not many minutes later that the staffroom door opened to admit a sheepish Andrew Smyth. Cynthia glanced up from the tidy salad she was pretending to enjoy.

'You're late, where have you been?' she greeted him.

'Just chatting to Mr Carter,' he mumbled, flicking the switch of the kettle and reaching into the murky sink to retrieve a cup.

'You've been smoking,' she said, more a statement than an accusation.

'Yes, well, I've been smoking since I was fourteen,' he said defensively. 'Not likely to stop now.'

'This is a no smoking area,' Cynthia reminded him. 'Even outside is considered school property.'

He gave the mug a quick rinse under the tap and added a large teaspoonful of instant coffee. The powder began to dissolve in the wet mug and leached dark brown across the stained white surface.

'You want a coffee?' he offered, refusing to rise to her attack. 'And we weren't on school property. We were round the corner, out of sight.'

'Well I saw you,' thought Cynthia, but realised she was lost should she admit that.

'Are you going to wash that properly? And no, thank you, I have partaken of sufficient caffeine for today.' She replaced the lid on her plastic container. It was old and slightly misshapen and she had to squeeze tightly on the corners before it snapped shut.

'Fourteen? Isn't that illegal?'

Andrew turned and looked at her. He looked at her for a long minute.

'Well,' she bustled, 'I can't stay here chatting all day. I need to prepare for the afternoon. I would like to discuss the grades which you have submitted to the computer document. Perhaps after the staff meeting we could meet? I do not anticipate it will extend more than a few minutes.' She balanced her lunch box on top of some files in her over-full bag and heaved herself to her feet. Nodding politely at Esther Pritchard, she trotted out.

Esther watched her go, then smiled at Andrew.

'Feeling the stress?' she asked kindly. 'It gets a bit fraught at the end of term, especially the winter term. At least we haven't had lots of snow this year, that really makes them sky high. Are you feeling better now?'

'A bit,' he admitted, carrying his coffee to a vacant chair. He avoided the chair where Cynthia had been sitting. He did not like sitting on chairs that were still warm from where other people had sat. Especially not her. The thought of sharing body heat with her nearly put him off his coffee.

'She hates me,' he stated.

'No, no,' smiled Esther, 'it's just her manner. She worries about things. But she's a good teacher.'

'That's what Mr Carter said,' Andrew muttered. 'But I don't see it.' He leaned forwards and pulled a tin of chocolates towards him. The small table was covered in chocolates and biscuits, gifts to the staff from governors and parents. He pushed his fingers through them, searching for a green triangle.

Esther Pritchard stood and smoothed her sweater. She planned to let the children paint this afternoon, so needed to smother every available surface in newspaper.

'You're doing fine,' she said kindly. 'You can't expect to know everything at once. Just keep trying.' She walked smiling from the room, closing the door quietly behind her.

Andrew was alone. He leaned back in the chair and closed his eyes, savouring the chocolate.

'Too many women,' he thought. 'Definitely too many women.' He wondered how easy it would be to find work in a junior school. They usually had a few males.

***

When lunchtime was over, Esther Pritchard let her class into the newspaper lined room. Pots of paint were centred on each table, with a selection of brushes. A large piece of creamy sugar paper sat waiting in each child's place.

She sat upright on the carver chair and smiled at her class.

'Maisie, you are sitting beautifully,' she said, knowing this would spur the rest of the class to stop talking and fidgeting. Everyone likes approval. When they were silent, she called the names in the register, then leaned forwards in her chair.

'Now, we have a busy afternoon, so I need you all to be especially sensible. I want each of you to create a beautiful painting and I am going to let you choose what the subject will be.' She explained the task.

'Now, who is sitting very nicely and they can go and start work.' The children all shuffled into an upright position, some of them hugging their crossed legs, all of them stretching their necks in an effort to look attentive and ready.

'Red group, would you like to go? No, Michael, we don't need silliness, you show me how sensibly you can find an apron. And Blue group can go. You can talk, but it must be little voices so I cannot hear. Felicity, can you talk in a quiet voice? That's lovely. And Yellow group may go. Jonathan, please come and let me help you with that apron. Jane, please can you take the register to the office for me?'

The class began to move around, finding aprons, walking to where they would work. The room was not silent but the noise was minimal, there was a general atmosphere of calmness as the children began to paint. Esther was pleased that she had already sent home most of the term's work. It always took longer than expected to distribute and there was enough to do in the last days of term. Jane Lancaster had been rather short with her and had told her that she should have left her wall displays in place until after the nativity play. She had apologised whilst feeling that no parents were likely to visit the classrooms and it was good use of time. This had proved to be correct. She was not however, going to argue her case with the head teacher. Better to appear repentant and forget about it, it was not important. The room now looked rather bare, though she had left the bright backing paper in place. There were dark patches where the children's work had been stapled and several holes, and she realised with a sigh that it would need to be replaced before next term.

She moved around the room, encouraging the children with their work and suggesting improvements. By the time the message arrived calling them to the hall, the newspaper had all been swept into the bin, the tables wiped and the aprons were mostly all hanging back on their peg. Esther made a mental note to take them home with her to wash so they would be fresh for next term.

***

Jane Lancaster did not enjoy the carol singing. She was nervous about the staff meeting and could barely concentrate on the words. She most certainly could not muster much enthusiasm as she gave a brief introduction to each song. Tommy Smith was silly, making faces across the hall to his friend and she gave him much too harsh a telling off. As she shouted at him to sit properly, she watched his big brown eyes fill with tears and his cheeks turned very pink. The school fell completely silent, as though each child was holding their breath. Feeling guilty, she quickly introduced the next carol and suggested the school might like to stand, hoping to distract them. It was meant to be a little treat, instead it had become an ordeal. Eventually it was over and she could bid the school farewell for the day. She frowned, feeling the beginnings of a headache as she watched them file out of the hall.

Andrew Smyth was the last teacher to arrive at the staff meeting. His class had taken forever to find their coats and collect the small piles of paintings that he had distributed earlier. Many of them struggled to carry their work as it constantly slid from their arms and he walked behind, picking up pieces of paper as they walked towards the door where they would be met by their parents. Some of the work he passed to the adult as they collected their child, some he kept hold of and disposed of when he returned to the empty classroom. He brushed his sweater, removing flecks of dried paint and staples and dust.

Jane Lancaster stopped talking when he entered the staffroom. They had been discussing the nativity play and she was writing a neat list of all the things that they could improve upon next year. She had discussed the necessity of leaving wall displays in place until after the play. Esther Pritchard remained expressionless. Cynthia Mott asked that all classes please arrive in the designated order. They discussed the lack of space, which could not be changed, the lukewarm feedback from the governors, which they felt showed lack of insight from the governors rather than any problem with the school and whether it would be better to have two performances rather than one. Most of this was discussed every year, the same suggestions and thoughts always arose, were considered and then ignored. Cynthia Mott felt it to be an utter waste of time though still felt the need to contribute at length. Esther Pritchard said very little, wanting to go home. Andrew Smyth, now he had arrived, listened but added nothing.

'Right,' said Jane Lancaster, shutting her book and clipping her pen to the cover. 'Thank you all for your thoughts. Now, there is another matter which I need to raise with you.' She looked at her staff.

Miss Mott was uptight, as normal. She sat on the edge of her chair, taking notes of everything that was said. Jane wondered what she did with all the notes she wrote. There were many bright files on a shelf in her room and she assumed they were all placed in there but had no idea if they were ever referred to again.

Mrs Pritchard looked tired. She was sitting peacefully with her hands in her lap but Jane had noticed she had checked her watch four times already. Jane knew this would be a busy time for the Pritchard family and when the school term eventually ended, Esther would be called upon to attend a succession of meetings and services in support of her husband. She did hope she would not return to school in January completely exhausted.

Mr Smyth waited expectantly. He always appeared slightly surprised, as though the day had been full of unexpected happenings, despite his supposedly being in control of the activities. Jane thought that this was probably true and that very little occurred in his classroom that was as he had foreseen. He seemed to have lurched through his first term. She wondered if he had enjoyed it.

Mr Carter could be heard whistling outside as he collected

rubbish to load into the incinerator. Jane drew a breath and continued.

'After the nativity play, James Bird, the chairman of the governors, told me some rather disturbing news. It seems that our numbers for next September are unexpectedly low. This is partly due to a fall in the birth rate five years ago and partly because they have now started to take little ones at Markham School, which will affect our numbers.' She paused, letting the news sink in.

'How low?' enquired Cynthia, wondering why Jane Lancaster was placing such emphasis on this. Surely it could be dealt with after the Christmas break?

'Very low, at this point,' said Jane, unwilling to give too much information. 'It looks unlikely we will be able to afford to retain three classes.'

There was silence. The teachers frowned, not quite sure they were grasping this news correctly.

'What do you mean?' asked Esther, forgetting now that she wanted to leave quickly.

'What I mean is, that unless there is a sudden unexpected rush, our numbers are too low for three classes. We will have to introduce vertical grouping and reduce to two classes. That means that we will only need two teachers. I know this will be a shock. It was a shock to me too. Mr Bird wanted me to keep it quiet, to not tell any of you until the governors have decided what to do. But I didn't think that was fair. I felt you should all know and should have as much time as possible, so you can think about different options. I would, however, ask that it remains confidential amongst the teaching staff at this point. Until we know exactly what is happening, it should not be discussed outside of this group. If ancillary staff or parents start to gossip about it, the consequences could be much worse.'

'I'm not sure I understand,' began Andrew slowly. 'Can they do that, can they just fire one of us? Don't we have contracts and stuff? And what is "vertical grouping"?'

'It's when they arrange the children into classes of mixed ages. So all of the reception age children would be together with some of year ones and the rest of year one would go with Year Two,' explained Esther.

'Or even, have a mix of all three year groups split between two classes,' added Jane Lancaster. 'And yes, they can terminate our contracts. They just have to give a term's notice. It's the same as if you decide to leave and work at a different school. Which is why I wanted to tell you. You all have time, over the Christmas break, to look at which jobs are available. If you see something you like, then I suggest you think about applying. There is still time to find something; it will be more difficult after next term.

'I don't want to lose any of you,' she said, looking at them all and hoping they believed her. She wanted them to know she was on their side; none of this was her doing. 'I don't know what the governors will do, how they will decide which staff members to retain and who should look elsewhere.' She paused. This sounded even worse now it was actually being said aloud. These were her colleagues, it was their livelihoods that the governors were making decisions about and she did not entirely trust them to make wise decisions. After all, none of them were teachers. They were merely volunteers from the community and parish. They liked the prestige it gave them and although some were there for altruistic reasons, their understanding of what the job entailed was sketchy at best.

'It'll be last in, first out, won't it?' said Andrew bitterly. 'It'll be me who's for the chop then. They're not going to keep an NQT over an established teacher.' He felt angry and muddled. He was not sure if he wanted to stay, but he was sure that he did not want to be pushed. He needed a job. It was one thing to want to look around, another to be given no choice. Staying suddenly felt rather attractive now it may not be possible.

'Not necessarily,' Esther told him. 'The longer a teacher stays, the more expensive they are. If they are needing to cut costs, it would be me or Cynthia who would be more attractive to get rid of. Not that they are allowed to say that.' She sounded angry. She too did not trust either the governing board or the process. 'I expect they will come up with some clever sounding strategy that looks fair from the outside and will be a lot of fuss and waste lots of energy to implement. Then they will fire whoever it is they secretly wanted to fire in the first place but without the unions being able to do anything about it.'

'Well, I think we should close the meeting now,' said Jane hurriedly. 'I really don't have any more information to give you. If I did, I would tell you.' This was true and was another reason for telling the staff now. If she had waited until strategies had been decided upon, it would be harder to only tell the staff what they were supposed to know. This way she could with all honestly tell them everything she knew.

For a moment, no one moved. The staff felt slightly dazed, as if what they had heard was not what Jane had actually said. Cynthia was the first to break the silence.

'Thank you for keeping us informed, Jane. If you will excuse me, I will return to finish tidying my room before I depart for the day.

'Andrew, perhaps we could defer our meeting until tomorrow morning? Eight thirty?' She gathered her bag and walked from the room, feeling unsteady.

Esther rose and wound a long scarf round and round her neck before pulling on her thick brown coat. It was not an attractive look but she had never really considered her appearance, only how warm it was. She gave Andrew a fleeting smile and left. He followed her out, wondering what he was going to do now.

Jane Lancaster wished she had something stronger than coffee in her office. She stretched her back and walked unseeing to her filing cabinet. It was done, the battles would commence. She wondered who the casualties would be.

Chapter Four

ESTHER drove home in a daze. As the news began to sink in she began to consider the implications. She felt very close to tears. She really did not need this. She was so tired; there was still so much to do in the church before Christmas and now this to worry about. Esther sometimes felt her job was the only thing that kept her sane. She knew some members in the church thought she should be a full time unpaid support for her husband's job but Esther knew that she might fold up if she did that. Rob's wage did not cover more than the essentials and her boys missed out on enough of 'normal life' without having to forgo school trips and clothes that were relatively acceptable to young teens. It was not as though they lived an affluent life as it was, they had holidays in her parents' caravan, shopped in cheaper supermarkets and rarely went out for dinner. Esther did not mind, she did not resent the long hours her husband worked, the lack of money for treats, the constant invasion of her privacy and the continual being looked at, noticed, evaluated which was part of her role as a minister's wife. However, having a job that was nothing to do with the church was important. It allowed her time to be herself, to have an identity that went beyond 'Rob's wife'. The money was also not insignificant.

Money was something Esther often worried about. People who did not understand, looked judgmentally at Rob's salary (how she hated the lack of privacy; every church member looked at Rob's salary each year and discussed whether it was appropriate). Some people, those who had only ever done manual labour or stayed at home, considered that his wage was excessive. 'How can he relate to the poor in society when he earns so much?' they argued. They were quick to point out that his house was provided, free of charge and many of the bills were also picked up by the 'church'. They were the church, it was a Baptist church, so all the bills were paid from the collection, which they gave, so they personally were helping to pay for a salary in excess of what they would ever earn and he lived in a house that was significantly nicer than they would ever live in. They dressed up their jealousy in words that sounded religious and kind, talking about the poor in society and the need for the pastor to relate to them, to not be held back by having possessions and encumbered with worldliness. Esther had no time for such arguments. She did not notice any of them selling their houses and living in a caravan so they could better relate to those who were poorer. She also knew that had Rob used his intellect to go into business, he would have earned a salary many multiples of what he was earning now.

She also was horribly aware that the 'perk' of free housing lasted only while Rob was working. When he retired, they would own nothing. They would have nowhere to live and would not be eligible for council housing having not stayed in one place for long enough. Nor would they have anything to leave their children when they died. They would be cast onto the goodwill of whichever charities were functioning at the time and would be housed wherever those charities were able and willing to place them. Some churches compensated for this by paying the minister a large enough salary so he could pay for a mortgage on a property, instead of providing a manse. Marksbridge Baptist did not. Rob was putting some of his salary into a pension fund, which would help when he retired but it would not buy them a house. Nor would it pay a commercial rent on anything nice enough for them to want to live there. Esther tried not to worry, to trust that the God who she claimed to follow would provide for them when the time came, but sometimes her fears came to the surface. The sudden potential loss of her job was enough for those worries to haunt her again. She knew she was unlikely to sleep well that night.

She parked in the driveway behind Rob's car.

'May have to go down to one car,' she told herself miserably as she walked past it and opened the front door. She could hear the television on and the boys arguing about something sports related and went into the lounge. Both boys looked up and waved vaguely in her direction.

'What can I eat?' asked Samuel.

'Hello Mum, how was your day?' corrected Esther crossly.

'Hello Mum, how was your day? What can I eat?' repeated Samuel. Joseph laughed and threw a cushion at him. It bounced off his head, knocking the lamp from the table. Samuel lunged at it and caught it with one hand. Both boys whooped.

'I cannot cope with you two right now,' stated Esther. 'Where is Dad? I need to talk to him.'

'Study,' said both boys in unison. Then, 'Jinx', followed by another cushion sailing across the room.

Esther went towards the study. She really wanted to talk to Rob, to tell him all about what had happened and to hear him tell her it would be alright. There was something so calming about her husband, so solid and grounded, she knew that simply telling him would make her feel better. She knew what he would say, that they were in God's hand, that he would provide what was needed and if Esther lost her job then that must be part of his plan, it was not some horrible accident. She was not sure if she believed that but she still wanted to hear him say it. It would make her feel better. If Rob was not worried then maybe she didn't need to be either.

She could hear his voice through the thin wooden door.

'Yes Roselyn, yes. I can see that but maybe it needn't be as bleak as you think. Maybe we can work this one out. What did your brother say?'

Esther opened the door. Rob was leaning back on his chair with his feet on the desk, wedged between large religious tomes and piles of paper. His computer was at one side, pushed out of the way when he settled for what was bound to be a lengthy phone call. He looked at Esther and made a face. She pointed at her watch and raised her eyebrows, indicating that she wanted him to finish. He shook his head, letting her know that this was not going to be quick, he needed to give Roselyn some time. Esther withdrew, forcing herself to shut the door quietly. She went to the kitchen.

The work surfaces were sticky with spilled sugar, milk and cereal. She ran a cloth under the tap and wiped, wondering if the boys noticed the mess and decided to leave it, or if they never actually saw it. She filled the kettle and made two cups of tea. Then, in an unexpected spurt of self-pity, she poured Rob's tea down the sink. She wanted to talk to him. If he was unavailable then she would not take him a drink.

Pushing open the bedroom door, she ignored the dirty clothes scattered across the floor and sat on the bed. Kicking her shoes to the floor she drew up her knees and rested her chin on them. She sipped the tea. She had made it too quickly and it was weak, tasting of hot water and sugar rather than tea. She balanced the mug on the book and Bible which sat next to her pillow and closed her eyes. She knew she might be worrying unnecessarily; that she might well not lose her job or may find another one just as good. However, she was not sure she had enough energy to either fight or look. There was so much to do at home and in the church, plus teaching her class. She had no reserves left for anything extra, anything creative.

The study door banged and Rob bounded up the stairs. He peered around the bedroom door at her.

'Sorry about that. Roselyn,' he explained.

'Yes, I heard,' said Esther. 'Can we talk? There's something I need to tell you.'

'Not now, I'm late. Oldies Afternoon today and I am meant to be giving a quick talk after their carols. Can it wait until later? I'll be home for dinner, then I have a deacons' meeting at eight.'

Esther nodded and he blew her a kiss and left. 'I need to make an appointment with my own husband,' she thought crossly. 'He's available for everyone's problems except mine.' She rolled onto her side and pulled a pillow over her face. She would allow herself ten minutes to wallow, then would prepare dinner and clean something.

After exactly three minutes, the doorbell rang. Esther held her breath for a moment, hoping one of the boys would answer it. There was no change to the volume of the television and after a few minutes, there was another knock on the front door. Punching the pillow in futile rebellion, Esther dragged herself downstairs and opened the door. She smiled a welcome to Mr Wykes, who stood awkwardly on the doorstep.

'Ah Esther, I wasn't sure if anyone could hear me over the television,' he said, managing to convey that now was an unsuitable time for anyone to be watching television.

Esther waited, declining to respond.

'I just popped round for the church key. I agreed to set up the chairs for the meeting tomorrow and I left mine at home. Do you have one I could borrow?'

'Yes, of course,' replied Esther, 'but do you think you could return it when you've finished? You can just pop it through the letterbox.' She had lost four keys already to absent-minded members who forgot to return them and she did not want to ask the church secretary for yet another copy. It was a definite drawback to the manse being so close to the church; everyone thought that to quickly borrow the church key was no inconvenience at all. They did not realise this meant the Pritchard family rarely watched a whole programme or ate an entire meal without at least one disturbance.

Esther passed him the key, waved a cheery goodbye and closed the door. She noticed a stack of unopened cards on the window sill and decided she would make herself another drink and open them before she began her chores. She walked through to the kitchen and pulled a chair close to the oven, switching it on. This house was always so cold. The gas fire was on in the sitting room but the noise from the television would disturb her and she needed a few more minutes of peace.

She liked Christmas cards. She liked their bright messages and colourful pictures. Some were from old friends who only ever corresponded at Christmas time and it was always interesting to find out their news and keep some kind of tentative track on where their lives were leading them. She pushed her finger into the first envelope and tore across the top in a jagged line. There was a letter enclosed and she unfolded it with anticipation. They often received Christmas letters. These varied in content. Some were full of the achievements of her friends' children and were quickly discarded.

However, this letter was from an old university friend and was full of humorous anecdotes that made Esther laugh. Esther and Rob sent out their own letter. Rob wrote it and it tended to be aimed at their more religious friends, full of prayer requests and items to give thanks for. She was never quite sure how her friends from school days responded when told to 'praise God for his work with X' and had sometimes considered writing her own, secular letter. Maybe one day, when she had more time.

Even the boasting or religious letters and cards were better, in Esther's eyes, than those people who sent none. It had become fashionable recently amongst some Christians to stop sending cards, saying that it was another stress point around Christmas that detracted from the true Biblical message and was a waste of both time and money. They told people that rather than send cards, they would be making a donation to charity. Esther had no idea if they actually did. She did, however, feel the logic was rather backwards. They were basically saying, 'I will not give you anything, I will send the money to the needy. But you can still send me a card.' It would be better she felt, if they instead informed people that they did not wish to receive cards but would still be sending them, as a sacrificial action of love and friendship. It was something she could rant about at length. Rob would smile at her and pat her knee and tell her it was not important. The boys would roll their eyes and say, 'Mum's off again.'

The kettle boiled and Esther poured water over the tea bag. She would let it infuse properly this time. The telephone shrilled and knowing Rob was out, she hurried to the study.

'Hello, Marksbridge Manse, this is Esther speaking.'

'Hello? Esther? Can I speak to Rob please? It's urgent.'

Esther recognised Roselyn's voice and was glad her husband was out. This woman was a nuisance, whatever her problems might be. Esther used the calm patient voice that she used for children who were rather dim, 'I'm sorry Roselyn but Rob is out. Can I give him a message when he comes home?'

'No, I need to speak to him. I cannot get through on his mobile' (That is because he knows your number, thought Esther but said nothing.) 'Please ask him to phone me as soon as he gets home,' demanded Roselyn adding, 'If he really is out, that is.'

Esther took a deep breath to prevent herself from responding as she would like to. She knew this lady had emotional problems and did not see the world as clearly as she should and that this rudeness was not really directed at Esther.

'Yes, of course. Bye bye,' she said calmly, ending the call, returning to the kitchen to flop the teabag from her mug into the dustbin. She still had time to drink some of it. Then when Rob returned she could tell him about school and ask his advice. She doubted she would mention Roselyn's message. She needed her husband herself this time.

***

Andrew opened his second can of beer before opening his laptop. He clicked onto the 'tes connect' website and scrolled down to see what jobs were available. He decided to start with the NQT positions. Although he would not strictly be 'newly qualified' in September, he reasoned that if a school were willing to take on someone new, they would not be hoping for someone with experience. Andrew could blag his way into many things, but experience spoke for itself and he was sadly lacking. There were not many positions available and none at all that interested him. He shut his computer and belched loudly.

He could not quite believe what he had heard at school. He had always been under the misapprehension that unless you did something bad enough to be fired, your job was safe. He certainly had not realised just how insecure it was. He was not sure what he was going to do. But he knew what he was not going to do. He was not going to go back and live with his parents. Not even temporarily.

Andrew's parents loved him, he had never doubted that. However, they had never really helped him. This was mainly because they themselves had never really been helped in life, plus they had neither the resources nor the knowledge to help much. Andrew sometimes wondered if it was a cultural trait. Some ethnic groups seemed to work hard, striving for their children to escape the lives that they felt trapped in. Others seemed to have children just so they could help and support them as parents. Andrew's father had been expected to leave school and go into the family business. His grandfather had needed help in the shop and therefore it was his son's duty to provide that. Although that had changed slightly with the next generation and Andrew's father had been keen for him to attend university, there was still the underlying belief that Andrew's first duty was to help his parents. They did not think they should forfeit anything for their children, the children had a duty to help their parents.

Andrew remembered doing his A levels and having to first complete his early morning paper round before rushing to catch the bus to school. He watched other pupils arrive, driven by their parents, arriving calm and fresh from the shower. He felt that he was behind in the competition of life before he had written his name on the first exam paper. Even when he went home during his time at university, if he was studying, his mother would often call him away from an essay or revision because she needed help with the accounts or wanted him to fill the car with petrol or to pick up something from the wholesalers. There was always the feeling that what he was doing was less important, that it could wait until he had finished doing what they needed to achieve.

They also had not been able to advise him when it came to finding a university or applying for a student loan. He had needed to find a helpful teacher or glean what he could from friends. They certainly did not have the resources to fund his university life, so Andrew had been able to apply to only the cheaper universities. If he wanted computers or books, or money to buy a suit for interviews, it had to come from his earnings in the student bar. It was hard not to envy those students who only had to worry about their studies because their parents could afford to pay their bills. He now had to pay back his loan. At the moment his salary was only just enough for him to begin paying back the loan but every year it would increase and so too would the amount that he owed.

He sometimes felt the weight of that loan like a physical burden that he was carrying. He felt that he would not be truly free to live as he wanted until that loan was paid off.

Andrew stretched his legs out along his bed and scrunched the pillow beneath his head. He wanted to decide on a plan, to know what his options were before he was forced into a position that he did not want. He had been independent since childhood, so this was his problem and he would have to solve it. He wondered if what Esther Pritchard had said was true, if his low salary made him an attractive employee. He doubted it. He sometimes felt that if Maddy was not there to watch his back the class would completely go to pot. He enjoyed teaching, even dared to think that he might be rather good at it, but classroom control was not something he had yet managed to grasp. He was getting better, he knew that. When he thought back to his first week, even he shuddered, but there was still a way to go. Some schools insisted on watching a lesson as part of the selection process. He was not keen on that, not at all confident his 'model lesson' would be anything other than embarrassing. He pulled off his socks. It was easier to think with bare feet.

No, he was not ready to leave Marksbridge just yet. In another couple of years he would be raring to go but if he was honest with himself, he was not yet a very marketable product. So, how to ensure that he could stay? Pritchard and Mott had all the experience that he was lacking, anyone who watched them teach would choose them over Andrew, he knew that. What he needed was something else, some edge that made him an attractive employee. He had no idea what. He would think about it over Christmas. Maybe his sister would have a clever idea.

***

Cynthia could feel the tension inside. She was already exhausted from the previous day's drama and now all that anxiety had come rushing back. Her head ached and her neck was stiff. She opened the door of her cottage and went briskly to the kitchen to make some tea. Carrying the tray none too steadily into her sitting room, she bent to light the fire before going to her chair. She watched the flames lick the kindling, letting the familiar crackle calm her nerves. She sipped her tea, remembering the mug she had been presented with by Mr Carter. She had avoided him today, not knowing what to say, feeling that their relationship had changed somehow and not sure where she stood now. Had he crossed the line from colleague to friend? That was unthinkable. Cynthia did not have friends. She decided he probably thought her a very silly woman and she sighed. Never mind, he was only the caretaker.

The new problem was less easy to dismiss. Cynthia could not begin to consider what would happen if she lost her job. Like Andrew, she had thought her position was secure, had never considered the possibility that one day she might need to leave before she reached retirement age. The very thought made her hands shake and the cup rattled as it made contact with her saucer. She could not entertain the idea of leaving; she would do whatever was necessary to remain at the school.

Cynthia had been working at Marksbridge Infant School longer than anyone. She had seen hundreds of children come and go and had now taught a few of their children in turn. She had worked under three different head teachers and with a whole selection of other staff. She had seen the school expand to four classes, then five, then reduce again when the age of transfer changed with the introduction of the national curriculum. She had begun teaching in an age when everything was 'child centred' and lessons were plucked from the teacher's mind each term. Now everything was tightly regulated and she welcomed the improved record keeping and continual monitoring. Cynthia liked stability.

Cynthia had grown up in a large and draughty Victorian vicarage. Her father had been a traditional leader of the local Anglican Church and her mother had arranged flowers and worn a hat to church. When Cynthia was four, her grandparents paid for her to attend the local prep school and when she was aged ten years she became a boarder. She slept in a dormitory of girls who all seemed to own ponies and enjoy ballet. Cynthia did neither, having not the means for a horse nor the figure for dance. She was a self-contained child, not especially gifted but very hard working. At first, she hated boarding, with the unfamiliar smells and the constant noise. She found the lack of privacy difficult as well as the forced sharing of communal spaces. Nowhere was her own.

Gradually she became accustomed to her new life and began to miss her home less. The routine suited her, meals at constant times and rooms designated for prep or television. The teachers were kind, mostly they were young and had no family of their own and the school provided an element of security for all of them with its regular patterns throughout the term.

When Cynthia returned home in the holidays she found her parents to be vague and preoccupied. Their main requirement of her and George, her younger brother, was that they remain quiet and polite and appear presentable when in public. They never asked if Cynthia liked school and so she never told them. They did not know what she was reading, they were just happy that she was quiet. They did not know what she liked or disliked or worried about, they were content that she seemed polite if somewhat uptight.

Cynthia's relationship with George was rather more uneven. She remembered well the pivotal low point. They had always bickered, vying for their parents' attention and easily irritated with each other. George was rather better than Cynthia at scoring points, having a quicker wit and a cruel mind. One weekend, Cynthia was upset. The school had arranged an outing for the final week of the semester and had taken the girls to the Natural History Museum in London. The trip itself had been uneventful, with a lonesome meandering around exhibits while attempting to complete a questionnaire that did little more than distract the girls from actually seeing what they were looking at. The answer to 4a became so much more important than the rather splendid display of extinct birds.

Anyway, all was as expected until the journey home. The girls had been transported by coach and on the return journey they were counted into their places by the teachers and then sat watching a wet London pass through rain spotted windows as they drove home. Cynthia was sitting next to Clara. She was another girl who did not bond easily with others and the two girls were often together by default. This was not a problem. The problem arose from the seat in front, where Juliette Mayers was seated. Juliette was a bully. Bigger than the other girls and maturing early, she strutted around with her oversized breasts and her superior attitude, pushing less confident girls out of her way. She particularly disliked Cynthia, perhaps because the other girl was so self-contained. Cynthia did not seek to befriend Juliette, nor did she look impressed when Juliette entertained the class with stories of her exploits with boys. When she realised that Cynthia was behind her, she saw her chance to release some of her irritations. She swivelled around in her seat, kneeling so that she was able to loom over Cynthia.

'Well, Swot, I expect you enjoyed that. Did the dinosaurs remind you of Mumsy and Pupsy?'

Cynthia turned away, pretending to be absorbed with the London streets as they flashed past. She watched a mother struggling with a pushchair hood and a cyclist dressed in a yellow waterproof, resembling a speeding buttercup.

'Hey, you flat-chested hippo, I am talking to you! Did no one teach you any manners?'

Cynthia felt herself blush. She loathed that her body seemed so slow to change from child to woman, that the only curves she possessed were on her stomach and thighs. She refused to turn her head, hoping that ignoring Juliette would make her a boring target and the girl would return to her seat. She concentrated hard on the park they were passing, filled with forlorn benches and broken litter bins. She felt something land on her face. A slimy glob of spittle had landed on her cheek and was now descending towards her neck.

'You seem to be enjoying the rain. You can have some in here if you want. You'll never get to enjoy much else in life. Poor little vicar's daughter, will be a virgin like Mother Mary your whole life.' Juliette was clearly trying her best to find relevant hurts. However, all that Cynthia could think was that she was muddled, confusing Catholics with Anglicans.

'We don't worship Mary,' she began, 'That's...' Another blob of spit landed on her face, her forehead this time. She reached for her handkerchief but Juliette pulled it roughly from her hand and threw it on the floor behind her. She was clearly angry. Cynthia had no idea how to defuse the situation. She glanced at Clara but the other girl was reading her book, staring at the page with every ounce of concentration, determined not to get involved and become a target herself. Juliette had weight on her side and a wild lack of respect for all authority that frightened the other girls.

The coach swung round a roundabout, causing Juliette to lose her balance and knock her elbow on the window. She decided this was not a good position to be sitting in. She produced one more particularly juicy mouthful of spittle and spat it into Cynthia's hair, then promising her she would 'talk more later', she turned back to her seat. Cynthia spent the rest of the journey miserably aware of the other girl's deposits contaminating her head but helpless as to what she could do. Involving a teacher was not an option. Being a 'sneak' was the worst thing that a girl could descend to and she did not want the prohibition of the other girls. She sat in helpless confusion and wished the journey would end.

Cynthia did not allow her fourteen-year-old self to cry a single tear until she was safely home for the Easter break and was relating the tale to her mother. She needed some advice as to what to do, worried that Juliette's bullying might escalate. As she sat in the garden, beneath the willow tree and explained what had happened, she felt tears sting her eyes and she stopped talking to blow her nose. It was at this point that George appeared. He saw his mother having a rare intimate moment with one of her children and it was not him. She was sitting on the wooden bench, half turned towards his sister and as Cynthia began to rummage for her handkerchief, his mother placed her hand on Cynthia's arm. He thought he could probably make his mother laugh so kicked his ball towards them.

'Hey, what's wrong with Cynth?' he called. 'Turning on the taps again? Dooo try not to be Silly Cynthia. Sillynthia. Get it? Don't be so silly Cynth.'

Their mother smiled at his teasing, the force of his personality making her re-examine her own response. She turned to face her daughter. 'Yes dear, maybe he is right; you must try not to be silly.'

Cynthia sat very still. She had allowed her mother a brief glimpse into her world of angst and instead of joining her and helping her to cope, she had laughed at her. It was not an event that Cynthia ever referred to again. Neither did she ever forget. George's taunt of 'Don't be so silly Cynth' became a regular part of his vocabulary and began to seep into her subconscious mind. If there was one trait which Cynthia strove to eliminate, it was silliness.

Cynthia pushed the poker into the embers and watched the sparks dance towards the chimney. She must decide what to do about her employment but it could wait until the holidays. Tomorrow would be a noisy endurance test with overexcited children and a disrupted routine. She did not enjoy the last day of term and the Christmas party. There was nothing to prepare, so she decided to have an early supper and read by the fire. She rose from her seat and went to collect some logs from the dwindling supply by the back door. It was dark and the logs were laced with cobwebs and dried leaves that had blown there from the garden. She selected an armful cautiously, unwilling to bring spiders into the cottage. Now that Mr James was gone she was unsure who would chop the remaining wood for her. She sighed, so many problems. She raised her chin, determined that she would overcome them. She fully intended to solve them and if that involved a fight, so be it. Miss Mott was not going quietly.

Chapter Five

ESTHER woke to the sound of rain pelting the window. She snuggled deeper under the cover and wondered if the church would ever pay for double glazing to be installed. Probably when they moved out. A manse was improved ready for a new minister, not while the old one was still in residence. She sat up slightly and looked down at Rob who was still asleep. He was exhaling little puffs of sour smelling air and his hair was clamped to his forehead. Esther smiled and bent to kiss his cheek. He was wonderfully warm. He stirred but did not wake, so she turned off the alarm and inched from the bed. It would be good for him to sleep.

Last night had been helter-skelter. He had phoned from the afternoon carols yesterday to say that he would not, after all, be home for dinner. Mrs Brown had suffered a stroke and was not expected to last the night. Her distraught daughter had phoned Rob, asking him to come to the hospital and he had gone straight there. He ate a burger in the car on the way home. Esther had needed to cover for him when the deacons arrived for their meeting. Once she had shooed her boys from the lounge and picked up stray socks and books, she had answered the door as the deacons arrived, showing them into her sitting room and explaining that Rob would arrive as soon as he could. They had arrived tired from their day and keen for the meeting to not last too long. The group consisted of three men and two women. No one thought to remove their shoes. They came in and sat on the sofas and the dining chairs that the boys had helped her to move. The circle was not quite perfect and one of the men got up and moved the sofa slightly, angling it to a better position. There were indentations on the carpet where the casters had sat and some crumbs that had scattered unnoticed. This irritated Esther, who would never have entered someone's home and rearranged their furniture. But she realised this was different, the manse belonged to the church, it was easily forgotten that it was also her home.

She had taken them a tray of tea and biscuits and spent the evening on the computer in Rob's study. The meeting had been a long one as the deacons heard Rob's plans for the new year and discussed some of the pastoral needs in the community. Esther had slipped upstairs to bed long before they had finished and Rob had arrived to find her asleep. She had woken and briefly told him about the school, too tired to elaborate. He had kissed her and said they would talk more tomorrow but she should try not to worry. She had then vaguely been aware of him going downstairs and switching on the television to unwind before he too came to bed.

She now went into the kitchen. The linoleum flooring was cold under her bare feet and she wished she had paused for her slippers. Dirty cups were strewn around the sink, waiting for her to wash them. The tray was missing, so she went to the lounge to find it. Empty chairs stood in their circle, making the room too full. It looked untidy. Joseph was already in front of the television and Esther sent him upstairs to dress and wake his brother. Samuel was beginning to be harder to wake now, which Esther guessed was part of being a teenager. How they had longed for the boys to sleep longer when they were small. Now it was almost impossible to stir Sam some mornings. She rescued the empty tray from where someone had leaned it against the Christmas tree. Lines of spilled coffee had run down its surface, puddling in the slight ridge at the edge. Esther checked the carpet had survived, then went to feed mugs into the dishwasher.

By the time she had fed her sons toast and cereal and hurried them out of the house, Esther felt frazzled. Rob emerged just as she was leaving. She leaned against him briefly in the hallway, breathing in his smell of toothpaste and soap. He kissed the top of her head and hoped she would have a good last day. She heaved her bag into the back seat of her car and reversed out of the driveway, cutting across the lawn to avoid Rob's car which was parked behind her. She had worn a skirt and heels in an effort to appear festive and the heels kept snagging on the floor mat as she drove. She knew her feet would hurt by the time she returned home and wondered why she was bothering.

As she drove, her mind wandered to the reading she had studied last night. She always read her Bible in the evening and she had a little book of notes that gave her a study for each day. The reading had been about angels. Angels featured heavily in the Biblical account of Jesus' birth. They were not, she thought smiling, anything like their own nativity angels, with their glittered halos and runny noses. Her notes had discussed the role of angels. How their messages had helped to remind those long ago people that after centuries of silence, God still existed, still cared for the world and planned to intervene. Esther found this comforting. Sometimes God seemed very remote in her own life, she struggled to hear what he was saying. She liked the idea that this did not mean he did not exist, his silence need not be a cause for alarm. Esther very much wanted to believe that God was in control at the moment. Life felt rather precarious.

She arrived at the school and parked approximately in a space. The car was not straight but she did not notice. Hers was the third car to arrive.

***

Cynthia arrived to find David Carter waiting for her. He was fiddling with a window which she knew was working perfectly well and he stopped as soon as she entered the room, so she knew it was a pretext and not a reason for being there. She bustled over to her desk and began to unload files from her bag.

'Good morning Mr Carter,' she said.

'Morning Miss Mott. I'm glad I caught you; I wanted to check how you were feeling now. Have things settled down again? After what happened?' He peered at her, concern showing in his face.

Cynthia felt herself redden. She did not need to be reminded of their last encounter.

'Yes thank you, I am perfectly well again. It will be most satisfactory to finish the term today, then we can all rest a little.'

'Yes, of course,' he agreed. 'Do you have anything nice planned for Christmas?'

Cynthia paused. She had no plans at all other than to remain quietly in her cottage. She supposed she might see her brother's family at some point, but on the whole the Christmas period loomed ahead like an empty planet. It was likely to be a depressingly lonely affair with very little human contact involved. This was not something she intended to tell the caretaker.

'I shall see my brother I expect,' she offered lamely, politeness forcing her to enquire, 'Will you also be with family?'

David Carter looked uncomfortable himself now.

'No, not really,' he muttered. 'My wife passed away three years ago and I haven't much enjoyed Christmas since. Better to sulk by myself than inflict that on others, I feel.' He looked so vulnerable, so deeply sad, that Cynthia felt something stir within her.

'Oh,' she said, surprised. She had not known he was a widower. In fact, she knew very little about him at all. They did not generally trade information. She felt that she should add something, that etiquette demanded a rather more sympathetic response. 'That must be very difficult for you,' she managed.

He smiled. 'Well, life is what it is. We all do what we need to, don't we.'

Keen to move the conversation on, Cynthia asked if the Christmas tree was still in the hall.

'I wondered if I might have a portion of it, you see. My cottage is not very festive at present and I thought I might take home the top two feet of the tree once the school had dispensed with it.'

'I'm sorry Miss Mott, I'm afraid I threw that out yesterday. It was nearly dead anyway, would've made a terrible mess, dropping all over your pretty room.'

Cynthia blushed again at the reminder that he had been inside her home. He noticed her unease and turned away. She was a funny kettle of fish. Picking up his tools he walked towards the door.

'If I don't see you before you leave, I hope you have a lovely time Miss Mott. I'll see you again in the new year.' He left the classroom, leaving it feeling strangely empty. Cynthia watched him leave, feeling rather muddled. He had always seemed so strong, a robust figure at the school, almost part of the fixtures. It was strange to glimpse inside, to see something of the man, and they now shared a common experience, all be it something she hoped to soon forget. She gave herself a little shake and began to prepare for the day.

***

Andrew Smyth arrived shortly before the children. Maddy Brown was already in the classroom and noticed that he smelled strongly of cigarettes and aftershave. He bounced through the door with a grin, clearly excited by the prospect of the last day. She grinned back at him, finding his enthusiasm infectious.

'I'm just off to meet Miss Mott,' he told her cheerfully. 'Wish me luck.' He grabbed his folder of grades and bounded from the room.

He found Miss Mott in the staffroom looking through his computer grades. She looked up when he entered and motioned for him to sit beside her. He pulled up a wooden chair with a sagging seat pad and a loose leg. It wobbled every time he adjusted his weight.

'These are really not adequate Mr Smyth,' stated Cynthia . 'Look, you have given all the children bar one grades A or B. That hardly leaves room for improvement during the rest of the school year. And single word comments? Not professional, not professional at all. I am very much afraid that you will need to alter these and add some comments that will be of use should another member of staff need to refer to them.'

Andrew looked at his grades, looked at Miss Mott and decided that whilst he did not care in the slightest, it was better to appear contrite.

'Yes, I see, sorry about that. I'll change them now.' He stood, waiting for her to move out of his way. After one term he knew these children inside out. If she wanted more words, that was hardly a problem. Cynthia moved and he pushed her chair to one side, preferring to sit on his wobbly one. He began to delete his initial grades and to add slightly less optimistic ones. He had given the class a maths test last week, he could base his grades on those results. He remembered their scores, it would not take him long.

Surprised at the briefness of their conference, Cynthia returned to her own room. She would check those grades later.

***

The children began to arrive. Maddy Brown was tidying books when Simon Davies' mother called her to the door. She was holding a small plastic bag which she passed to Maddy.

'Simon came home wearing two pairs of trousers yesterday,' she explained. 'I don't know how he managed to fit them both on. I think he did it without thinking, probably talking too much to pay attention. I washed them. They have Jimmy McFee's name in.'

Maddy laughed, 'That's funny. We were wondering where those trousers had got to. Thanks, I'll hang them on Jimmy's peg.'

She followed Mrs Davies to the cloakroom, it smelled of damp coats and feet. Children were pulling wellingtons from their feet and changing into plimsolls or wiping their wet shoes vigorously on the mat. The floor was beginning to be dangerously slippery and Maddy pulled an old piece of carpet from underneath the shoe rack and spread it across the floor so arriving children could walk along it. It was brown with age and none too clean. She went to wash her hands.

Most of the children were laden with bags of gifts. Some were shop bought gift bags, complete with ribbons and tags addressed to Mr Smyth. Some clutched damp carrier bags and withdrew crumpled gifts that looked rather squashed. Maddy cleared a space on Andrew's table. George and Susie had also bought gifts for her. She thanked them and put them in her bag feeling pleased. It was always nice when parents acknowledged her own contribution to their child's education. Most of them only bought a gift for the teacher, but she usually received a smattering of gifts herself. She would open them at home later, it was a treat that she enjoyed.

Another table had been cleared for their food offerings. They were to have a 'special snack' after playtime and had been invited to bring in a contribution. Maddy watched as the heap of chocolate and crisps grew ever larger. There were multipacks of savouries and large boxes of fancy biscuits. There were chocolate fingers, chocolate muffins and tiny cakes coated in pink icing. Someone had sent a bowl of grapes, sealed cleanly with cling film, and there were also plates of homemade cakes which looked rather battered in their plastic boxes.

There were presents in Pear Class too. Esther was sitting at her desk, welcoming the children as they arrived and she had accumulated quite a large heap of brightly wrapped gifts. Some were small and heavy, others obviously bottles of wine. She would pass those on to Judy Mann, her teaching assistant. Rob did not like to have alcohol in the house. Although they both enjoyed a drink on occasion, he said that if he was going to counsel people battling alcohol addiction, then it would be unhelpful to have bottles of wine sitting on the table. The idea of hiding them, only getting them out when they were alone, seemed underhand to him. He was not prepared to risk an undignified scramble to hide the alcohol should someone visit unexpectedly. So the manse remained a 'dry' zone. Esther understood and supported him in this but it did seem a shame when parents were particularly generous and gave her some rather special bottles to enjoy. Never mind, she would give them to Judy, who probably deserved more gifts than she would receive.

The children were not wearing their uniform today and they sat on the carpet with their books looking happy and colourful. Some of the girls wore shiny patent shoes and party dresses with white tights. Esther wondered what colour the tights would be by the time they left. They all sat proudly, feeling special. The boys were in an array of corduroy and denim. They looked younger out of their uniforms. Bill Sanders seemed to be having difficulty with his trousers and constantly pulled them up as he walked. Harry Smith, with his pink cheeks and damp hair, smelled strongly of his father's aftershave. Lucy Williams had a complicated plait in her hair, fastened with numerous ribbons. Esther wondered how long her mother had spent knotting it and how easy it would be to untie. She reached for the register and her pen, and began to read their names, marking who was present. It was an oddly calming activity, for both the children and herself.

'I need this,' she reminded herself. 'I need this normality, this stability amidst the lurching wheel of the church. I need to cling on, to find a strategy that allows me to stay.' She felt suddenly emotional and closed the register with a quick breath and a forced smile.

'Now,' she told the class, 'let's have a fashion parade and look at all your wonderful clothes.'

***

When Andrew arrived back at his classroom he paused in the doorway, shocked by the tables of food and gifts. He hadn't realised that the children would bring presents or so much food. The stack of gifts on his desk was quite overwhelming. Maddy smiled at his surprised face and the children crowded round him, eager to tell him they had bought him a gift. He sat on his chair and gazed at the mound of presents. Every child had brought one, so he had twenty-nine to open.

'Wow,' he said to Maddy. 'Do I open these now or take them home?'

'That's up to you,' she smiled. 'I always like to take them home and open them quietly. I try to write a little thank you note for each child to give them in the new year. But some teachers open them with the class. I expect the children would like to see you open them,' she added, guessing correctly that he was rather keen to unwrap them.

'What do you think?' he asked, turning to the class. 'Shall I open them now?'

'Yes,' called the class, all eager to see inside themselves, each child sure that their gift was the best, even those who could not quite remember what their mothers had bought.

'Register first,' announced Andrew, searching for a black pen.

His desk was a mass of paper and ribbons and gift bags. There was no pen in sight. He went to the side and selected a green felt pen from the pot that the children used. He could not think that green would be a problem; it was marking their attendance that was important, not the colour of pen. He began to call their names, placing a fat green stroke next to each one. He thought it made the register look rather festive. When it was complete he sent a child with it to the office and selected a gift.

'That's mine,' called Justin Brown. 'It's a book.'

'Well, thank you, Justin,' laughed Andrew, 'maybe you shouldn't tell me what it is until I have opened it.' The class all laughed, enjoying the moment and Justin mimed a faint of embarrassment on the carpet.

Thus, with much giggling and calling and general happiness, Andrew opened each of his gifts while the children watched. Their excitement probably exceeded his, though not by much. He was beginning to love his job. He had never in his life received so many gifts all at once. He felt like it was his birthday and was briefly unable to speak. He looked at his class, suffused with emotion and fondness. This had not been an easy term, but he had struggled through to the end and these children had staggered along with him, never critical and always willing to try what he prepared for them. These gifts signified so much more to him than mere token gestures from the parents and he knew he would never forget each one of these children. As he gazed now at their shining faces he realised he needed to bring the chaos down a notch.

'Right,' he said loudly, 'let's have you quiet and I'll explain what we're doing today. I'm only saying it once so you need to listen.' The children shuffled onto their bottoms and mostly stopped talking. Jimmy and Gavin were still having a chat but it was not loud so Andrew chose to ignore it. You couldn't expect every one of them to be silent at the same time. 'We are going to start by making hats for our party,' he began.

***

By ten o'clock, when all the classes were sent by their teachers to find their coats for playtime, the children were slightly calmer. Andrew Smyth was very pleased that he did not have to supervise them and went quickly to the staffroom.

Someone had turned up the gas fire to full and the room felt stuffy as he entered. All the staff and assistants were present, as Jane Lancaster had arranged for two of the dinner staff to cover the last duty.

'We never see them,' thought Andrew. 'They are like night shift workers, in a different world to the rest of the staff.'

He made a coffee and went to sit next to Esther, who was looking tired. She smiled up at him and asked how his morning had gone. He began to tell her how surprised he had been by all the gifts when Jane Lancaster called them to quiet.

'Now, the teaching staff have bought a small gift for the assistants,' she began, pulling some presents from her bag. All the assistants shuffled, looking either expectant or slightly embarrassed. This charade was played out every year. They were always given a gift by the teachers and it was always meant to be a surprise. The assistants slipped the gifts into their own bags, not wanting to have to react enthusiastically in front of an audience. The staff sat in the warm fug, sipping their drinks and eating chocolates, each lost in their own world of thoughts.

'I am a good teacher,' thought Esther. 'I just need a chance to show off my skills. We almost need a teacher competition, a test to see who is best. I'm sure they would keep me then.'

Cynthia was reading Mr Smyth's new grades on the computer.

She shuffled slightly in her seat to reach her coffee. The chair wobbled alarmingly and she clutched the table until she was sure it was stable.

'These grades are much better,' she thought reluctantly. 'However, record keeping is of the utmost importance if one is going to both teach effectively and give relevant feedback to the authorities. One needs to be able to justify one's practice. Perhaps greater importance could be placed on our records and plans. I am sure that mine will quickly illustrate the value that I add to the school. One's salary reflects one's value; it should not be used as a negative judgement. My records are exemplary, I am sure they will show I should be chosen over inexperienced staff.'

Andrew sunk into his chair, feeling the cushion sag beneath him, making his back ache. He looked around. No one was talking and he wondered what thoughts were racing through his colleagues' minds. He reached for the stack of papers which were always on the table and rarely touched. There were some educational journals and a couple of local papers. He chose one of those; he fancied thinking about something other than school. There were some photographs of a local celebrity who had been called upon to open a Christmas Fair and some angry letters from residents complaining about the proposed cut to the bus service. He thought there was something ubiquitous about local news and wondered if journalists were ever tempted to copy and paste articles from other areas. He was sure no one would notice. He flicked through to the classified section. There was the usual stuff for sale and a whole section devoted to used cars. He scanned down to the portion marked 'Education'. There were adverts for Pilates classes and Zumba. You could spend the evening learning to draw portraits or paint in watercolours. Then he noticed, nestling under a coffee stain, an advert for Mandarin classes.

'Come and learn Chinese,' the article read. 'Beginners welcome.

Learn to speak, read and write Mandarin Chinese. Flexible times to suit. £15 per hour. Native Mandarin speaker teacher.' There was then a telephone number which Andrew knew from the code was local.

'Mandarin,' he thought, 'that might give me an edge.' He had seen some reports on the news recently and knew that China was thought to be the next big economy and the government was considering plans to introduce Mandarin into schools. 'How difficult can it be?' he asked as he reached into his inside pocket for a pen. He wrote the number on the back of his hand then folded the paper and replaced it on the table.

Judy was seated between Maddy and June. They sipped their tea and watched the teachers. Something was wrong. Usually the last day of term was full of funny stories and plans for the holidays. Even tiredness could not account for such sombre staff. June leaned across her.

'What's going on?' she whispered. 'Who died?'

'No idea,' answered Maddy quietly, 'but I'll ask Andrew later. There's no way he'll be able to keep a secret for long. I'll let you both know when I know.' They nodded their understanding and returned to their drinks.

***

At the end of playtime, Cynthia walked briskly back to her room. The children were pulling off their coats, full of fresh air, their cheeks glowing from running around for almost the entirety of the break. With damp hair sticking to their foreheads they kicked off wellingtons and forced feet into plimsolls, hurrying so as to not miss a second of their 'party'. She was always surprised at the ease with which an event could be made special for young children.

Felicity was trying to cram her foot into a plimsoll with her tights all bunched up around her toes. It would not go on and her face began to crumple in the precursor to tears. Miss Mott bent down to help her.

'There is no need to hurry Felicity, we won't start anything until everyone is ready.'

Felicity's face flushed.

'It won't go on,' she explained, gritting her teeth, 'it's got smaller.'

'No, it's the same size,' reassured Miss Mott, 'but your foot has got bigger. Look at how your tights have fallen down, there's too much material around your toes. Come along, let's pull them up properly and then your shoes will fit.'

Cynthia did not hurry. She wanted the next session to take the whole of the period until lunchtime. The children were not in any sort of mood for working and even being moderately quiet would be an effort today. Let them wait a while, then enjoy their food. She wondered at the sense of them then going into lunch but that was not her problem. If the staff took the afternoon register, they were allowed to include that as a whole day in their allocated number in the year. They could not open the afternoon session unless there had been a lunchtime. She sighed, wishing the day was over.

***

Miss Mott did not see Andrew Smyth until she was leaving. As she loaded plants and bags of unopened gifts into her car he trotted over to her from the school.

'Miss Mott, sorry to trouble you, but what do I do with the party food?'

She looked somewhat confused.

'Party food? Did the children not eat it before lunch break?'

'Well, yes, they did,' he explained, 'but they brought loads. What should I do with all the leftovers?'

'Did you not check the "Use by" dates during lunch break, enabling you to return all the perishables and keep the rest until next term?'

'Er, no.'

'Obviously,' he thought. 'Or I wouldn't be asking.'

'Well in that case I suggest you dispose of anything that will go bad in whatever way you think fit. Next term we usually try to incorporate a little snack at some point so the children can finish the food that was left over.' She shuffled the items in her boot. The plant was really too big, she was concerned that closing the boot would break the longest shoots. Deciding it would be safer in the footwell she pulled it out and moved around to the side of her car. Realising their conversation had ended, Andrew moved away.

'Happy Christmas Miss Mott,' he called as he walked back to the school.

He was surprised to find Maddy in the classroom sorting out the food into three piles. He had thought she had already left for the day. Maybe she had been in the toilet.

'That's stuff that will keep for next year, that's stuff for you to take home and that's for me,' she stated. Andrew looked at the mound of food, wondering if he especially wanted three bags of assorted crisps, some cheese strings and two half empty boxes of cupcakes. Maddy's pile looked somewhat nicer and the thought entered his mind that maybe she had known this was the tradition each year and had therefore not opened certain packets when the children were eating, in order that she might take it home. Surely not.

'I won't eat the cheese,' he told her. 'Do you want it?'

She smiled and stuffed it into an empty carrier bag with the rest of her food. She passed another bag to Andrew.

'Here you go; you can put your gifts and food in here.'

'No, thanks,' he said, heaving his satchel from the floor. It was hard enough to feel masculine working in a primary school as it was, he was not about to start carrying shopping bags. He would manage with his arms and satchel.

In Pear class, Esther was also looking at all the food that was left. She too had forgotten to send home the leftovers, having spent the lunch break removing backing paper from the walls so she could spend less time here during the holidays. She was now in something of a dilemma, unsure of what was morally right. Clearly the parents had not intended for her to take home the uneaten food, however, she had forgotten to return it and to simply throw it away seemed more wrong than taking it. Plus she knew how much her boys would love what was left. The cakes and snacks were the sort of food she rarely bought, feeling it was too extravagant for their budget. Judy watched her, waiting for a decision.

'Seems a pity to waste it,' she said helpfully, 'I'll take it if you don't want it.' There were some toffee filled cakes she particularly fancied, they sat in their cellophane container brown and smug with small drips of caramel oozing from their centres. The grapes looked nice too.

'Yes, you're right, of course,' decided Esther. 'Let's share it. You can divide it, use those empty bags while I go and get some fresh backing paper.' At least she would not be making the choice of what to take herself she reasoned, that must absolve her a little. She wished her classroom assistant a Merry Christmas and hurried to the stockroom. Her heels rubbed painfully against the back of her shoes as she walked and she tried to balance mainly on her toes. She hoped to have her room looking presentable before she left and she could not be late. The church had been invited to meet at the manse this evening before they sang carols in the town centre. Maybe the family could eat cupcakes for tea.

Chapter Six

As soon as Andrew reached home he dialled the number from the newspaper. The signal in his room was rather unreliable, so he perched uncomfortably on the window ledge, looking down at the garden below. It was brown and forlorn with tufts of grass growing amongst the rose stubs. His call was answered by a woman with a pronounced Chinese accent. Andrew shut his eyes to better concentrate and listened hard. He explained that he had seen the advert and was enquiring about having Mandarin lessons. Most of what was said in reply he did not understand. After ten minutes, the call ended. Andrew was pretty certain he had booked himself a place in the class.

***

Three days later, Andrew arrived at the library. The night air felt frosty so he walked with care up the metal steps that led to the small meeting room above the main hall. The door was slightly ajar and he tentatively pushed it open. Seated around a table were three men and two women with notebooks in front of them. They turned when they felt the draught from the door and welcomed him with nervous smiles. One of the women was a tall Chinese lady. She stood as he entered and indicated a chair, saying something very fast that he did not understand. He noticed she had a mass of curly black hair, very bad teeth and wore a smart red suit. This, he assumed, was Mrs Wang. The room was painted a sickly pale green and had a synthetic carpet. There was an overflowing noticeboard on one wall and a rack full of leaflets. Some had slipped from their holder and were scattered on the floor, others bent over as though in despair of ever being read. There were grey chairs stacked along one wall and a broken blind at the window that did nothing to hide the yellow night sky that pushed feebly against the glass. In one corner was a coffee machine. No one had a drink so Andrew did not feel it would appropriate to get one for himself. The table was actually four tables pushed together, the wooden surface carved with initials and indeterminate doodles. There was a mobile whiteboard and Mrs Wang had pulled it into position behind her.

It seemed Andrew was the last to arrive as Mrs Wang remained standing, went to close the door and then began to speak. At first Andrew assumed she was speaking Mandarin but gradually his listening adjusted and he began to recognise the words as English. He understood roughly one in every four. He looked around the table.

The lone female pupil was looking slightly anxious. She wore a thick coat which she did not look like she planned to remove and she drew her head further down into the collar, like a tortoise withdrawing into its shell. Her eyes looked very worried and she had a slight frown beneath a very heavy blond fringe. Next to her was a man of about sixty. He had thin grey hair and wore a suit. His expression was impatient and he tapped his pencil on his pad as he listened. Andrew wondered if he was understanding more than himself. The next man was chubbier and wore a sweater and jeans. He looked as if he might burst into laughter at any minute. He had curly brown hair and needed a shave. The last student was about the same age as himself but also dressed in a suit and Andrew guessed he may have come straight from work. He was listening attentively and nodding.

Mrs Wang paused, looking at the woman, who now looked terrified. She was clearly expecting a response and the woman obviously had not the first idea what had been said. The younger man came to her assistance.

'Mrs Wang suggested we should introduce ourselves,' he explained. 'Did you have trouble understanding her?'

'Yes, I wasn't even sure she was speaking English,' admitted the woman, adding that she was called Heather Smith and worked in Waitrose.

At this, the curly haired man did laugh, admitting that he too had not understood much. His name was Trevor and he worked in a bank. The older gentleman was called Nigel and he was an accountant. The young man was called Harry and he was an actuary. He spoke several other languages and had studied Mandarin before but not got very far with it. He assured everyone that they would get used to the accent. Mrs Wang listened to them all, nodding energetically. Andrew wondered how much she understood herself.

They were first taught a little about pronunciation. Mrs Wang waved her arms energetically while saying,

'Ma, ma, ma, ma, ma.' Each one sounded slightly different. She wrote the words on the white board, adding a symbol above each that indicated whether the voice should go up or down as they were spoken. These were tones. They completely altered the meaning of the words the class learned.

'Ma, ma, ma, ma, ma,' the group chanted, desperately trying to make each one sound different. Andrew noticed that most of them were moving their heads in the direction that the tones were meant to go, though audibly they were identical.

'Ma,' said lightly, meant 'mother'. 'Ma' said with a voice that fell then rose, meant 'horse'. Andrew felt there was great potential for disaster with this language.

They were then passed work sheets and Mrs Wang began to write on the board. She showed them two symbols.

'Woman,' she said, pointing to a squat looking crisscross shape. 'Child,' she announced, pointing to an upturned 'L' with a line crossing through the middle. At least, Andrew thought that was what she had said, it sounded like 'chiyel'.

'Woman and child mean "good."'

Andrew began to think that this might be harder than he was expecting, not least because he could not understand the English content of the lesson. The group all tried to copy the symbols in the boxes marked on their worksheets. They resembled the attempts of reception children when first given a pencil. Mrs Wang indicated that they should fill their paper with practice attempts and they began to do so, peeking at their neighbour's work and deciding that theirs may not be the worst.

By the time the lesson finished an hour later, Andrew felt that his brain had been through a mangle. How did one begin to learn something so unlike anything he had previously encountered? As he clanged noisily down the metal steps, he heard someone shout his name. It was Harry. He and Trevor were going to the pub and they asked Andrew to join them. He figured there was no school the next day, why not? Perhaps Harry could shed some light on what he had not understood.

The Bell was full of people merry from office parties and the countdown to Christmas. The men found a table near the door being careful to avoid putting their arms on its sticky surface. Harry bought the first round and carried them through the teeming mass of coats and hats to where they sat, adding to the general stickiness when he put down the overflowing glasses. There was a fire billowing heat into the already hot room and giant baubles hung from the Tudor beams, brushing people's heads as they passed beneath. Trevor raised his glass.

'Cheers,' he said before taking a long swallow. The men nodded and took a serious drink before lowering their glasses and looking more closely at each other. Trevor had an open face, Andrew guessed he probably laughed easily. He asked Harry about the lesson.

'Didn't have the first idea what she was saying most of the time,' he confessed. 'What was all that *"ma ma ma"* stuff for?'

'That was to learn the tones,' explained Harry. 'Mandarin doesn't seem to have many words, so they just reuse them. But they say them differently, so they know the meaning from the tone. That's why they sound almost like they're chanting when they speak; it's not a very even language to listen to. They also mostly learned to speak English from a Chinese person, so their accents are terrible. You'll get used to it though – eventually. I expect we'll sound as bad to them when we start speaking Mandarin.'

'What do you mean, they reuse words?' asked Andrew, 'Surely that can't work.'

'Well, we do it a bit,' said Harry. 'We might say "right" as in you need to turn right, or "right" as in that's correct. You probably don't ever get them muddled up though. You know from the context which meaning is meant. They do the same, it's just they have tons of meanings for the same word. Look, I'll show you.' He pulled his phone from his pocket and touched the screen, scrolling through a few menus until he found what he was looking for. 'This is a Chinese dictionary app. It's free and makes life much easier. You should get one.' He frowned at the screen for a few minutes, then smiled. 'Here you go, today we learned *"ni"*, the word for "you". Well, depending on how you say it, *"ni"* can also mean: a Buddhist nun, a woollen cloth, mud, to imitate, plaster, to hide, fatty, drown…'

Trevor mimed shooting himself and falling dead across the table.

'Enough, stop mate, you're doing my head in. This is going to be impossible. I only wanted to learn to impress the missus. We're going to Beijing next year, thought I would learn some of the lingo before we got there. Sounds too hard though, much too hard.'

Harry paused. 'It is hard,' he agreed, 'but you should be able to learn a bit before you go. Just a few sentences, like "hello" and "thank you."' He smiled. 'I tried to learn it at uni, just for fun. Got bogged down with course work and had to stop, didn't have the time. But I think it's a really cool language to know so thought I'd have another crack. Plus there are Chinese people everywhere, whichever country you go to there are sure to be some, so I reckon it's the most useful one to learn. It'll be good for work too, so few Brits speak it. What about you Andrew, why are you learning? And what do you teach? Languages?'

It was the question that Andrew had grown to dread. When he said he was a teacher, people always assumed he worked in a senior school and taught a specific subject. That was what men did. He always felt like a wimp admitting that he worked with little children. He never knew whether to answer, 'Children' or 'Everything'. He opted for a combination.

'Everything really, I teach younger kids, so we do all the subjects. But like you, I was hoping it might give me bit of an edge, something different. I could teach the older kids a bit of Chinese after school. Run a club or something. But like Trevor, I'm wondering if it's too hard. I mean, I couldn't even understand the English bits.'

'Wonder when we'll learn how to say "my brother has brown hair."' said Trevor. Andrew and Harry looked confused, so he continued, 'Didn't you learn a language at school? You always learn how to say how many brothers and sisters you have and what their hair colour is. Strange thing is, I've been to Paris a dozen times and no one has ever asked me what colour hair my brother has. Someone needs to let the schools know...'

They laughed and talk turned to work and sport. Their conversation was smattered with the occasional Chinese joke. Andrew, who had spent four years being drilled about equality, was not sure whether they were racist and he should try not to laugh. Somehow, making fun of Chinese people seemed less bad than laughing at black people.

They were all driving so it was a relatively short evening. Before they left, Andrew and Trevor promised to attempt at least a second lesson. They obediently took the name of the dictionary app. There was one more lesson scheduled before Christmas. Mrs Wang had been slightly shocked that everyone wanted a break over Christmas. It was not something she had encountered in China and had assumed it was some kind of tree festival, given the number of decorated trees she had seen in shops. No one had felt inclined to explain further given the language barrier.

***

Wednesday morning, Cynthia had a visitor. She opened her cottage door to find Mr Carter standing awkwardly on the path that passed her home. He was clutching a small Christmas tree in a pot and she noticed that some of the soil had dislodged and now speckled his grey sweater.

'Ah, Miss Mott,' he began as she peered around the heavy wooden door.

'Who else was he expecting?' wondered Miss Mott, bemused.

'I hope this is not too early for you' (it was not; at ten o'clock she had been up for nearly four hours) 'but I was at the garden centre and they were giving away the last of their little trees, so I picked one up but then didn't quite know what to do with it and I remembered you saying you wanted one, so here I am.' He spoke in a rush, all one sentence, as though he had rehearsed the words in his mind. He stopped, looking unsure.

Cynthia smiled, it was a lovely thought and she was rather touched. She opened the door wider, aware that heat was escaping.

'That is most kind of you. Please, won't you step inside for a moment?'

Mr Carter walked round her, into the small sitting room. There was a fire already burning in the hearth and he noticed that she had hung her cards from ribbons to decorate the doorposts. A small heap of gifts waited on a small table and she went across to move them, piling them on the floor to make space for the tree.

'If you would be so kind as to place it here,' she said, pulling a magazine from her rack to protect the surface. 'These are from the children; I shall open them Christmas morning. It will be rather splendid to have them under a tree.' Her face was shining and Mr Carter glimpsed the child she might have been, excited by an unexpected treat. He was struck by how lonesome her existence was and he wondered if this was through choice or circumstance. She was a difficult person to know but that did not necessarily mean she did not want friends.

'Might I offer you a beverage?'

'No, but thank you. I need to get on, it's quite a busy day for me, I just wanted to drop off the tree. I'm glad you like it.' He paused, unsure why he had refused the drink. He could have stayed and wondered if he should have done. He had been so sure that she would try to rebuff the offer of a tree, so had decided that he would simply arrive, present it and leave so as not to cause her inconvenience. He had been taken aback by her obvious delight.

'Yes, yes, of course,' she said hurriedly, anxious to not be a hindrance if he was busy. She went to open the door. 'Well, thank you again. I have some decorations; I shall spend a happy few minutes making it look festive. It was so very kind of you.' Her eyes clouded for a moment, as if suddenly aware of how seldom people were kind to her. Her mouth smiled. He raised his hand, wished her a Merry Christmas and left.

She did not watch him leave, not wishing for more heat to escape than was necessary. She did however lean against the closed door and listen as his car started and then drove away. She smiled a small secret smile. What a lovely treat. She opened the small wooden door that concealed her stairs and ascended the steep steps in search of her box of decorations. There was a rope hung on the wall beside her and she held it lightly as she climbed, feeling the temperature drop as she reached the second floor. There were just two rooms upstairs. Originally they had both been bedrooms, with a lavatory in an outbuilding in the garden. A previous resident had transformed the smaller bedroom into a bathroom and when Cynthia had moved in she had updated it, adding a shower and new white goods. It was now a rather luxurious space, though it tended to be too cold in the winter. She had added a large heated towel rail but had wanted to retain the fireplace and it had proved more draughty than pretty.

She went now into her bedroom on the opposite side of the tiny landing. Reaching above her wardrobe, she felt for the shoebox that contained some tinsel and baubles. They had only been used once, the Christmas when her nephews had come for tea. She doubted she would have any visitors this year but she found she wanted the house to look festive for herself. Perhaps she was getting old, she thought, carrying the box back to the sitting room.

As she sorted the twisted tinsel, showering her carpet with glitter, she thought about Mr Carter and his kindness. She was not a person who was comfortable receiving from others. If one accepted, then one owed, was her rather twisted logic. Had the tree not been free, she might not have accepted it, though she did really want one so she might have been tempted. She would like to give Mr Carter something in return, to balance the gesture with one of her own. But with what? She did not consider their relationship one where she could reciprocate with a gift, that would be too much. No, it would need to be something not bought.

'Gingerbread,' she thought, 'I could make some gingerbread and deliver a few pieces to him. In a box, so they look nice. But it won't be a shop bought gift, so it won't look as though I have gone to any effort, more just made some for myself and given him the extra pieces. That will make us equal. Excellent. I will need to discover his address but I am sure he will be listed on our Emergency Contacts sheet.'

She looked across the room at her tree. She had wrapped some paper around the pot and planned to stand it on an old saucer. It stood proudly, festooned with sparkles and stars as the tinsel and baubles caught the flickering light from the fire. There was slightly too much decoration for the size of tree and it resembled a child who had dressed in their parent's clothes and was now standing proudly on a chair swathed in too much silk and finery. But Cynthia did not care. She was extremely pleased with her tree.

'I had better water it or this room will be too warm for it,' she decided, going to the kitchen. Then she would find her recipe book and check she had all she required to bake gingerbread. She found she was humming as she went, content with the shape her day was taking.

***

Esther Pritchard was not humming, nor was she content. She stared grumpily at the box of children's stories that had been dumped on her dining room table. In a few days it would be the church carol service. This was an event that tended to be popular with local residents and several families came to solely that service during the year. It had been decided that this year, every visitor would be given a small tract which explained the Christian message of Christmas and each child would be given a little book. It was these booklets which now sat on her table. The member who had been responsible for buying them had just delivered them, explaining that although initially she had agreed to wrap them, she now found she did not have time. So here were the books, the wrapping paper was all in the carrier bag ready, if Esther did not mind, maybe she could just wrap them. After all, now school had broken up she was probably looking for something to occupy herself.

However, Esther did mind. She had quite enough to do for her own family which is why she did not offer in the first place. She scowled at the books. The idea had been a good one. She knew that many people had almost no contact with the church, that this was the only chance they had to hear about God and that taking home a book might remind them in the future of what they had heard. She did not personally have time to buy and wrap them so had been happy when someone else had volunteered. Now they had been dumped. On her table.

She thought through her options. She could refuse, take them unwrapped to the church and they would still be given out. There was a high possibility that some people would see it was a religious booklet, decide they did not want it and leave it unread in the church when they left, hence resulting in both a missed opportunity and a waste of church resources. A second option was to tell Rob he needed to find a new volunteer. But Rob was at full stretch at the moment. He had three members who were seriously ill and all the extra events and services that came with Christmas to plan for. If she told him she was cross he would take the responsibility into his already overloaded schedule. She could not burden him with that. She thought, not for the first time, that when God was your husband's boss, it was very difficult to complain. She wondered if the boys would help her then quickly dismissed that idea. They would find it amusing to smuggle extra items into the packages and their wrapping was sloppy at the best of times and she did not have time to buy more wrapping paper to compensate for the amount they would waste. It was also too near Christmas to lumber someone else with the job. Though the member, Stacey, who had left them with her had clearly not thought so.

'People think I am different,' thought Esther, 'I am the minister's wife and therefore they assume I have different priorities to everyone else, less pressures, more free time to devote to church duties.' She sometimes felt that although they only paid Rob, they expected them both to give all their time to the church. 'Buy one, get one free,' she thought bitterly.

The doorbell rang. Margery stood on the doorstep, her hair firmly hidden under a headscarf of swirling paisley, her green coat buttoned to the collar.

'Ah Esther, so sorry to disturb you dear but do you have any milk we could borrow? I've come to help sort out the seating and I told the others I would make tea but completely forgot the milk. So much to think about at this time of year isn't there. Do you have a little drop I could have? Save me going to the shops?'

Esther wondered if she should point out that giving away her own milk would mean that she would have to go to the shops herself. She decided that getting rid of the woman was the main priority and allowed herself to smile.

'Yes of course, Margery. Do step inside for a minute; it's such a cold day isn't it. I'll just get you some. I probably have an empty water bottle that I could put some into.' She hurried to the kitchen. She had plenty of milk, it was probably fine. 'How much do you need?' she called to the hallway.

She poured some milk, her milk, into a plastic bottle. It smelled a bit stale but she was sure it would be okay, the milk wouldn't be there for long, they wouldn't notice. She took it back to Margery, thanked her for all she was doing, hoped to see her at the service. Then she shut the door gently and returned to the books.

She heaved the box into the lounge and lowered it onto the rug.

She would sit and watch television while she wrapped, maybe that would help her to feel more festive. There were rolls of paper in the bag but no sticky tape. Esther went to find her own supply in the study, stopping to add it to her shopping list in the kitchen. She still needed to wrap their own gifts for the boys and this was going to use all she had. She looked at the small reel in her hand and settled down on the carpet. It did not look like there was enough.

'Okay God,' she prayed, 'You made two fish and five rolls feed five thousand. Please could you now make one roll of Sellotape wrap all these presents? I do not have time to buy more.' Doubting the effectiveness of her prayer, she began to wrap. The television was showing a variety of festive programmes and she selected an old black and white movie. 'This might not be so bad after all,' she thought just before the telephone shrilled.

'Mum!' she heard a few minutes later, 'That Roselyn woman is on the phone. She says it's urgent.'

***

Cynthia was still humming as she made her gingerbread. The recipe book was old, she had been given it when she was still a child but she found the quantities and instructions to be reliable. Some of the books she had bought more recently looked rather more glamorous but the recipes rarely worked. There was one book, supposedly written by a television chef, which seemed to have strange quantities for every recipe. Cynthia had used it a few times, each one resulting in disaster. She wondered if the celebrity had actually made the food herself or if someone had presented her with the recipes and she had merely added her name to the glossy cover. As she tended to be disparaging of other people's cooking on her programme, Cynthia would rather enjoy meeting her one day and informing her of the ineffectiveness of her own recipes.

She turned the thick pages of her book with care. It was splattered with grease and the pages had come loose over time. There were many happy memories in that book. She had enjoyed baking as a child and George had tended to avoid the kitchen lest he be called upon to help. She had therefore spent many contented hours creating in peace. She still found it relaxing to bake and often wished she had more energy at the end of the school day to indulge in her hobby.

She added butter and sugar to a pan and set them to melt while she weighed out the dry ingredients. The kitchen filled with the tang of ginger and a sizzle alerted her that the butter was beginning to boil. She combined the ingredients, gently turning the heavy mixture with her spoon, watching the grease seep out as she pressed them together. She then floured a board and her rolling pin and turned the mixture out of the pan. It was hot to touch at first, so she added extra flour and lightly kneaded the dough. Soon the burning dulled to a comforting heat and the soft mixture was soothing to touch as she rolled and cut it to shape. She placed the biscuits onto her greased tins, seeing the light shine on the surface. When all the dough was cut, she put them into the hot oven and set the timer, running water into the saucepan. The water foamed as it combined with the detergent and she reached for her brush and began to scrub. The warm kitchen was suffused with the smell of ginger and baking sugar now and Cynthia felt very happy as she cleaned her kitchen and washed her utensils. When the gingerbread was cooked, she removed it from the cooker and left it to harden on the trays while she went in search of a box. She had a box of tea bags in her larder, she could empty that and cover it in Christmas paper. The biscuits could be placed on some greaseproof paper and it would look delightful. Then she stopped.

She imagined herself driving to Mr Carter's house and presenting him with the gift. Rather than being 'leftovers', it would appear rather a personal offering. What would she say? How could she casually explain that she had made him some biscuits? What would his reaction be? Her mood changed as suddenly as if someone had thrown cold water over her.

She abandoned her kitchen and went to stoke the fire. There was the tree, happily festooned in decorations, mocking her naivety. He might think she was stalking him. Or trying to ingratiate herself. Or worse, he might think there was a romantic element to her gift. She felt her cheeks burn at this thought and she quickly sat down and put her hands to her face. Oh dear, she could not think what to do. To even see Mr Carter now would be embarrassing. Yet if she did not reciprocate his kindness in some way it would hang over her, an unresolved debt. The more she considered the problem, the more certain she became that she could not possibly give him the gift. The disappointment within her was immense, like a physical weight it took all the lightness that had been within her and turned it to despondency. She collected more wood from her dwindling supply. She placed a plastic saucer beneath the tree. She dried and put away all the utensils she had used. She arranged her gifts into a more pleasing shape. She browsed through the television magazine, choosing which programmes she might like to watch.

Then she tilted her chin and took a deep breath. Cynthia Mott was not a coward. She had enjoyed baking that gingerbread and she very much wanted to give some to Mr Carter. She was not going to be thwarted through fear of mistaken assumptions concerning her motives.

***

It was about ten o'clock that evening when David Carter was sitting in his lounge deciding what he would watch before he went to bed.

His back ached. On returning from the garden centre he had carried the shrubs he had bought to the garden shed so they would be protected from the frost. It was completely the wrong time of year to buy shrubs. He knew that, but he had felt the need to do something. Wherever he turned, Christmas loomed, with its jangling songs and over bright colours and stuff. There was too much stuff. He had always loved Christmas in the past, had immersed himself happily in the festivities, applied for the maximum leave from work and revelled in it all. That was before Sally got sick. He ran his fingers through his hair, leaving it dishevelled.

How he missed her. It was not getting any easier. He remembered those early worries, forcing her to visit the GP, telling her the lump was probably nothing but she should get it checked. Offering to go with her and then having an awkward shift so not being able to. Then coming home from work to be told that it was probably nothing but she had been referred to the hospital clinic. Just to be safe, just for a check. It had seemed an age before the appointment came through, though it was within the promised two weeks.

This time he made sure he had time off work and went with her. The hospital had been modern, with computerised screens directing everyone, saying how long they should expect to wait, which rooms to move to. They went from one waiting room to another, the psychology clearly being that they would feel they were making progress if they were not in the same chair for the entire wait. It didn't work. They were both nervous, both being jolly, reassuring the other that it was all going to be fine. A waste of time really. They could have a nice meal afterwards, maybe get a curry. It was better to know, to get it checked, than to worry needlessly.

Then waiting on his own while she went in to see the doctor and have the mammogram. It seemed like an age before she reappeared, looking tiny, as if they had shrunk her. It was probably nothing but they wanted to just do an ultra sound, check that what they could see was just a cyst and nothing to worry about. Waiting in that stuffy room again. No windows, no weather, no time. Just an endless uncomfortable wait. Sally clutching her clothes and wearing a thin gown. Shivering despite the heat. Holding hands miserably and pretending they were fine, just a bit bored really, shame they hadn't thought to bring a book to read.

She had been longer in the second consultation and he had begun to pace. It was harder to stay positive without her there to pretend to. He wondered if he had time to slip out for a smoke, was worried she might come out and not find him there. Then she emerged and he could tell she was near tears. They did not speak as they left, he just guided her out towards the car park, steering her with a strong arm through the over bright corridors and out into the fresh air. Paying a fortune for the parking ticket. Then holding her close. Feeling her body melt against his as he stroked her hair, told her it was going to be alright. They had done a biopsy, sent the sample for testing, they would know in a week. A week that was more than an age. A week when nothing else mattered, when neither of them really ate or slept. When they avoided looking into each other's eyes in case they saw their own fear mirrored there.

Finally, the consultation. Sitting next to each other, talking across a desk to a woman who held their lives in the balance. Hearing that their fears were well grounded. That there were treatments but knowing, knowing in their hearts that nothing would ever be the same again.

Now, as he approached another lonely Christmas, David Carter felt tears well in his eyes at the memory. Even now, years later, that moment still felt like a pivot when his world had tipped. It had remained off-kilter ever since. He did not expect it to ever be righted. There was also a strange sense of guilt, an irrational feeling that if he had never made her go to the doctor in the first place she would never have known, never have been ill, never have slipped away from him. He made himself get out of his chair and go to boil the kettle. Maybe a strong brew would stop him feeling so morbid.

He was in the kitchen when he heard the sound. He had not seen any lights or heard a car, but there was someone at his front door. He listened. Maybe he had imagined it. He poured boiling water over the tea bag and decided to go and check while it brewed. The key was on a little shelf next to the front door and he unlocked the door and turned on the outside light. There, on the step, was a small box wrapped in cling film. He picked it up. It was very light and he could smell spices. There was a tiny card attached. He took it into the kitchen and pushed old newspapers onto the floor so he could sit at the table. It was a box containing four Christmas tree shaped ginger biscuits. The card read:

Season's Greetings. Regards. Cynthia Mott

'Well,' he chuckled, 'at least she used her first name.' He took a bite. They were really rather good, sweet and crispy with a softer centre. He would enjoy those with his tea.

Chapter Seven

CYNTHIA decided to go to a carol service. It was Christmas Eve, her single turkey leg was safely in the refrigerator, her tiny pudding was sitting in the larder, she had made her own stuffing and tomorrow she would open a half bottle of wine, which was cooling. There was nothing to prepare and there was a limit to how much television one could stomach at this time of year. Sickly romances and false jollity were not to her taste. No, better to go out in the fresh air, greet some neighbours and sing something familiar. The local Anglican church was holding services both mid-afternoon and midnight, so Cynthia chose the former. She selected a cheery scarf to brighten her winter coat and found some gloves in the drawer beside her bed. They smelled of lavender and were rather pleasing. She changed into a kilt and thick tights, pulled on her fur lined boots and picked up her bag. A glance in the small mirror next to the door confirmed her hair was acceptable and she set off.

As she drove towards the church, she wondered who else might attend.

'Gosh,' she thought, 'I do hope Mr Carter doesn't venture out. That might prove rather embarrassing. I would prefer not to encounter him again until we are safely back at school.

'Now, where should one park? There seem to be more cars than spaces. How inconvenient.' She followed the line of cars that were parked along the length of the church wall, finding a space at the end, tucked beneath the thick trunk of an elm. There was only just room for her car and if she had been carrying a passenger, which she never did, there would not have been room for them to open the door. She hurried back to the church, thinking that perhaps she should have allowed more time.

***

Esther was also hurrying to church. The day had been a mass of activity, not helped by the boys' constant bickering. She wanted them next to her, she was wearing them like armour despite their grumpy faces and whispered gibes at each other.

'Bet you can't work out four to the power of ten,' whispered Joseph.

'You are such a baby,' hissed back Samuel. 'We did that years ago, years and years ago.'

There was a plastic nativity scene in the foyer of the church. Baby Jesus seemed to be riding a camel and Joseph was on the roof for some reason, leaving Mary and the shepherds to welcome the wise men. They seemed to be lost and were scattered across the bookshelf opposite. Samuel wished he had been the one responsible. It added interest to the tableau he felt.

As they arrived at the church, Bob Sayer welcomed them and handed them a small white candle encircled with a small piece of card.

'Lovely to see you all,' he smiled, 'these are for later. No idea what they're for but all will be revealed.' He winked at Samuel, who wondered for a second if he was making a dodgy joke, then decided that he could not possibly be. This was church. And he was old, about a hundred from the looks of him.

'Now,' Bob continued, 'we are hoping for lots of visitors but we don't necessarily have lots of seats. If we run out of chairs, I can rely on you youngsters to stand at the back, can't I?'

'Yes, of course,' Esther answered for them with a smile. She hurried them through the door quickly so Bob would not hear their cries of complaint about having been forced to come, they had already been to church twice this week and why did they have to stand? Why can't old people stand? They were still growing their legs, they needed to conserve their energy. This became slightly modified to a quick discussion about all the people who they did not, under any circumstances, want to sit next to and if Esther did sit near them they would leave and spend the entire service in the toilets. Esther wondered what it would be like to come to church as a family, to sit with her husband and have him help discipline the children. She ignored them and sat where she wanted, glad for the general volume of chatter so her boys' whining was unlikely to be overheard. They slouched either side of her and scowled at anyone who looked likely to approach.

***

Cynthia was also unsure where to sit when she arrived at the Anglican Church. She walked past the porcelain nativity scene that decorated the entrance hall and through the nave into the main body of the church. It smelled of incense and candle wax. She was handed a solid green book and a smaller red one and she meandered down the aisle, choosing where to sit. There was an empty pew near the back and she slid into it and bowed her head. If people assumed she was praying they were less likely to speak to her. She studied her boots. They could do with a polish; she would do that when she returned home. The organ filled the hall with majestic volume and the congregation rose as one. Cynthia was pleased she had come. It was nice to feel part of something. There was something comforting about the familiarity of carols and she listened to the choir as they sang their way to the front, their crimson tunics billowing as they walked, their expressions stern. If she had the right voice, thought Cynthia, she would have joined a choir. The discipline and structure would have suited her. Unfortunately her soprano efforts were often rather sharp and off key, as George had persistently pointed out when they were younger. Better to stick to something she could excel at.

The congregation fumbled through their books and the service began. Cynthia remembered much of it from her childhood and barely needed to look at her book. She noticed that others were less comfortable with the service and looked anxiously at each other as they sought to find the correct page and give the correct responses. In the flickering candle light, the old church echoed with history. The high ceiling and majestic arches lifted one's eyes and thoughts upwards, beyond self towards a higher being. For ages past people had observed these rituals, letting tradition add structure to their year. Cynthia wondered how many people regularly attended. It was not something she found the time to indulge in very often.

***

In the Baptist church, Rob was encouraging the latecomers to find their seats and join the congregation. His face was shining and Esther knew he was excited. He enjoyed preaching and spent hours preparing what he hoped were interesting talks. So much more fulfilling if they were delivered to a packed church rather than a handful of faithful regulars. She smiled up at him, enjoying how good-looking he was. She wondered how many other women were thinking the same thing. Strange to have such a public husband, at times like this she felt she shared him with a hundred other people. And God. She was always aware that hers was not the first claim on him, first came God.

'Is it allowed for someone to be jealous of God?' she wondered.

'It's not like I can compete really.' She began to listen to what Rob was saying. He was explaining what the Bible meant by 'God became flesh'.

'I remember when Samuel was about three,' he began.

Samuel slunk lower in his seat. He hated being discussed from the pulpit, it was so embarrassing and his father always managed to make him sound a complete plonker. He drew up his shoulders and stared hard at his feet, wishing he was somewhere else, fearing what piece of personal family history was about to be sacrificed on the altar of a good illustration.

'We had gone to see a friend whose dog was pregnant,' continued Rob, warming to his theme and oblivious to his son's discomfort. 'We all discussed how many puppies she was likely to produce and then Sam spoke up and asked if she could have kittens next time because he was allowed a cat but not a dog.' He paused, waiting for polite sniggers which were dutifully delivered. 'Now, it is obvious to us as adults that a pregnant dog can only produce puppies. And a cat can only produce kittens. And when my wife was pregnant, she could only produce a child. But what about God? If Jesus was God's baby, what was that baby? And if Mary, a woman, was the mother, then does that not mean that Jesus was both human and God?

'Think about it for a minute. Consider what that means. A real baby, that cried and pooped and fed, just like our babies. Yet also God, God who created the world, who is beyond anything we can imagine. That God, still God, but limited now to human form. Why would he do that? What was the point of that first Christmas? We will consider that after our next carol.'

The congregation shuffled to their feet as the band began to play. The words were displayed on a large screen at the front of the church. Samuel stood with his mother, glad that the story had only been moderately embarrassing. He refused to meet his brother's eye, who he knew would be bursting to tease him about his stupidity.

★★★

In the Anglican Church, Cynthia was scanning the congregation as they stood for the final carol. It was one of her favourites, with a beautiful descant that the choir sang, imitating the angels of long ago. She held her hymnal high and sang out, confident that she would not be heard above the volume of the choir. She was looking around to see who she might recognise. There was the lady from the greengrocers and a couple of parents from the school. She would speak to them as she left; offer them the compliments of the season. She was searching for a familiar head of grey hair.

'Not that I would want to speak to him if he was here,' she thought to herself. But it would help her to decide which door to leave through. She twisted as much as she considered appropriate to look to each side but to no avail. It seemed that he had not come. Not that there was any reason to suppose that he would. He was possibly visiting relatives. He might not even be religious, very few people were it seemed. She felt oddly disappointed as she decided that he was not there. She would not see him again until school recommenced. Which was good, she reminded herself, much better to keep the relationship strictly professional. He was a work colleague, that was all.

The children were now processing down the central aisle, each one carrying a small candle stuck into an orange. The tiny flames twinkled in the dark church, making a pathway of light towards the altar as the organ softly played. The shadows in the ancient building deepened, casting the congregation on either side into near darkness. Parents and grandparents strained in their seats to watch their child, the young faces shining as the light flickered across their cheeks. The atmosphere was magical and the scent of melted wax mingled with the incense to further warm the church.

They seemed terribly near to each other and all her instincts as a teacher made Cynthia feel that this was a ritual that would soon be deemed too dangerous to continue. The possibilities of setting on fire the hair of the child in front was very great. She watched tensely, noting where the font was as a ready supply of water, ready to spring into action should it be necessary. It was not. All the children safely reached the altar rail and the candles were removed from them. She felt herself relax a fraction. The vicar began to say the benediction and she bowed her head.

***

The candles were also being lit in the Baptist church. They represented the light that Jesus had brought into the world, which individuals had talked about until the whole world and every generation knew that Jesus had come. Rob stepped forward and lit the first candle from the large white candle that stood at the front. The woman holding that candle, then shared the flame with people on either side, who in turn shared the flame with others. Gradually the flame was shared along the rows of people, more and more of the congregation holding a tiny lit candle. Someone in the back row was either anxious about how long it was taking or did not quite understand the illustration, as they took out their lighter and lit their own candle. Esther felt there was an illustration there in itself, but not one that could tactfully be used from the pulpit.

The tiny candles burned brightly, casting their light throughout the building, lending a rosy hue to everyone's face and making the church feel very festive. Joseph had placed his ring of cardboard upside down and instead of protecting his fingers, it channelled hot wax onto his skin. He gasped and quickly blew out his candle, much to his brother's amusement. He felt rather pleased with himself for not swearing and smiled angelically back, picking hardening wax off his hand and placing it in the handbag of the woman seated in front. Esther was absorbing the peaceful atmosphere and did not notice. Samuel passed him some more wax from his own candle. There was a final prayer and the service ended. The boys wondered just how many hours their parents would now talk for before they could all go home.

The threesome wended their way through to the hall, where coffee and mince pies were being served. Esther would have loved a mulled wine. A strong one.

There was a general hum of noise as most people chatted enthusiastically, happy to see each other and excited by the season. A few people hung back awkwardly, clinging to the sides of the hall for security and looking absorbed by their drink. Esther headed towards them. They were visitors and she was keen to make them feel welcome and find out who they were. Rob would be standing at the main door, greeting people as they left and thanking them for coming. It was her role to notice the people who left via the side door, to make sure no one left without being spoken to, being acknowledged and offered a friendly smile. It was a role she was happy to fulfil. The boys watched as their mother walked towards someone they did not recognise and resigned themselves to a long wait. Their family was always the last to leave, even if there was something they wanted to watch on television or somewhere they wanted to go. Nothing could cause their parents to hurry. Even if they felt ill, they were always required to stand quietly out of the way until the very last person had been greeted and chatted to. Sometimes for what felt like hours and hours. Samuel reached into his pocket.

'I got this tongue-twister from Tom,' he said. 'See if you can say it. It might be too hard for someone your age.'

Joseph took the paper and read the rhyme. He giggled, spotting quickly what the mispronounced words would say.

'Go on,' urged his brother, 'see if you can say it. I can do it at double speed. If you say it into the microphone, I'll give you a fiver. Go on, I dare you.'

Joseph considered. Five pounds was a lot of money. However, his father was quite likely to kill him if he said what he thought he would probably say, at high volume and in a church packed with visitors. He did not dare. Not even for five pounds. It would be funny if Samuel did though.

'No, I'm not that stupid,' he replied. 'You can though, if you're so clever, you say it.'

Samuel leaned towards him and whispered in his ear. Both boys collapsed into a giggling heap. Esther reappeared at their side.

'What are you two laughing at?' she asked, 'And do you want to get a drink? There should be some juice if you want it.' The boys shook their heads, knowing the 'juice' would be orange squash, diluted to almost nonexistence and tasting like sweet urine.

'I got a tongue-twister at school,' said Samuel, giving his mother the paper. 'It's quite a good one.'

Esther saw Roselyn approaching and looked down, preferring to be absorbed in reading than to be open to an unwelcome conversation with someone she disliked.

'I am not a pheasant plucker, I'm a pheasant plucker's mate,' she began to read.

'You have to say it out loud,' urged Samuel.

'Yeah Mum, see if you can,' said Joseph, removing the paper.

'I'm not a pleasant fucker,' began Esther and stopped. 'Oh.' She covered her mouth and giggled.

Roselyn stood very still. She was not sure that she had heard correctly. The Pritchard family appeared to be having a cosy time together laughing. They obviously did not care that she was finding life very difficult at the moment. She was not even sure she could carry on. Christmas was such a difficult time for her. She did so need to talk to someone, be listened to. She was sure it would help. She turned away. Esther did not appear to be in an overly sympathetic mood. She would go to the front door, perhaps Rob would have time to listen. It was his job, after all and she did need help, she felt so horribly lonely. She left the hall. Esther watched her leave and smiled. That was one less thing to spoil her evening. She told the boys they were terrible and went in search of more visitors.

Stacey entered the hall, struggling with several bags that were clearly too heavy for her. Esther was somewhat surprised to see Samuel go towards her and take some of the bags to help. They carried them through to the church kitchen. Esther finished her conversation and went over to investigate.

Stacey was unloading food from the carriers into the fridge. Samuel was leaning against a cupboard door watching her. Esther wondered why. It was most unlike her son to show any interest in anything at all that was church related.

'I've got a really cool tongue-twister,' she heard him say, 'do you want to try it?'

'I hardly think Stacey wants to say that, thank you Samuel,' she said, keen to stop him. 'What's all this food for?'

'It's for the church Christmas lunch tomorrow, you know, the one for people who would be on their own? I think we might get a few homeless people too because I know Rob mentioned it at the shelter last week when he was there.'

'Oh, of course,' said Esther, embarrassed that she had forgotten. She was not involved and there had been so much else to think about.

'Sarah was meant to be organising it,' continued Stacey as she heaved a sack of potatoes onto the surface next to the sink. 'But her mum was ill so she asked me to cover for her. That's why I dumped you with the gifts to wrap. Did you manage them all?' She pulled open a drawer, searched for a peeler, then settled for a knife that looked sharp and pulled out the first potato. The knife was blunt. It was like trying to remove the skin with a spoon. She had another rummage through the drawer.

Esther was feeling somewhat guilty. All those uncharitable thoughts she had had and Stacey must have been flat out, organising everything for the lunch. She felt like a very bad person.

'Sorry God,' she thought, 'I shouldn't have jumped to conclusions.' Stacey did not appear to notice her discomfort and was peeling potatoes at high speed. Water had splashed from the saucepan, wetting her apron. The dirty peelings were a growing mound in an empty carrier bag. Esther wondered if she should offer to help. Samuel guessed her thoughts and was glaring at her. She decided not to.

'I think Rob is going to pop in after he's eaten with you lot,' Stacey continued. 'He said he would. Will you come too?'

Esther stopped smiling. Her voice sounded very strange as she heard herself ask,

'Did he? What, tomorrow? Christmas Day? He hasn't mentioned it to me yet.' She regretted saying it as soon as the words were spoken. Now it looked like they did not communicate. If she persuaded him not to come, everyone would guess that it was Esther who had stopped him. People would talk. People always talked.

'Come on Mum, we should find Jo,' said Samuel. He did not know exactly why his mother was pulling strange faces but he did think it was time they left. He did not want to witness a tense conversation between two women and he felt one brewing. Women could behave very strangely sometimes. Esther allowed herself to be pulled away. They went to find Joseph and, to the boys great joy, decided to go home. Rob would follow later, when everyone had gone. She would talk to him at home. Where they could speak in private. As they walked home, Esther reflected that the carol service had been rather lovely but the minefield of human interaction afterwards would have been better avoided.

***

Andrew had not attended a carol service, opting instead to go on a pub crawl with some old school friends. He would be staying at his parents' house and was glad for an excuse to escape for a few hours. He drove down late afternoon on Christmas Eve and used his key to let himself in, shouting hello as he slammed the front door behind him, shutting out the cold evening air. The smell of the house brought back so many childhood memories. It was like a time machine. He arrived, walked through the front door and within seconds he was a child again, trying to avoid jobs and looking for something to eat. His mother had met him in the gloomy hallway, kissed him and told him he was too thin. She wiped her hands on a tea towel she was holding and told him to come and have a cup of tea. His father had punched his arm and told him he was too tall. He had then handed him a red plastic price gun and asked if he would mind pricing up a box of tins that he wanted to get on the shelves before Christmas.

'I won't work Christmas Day, your mother will make a fuss,' said his father, 'but I would like to get this last lot of stuff from the wholesalers out before tomorrow. Then I can open for a couple of hours on Boxing Day. You'll give me a hand won't you? I don't want to be paying staff double time for a bank holiday. It'll only be an hour or two; you never know what people might have run out of. Have to keep the customers sweet or I'll lose them to the supermarkets.'

Andrew followed his father into the shop. It always felt cold and empty when it was closed. There was only one strip light on and the shelves loomed greyly towards the ceiling. It was silent except for the whir from the fridges. The till was placed near the door, with a stack of wire baskets on the floor next to it. Behind the till, out of thieving schoolchildren's reach, were the sweets. Most were wrapped but there were some old fashioned jars of multicoloured boiled sweets, cough candy, jelly animals, butterscotch and pear drops. There were small white paper bags hanging from a meat hook and a set of scales standing next to them. The vegetables were there too, displayed in large bins that needed to be emptied regularly or the bottom filled up with rotting vegetation and the whole shop stank. Andrew remembered the day the family cat had used the potato sack as a litter tray, unnoticed until his father had scooped out a handful of potatoes and cat poo. It was one of those stories that his mother loved to tell while his father glowered in the background.

The smells of sugar and dust and new plastic stimulated a kaleidoscope of memories, images fighting for space in his mind: Reaching up to stack shelves with a pyramid of tins. Using a broom taller than himself to sweep the floor. Loitering near the till in the hope a customer would buy him sweets. Setting up his train set one Christmas along the aisles and then searching for a lost carriage amongst dust balls and rotting potatoes behind a unit. He stood, holding the plastic price gun, watching his own image through the ages, seeing himself change in an unchanging landscape. Knowing that he was different now, that this place was no longer part of him, though should he choose to return, he would always belong.

He smiled and bent to pick up the heavy box of canned produce, groaning as he heaved it next to the shelf. His father was at the other end; straightening boxes, turning cans so their labels faced outwards, pushing toilet rolls to a more secure position. The business was a small corner shop, well positioned on the main road at the intersection of four residential roads. In the early years, most customers had lived within a few hundred yards of the shop. They had come almost daily to buy their staples, walking or cycling, knowing each other and chatting for many hours under the bright awning at the front. Then the supermarkets had arrived in town, with their lower prices and bigger range of products. The shop adapted, opening at odd times to sweep up the shoppers who had run out of something essential and wanted to buy an item quickly or on a Sunday when the larger shops were legally closed. There was still an early morning paper round, which provided a small but steady income and they had opened an off-licence section where teenagers of indeterminate age bought alcohol for parties. Andrew constantly nagged his father to be more vigilant about checking their id, telling him he could receive a large fine if caught, but there was a good profit margin so his father only half listened. They had also recently agreed to be a receiver point for returned Amazon goods. They had installed a computer programme and cleared a space under one counter for products waiting to be returned. This did not bring in much money but did bring in more customers, many of whom would buy the odd thing while they were there.

Andrew finished pricing and stacking and went back through the door that led to the house. The kitchen and a small lounge were behind the shop. There was an outside toilet which the staff used and his mother complained about cleaning. Upstairs were the bedrooms and over the shop was one large room. For as long as he could remember, Andrew's parents had planned to divide the room, making a study and another sitting room. It was unlikely to ever happen. The room was large, ideal for parties that also never happened. It was always cold, having only one fireplace and two small radiators and facing north.

Andrew went into the kitchen. His mother was removing

crockery from the dishwasher and stacking it in cupboards. She handed him a bowl and pointed to a shelf she could not reach.

'Save me standing on a chair,' she said.

He leaned across the sink and put the bowl on the top shelf. The kitchen was a mess. There were crumbs where his mother had been making stuffing and the heavy scent of sage fought with the tang of raw onion. Sausages were neatly wrapped in bacon, the discarded wrappers on the table with knives and peelings and spilled peppercorns. His mother grinned at him.

'Lucky I'm not a chef on telly,' she said, following his gaze. 'What time are you meeting your friends? Could you empty the bins before you go?'

'It all smells good,' smiled Andrew, feeling the excitement building inside. This was what Christmas should smell like. It was always a flurry of cooking, preparing food for the next day. Every surface was dirty, every knife had been used and there were saucepans heaped in the sink. His mother always prepared a feast and she always left it until the day before to prepare, mainly because the shop absorbed all her time until the very last minute. Andrew fished a cloth from the sink. It was full of greasy tepid water and he squeezed it out before running it under the tap.

'There's no hot water,' his mother explained, 'I used it all having a shower after we shut the shop.' Andrew sighed. His parents would not want the expense of putting the boiler on for longer during the day, which meant there would be no hot water until about seven o'clock. Too late for a bath before he went out. In the morning he would have to race to the bathroom before his sister or it would be a cold shower in the morning too.

He rinsed the cloth as well as he could and began to wipe surfaces, listening while his mother updated him on all the family news. A cousin had left her husband but had not wanted to take the children so they were living with his aunt. His uncle had decided to take early retirement. Mrs Jones from two doors away had lost her cat and had spent the last three days posting notices through everyone's doors. They were resurfacing the High Street and were going to build a new car park near the station.

Andrew let the news wash over him, content to be home, secure that very little had changed. He had no interest in what his mother was saying but he liked hearing her voice, knowing that no response was expected from him. It was relaxing. He finished wiping the last surface and threw the bits into the bin and the sticky cloth into the sink. It floated in the grey water, spreading crumbs and dirt across the greasy surface. He scooped the bag out of the bin and headed towards the dustbins by the back gate. His mother reached up and kissed his cheek as he passed, happy to have him home again. The house felt complete when he was there.

Andrew put the dustbin lid back on and looked up at the sky. It was a clear night and even through the haze of orange street lights he could make out some stars in the blackness. He remembered the Christmas Eves of childhood, gazing at the sky in search of Father Christmas, straining to hear sleigh bells. The air always seemed cleaner on this night, as if tingling with a contagious excitement. The back door burst open and Emily appeared.

'Hello, heard you were home,' she grinned. 'Mum's put you to work already I see. Has Dad asked you to help in the shop yet?'

He gave her a rueful look.

'It wouldn't be home if anything changed,' he said, wanting to defend his parents. His sister could be pretty negative when she got going and he wanted the evening to be pleasant, to wallow in nostalgia for a bit longer.

'Well, I think it's just rude,' she declared. 'You've only been home about an hour and they're already giving you jobs. They should treat us like guests for a little while. We're adults now.'

Andrew poked her as he passed. She was almost as tall as him, with a willowy figure. Her hair was more red than golden and fell in a heap of untidy curls across her shoulders. Her face was serious, her forehead puckered in a frown above the scattering of freckles that covered most of her skin. He preferred it when her green eyes were dancing with fun. His sister had the ability to change the atmosphere simply by entering a room. When she was happy, everyone had a party. When she was cross, which was fairly often these days, her disapproval pervaded every corner and made everyone present feel discontent. This was not the mood that Andrew wanted for Christmas.

'Come on you, it really doesn't matter. It's just how they are and I don't mind.

'How are you anyway. Any decent men yet?'

She made a face at him and followed him back inside.

'I'm beginning to think decent men don't exist any more. Even the married ones seem a bit weird.

'And don't ask me in front of Mum. I do not need the whole "body clock" lecture. I like to think that even if I never marry or (horrors) do not produce children, I might still be a successful individual. I'm not sure that being single has to be a fault. I'm beginning to quite like it actually.'

Andrew smiled quietly to himself. Clearly she had her eye on someone but was choosing to keep it secret until things were more concrete. Fine with him. He did not much enjoy the relationship scrutiny that tended to be inflicted during visits home either.

She sniffed loudly at his back, leaning forwards so her face was almost touching his hair.

'Not given up yet then. How's the smoker's cough coming along?'

Andrew turned and stuck out his tongue, then went to wash his hands. He peered at his reflection in the mirror, trying to decide whether he needed to shave before he went out.

Chapter Eight

THREE days after Christmas, Andrew drove back to his lodgings. He felt fatter. It had been a good Christmas, full of his mother's cooking, his father's jokes and his sister's sagas. As he drove, he listened to the Mandarin CD his sister had given him. He was always difficult to buy for, not being especially interested in music, sport or clothes and his family had clearly pounced on the idea of his new hobby. He had received a couple of children's books, printed in Singapore and aimed at children learning Mandarin, a book about Chinese grammar, some films and some language CDs.

'*Wo jiao* David. My name is David,' chanted the CD.

'*Wo jiao* Andrew,' he repeated. He sounded very English, even to his own ears. He tried again, adjusting the tone of his words to the chant of the voice he was copying. It sounded a bit better. He indicated right and joined the flow of traffic on the motorway. He really wanted to get this right. It was a good language to learn, he just had to keep going. Every language was hard to learn at first, he would just start slow, try to learn a sentence or two a week. He did not have to ever be fluent, just good enough to teach the basics to a few British infants, something to put on his CV, a little boost to his credentials.

He could already say, 'Hello, how are you?' He had changed the words '*Ni hao*' into the English version of 'knee', followed by an American Indian greeting of 'How', copied from old western movies, so as to better remember how to say them. He knew he needed to dip his voice for both words because he had to dip to touch his knees. He was rather pleased with himself for having applied his teaching skills to his own learning. The children's books would be useful too.

He intended to try and learn Mandarin in the same way that a Chinese child would learn, constantly reading books, gradually increasing the vocabulary within a context that he understood. He had never been able to learn lists of new words when he was studying languages at school, it seemed to rely too heavily on the mathematical part of his brain. He knew that time and space relied on the right side of the brain, so when he was teach drawing he avoided using words like 'leg' or 'eye' which would evoke language and talked instead about curves, lines and lengths. Mandarin was a language, he therefore intended to learn it with the left side of his brain, the part that thought in words and stories and meaning, not symbols which related to little else.

'I may not know languages,' he thought, 'but I do know how to teach. I can teach myself this, I just need to start small and take little steps.'

He leaned down and ejected the CD, fiddling on the seat beside him for a different one. The car swerved slightly, earning him a honk from a passing Volvo. He checked his mirrors and moved into the slow lane, deciding he could concentrate less on his driving by reducing his speed a little. The traffic was light and he could listen intently as he drove. He was aware that he was happy. He liked a new challenge and his slightly compulsive personality was beginning to urge him forwards. It was possible that this hobby would be all consuming and then quietly die, like his kick boxing and fine art passions of earlier years. But he doubted it. There was something about the challenge of Mandarin that appealed to him and it was certainly more useful than fighting in a gym. He realised he was beginning to hum along with the childish rhymes, whilst not understanding a single word that was said. Never mind, he could look up a few words when he got home. Then perhaps he would watch a DVD. His sister had given him four. That would be a nice way to relax.

***

Esther was tired. The rush of Christmas was finally over and as the adrenaline seeped away a deep weariness set in. The Christmas services had all gone well, with a smattering of visitors at both the carol service and the one on Christmas morning. She wondered if any of them had enjoyed it enough to visit again before next Advent. Christmas lunch had been late. It was always late because if anyone at all wanted to chat, Rob was available. The weather had been cold and wet, too unpleasant to walk the short distance to church so she had driven herself and the boys. As soon as she was sure all new people had been welcomed and all regular members had been suitably greeted, she left.

Dinner was a chore but she felt she had accomplished it okay. The vegetables had all been prepared the previous day and the turkey roll went in the oven as soon as they got home. It was then a marathon of boiling pans and opening packets of stuffing and bread sauce, juggling timings and temperatures until everything was cooked at roughly the same time. She always cooked the same things, though was not really sure why. Neither boy liked sprouts or bread sauce but they always had a tiny portion of both on their plates. It was one of those weird traditions that everyone liked but no one really knew why. She remembered the year they had hosted visitors from Canada. They had clearly been disappointed by the lack of sweet potatoes and were perplexed by why she had served them 'oatmeal'.

After lunch, she and Rob had returned to church to visit the lunch being served there. They had tensely discussed it after the carol service, Rob insisting that it was important that he support an initiative being trialled by the membership, that surely the point of Christmas was to remember what God had given to them and to share a little of that joy with other people. Esther had argued that he had done enough, that there had to be some point at which the family became his priority. She had known from the outset that it was a futile argument. Much like teaching, there was no cut-off point with being a minister, you never finished, there was always more that you could do. She saw her role as trying to balance Rob's natural enthusiasm for his work with his responsibilities for his family. However, it was hard to argue against helping homeless people enjoy one good meal a year, so they had gone. Even when she felt she was right, Esther thought that her arguments sounded selfish when compared with what Rob was trying to achieve. It felt like she was arguing with God and who could hope to win that battle?

The boys had not even opened their presents, as they left almost straight after eating. Esther had pulled on her thick coat and attempted to not appear truculent as she told the boys they would try to be quick. They had looked at her sombrely, resignation deeply ingrained in their expectations of life.

They had driven to the church in silence, her anger needing no words for it to be felt. The windscreen wipers' regular sweep of the glass was the only sound, one of them emitting an annoying squeak each time it moved. Rob stared at the road as he drove, knowing that his decision was right but not knowing how to impart that to his wife.

When they walked into the church hall, they saw that the lunch was almost finished. People sat around tables, wearing ridiculous paper hats and smiling. There were bright paper cloths on the tables and each one had a centrepiece of a candle stuck into some oasis and surrounded by holly. The debris on the table showed the remains of crackers, jokes and plastic toys strewn next to dirty cutlery. A CD of carols played quietly in the background and everyone looked happy and slightly sleepy.

The room smelled of boiled vegetables and roasted meat with a strong undercurrent of unwashed bodies. There was another smell wafting through the air and Esther guessed that many of the guests usually indulged in a rather more liquid lunch. Everyone turned as they arrived and Rob grinned happily and called a loud 'Happy Christmas' to everyone. He then went to a far table, pulled up a chair and introduced himself. He was smiling and relaxed, and soon in deep conversation. Stacey emerged from the kitchen and waved at Esther on her way to collecting a stack of dirty plates.

Esther chose a table near the door and slid into an empty chair next to a wrinkled woman of indeterminate age. Her bright yellow hair was streaked with grey and she wore an eclectic selection of knitted items. Next to her was an outsized shopping cart and Esther guessed that it contained all that she owned in the world. The woman leaned towards her, eyes shining with tears.

'That was best food ever,' she announced through a wave of stagnant breath. 'This church is what God is wanting,' she continued firmly. 'No one else cares you know. Most folks don't even see us.' She patted Esther's hand absently.

Esther was not sure that the woman was quite right in the head. However, the sentiment was genuine. This had clearly been special for her, an oasis of comfort in a life that was a continual struggle with cold and hunger and clarity of thought. An old man on her other side also leaned towards her.

'Your husband is a saint,' he stated. 'Every year I dread Christmas, sitting on my own all day thinking about all them friends what have gone now. First time since the war that I've had proper company and proper food. It's kind of you people to bother about us.'

Esther was beginning to feel somewhat uncomfortable. It was

hard to resent being somewhere when people were clearly touched by their presence, who felt significant just because the minister and his wife were there. She reached out and touched the man's hand.

'I'm glad you had a good lunch,' she said. 'Happy Christmas to you.'

The drive home was again silent. Esther was no longer angry, Rob had been right to come. But her feelings were a muddle. She found the amount of his time that was reserved for her and the boys was not enough. She needed to know that she was more special than his work. But did that mean she needed to be more special than God? Than what Rob felt God was asking him to do? She had never wanted to be a minister's wife. She often told people lightly, 'I did not fall in love with the minister; I fell in love with the man. He just decided to become a minister after it was too late for me to change.'

She thought those words again, a week after Christmas, when she was beginning to give in to tiredness, to get up later and spend more time reading and watching bad television with the boys. They were watching a rerun of a James Bond film when she began to evaluate her role. The boys were engrossed in the film, watching a daring chase through a crowded market where miraculously everyone avoided being struck by a speeding car. Esther sipped her coffee and allowed her mind to wander.

She had met Rob while at university. She had been studying English, him theology. A year into their relationship she decided to stay on and do a PGCE, qualifying her to teach primary school children. He decided to modify his course and study to be a minister. He was ordained the same year she graduated and they became engaged. It had all felt wonderfully romantic. She remembered taking him home, proudly introducing him to her parents when they were first dating. Feeling proud of his dark good looks and the confidence with which he spoke to her father. Her parents had loved him. Of course. Everyone loved Rob. He was one of those easy going personalities who embraced life with enthusiasm and found people interesting.

Rob had worked as an assistant minister in a fairly large church for a year, then they had married and moved to a small village where they worked at the local chapel and the village school respectively. Esther liked the harmony of both inputting to the same community in their own field of expertise.

She had stopped working when the boys were born. At first, motherhood was all she had dreamed of and she thought she would never teach again. But after Joseph was born, she began to feel restless. Her identity had reduced to 'Samuel's or Joseph's mummy' or 'Rob's wife' and she began to want to use her skills again.

'I need to use my brain again,' she told Rob, 'to speak to someone who's more than two foot tall.'

Initially she took on supply work, covering odd lessons and days when teachers were ill or away on courses. She felt alive again when she taught. Standing in front of a class, holding them all in her spell, making them laugh or concentrate on something difficult. If she was honest, she loved the power she felt, the total control over thirty small people. There was also the satisfaction of a job well done when a child finally started to read, or grow in confidence sufficiently to speak out in a class discussion.

Now Esther realised how important that role was to her stability. Being married to the minister entailed a lot of public scrutiny, not all of it kindly. People would comment at how late the manse curtains had been opened, implying that she and Rob slept far too late each morning. They did not take into account that often Rob had been leading meetings until late the night before and by the time he had relaxed and gone to bed, it was after midnight. They noticed when she and the boys were late for church, if they had a new car or a longer holiday than was expected. It was also hard to have friends within the church. Some people assumed that her friends would become privy to confidential details, others were just plainly jealous of the attention that the minister was giving them. Esther had to be careful to sit next to different people each Sunday, to not be seen to be too close to any one member. Her role was often a lonely one.

The boys lay on the floor facing the television. Joseph was surrounded by sweet wrappers and was chewing contentedly. Samuel kept glancing at his mobile. The phone had been his Christmas gift, more than they could sensibly afford but Esther felt that given his age and increased independence, it was a necessary safety measure. He had been delighted and was already deciding how he could smuggle it undetected to school.

She thought about her job. She could not afford to lose it, not if she intended to remain sane. She would have to prove that she was worth keeping. She did not doubt her classroom skills, she just needed to concoct some method for displaying them. She could not help seeing this situation as a competition. One that she intended to win.

The telephone rang. They all pretended they had not heard it. At the fourth ring Esther slowly put down her cup and went into the study to answer it. It was Roselyn.

***

Cynthia had enjoyed her Christmas. She had seen no one but that was to be expected. She had dressed carefully in the morning, choosing to wear a rather special satin camisole top and silk shirt under her Arran sweater. Her lunch had been pleasant and she had enjoyed a walk in the sunshine before settling beside the fire with a book. Before she ate her tea, she telephoned her brother. They always spoke on Christmas day, alternating each year who called.

They spoke about nothing for about fifteen minutes, ascertaining little more than that they were all still alive and doing the same jobs and living in the same houses. Then, with relief on both sides, the call ended.

Cynthia did not expect to speak to anyone else until the beginning of term, so she was surprised a week later to hear a loud knock on her door. She opened it to find Mr Carter and a young man standing on her step. She found that she was pleased and smiled a welcome, though did not invite them inside as she did not recognise the young man.

'Hello Miss Mott, and Happy New Year to you,' began Mr Carter.

'Yes, well it is still only New Year's Eve, but season's greeting to you too,' she corrected. Mr Carter smiled. Some things would never change.

'This is Tommy Martin. He's just left school and is looking for an apprenticeship at college, wants to be a mechanic. I thought you might be needing a gardener. You'll need to train him a bit but he's strong and willing, aren't you Tommy?' He turned towards the youth, who grinned broadly, showing a mouth full of uneven teeth.

'Yep,' he said.

'He's helped me out a couple of times; I can vouch for his honesty. What do you think? Do you still need someone?'

Cynthia looked at the young man, unsure of her feelings. He was very tall and very thin, with a tangle of brown hair that needed a cut. She wondered if it had ever been combed. She did not enjoy surprises and felt uncomfortable. However, she did need some help in the garden and was unsure how she would find someone. This could solve a problem for her.

'Well, that is very kind of you, Mr Carter,' she replied. 'What were you thinking?' she asked the silent Tommy. 'I can pay ten pounds an hour for three hours once a week. Would that be sufficient? At this time of year it only involves chopping wood and

129

keeping the hedges trimmed, moving compost, that sort of thing. In the summer I have a small vegetable patch that needs weeding and a lawn that needs to be cut. In the autumn I need help raking the leaves and digging over the beds. What do you think?'

'Ten pounds is alright,' said Tommy, who appeared to have no opinions about the actual work.

'Do you want to show him the garden now?' asked Mr Carter, moving as if to enter the cottage.

'Yes, of course,' answered Miss Mott, blocking the doorway. 'If you walk to the end of the terrace you will see a gate. Follow the footpath along the end of all the gardens and I will meet you by my gate. Do take care of the brambles, they can be rather ferocious.' She did not intend for this stranger to ever enter her cottage. He did not look at all tidy. Mr James had only ever entered it once and that was when he was dead.

The two men sauntered down the road, Mr Carter smiling to himself, Tommy walking beside him whistling a tune through his teeth. They found the gate and the brambles and fought their way along to where Miss Mott was waiting at the end of her garden. Her hedge was laurel and rather thick and the gate was low, stiff and slightly rotten.

'You could give this a bit of an oil,' suggested Mr Carter. 'Maybe replace some of that wood too. I expect it gets rather damp back here, not much sun.'

Cynthia showed the men her wood supply, her garden tools and the beds of bare earth that contained either flowers or vegetables when the weather was better. The garden was not wide but it was fairly long and she did not have the time to maintain it properly herself. She told Tommy that he could let himself in through the back gate. He agreed to come every Wednesday and she said she would leave his money in the shed with a note of instructions.

'It'd be better to just tell me,' he commented.

'Yes, well, I may not be in attendance when term recommences,' she informed him.

'I'll start with chopping wood then,' he said, 'and fixing the gate.'

Cynthia agreed and the two men left.

They walked back along the narrow footpath, peering into the backs of gardens as they went. Most were well kept, even during the winter. Some had small ponds and one even had a miniature bridge and gnomes fishing. Tommy snorted. David Carter grinned at him. He had known the family for decades. He knew that he had rather sprung this on Miss Mott but felt that giving her little choice was probably a good thing. Tommy needed a job and she needed a gardener. It was better than her employing someone unknown. He did not know why he felt slightly protective towards her but he did. Perhaps it was because she tried so hard to keep him at a distance.

'She always talk like that?' asked Tommy.

'Yes,' said David. 'But you'll get used to her. Besides, you'll hardly see her during term time, she'll be at work. Just try and tidy up after yourself, she won't like mess.'

'Yeah, I got that much,' grinned Tommy. He was pleased. Thirty pounds a week was better than nothing and maybe it would be the start of something. Perhaps he should forget being a mechanic and do gardening instead. He thought he could do that. He would tell his mates he had started a landscaping business, that sounded good. Couldn't be too hard, pulling up a few weeds and a bit of digging. Would help keep him fit, he reasoned and it would be nice to work outside in the fresh air. It was nice of Mr Carter to help him. He waved his thanks and trundled happily off to catch his bus home.

***

On New Year's Eve, Andrew decided to get a Chinese takeaway before meeting his friends. They had planned a night of heavy drinking, and he thought that some solid greasy food would enable him to drink slightly more for slightly longer. He parked in the supermarket car park and walked up the High Street to the restaurant. He would order while he was there and read the paper while he waited. The door jangled as he entered.

The Chinese restaurant had a front section where takeaway food could be ordered. It had a long bench where people could wait and a table of old magazines. The walls were mostly bare, with a Chinese calendar hung on a nail and an elaborate paper butterfly cut out from thin red tissue. There were pictures showing the Chinese zodiac and a large copy of the menu. Some of the prices had stickers over them and corrections written with a red pen. On the counter sat a plastic cat. It had an inane grin and waved its arm. There were two customers ahead of Andrew, so he took a magazine.

Someone was just arriving in the back of the shop and the girl at the counter turned and greeted them. Andrew listened while deciding what he would order.

'*Ni hao*,' he heard, followed by a string of words that blended into one long stream of Chinese.

'I know what that means,' he thought, recognising the first two words and feeling rather pleased with himself, they must be speaking Mandarin. Suddenly, an idea presented itself. He had diligently been watching Chinese films, listening to CDs and reading books. But there was no opportunity for him to actually speak. It was all taking in and no practice. What if he came here once a week and taught them English? His Mandarin was still limited to a handful of words but his English was excellent. Surely in teaching them, he would pick up some words and he could practise those he already knew. It felt like a good plan. He smiled at the girl who was waiting to take his order.

'Is the manager here?' he asked. The girl looked worried, nodded and left. She reappeared a few minutes later with a stockily built woman with short black hair and a frown.

'I am manager. What matter?' she asked defensively.

'*Ni hao, ni hao ma?*' said Andrew, trying to impress with his 'Hello, how are you?' in Mandarin. The woman looked momentarily confused. Why was this strange young man calling her a dirty horse? Then she understood what he was trying to say and smiled.

'You speak Chinese?' she asked.

'Yes,' said Andrew, glad she had not answered in Chinese. 'I am just learning. *Xue sheng*. I am a teacher. *Lao shi*. Does anyone here want to learn English?'

She frowned. 'How much?' she asked.

'No, no cost,' said Andrew, wishing he had prepared a few sentences before he had come. 'You help me learn Mandarin, I help you learn English.' He wondered why he was now speaking in pidgin English. It must be contagious.

The older woman was still for a moment while she worked out what he was saying and whether this could work to her advantage. She decided the decision was too important for her to make.

'Come,' she said, pushing the dividing hatch open and gesturing that Andrew should come to the other side of the counter. 'You talk to owner.'

Andrew grinned, this was rather fun. He went to her side of the counter and followed her through the door at the back. They walked through the restaurant, which was busy, waiters scurrying to deliver orders and couples talking over candles. They then walked along a dim corridor, past a kitchen full of steam and bubbling fat and men shouting and towards a door which needed painting. Beyond it he heard a scream. It was a noise of pure terror. For a fleeting moment, Andrew wondered if he had made a terrible mistake. Images from the film *Sweeney Todd* flitted through his mind. Were all the horror stories about what is served in Chinese restaurants even more horrible than people imagined? The manager opened the door and led him into a floodlit courtyard. A squat Chinese man sat on a low stool. On the floor was a dead chicken, its body still twitching. In one hand he held its head, in the other a large cleaver.

He looked up as they approached and spoke to the manager. He seemed extremely angry. The manager shouted something in reply, sounding equally cross. Andrew recognised the word for teacher, *lao shi*, but nothing else. They spoke quickly and both seemed cross. The manager turned again to Andrew.

'You say free, right?' she checked. Andrew nodded.

'When you start?' she asked.

Andrew said he could come one evening a week.

'Evening no good. Restaurant open. You come afternoon.'

Andrew thought quickly, wishing he had planned this a little better.

'On Fridays I could come at four o'clock,' he said. 'In the holidays I could come earlier.'

'Two clock,' stated the manager.

'Next week on Monday I could come at two o'clock,' agreed Andrew, 'after that four o'clock.'

The manager translated for the owner. He still sounded cross but Andrew was beginning to realise that this was just how Chinese people sounded when they were speaking to each other. They both nodded and the owner stood. He came across to where Andrew stood and gave a slight bow and smiled widely.

'*Xie, xie,*' he said, which Andrew knew meant thank you. He seemed to have passed the test. He grinned back and pointed at the cleaver, which the owner still held. Blood was dripping onto the paving slabs.

'*Sha ren*, assassin,' he said, using a word learned from one of his films. The owner laughed, a loud short burst of joy. He pointed gleefully at Andrew.

'*Sha ren, sha ren*,' he repeated, enjoying both the joke and the strange way that this tall foreigner had pronounced it.

Andrew turned back to the manager.

'For the restaurant?' he asked, pointing to the chicken carcass. It was mostly still now, though every so often gave a great twitch, as if it would at any moment rise up and be reunited with its head.

'No, no. Very strict rule. Only buy meat for restaurant. From…' she paused, clearly unsure of the word.

'Wholesaler?' suggested Andrew. The woman nodded, looking confused.

The owner was heading back towards the restaurant. He was saying something which Andrew did not understand, though it sounded like '*shui*', the word for water. He stood and looked around the small courtyard. There was some blood where the chicken had been killed, though not a great amount. Dustbins were off to one side, with a bike leaning against one. He could see the backs of other shops, each one opening onto a small patio. Only theirs was lit, the strong light piercing the darkness so that it almost felt like daytime.

The door opened and the owner reappeared. He was indeed carrying water. A great steaming bucket of it. He put it down and reached for the chicken's body, dunking it until it was completely submerged. He was careful to avoid putting his hands in the water and Andrew guessed it was near boiling. The legs discoloured as the proteins coagulated, losing their pinkness. He withdrew the bird and began to tug at the feathers. They came off in great chunks, offering little resistance. Within minutes the bird began to resemble the poultry in the supermarket, though with legs attached. Andrew was fascinated.

The manager clearly thought Andrew had stayed long enough and was heading back into the shop, holding open the door for Andrew to follow her. They went back to the takeaway section.

'You want food?' she asked.

Andrew ordered his food. It arrived within minutes and he wondered if he was receiving special service. As he walked back to his car, carrying his white plastic bag of food he thought about what he had arranged, unsure if he was excited or alarmed by his impetuous decision. It had certainly been an experience and he had not even started yet.

Chapter Nine

ANDREW woke to the alarm. He staggered across the room, turned it off then fell back into bed. His eyes were heavy and the bed was warm and comfortable. He felt the heaviness of sleep start to seep back into his brain and forced his eyes open. So tired. He stretched, tensing every muscle in his body then heaved himself out of bed. He walked unseeing into the shower and let the cascading water finish waking him.

He had to be at school at nine o'clock for a staff meeting ready for the new term tomorrow. He would spend a couple of hours in his classroom, then would go to the restaurant for two o'clock. What had felt new and exciting, now just seemed like a burden. He was not at all sure that he could fill an hour with anything worthwhile given his meagre understanding of Chinese. He could say about five sentences and understood a smattering of other words. It would not be easy. Nor would the staff meeting. If the female teachers had been stressy before, he could just imagine what three weeks of worrying about their jobs would have done to them. Tensionville.

He finished rubbing himself with the towel, tied it around his waist and went back to his room. His bed beckoned enticingly, the tangled duvet looking especially inviting. He considered phoning in sick, then dismissed the idea. This was life, being grown up, no choices. He started to dress.

***

He was the last to arrive in the staffroom. The other staff greeted him politely when he walked in but only Esther actually looked pleased to see him. She asked how his Christmas had been and he started to tell her when Jane Lancaster coughed loudly and suggested they should start if they wanted to finish on time. The women all had their big red school diaries on their laps. Andrew had a vague idea that his might be in the back of his cupboard somewhere. They had all been issued with them in September but he had opted for adding dates to his online calendar on his mobile instead. It was smaller and he could set alarms to remind him of things in advance, so no nasty surprises when he turned a page and realised that today was the morning his class was meant to be leading the school assembly.

Jane thanked them all for coming (like they had a choice) and began to give them a list of dates. They started with when they would finish for Easter and then worked backwards, adding assembly dates, outings, special visitors and deadlines for grades, reports and parents' evenings. It did not sound a fun term. Jane then briefly mentioned the probable redundancy.

'I don't have any more details to give you but I'm fairly certain they will trim the staff by one person,' she said. 'The governors are still discussing procedure. I think you will all be interviewed and given a chance to say what you will bring to the job, but ultimately I think it will be decided on cost.'

Cynthia and Esther exchanged looks.

'That is so unfair,' said Esther. 'We are not allowed to opt for less money, our salary is automatically increased as agreed by the unions decades ago. If we have more experience it could be argued that we are better teachers, it seems illogical to now penalise us for that.'

'I know,' said Jane, 'but they have to work out a way to save money.'

'A school is so much more than just a business,' argued Esther.

'Do most of the governors have the first idea what is involved in teaching? When did most of them last visit the school on a normal day to watch teaching in progress? They can't just judge us by a balance sheet and a few wall displays and school plays. They need to come, to watch us teach, then make their decision.' She leaned forward, warming to her theme. 'I think we ought to plan something special, put on a sort of display of normal school life and invite the governors to come and see. What do you think?'

Andrew looked worried. He was much happier with the thought that this would all be decided numerically, he was cheap, therefore safe. Cynthia, however, was looking interested. This might work to her advantage. Maybe Esther was not the soppy woman that she had always assumed. Jane Lancaster looked resigned. It would not make any difference to the decision, she was sure of that. But maybe the staff needed to feel like they had tried. Maybe this was more about staff motivation than changing the outcome. Perhaps if they felt they had been given a chance to fight, to try and keep their jobs, they would feel less bad about losing them. She nodded at Esther.

'Go on, what did you have in mind?'

'Well, I'm not really sure; I haven't thought it through fully. What about an Art Week? We could each take an artist and teach about their life, show their work and teach the children to create something in the style of that artist. Perhaps, instead of all teaching our own class about several artists, we could all just do one artist and each class could have a session with each of us. So, for example, on Monday I would teach my class about Monet. Then on Tuesday I could do the same lesson but with Cherry class and on Wednesday with Oak. We could display all the work, I'm sure the children would enjoy seeing each other's attempts at what they themselves have done. We can turn the hall into an art gallery, invite the parents to come and see it at home time on Friday, something like that. Maybe even advertise it in the newspaper, raise the profile of the school a bit. Who knows, maybe the interest will result in better numbers for next year.'

She finished and smiled around at her colleagues.

Andrew ran his fingers through his hair. For someone who had not 'thought it through' she had given a fairly detailed outline of a plan. A plan that would show how an experienced teacher could cope with any age group, who could have a calm classroom and get the children to produce some quality work. A plan that would allow herself to shine. He, on the other hand, would flounder. Probably. True, it was art and he was good at art. He wondered if she had chosen art so that he would have bit of a chance. She was kind like that. He could produce a decent display, he was sure about that. Plus his knowledge of artists was pretty good so he could find someone to enthuse the children about. But teaching different age groups? Teaching classes who he had never taught before? That was huge. That could end in all kinds of chaos.

Cynthia was frowning.

'I am not at all convinced that public demonstration is in keeping with the ethos of the school,' she began.

'Well, I think it's an excellent idea,' said Jane. She did not want this to turn into a long debate about the merits of the plan. She was the head teacher, she would make the decision. It sounded good to her. It would give the term a focus, raise the profile of the school if done well and would give the staff something concrete to work on. Stop them all just worrying. It might turn into a 'competition' or even a mild fight, but did that matter? Better that they should have a fair fight, if that is what it turned out to be. She turned the pages of her diary.

'Perhaps at our next meeting you could all tell me which artist you will be teaching about. Thank you Esther, good idea,' she gave her a brief smile. 'Now, which date shall we choose? How about a week in February? Just before half term?'

Cynthia scowled. She hated to be thwarted. She looked in her diary, searching for some reason to stop it. There was none. Everyone was adding the dates to their calendars and looking optimistic. Jane was speaking again.

'Talking of new children, we have a little boy starting. He's only just moved to the area, I think there has been some family trouble and they moved unexpectedly. Cynthia, he'll be in your class. He's called James Buchan. I'll let you have a copy of the records from his previous school after the meeting. I met the family last week and I don't foresee any problems. He came in with both his mothers and they seem a nice little family.'

'Both his mothers?' said Cynthia. 'What does that mean?'

'It means he has two mothers. They are married.'

'Homosexual you mean? They are two lesbians? Who have been allowed to adopt? Well.' Cynthia stopped, indignation clear on her face. This was not the sort of family that they wanted at their school. She was surprised that Jane had accepted the child. She turned to Esther, confident that her disapproval would be shared by someone religious.

Jane Lancaster frowned at her. 'We are an equal opportunities school Miss Mott,' she reminded her. 'It is not our place to have views about how other people choose to live. And James may not be adopted, he may have been conceived by artificial insemination. That is not our concern. If the other children tease him at all, you may have to consider some additional lessons about equality and acceptance. It is an important part of the syllabus. There is no "right" kind of family group any more. All prejudice is wrong, whether it is based on race, gender or sexual preference. I'm sure you would agree?'

Cynthia had the good sense to nod, though her expression said clearly that she did not agree.

The staff meeting moved on to other matters and then finally the teachers escaped to their classrooms to prepare for the following day. They did not meet again until midday, when they took their lunches into the staffroom. Jane was still working in her office and Cynthia was keen to raise the question of homosexuality in her absence. It seemed to her grossly inappropriate to introduce such a topic with infants, even if they were forced to accept a child with a dysfunctional family. Surely, by promoting such behaviour they were actually encouraging it, teaching the children that this was a good option. That seemed very wrong to her mind. Children were meant to be raised by a man and a woman. True, that often was not possible in today's society, but that was best, that was what they should be encouraging these children to strive for. It was one thing to accept the problems that society threw at them; it was another entirely to promote them. She leaned towards Esther.

'What are your views concerning this new addition to our school?' she asked

Esther chewed her sandwich quickly, wondering if Cynthia was referring to the Art Week or the governor's decision. Then she realised that she meant the new child, the one with two mothers. She swallowed. The bread was not properly soft and she felt the hard lump of it going painfully down her throat. She coughed.

'Well, it will be a challenge possibly, especially if the other children are told unhelpful things by their parents and then repeat them at school. But I'm sure you will handle it wonderfully Cynthia, you have so much experience with that age group. Why, are you worried?'

Cynthia wondered if the wretched woman had purposefully misunderstood. Obviously she was not worried about maintaining peace in her classroom, she had never suffered bullies. It was the issue she wanted to discuss, not her teaching techniques.

'Do you not find it rather distasteful? Two women? In the bedroom? It is an abomination. Completely against the laws of nature. And God's laws come to that; I would have thought you might have wanted to stand against this, given your husband's job.'

Esther sighed. She really did not want to be drawn into this discussion with Cynthia.

'Well, Cynthia, I try my best not to imagine the parents in bed. I think I would find it rather distracting at parents' evenings.'

Andrew, sitting at the far end of the room, exploded, showering crumbs across the floor. Cynthia gave Esther a withering look and gathered her things.

'I am somewhat perplexed that you find it a matter for amusement,' she said as she stood. 'I will return to my classroom and commence naming books.' She strode from the room.

Andrew grinned across at Esther.

'Oh dear,' she said, 'that was a bit naughty of me. I didn't really mean to upset her, I just didn't want to get into the conversation. Not with Cynthia. It would just have been a disagreement and we have enough to worry about without getting into theology.'

'Why? What do you think about all that?' asked Andrew. He was interested. He did not actually know any gay parents, but he had a few friends who were gay. It was no big deal really. Two were in a stable relationship, if they decided they wanted children, he couldn't see it would be a problem. They would probably make quite good parents. He would be interested to see the two new mothers though. He fully expected one to be plain, slightly podgy with very short hair, masculine body language and the other to be your regular feminine woman. He was unsure if this was based on experience or stereotype, he would be interested to put it to the test.

He was a bit surprised by Miss Mott's outburst. She was usually so proper. He knew lots of her generation had a problem with gay people. Especially his dad. He would not have wanted to 'come out' if he had been gay. But he was a bit surprised by someone educated being so prejudiced, someone who worked with the public. He was not so sure about Esther. There had been a lot in the newspapers about churches being against gay marriage when it was proposed. He was interested to hear what she had to say.

Esther looked at him and lowered her sandwich. It seemed she was not going to be eating much this lunchtime.

'Well, I don't think it's as simple as some people think,' she began. 'A lot of churches quote Bible passages that condemn homosexuality, talk about it being wrong. That's where Cynthia got that word from; there is a quote where it is called an "abomination". However, they tend to ignore that it also says that eating prawn sandwiches or wearing cotton and wool mixed clothes is also an "abomination". No one would think those bits of the Bible are relevant today, they only pick out the parts that talk about homosexuality.'

Andrew looked surprised, so Esther continued, 'But I don't think that's the true picture. You see, the Bible is an interpretation. Unless we are reading it in the ancient Hebrew and Greek, every Bible we read is translated and when you translate something, it's never straightforward, we have to make decisions about the meaning of words, we add interpretations.'

Andrew knew this was true. A sentence in Mandarin was impossible to translate word for word into English; you just had to write the meaning. He nodded, wondering where this was going.

'There's also a problem because in the days when the Bible was written, there were no stable relationships of loving homosexual couples. So, when it refers to homosexuals, it is talking about the abuse of young boys in the Greek temples or the promiscuity of casual sexual partners. I do think absolutely that child abuse and promiscuity are wrong. I think that's how people get damaged.'

Andrew nodded. He agreed on the child abuse point, was not

quite so sure on promiscuity. It sounded bad but might be fun in practice.

'In fact, they didn't really have a word that can be directly translated as "homosexual", there is a word that Paul uses but it is a made up word, not found in any other writings. He was trying to find a way to explain something which they had no words to express. So, I think that maybe we have been interpreting the Bible wrongly all these years, that the church is ostracising a whole group of people who actually it should have been accepting. It just doesn't sit comfortably with me, it seems against what I know about God. In the Bible, I see God as a loving God, someone who cares and accepts. I cannot understand how something that people are born being, can be contrary to what God wants. I'm just not sure that it's wrong.

'And we can't argue that it's "unnatural". Look in any field of animals – bulls are clearly gay, so are some dogs, so are male ducks in the spring! Nor does the reason that we are meant to produce children seem right as an argument, or that would mean that any single or barren person was not living how God intended. Not everyone is meant to have children.

'We've made mistakes before, like with slavery. Go back two hundred years and many Christians believed that slavery was fine, was advocated by the Bible, whereas now we look at those same passages and translate them very differently. We are shocked by what the church used to preach. I wonder if it will be the same with homosexuality, if my grandchildren will be horrified that the church of today shut out homosexuals unless they admitted they were wrong and did not practice.' She paused, rubbing her eyes.

'But it's not that simple either. Because actually, some people are born being something that they have to deny if they want to live as God wants. Someone who naturally finds children sexually attractive has to repent of that and not practice it. Someone who likes to steal has to stop. Someone who is a gossip has to get over it and stop being malicious if they want to live how God wants them to live. My arguments don't really stand up to close scrutiny; they are more based on how I feel.

'I think God might be very angry with us church people for rejecting a whole lot of people. I hated walking past churches when the marriage debate was on that had big signs outside that talked about marriage being for one man and one woman. How must that have made gay couples feel? It made churches the very last places they would ever willing go into, and that has to be wrong.

'Some people say that you can love the person but hate the sin. They mean that homosexuality is wrong but we should still welcome gay people into church, just show them that what they are doing is wrong. But I don't think so.' Esther was enjoying the discussion now, finding lots of arguments to support her view. It was nice to be able to discuss, to share her views with someone new. Andrew was beginning to regret he had asked. He offered her a coffee.

'No, thanks, I already had one.

'There is no other group of people that we would invite into church just to show them that how they are living is wrong. If someone is a gossip, we do not see it as our mission to stop her gossiping. We welcome her into the church and then leave it up to God to change her, in his time. The church is not about changing people, it's about being a safe place where people can get a bit closer to God. And as I said, I don't even think being homosexual is necessarily wrong.' She smiled, aware that she was ranting slightly now.

'Sorry, was that a bit too detailed? I don't expect you wanted the whole sermon did you. It's very hard being a Christian you know. God never gave us a list of rules like other religions, he just gave us principles and showed us how to live. Sometimes people think we're weak but actually it's hard to live like God wants.'

'Like when Jane talks about leaving up wall displays and you keep quiet when really you want to tell her to fuck off?' said Andrew.

Esther laughed. 'You are more perceptive than you like to let on,' she said. 'Talking of which, my boys gave me a tongue-twister over Christmas, they are so bad, they made me say it in church.' She told him the story and they both laughed. He was glad to have moved the conversation on. He was interested in her views, just maybe not quite *that* interested.

Andrew returned to his classroom laden with rolls of paper and a thick piece of cardboard. The paper was for his display boards, the cardboard was to make a game for the Chinese restaurant. He was using card from the school stock cupboard. It had not really occurred to him not to. After all, the school would benefit if he learned Mandarin, so they could help with some of the material costs.

***

At one thirty, Andrew left school. He slipped out a side door, hoping no other staff would notice he was leaving early. There had been no specific timings given for the day, just a morning staff meeting followed by time to prepare their rooms for the new term. It did not look good to be leaving first, though there was no logical reason for him to stay if he was fully prepared, which no one could challenge even if he was not.

He parked at the supermarket and walked up to the restaurant. When he arrived there were a few customers waiting to collect takeaway food, though the sign clearly said they shut at two o'clock. The manager was behind the counter and when she saw him she opened the hatch and beckoned him into the shop.

'Good, you come,' she said, as if she had not assumed that he would. She led him into the restaurant area and to a round table

147

near the window. It was quite cold in the room and there were no lights on, so it was fairly dim. Andrew hoped there would be enough light from outside.

The manager began to clear the table, carefully placing folded napkins and chopsticks on the table next to it. The chopsticks rested on a wedge of porcelain and the napkins were peach coloured and folded into fans. Andrew saw she was careful to keep them clean and in their folded shapes. She handled the glasses by their stems and moved the vase of plastic roses. When the table was clear, he moved to put his satchel down on the white cloth. The manager lifted it back to him.

'Not table, use chair,' she directed before leaving him and heading off towards the kitchen.

Andrew obediently put his bag onto a chair and began to withdraw his things. He knew that explaining the game would be much too difficult, so he had written the instructions using his Mandarin dictionary. He had also found a photograph of his family to use as a starting point. While he was waiting he looked around the restaurant, wondering if it was a nice place to eat.

Most of the larger tables were round, all laid up with chopsticks and cloth napkins, with a turning circle in the centre. The chairs were grey, padded and comfortable. His mum would like that, she always complained if they ate out and her seat was uncomfortable.

At one end of the restaurant was a bar, with glasses and bottles glinting through the dimness. It all smelled warm, of Chinese food residue, garlic and fried vegetables.

The manager returned. She carried a small tray with a Chinese teapot and a delicate bowl and saucer. She was followed by seven other people. She set the tea things on the table in front of Andrew.

'Tea. You drink,' she directed, pouring a thin green liquid that steamed.

Andrew was not sure that he had ever tried Chinese tea or that he wanted to. He obediently took a sip. It was hot and bitter but not unpleasant. He thanked the manager and set the bowl back on its saucer.

Four people were sitting at the table, two men and two women. They stared at him with their black eyes, unsmiling. The others stood behind, watching. Andrew felt very foreign. It was as though he had walked into a different country, a place of unsmiling eyes that watched intently. It was not a comfortable feeling.

'You teach them,' said the manager, 'they speak not good.' She pointed at the men standing behind. 'Them cooks. No speak, they watch.' Then she left.

Andrew looked around. This was slightly scary.

'*Ni hao*,' he began with a smile. 'Hello.'

Everyone smiled. Their eyes sparkled with laughter.

'*Wo jiao* Andrew,' he continued. 'My name is Andrew. *Ni ne*? And you?'

He turned to the girl on his left. 'And you?' he repeated.

'My name Bai Yun,' she told him slowly, repeating the words with care.

'My name is Ben,' said the next person.

'Ben?' queried Andrew surprised.

'Yes,' answered the boy, 'I have English name. Chinese name is Lao but I change it when I come England.' He pointed at his colleagues. 'They want English names too. You give them please.'

Andrew nodded. This was unexpected. Why would they want English names? He supposed it made sense, made them feel more part of the community, perhaps stopped English people mangling the pronunciation every time they said it. Bit of a shame though, to give up your culture so easily. Perhaps that is where England had been going wrong though, being determined to be British wherever they were. 'Next time,' he promised, wanting time to think about it. He had never named anyone before, it felt important.

'*Wo jiao* Cheng Zhi,' said the next man.

'English?' prompted Andrew.

'I na i Cheng Zhi,' said the man, clearly uncomfortable at being forced to speak in English. His friends laughed at his distorted English and he turned pink.

'He not speak good,' said Lao.

'Well, my Mandarin is not very good, so that's okay,' said Andrew.

'No, you speak Mandarin very good,' said Lao. Andrew assumed that flattery was another part of this culture which he needed to learn. He turned to the last girl.

'My na i Shao Ling,' she told him.

Andrew showed them the photograph. 'This is my family, *zhe shi wo de jia ren*,' he said. The men standing at the back laughed loudly and said something to Lao. He turned to Andrew.

'They never hear English man talk Chinese before. Plea you say it again,' he asked.

Andrew felt something of a spectacle but he obliged. They laughed again and one repeated what he had said. They obviously found him hilarious. They were also deeply interested in the photograph. They took it from him and passed it around, staring intently at the faces.

'*Ba ba, ma ma?*' they asked him and he said yes, it was his father and mother. They handed it back. Andrew asked Lao if he thought that he looked like his sister. Lao leaned forwards and spoke quietly.

'Teacher, I very embarrass. All English people look same to us.'

Andrew laughed. That was so funny. All these years that people had said Chinese people looked exactly the same and now it turned out that they thought English people did too. He was rather enjoying this now. It was difficult and he had not expected an audience but he realised that his pupils were just as nervous as he was. He sipped some more tea. It seemed less bitter, so he took a few swallows, then pulled his game from his bag. Now this would be a challenge.

They read the instructions and had a few discussions in Chinese which Andrew did not understand at all but he assumed they were sorting out his bad Chinese and what the instructions meant. They then attempted to play the game. Andrew managed to both use and recognise a few words and they all spoke some English. He felt rather pleased with himself.

During the hour long lesson, the men standing behind them gradually left. They did not say they were leaving nor say goodbye, they just melted away, leaving the class to continue without an audience. Andrew was not sorry to see them go. They had mainly laughed at his Chinese and his pupil's attempts at English. It was not especially helpful.

'Right,' said Andrew, 'that's the end of the lesson. Shall I come next week? Four o'clock?'

'You come different day?' asked Lao.

'Er, yes, probably. When were you thinking?'

'Tomorrow? You come every day?' said Lao.

'Oh, no, no I can't do that,' said Andrew, 'no time mate, need to get my school work sorted too. But I could come a different day if that's easier?' He took out his mobile and turned to the calendar. Lao reached across and took it. He started to scroll down the days.

'It say Wednesday seven o'clock Chinese,' he said, puzzled.

'That's my own lesson,' said Andrew, taking his phone back into his own possession and holding it firmly.

'You come Tuesday?' asked, Lao. 'Monday my day off.'

'Well, after this week I was going to come on Fridays,' said Andrew. 'Are Fridays any good?'

Lao frowned. 'Friday busy,' he said, then remembering his day off smiled and nodded. 'Yes, Friday good day.'

'Okay, Friday. Four o'clock,' said Andrew, adding it to his calendar.

The door opened and the manager appeared. She was carrying a bulging white plastic bag, which she passed to Andrew.

'For you,' she said, 'you come again next week.'

Andrew took the bag, savouring the sweet smells of Chinese spices. He thanked her, said he would return next Friday and waved goodbye. They unlocked the door for him and he left. The day was already beginning to fade and he walked quickly to his car.

As he sat in his seat he peered into the bag. There were prawn crackers and a plastic tub of savoury rice and some sweet and sour chicken and what looked like a curry. It smelled delicious. He smiled broadly. This was exhausting but rather fun and he seemed to have got dinner out of it too. He felt that he had glimpsed a whole new culture, been allowed inside a closed community. It felt rather special. He thought about how Lao had looked through his diary. That would never happen with English people. English people have great respect for the individual and privacy. He guessed that in China it was the opposite, the masses were important but individuals had few rights. It was weird how different their cultures were. Andrew wondered if he had done anything that seemed rude to them. He hoped not.

He put his food in the footwell and turned the key. As he pulled out from the parking space he turned on the radio. His brain was way too tired for more Chinese, even nursery rhymes. He started to tap the steering wheel to the beat of something by the Plain White T's. He was very happy.

Chapter Ten

ESTHER had also slipped away from school soon after lunch. She had agreed before Christmas to speak at the Afternoon Tea Club, a group where the elderly people met once a week for tea and a short devotional talk and prayer. She had assumed it would be during the holidays but today was their first meeting of the year. Esther often felt pressure to do more in the church. She knew that many members were disappointed that she had a job apart from the church and they missed seeing her at groups other than on a Sunday. When she could, she therefore tried to accommodate them and be available occasionally for meetings and 'minister's wife' activities.

She parked in the church car park, avoiding the potholes. It desperately needed resurfacing but the church had been re-roofed last year and the congregation would be unable to fund another big project for a while. She checked that there was nothing valuable on show in the car, grabbed her handbag and hurried through the damp afternoon into the hall. It was one of those grey days where afternoon and evening were hardly distinguishable, both being dull and devoid of colour.

Most of the elderly people had already arrived. Some had walked, painfully leaning on sticks or frames, some had come on the dial-a-ride bus or used their taxi vouchers to be driven. A few had come on motorised disabled vehicles, narrowly avoiding pedestrians and swerving onto the road when the pavements dipped, often being sworn at by car drivers. They either did not care or enjoyed the thrill of being still able to rebel. They had parked them at the top of the ramp, just inside the double doors and Esther walked through them as she entered. They rather reminded her of the scooters that Mods used to drive in the old movies. One had large flags on posts at the back, another was personalised with a row of multi-coloured teddy bears on a small shelf behind the seat. Esther wondered if they were glued in place and if they would smell after it rained.

She wound her way through them, taking care not to snag her tights. It was rare for her to wear a skirt but she had felt it appropriate for when speaking to a group of elderly people. They often felt that jeans and trousers were for casual wear only and so to speak in them would appear disrespectful.

The hall had been set up ready for the meeting. Three rows of chairs had been carried in from the main sanctuary and arranged around small tables. Each had a cloth, paper napkins and a small pile of tea plates. Esther could smell freshly baked scones and two women were distributing plates laden with cakes. In one corner the urn had been set up, trays of smoked glass mugs crowded with bowls of sweeteners and sugar that had a week old crust on top. The leader, Carrie Whyte, came over when she saw Esther. She was an anxious woman, mid-sixties, sturdily built but of a fragile disposition.

'Hello dear, so lovely of you to come. We are all ready for you I think. I will introduce you and you can speak for about five minutes. Then we'll have our tea. It's not worth talking for longer than that dear or they start to fall asleep.' She turned to the group and clapped her hands. Most of them stopped talking and looked at her expectantly. Two ladies comparing knitting patterns continued their conversation.

'Now then everyone, we are very fortunate today that our lovely pastor's wife is able to come and speak to us.' Her voice was high and thin, nervous to be speaking to a large group. Her tight grey curls fluttered as she shook slightly. 'We all know how busy she is and so this is a rare treat for us.' She turned to Esther and smiled, 'Thank you pastor's wife.'

Esther went to stand at the front. She smiled at them, noting the wrinkled faces, the short grey hair and the hand knitted jumpers. She hoped she would not be expected to remember their names; there was something indistinguishable about a group of elderly people. She said hello and unfolded the poem she wanted to read to them as the introduction to her talk. As she did when at school, she waited for them to be silent.

The two knitting pattern ladies continued their discussion. They were passing shiny patterns to each other and comparing wool quantities. The patterns were well used, with dozens of folds breaking the surface, as wrinkled as the skin on their weathered hands. They saw Esther was waiting and lowered their voices, leaning closer together. Esther realised that they did not intend to finish their conversation. Could you ask people older than you to be quiet? Was it appropriate to frown at them? No, probably not. Quelling a desire to giggle, she began her talk.

She read her poem and began to explain why it was significant for her.

'I can't hear her, can you?' bellowed an old man at the back.

'Yes, you old fool, put your hearing aid up a bit. You're disturbing us.'

'It's already up. Oh no, wait, stupid thing, can you do it?' He leaned towards his friend, frantically twisting his hearing device, trying to raise the volume. His friend peered at him and frowned. There was a high pitched squeal emitted, then silence. The man smiled up at Esther.

'Still can't hear you,' he informed her, 'but I'll just enjoy the view. You're better looking than most of our speakers.'

Esther was somewhat thrown. She finished with a short prayer, which ended with loud Amens from everyone, including the knitting ladies. Esther was unsure if this was in approval of her prayer or the fact that she had finished on time and they could now have tea. Carrie Whyte bustled back to the front.

'Thank you so very much pastor's wife, that was most interesting.'

Esther wondered if perhaps Carrie had forgotten her name and did not like to ask for it. She was unfolding a copy of the local paper and holding it up.

'Now, have you all seen the paper this week? It is rather exciting.' She smiled at the group.

'Is it a photo of you naked?' asked one of the men at the back.

Carrie blushed, obviously having no idea how to respond.

'Thank you Eddie, it is a photograph of our dear member Dot. She helped to raise some money for the children's gardening charity. Now, perhaps we would all like to have our tea. ' She moved towards Esther. 'Come and sit over here pastor's wife, those man can be rather naughty I'm afraid. There's room here with Jean and Edna.' She led Esther to where two empty chairs waited in a group of ladies. They all smiled at Esther as she sat down.

'We do love your husband, dear,' said one, leaning forward and talking loudly. 'He always has time for us you know, time for a chat and a laugh. Even if we see him in the town, he'll always stop you know. You must be very proud of him.'

Esther nodded. She would have preferred to sit with the men. They reminded her of her boys, looking for fun and not afraid to shock if they thought it would get a laugh. She wondered if men changed as they aged or if their humour and inquisitiveness remained whatever their age, becoming hidden in a decaying body. Old women seemed old to her, they appeared to mature with time, seeing the world through responsible eyes which often worried at change. They noticed the problems in life, to know that things needed to be planned and organised. It seemed to Esther that the men had lurched through life, bouncing from experience to experience, happy to just survive unscathed. They seemed at some point to have switched their mothers for wives and then continued to concentrate on doing rather than thinking. Then one day they woke up and realised their bodies were old, their skin wrinkled and their bones aching. She wondered what it would be like to be old, to gradually watch each of your friends and relatives die, to become ever more alone. Morbid thoughts. Carrie was offering her a plate of cakes.

Esther took a slice of lemon sponge and balanced the plate on her knee. The helpers were going round, taking people cups of tea, moving napkins, passing cakes. The old people tucked in to the tea with enthusiasm. Some of them had piled their plates with cakes, a whole meal of sugar and frosting. Esther glanced at the clock. She might have time to nip back to school if this did not take too long. She was almost ready for tomorrow but it would be nice to have another half hour, time to put out a display of readers for when the children first arrived. Maybe look through some books and decide which artist she wanted to teach about.

She nibbled her cake. It was beautifully moist but had been stacked on the plate with a whole array of other cakes and the flavours had leached into each other. It no longer had the clean sharpness of just lemon and contained a hint of coffee and chocolate too. What a pity. She knew that several people in the church made cakes for the Afternoon Tea Club. It would have been so much nicer if each one had been presented on a separate plate. She supposed that it was easier to slice them all and put a selection on each plate. As was often the case at church, the volunteers did not always have the time or the imagination to do things properly.

Her tea arrived. It was hot and strong, and she listened to the general chatter while she enjoyed it. Carrie was talking to the lady next to her about the supermarket, bemoaning prices and opening hours. Esther finished drinking and started to pile the empty plates next to her.

'Oh, you leave those,' said Carrie, 'we don't expect our pastor's wife to clear up. You enjoy a break dear; we know how busy you are.'

Esther forced a smile. She knew that Carrie was being kind but she thought she might start twitching if she had to sit and listen to them any longer. The room was warm. Too warm. She needed to move around a little and was happy to help clear up. She collected the plates and carried them to the kitchen, then returned for some empty tea cups. The men were mostly finished so she began to clear their table. She noticed that some of them were stuffing their pockets with pieces of cake and wondered if they were meant to. Maybe they should give them all a plastic bag of leftovers, they would be stale by next week and not worth saving. She would suggest it to Rob; it would be listened to if the idea came from him.

Esther collected more dirty crockery and went back to the kitchen. She found she was smiling as she loaded plates into the dishwasher. They were interesting characters and she had enjoyed being with them. She checked the time. Too late to be worth going back to school. She went and said her goodbyes to Carrie, thanked the ladies for the tea and left.

As she pushed open their front door, Rob was emerging from his study.

'Hello, do you have time for a chat before you go out?' she asked, raising her cheek for a kiss.

'A quick one,' he said, 'I'm due at the hospital in half an hour but a few minutes won't make any difference.' He wandered into the sitting room and slumped onto the sofa. Esther sat beside him, tucking her legs beneath her and smoothing her skirt over her legs. She told him about the Tea Club, telling him that Carrie refused to call her Esther and after her talk the old ladies had told her how much they admired him but had not acknowledged her talk at all.

'Oh dear, poor you,' said Rob, 'that's just rude. But women of that age sometimes have trouble accepting that the sexes are equal now. They probably thought that praising me was what you wanted to hear.'

'Yes I know, it's okay, you don't need to explain,' said Esther. 'It was kind of funny.'

She told him that she had seen some of the men putting cake into their pockets. 'Couldn't we have a supply of sandwich bags there for them to take home the leftovers? They'll be stale by the next week and it would be nice if they could take them home.'

'Good idea, I'll suggest it,' agreed Rob. He smiled at her fondly. She was usually so busy, it was nice to have her able to help with church things for once. Plus she was very good at it, observant and thoughtful. She liked things to be done properly, had some good organisational skills. He sighed. He understood why she wanted to work, knew that she found the lack of money a strain and wanted to protect the boys from the worst of it. But sometimes he wished that it could be like this more often, both sharing the church work, giving their input to the same place. Too often he felt like it was his job and she was helping him rather than being a partner in the same work. It didn't exactly cause a tension point but it nearly did. He looked at his watch.

'Oops, better go if I'm not going to be late.' He rose and kissed the top of her head. 'Thanks for going along Esther, it was nice of you. I hope you managed to get your school stuff done in time.' He paused; wanting to tell her how significant it was to him that she had gone to the meeting but not knowing how to voice it without it sounding like a criticism. He decided it was better left unsaid and chose instead to kiss her again.

'See you later.'

The door burst open and Samuel appeared.

'Dad. Before you go I need my school stuff, it's in the back of your car. It's school tomorrow.'

'What stuff?' asked Esther, with a sense of dread.

'I put my bag there at the end of term,' he explained, 'it has my sports stuff, homework, stuff like that.'

'Homework. Your homework has been in the back of Dad's car all holiday?'

He grinned at her, 'Obviously. So now I need it so I can do it before tomorrow.'

Rob raised his eyebrows and collected the bulging bag from his car. Samuel opened it in the hall, digging for his books and papers and carrying them into the kitchen so he could sit at the table to work. Esther looked at the heap of smelly clothes that now littered the floor. She waved to Rob and carried them to the washing machine.

There were tee shirts and vests, heavy with old sweat and dirt, tangled with a Christmas card and a homework diary. Shorts caked in mud, socks which she managed to tip into the machine without touching. Would he have worn these clothes unwashed if she had not found them? Did boys notice when things were dirty, stank of mildew and sweat? Were all children like this or had she missed some vital parenting point along the way? It was hard to be annoyed; she felt it was her fault somehow for neglecting to ask where his bag was earlier. She doubted that other mothers were washing kit today that would be needed tomorrow. She felt like the worst mother. Again. Flakes of mud had drifted onto the floor so she found a cloth and wiped them away.

She also knew what Rob had left unsaid, that before they were married he had imagined that more of their life would be like it had been this afternoon, both leading groups in the church, both giving all their energy and skills to the same organisation. But the afternoon had done nothing but underline to her how important her job was. She did not really mind being referred to as 'the pastor's wife' but that was because she had her own identity at work. She was not just Rob's appendage; she was a person in her own right. Whenever she was introduced to someone new at church, she was always described as 'the pastor's wife' and that was okay, she understood that it was just an easy way to reference her. But it would matter more if that was all that she was. Other than members of parliament, or a head teacher, she did not think there was another job in the world where the wife was introduced by the job of the husband. No one ever said, 'Ah, this is the dentist's wife', or 'Do come and meet the lawyer's wife'.

She went into the study and scanned the shelves. Somewhere she had some children's art books. She could make a start on planning the art week. It was exciting that Jane had accepted the suggestion. Esther felt she had a real chance now to showcase her teaching skills.

The study was a good space to work in. Though too small for meetings, it was ideal for one person. There was a large window at one end which flooded the desk with lots of natural light. There were also two upright but comfortable chairs, angled towards each other on a small round rug, ready for when Rob needed to counsel someone. Along one wall was a bookshelf that ran from floor to ceiling. She found a book on Monet and pulled it from the shelf. The telephone on Rob's desk shrilled.

Esther picked up the phone and said hello, flicking through the book with her spare hand. It was Rachel Blogs, her father had died, Rob was taking the funeral next week and she wanted to leave details of the undertaker. Esther put down the book, reached for a pen and made a note on a pad of paper. She asked Rachel how she was feeling, how the arrangements were going. She did not ask if there was anything she could do to help, knowing that she had no time. She listened sympathetically, not allowing herself to flick through the book at the same time, feeling she owed this poor woman her full attention. When the call ended she made some notes for Rob and opened the book. The doorbell rang.

Abandoning the book, Esther answered the door. It was Mr Thomas, just passing and thought he would pop in to tell Rob that he had arranged for the health and safety officer to visit the church next Wednesday. Was that alright? Esther did not know but promised she would tell Rob and he would be in touch. She asked him if he would like a cup of tea and was relieved when he refused. He was just passing, no time to stop. She thanked him warmly, happy he had refused the tea and shut the door. She returned to the study.

She settled into the chair and opened the book. Joseph put his head round the door to ask what was for dinner. She told him sausages and he went away happy. She looked at the book. Her mobile buzzed. She checked the screen, saw it was Rob and answered.

'Hi love, are you busy?'

'I'm trying to get some plans sorted out for school, nothing important, is everything okay?' she said, trying to sound less irritable than she felt. He often phoned her when something occurred to him, not trusting his own memory and wanting to tell her immediately. It was annoying, broke her train of thought and was usually nothing that could not have waited until later. But to say so would look unloving and selfish. She was supposed to cherish calls from her husband, delight to hear his voice at unexpected moments. She tried not to frown at the book in her hand.

'Good. I just had a thought and wanted to tell you about it before I forget. I've got to wait for the doctor to have finished before I can see Carol so I've got a few minutes. Is that okay? It's not important if you're busy.'

Esther resisted the urge to tell him that yes she was and maybe he could tell her later.

'It's about the children's talk on Sunday,' he explained. 'I'm going to preach from 1 Peter 2, the bit about being "a chosen race, a royal priesthood, a people who God possesses". I want the kids' talk to link in, so I thought I would talk about how a thing has value sometimes just because of who owns it. A pen is just a pen, but if we knew that Charles Dickens had owned it, it would be worth millions. A pair of gloves is just a pair of gloves, but if we know a famous goal keeper owned them, they would have lots of value.' He paused; Esther thought he was distracted by something at the hospital. She waited.

'Anyway, can you help me think of examples and maybe collect a few props for me? I thought I would do a spoof auction, get the kids to guess the value, then reveal who owned the objects previously and let them change the price. Then I'll talk about God owning us, about how that gives us ultimate value, that we are extremely precious just because he chose to possess us and what that means. Hello? Are you still there?'

'Yes, sorry, was just looking at something,' said Esther, who was controlling her anger. It was a good talk, he always did good children's talks, often preaching as much to the adults as to the children. But she was cross. Here she was, struggling to even read a book for her own planning and he was asking her to help him with his. She knew that this was what her role was, she knew that she would resent it if he asked someone else for help. But today, at this very moment, she wanted to refuse, to tell him she was too busy.

'That sounds good,' she forced herself to say, 'I'll have a think.'

'Oh, doctor seems to be emerging, I better go. Thanks love, see you later,' and he was gone.

Her phone buzzed again. The screen showed it was Carrie.

Probably wanted to thank her for this afternoon. She would speak to her later or wait for a text. The house phone rang. She considered leaving it but forced herself to answer, taking the book with her.

'Hello Esther? It's Roselyn, is Rob there? I can't reach him on his mobile.'

'He's doing hospital visiting Roselyn, can I take a message?'

'Not really, it's terribly urgent...' Esther settled in the chair and opened the book. She held the telephone to her ear and every few minutes said something sympathetic whilst concentrating on her book. She only really needed to monitor the ebb and flow of Roselyn's voice, nothing that she actually said really mattered, it was always the same. Roselyn was finding it hard to cope, no one cared, she felt alone, she couldn't sleep, she wouldn't go to the doctor because they just gave her pills and she felt worse with pills than without, someone had avoided her in the street, she might consider the counsellor that Rob had suggested but wasn't sure she was quite ready to go yet, she couldn't eat. Esther let the words wash over her, words she had heard a hundred times before. Roselyn needed help but refused to either seek medical help or talk to a trained counsellor. What she wanted to do was recite the same feelings over and over again to someone who would listen. Which was usually Rob but this afternoon was Esther. It was easy enough to listen and scan the book at the same time.

There was nothing in the book that sparked an idea, so Esther drew Rob's laptop towards her. Roselyn was still talking, whining really, and Esther made a noise that could be taken as agreeing. She clicked onto Google and began to search. Flowers was a common theme, maybe they could all chose a different artist but look at the style in which they had painted flowers. Monet and Van Gogh would be easy. They could also choose a Dutch artist, one that used intricate realism. Then they could compare the three. Flowers always looked good; they could have some big arrangements in each classroom for the children to paint. It would make the school look lovely. Lots of bright colours. It would link well with Mother's Day cards too. When was Mother's Day? She would need to check. She logged off the computer.

'Well Roselyn, it has been lovely to chat but I really must go now,' she lied. 'I will tell Rob that you phoned and I expect he'll want to call you when he gets a minute.' He wouldn't, but hopefully it might delay the next call for a few days. Esther wondered what on earth Roselyn's phone bill must be. Maybe she got free calls with a special deal. These companies ought to consider the loss of valuable time to busy people before they offered free phone calls to all and sundry. She smiled at her thoughts and rose, ending the call as gently as she could bear to.

***

Samuel was working at the kitchen table. He pulled a book across a piece of paper when Esther entered. He was supposed to be studying geography, drawing diagrams that showed how the earth's plates moved. But he was thinking about Clare Beackon. Clare was in his geography class. She was fairly tall with blond hair and very impressive breasts. Very impressive. Samuel had started noticing breasts. He sometimes realised that he was not actually looking at a female's face when speaking to her and had to drag his gaze upwards before she noticed. He could have written a detailed description on the breasts of every female that he knew. Even the old ones. He could not have told you their hair colour, eye colour or possibly their names. But breasts were his speciality. He was not entirely sure if this was normal and occasionally worried it might be classified as sinful. It was not however something he felt inclined to ask his father about.

When his mother had come into the kitchen he had been

doodling a sketch of Clare's breasts on a scrap of paper. It was a fairly crude representation but he was fairly sure he had the contours about right. He would put it in his bag later and throw it away at school tomorrow. You had to be careful about litter at home. You never knew if it was going to be looked at before it made it to the dustbin. He gazed down at his geography book. Geography was so boring. Did anyone actually care about how the world worked? It was meant to be lived on not studied. School was okay, he had his mates and they all had a laugh but he did resent when it spilled into home life. Homework was an invasion of his personal space. If teachers wanted to teach they should manage to do it during school hours, not send them home burdened with all this rubbish to do. He was missing some quality telly for this.

Esther glanced at him and he lowered his head and sighed. Hopefully that would give the impression of deep concentration. He knew his mum in these moods, she would ask him to help with something if she spotted an opening but she would not disturb school work. Homework always took high priority in their house. It was something he was learning to use to his advantage.

***

When Rob arrived home it was late. Esther had eaten with the boys and left his dinner on a plate. It was congealing in the fridge and he was not sure he could face eating it. He grabbed some bread and cheese and took it into the lounge where Esther was watching television.

'Not sure I can manage a full meal, do you mind?' he asked, holding up the bread and knife, and moving to sit opposite her.

'No, of course not, it's sausages so one of the boys will eat them cold tomorrow. How was it?'

'Pretty tough actually.' He chewed the bread and broke off a piece of cheese.

'I'll make you some tea,' said Esther, rolling out of the sofa.

'No, stay for a bit,' he said, looking up at her. 'Make the tea in a minute. I could do with some company.' He always felt like this after sitting with someone when they died. He was full of adrenaline and physically exhausted and he wanted Esther near him, to tell her what had happened. 'Edith slipped away while I was there.'

'Oh dear, her poor family. Were you with her?'

'Yes, by chance really. I went in to see Carol first. The doctor was with her when I first arrived, that's why I had to wait. He told me that all had gone to plan, the mastectomy was a nice clean op and she'll have further tests next week, find out if it's in her lymph glands.'

'How was she? Poor thing, she must be worried.'

'She seemed fine actually, very strong. I think she almost feels glad she is doing something, sees the op as a chance to fight back, be proactive. She was tired of course, but very cheerful considering. I thought she might be tearful but she wasn't. I stayed for a while, prayed with her and chatted. Then her family came so I left them to it. I'll try to visit her again next week, though she might be home by then, they don't keep them in long these days.'

He thought of Carol, how she had worn an obviously new dressing gown and had bothered to put on make-up. She was determined not to let go, not to become a patient devoid of all personality, refusing to see this as anything more than an illness. An illness she would defeat. She had been pleased to see him but he had also sensed a wariness, as if she was worried he might get too close, touch a nerve that she was protecting. So he had kept the visit cheerful and bland, praying with her but not asking probing questions about how she was really feeling. Some people liked armour when they were in hospital and he was careful not to find chinks in it. He was there if she needed to talk but he was not going to force anything.

'Did you get to see David's brother? I know he's worried about him,' asked Esther, remembering that David had asked people to pray for his brother at the service on Sunday. He was not a church member, David was not sure he even believed in God, but no one minds being prayed for when they are ill. He had asked Rob if he could pop in and see his brother and Esther wondered if that had been awkward, visiting someone who you had never met.

'Yes I did; popped in after seeing Carol. I got there before any visitors so I explained I was David's pastor and asked how he was, if he needed anything. He was a nice chap. I didn't offer to pray or anything, didn't seem appropriate, but it was good to make contact. You never know when people are going to be looking for something more and it helps if they've already met you, makes it easier for them to approach you.

'Then I went in to Edith. Her son and daughter were both there but they asked me to stay. They wanted me to read to her, she's been asking for Psalm 23. So I read, held her hand and we prayed. She squeezed my fingers while I prayed, so I know she was listening. Then she just slipped away. It's always so gradual, you're never sure which breath will be the last.' He thought of those long minutes, sitting next to her bed, listening to the machines and her daughter's sobs. It was hard seeing people suffer. Edith was old. She was sure of her God, knew that he would be waiting for her and felt ready to go, to leave her painful body behind. It was never easy for the family though, nothing really prepared you for the finality of death.

The room was a private one, not part of the main ward. It was very bland, no colours and lots of shiny surfaces. Nothing personal, nothing you would want to look at. He often thought that he would rather die in a field than a hospital. Somewhere that he could smell the earth and see the sky.

'Her daughter was crying, of course, could hardly speak poor woman. The son was upset too but he didn't really show it, just kept shaking my hand and thanking me for coming. They want me to do the funeral so I'll phone them tomorrow.' He rubbed his hands across his face. His eyes itched and he could feel tension in his forehead.

Esther came to him, smoothing his hair and holding him close.

'Ah Esther, it's hard sometimes,' he said through the warmth of her shoulder. 'It's such a privilege to be there when someone finishes with their body, goes off to live as they are intended to live. But it's hard too. Watching that body cease to be a person, feeling the weight of the family's despair as they start to realise their loss.' He sighed, pulling her tight. 'A privilege and a burden, all rolled up in one.' He kissed her hard, wanting to escape into her for a while. He was tired now, beginning to feel drained of all energy. He just wanted to take his wife to bed and be a man again, to leave the minister bit of him on a peg until tomorrow.

'Were there any messages?' he asked.

'No, nothing that can't wait. I would've texted if anything had been urgent.' She knew he was empty now, everything could wait until he had rested.

Esther allowed herself to be led upstairs. She would tidy the supper things tomorrow before school. She knew that he had no space left inside him to listen to her plans, to hear about the Art Week. It seemed rather inconsequential compared with his day. She did not even mention the drawing she had found when putting Samuel's sports kit back in his bag. Tomorrow would be busy. She hoped he would soon go to sleep.

Chapter Eleven

IT was nearly midnight when Cynthia gave up on sleep. She had lain in her bed restlessly for two hours and she felt that she might as well get up, have some tea and see if she could relax her brain. She wore a white towelling dressing gown that stretched around her ample form. It was unflattering but warm.

It was some time later than the other teachers that Cynthia had driven home. Her display boards were neatly lined with colourful paper, a contrasting border edging each one. The children's books stood in neat stacks on her table, a new one for each subject named ready for James Buchan. She had read his record from his previous school, not that a term in a reception class had produced much. She had gleaned that there were no medical or behavioural problems, and from his reading book he was likely to be a clever child. She felt very uneasy about his home arrangements and hoped she would have no cause to communicate frequently with his mother. Mothers.

She knew that people laughed at her, thought her old fashioned but they were wrong. Cynthia had been teaching for years and when you taught, especially young children, you became involved in their lives. Cynthia had seen a lot of heartbreak over the years. She thought that people often treated each other very shoddily. She had seen what the break-up of a marriage could do to a five-year-old, had sat with children disturbed because of happenings in the adult world which they did not understand but they were aware of. They were left feeling lost and insecure. Sometimes a child was all but broken due to the selfishness of his parents.

The thoughts had spun around her head constantly, chasing away any chance of sleep. She slid her feet into fluffy slippers and used the toilet.

She wondered how this new young man would fare in her garden. His visit last week had been unremarkable, which was good. She now had a replenished supply of firewood and a gate which did not creak. She had taken him tea and his money when he arrived and checked he knew what to do. She had not seen him leave but was surprised the empty mug had not been returned. Nor was it in the shed. She had, somewhat perplexed, assumed he had taken it home. Then on Saturday, when enjoying some late afternoon sunshine, she had spied it. In a bush. The bright yellow handle shining merrily through the foliage. It had not been where one might have expected to find a returned mug. She would need to remember to write a note to that effect with his instructions for this week.

She thought about this idea of an art display. Something to impress the governors and show Esther's skills, no doubt. Well Cynthia had some skills of her own. She had taught a project on Monet a few years ago, she would find her notes and put some of those ideas to use. She had no concerns as to her ability to teach but was unhappy about being watched. However, if that was the challenge she would rise to it. She yawned. She was terribly tired. The last few nights she had not slept at all well, her mind constantly full of the worries about her job. It was impossible to 'not think' and she had spent the nights tossing sleeplessly in a muddle of thoughts. Could she afford to stay in the cottage if she lost her job? What would happen to her pension? Would any school consider employing someone of her age?

Descending the stairs while holding on to the rope fixed to the wall, she went through the wooden door into her sitting room. It was dark and cold. A car passed on the road outside, casting a display of shadow puppets across the walls. A kaleidoscope of movement then nothing. In the waste basket were some fliers that had arrived while she was at school. Nothing of importance, just a selection of vouchers and advertisements. People did waste so much paper these days. She scrumpled it into neat balls. She would light a fire; she had lots of wood and kindling now.

Kneeling on the hearth rug she placed the screwed up paper on the grate and covered it with small sticks. The matches were on the mantelpiece in a china box. She struck one and watched the flame lick the paper, growing and taking on the falsely bright colours of the printed sheet. Green, blue, yellow, the flames grew larger and warmer, hungrily searching for fuel. Slowly she added more sticks, increasing their size until the flames were surrounded in a cage of logs. They flickered through, like snake tongues seeking oxygen. The smoke curled up the chimney and Cynthia went to wash her hands. When she returned, the fire was crackling cheerfully in the grate. She was good at fires.

Sitting in her chair with a cup of tea, she flicked through the television channels. There was an old musical being shown but the pictures and sounds jarred her nerves. She turned it off. The room returned to the dancing light from the fire. She had found the television very irritating lately, too much stimulation for her already over loaded mind. She could not stop thinking, worrying, playing out possibilities. She snapped on the lamp next to her and tried reading a book but after reading every word on four consecutive pages without a glimmer of understanding she closed it.

She watched the flames reaching towards the chimney, restlessly stretching higher like a thing that was alive. She had always loved fires. They reminded her of precious times spent at the end of her garden with her father. Just the two of them, peacefully feeding logs into the smoking leaves. Adding branches from the pine tree and listening to the sizzle as the flames flashed into life. She remembered the day she had burned her diary, page by traitorous page, after George had found it and read snippets aloud at lunch. There was something cleansingly permanent about burning something.

Cynthia rose. She was no nearer sleep than when she had come down. Perhaps she needed some of those pills that so many women seemed to swallow to calm their nerves. She thought not. Cynthia did not approve of unnecessary medication. She visited the doctor only when suffering from the most extreme of illnesses. She decided to go outside for a walk. It was rather a daring idea, one that caused her heart to race slightly. An adventure. She liked walking, it often helped to calm her mood. She had never walked at night though, not alone, not without a reason. However it would be better than sitting and fretting in her cottage. A brisk walk down to the little bridge that crossed the stream half a mile down the road. Then home to bed, where she would remain until morning.

Glad to have made a plan, to be doing something other than trying to not think, she went back to her room and dressed. She chose some woollen trousers with an elasticated waist for their warmth and comfort, a thick Arran sweater and some socks. Rather daringly she decided to pull on the outer garments over her pyjamas. It felt reckless, fitted the mood of her naughty child adventure.

The wind caught the door as she opened it, making her gasp. It was cold but not raining and she checked she had her key, then slammed the door shut behind her. The road was quiet. Somewhere in the distance she could hear a dog barking but there was no sound of traffic, no other people. The houses opposite had dark windows that stared unseeing into the lane. The world felt empty. Under the yellow glow from the street lights she began to walk towards the bridge. Her shoes clicked as they touched the pavement and she found the rhythmical sound comforting. The air was fresher than during the day and she felt very alive. It was rather exciting. She was not sure if she would feel nervous if she met anyone but she thought not. She did not consider herself a likely target for attack of any kind.

It was extremely rare for Cynthia to break with convention and she found she enjoyed it. She stood for a moment when she reached the bridge, listening to the water as it gurgled away from town. It was too dark to see anything, the bridge cast a black shadow. But she had looked down many times and knew that the bank was covered in brambles that had snagged pieces of litter and they would be fluttering like small flags in the wind. The same wind that was beginning to penetrate her coat. She turned and retraced her steps.

When she opened the cottage door the fire seemed particularly welcoming. It made the whole room cosy, warm after the cold of outside. She smiled as she removed her shoes. That had been fun. She had felt like a secret agent, someone on a mission, quite unlike the staid and predictable Miss Mott. She found she liked the feeling.

She checked the fire was safe for the remainder of the night, took her dirty tea cup to the kitchen sink then went back upstairs. She removed her thick jumper and trousers and slid into bed. She would not look at the clock, better to not know how much sleep she was going to have. Lying back on pillows that felt especially comfortable she closed her eyes.

***

An unwelcome surprise greeted Cynthia when she arrived at school in the morning. She was tired and getting ready had been an effort. She was usually a cheerful riser but the lack of sleep was beginning to take its toll. She had made toast for breakfast but been unable to eat more than half a slice, due to both lack of time and appetite. It seemed that her appetite had disappeared with her sleeping ability. Both left her feeling ragged.

She was the first person to enter her room that morning. She pushed open the door, laden with pieces of paper and worksheets ready for the day and stopped. There was a sound. A rustling followed by a flash of brown that disappeared up the brick wall next to the chimney breast. It was a rat. Miss Mott screamed.

She was not really afraid of rats, she had after all grown up in a vicarage in a village where rodents and other wildlife were a regular part of life. It was the shock of seeing it so unexpectedly and the speed at which it moved that made her cry out. An involuntary sound which she instantly regretted, especially as she immediately heard footsteps running towards her.

Mr Carter and Andrew Smyth both arrived at her door looking concerned.

'What's...' began Andrew, then stopped as he saw the remains of the children's party food strewn from the cupboard where it had been stored and littering the floor. Chewed pieces of plastic wrapping and rat droppings were scattered amongst the crumbs.

'Mouse?' said Mr Carter.

'Rat,' corrected Cynthia. 'A very large rat. And I apologise for screaming, that is most out of character. I think it was the shock at seeing it so unexpectedly. It made me jump. One does not usually give way to hysterics over something so trivial.'

Andrew grinned at her. 'At least we didn't find you standing on a chair,' he said. 'Is there anything I can do or shall I leave you to it?'

'No, no, you get back to work,' said Mr Carter, 'I've got some traps I can put down. Nasty little critters, I'm not surprised they gave you a fright. Don't like rats, they carry disease. I'll get my broom and sweep up that mess. Perhaps throw the rest of the food away now, you don't know what it walked over with its dirty little feet.'

Cynthia bent down and began to sweep the debris into an empty plastic bag. She wished she had some gloves. The carpet was old, worn away in several patches and it made sweeping up easy. She worked quickly, keen to have it cleaned away before the children started to arrive. She still had the paper to prepare for her maths lesson. It was most inconvenient.

Mr Carter returned after a few minutes carrying what looked like a cage.

'Are we going to catch it?' asked Cynthia, feeling cross.

'It's a humane trap,' he explained. 'When we've caught one I'll take it into the woods away from the school and release it. No need to kill something if we don't need to, that would give the wrong message to the kids. You don't want to be opening the cupboard to find a dead rat do you?'

Cynthia thought she would prefer it to finding a live one but keeping up appearances was something she understood very well, so she said nothing.

'Course, if we've seen one, there'll be at least twenty somewhere. The previous chap used to put down black boxes of poison. They were safe enough I suppose because only a rodent could get inside. Not very nice though. They're still in the caretaker's shed, I cleared them all up when I arrived.

'It's a shame you all left food in the school,' he continued as a gentle reprimand. 'Rats are almost impossible to get rid of once they realise there's a food source. We're going to have to be very careful to dispose of edible rubbish properly before they get hold of it. Won't be good for the school's reputation if people start seeing rats around.

'They're clever little buggers, avoid anything new. I'll put the trap in your cupboard, where they found the food, but I doubt they'll go near it. They don't walk into things they don't recognise, don't eat food they've never had before. Makes trapping them very hard. They do tend to visit the same places though, so we might get lucky. Now, which shelf was the food on?'

Cynthia opened the big wooden cupboard by the door and showed him the shelf. It was an old cupboard, at one time it had a lock but the key had been lost long ago and now the doors did not stay properly shut. She guessed that was how the rat had got in. Horrible creature. She shivered at the thought of it running up the wall, straight up, as if it were climbing a ladder. A ghastly image. She began to prepare for the children. They would begin with a maths lesson.

By the time the children arrived the classroom was tidy and games were waiting on each table. They came in, full of fresh air and the excitement of a new term. Cynthia settled them, listened to their news and took the register. She introduced James to them.

He was a small child, recently cut blond hair, ears that stuck out and very large eyes. He watched the class silently, deciding whether or not he wanted to stay. Miss Mott did not call him to the front, so he could sit at the back while she told the class that he had arrived. She chose a girl, Mandy, to be his special friend and to help him find his way around. Mandy looked at him. She had three younger brothers and liked to organise people. She would enjoy being his helper.

Miss Mott sent most of them off to various activities. Mrs Fuller sat at the creative table and helped a group to push various objects into wet clay. They were supposed to be making a repeating pattern but most of them just enjoyed the feel of the cold slab and spent many minutes squeezing and moulding it into shapes.

Miss Mott gathered a group, which included James and Mandy, onto the carpet. She was careful to avoid sitting where she knew the rat had been. She had a large tray of coloured cubes, which could be interlocked into towers. She joined four, counted them and asked the group how many she had. How many towers of four bricks? Any more towers? The children confirmed that she had one tower. She then showed them on a large piece of paper how they could write this down, one tower of four, or one four and no more. She asked them to all make their own tower while she went to check how the children on the drawing table were getting on.

The children all dipped into the cubes box and began to build towers. Mandy wanted all yellow cubes, so she took quite a long time picking her cubes. She suggested that James might like red cubes. He did not. He did not really want any cubes but he was still unsure of this plump lady with a round face who seemed very much in charge. He did not yet dare to defy her and so obediently made a tower of four bricks.

Miss Mott returned and made another tower. They then all counted and verified that she now had two lots of four and that was eight cubes in total. She showed them how that could be written down. Four and four makes eight altogether. Lauren was making a striped tower, using alternate green and yellow cubes. She was concentrating on collecting the colours and forgot to count. One of her towers was too long. James noticed but decided not to tell her. He watched with interest as she wrote four and four made ten. Miss Mott also noticed and told Lauren to count the cubes in each of her towers again, while she went to see the clay children. She realised her mistake and scribbled across the ten with a green crayon until it was obliterated. Mandy then said that she needed Lauren's yellow cubes. Lauren planned to keep them for her next tower and moved them out of Mandy's reach. Mandy told James to get them. He looked at her silently but did not obey. She pinched him and reached across to grab them, just as Miss Mott returned. James considered crying but decided that then the round teacher would take him to one side. He gave Mandy his angry look, the one that could kill monsters. She did not die.

By the time the children had cleared up ready for assembly, three groups of children had made and added towers and everyone had made clay patterns. Cynthia considered it to have been a nicely productive morning. She left June Fuller to wipe all the tables clean of clay dust and took the children to the hall.

When all the children were settled in an almost straight line on the floor, Cynthia took her seat at the side and listened as Jane Lancaster greeted the school and told them a story. It was meant to have a moral but Cynthia was unsure what it was. She was barely listening. She stood for the hymn and she moved her mouth to the correct song but her mind was elsewhere. She was so tired and her head ached. The day stretched before her like a yawning chasm, it seemed too wide to pass. The chair was uncomfortable, the singing was too loud and the children were twitching in a most irritating fashion. How she longed to be curled up in her bed.

**

The following day, Cynthia entered her classroom very cautiously. There was no sign of life so she went to the cupboard and tentatively opened the door. She did not scream. But she nearly did. There, in the trap, was a rat. It was very much alive. It was brown and fat, about the size of her shoe. It had small round ears and little pink feet and it was extremely angry. When it saw Cynthia it let out a series of high pitched screams and began to leap frantically around the trap. It thrust its nose through the bars and showed it teeth. Cynthia was unsure if it was trying to bite her or chew its way out of the trap. But she was very sure of her own feelings. She hated it.

There seemed to be no way that it could escape, so Cynthia closed the cupboard door and went in search or Mr Carter. He was not in his shed, nor the hall nor the playground. She went to the office.

'Has anyone seen Mr Carter today? I am unable to locate him,' she asked Pauline Brookes, the School Administrator. A secretary really, but in this modern age one must refer to the ancillary staff by their correct titles. She waited impatiently while Mrs Brookes finished typing and looked up from her computer.

'I'm afraid he isn't here today Miss Mott. He came earlier to open the school but he won't be in until this afternoon. I think he has to sort out his car at the garage or something. He booked the time off ages ago. Can I help with anything?'

'Absolutely not. Thank you. One expects the staff will all be present during school hours. I shall sort the issue myself' said Cynthia and strode from the room.

Pauline Brookes watched her leave with raised eyebrows and pursed lips. 'Stupid woman,' she thought.

Cynthia checked the time. The children would soon arrive and she needed to prepare. She returned to her classroom. The rat was where she had left it. She stared at it for a long moment.

'You must die,' she decided. She felt strangely powerful. This repugnant creature had dared to come into her room, to invade her space and was now threatening her with its screams and leaping around, as if the roles were reversed and it would happily dispose of Miss Mott. But they were not reversed and she had all the strength and all the power and she was going to destroy this animal.

Cynthia moved the furniture slightly, blocking the door to the cupboard with the back of a chair. Now nobody would be able to open the door and see the cage. She stood in the centre of the room for a few minutes, thinking. She didn't think she could bear to touch the cage, to lift it while the creature within leaped around, snapping at her through the bars. She would need to kill it while it was in the cage. Stabbing it was too brutal; she needed a method which involved no contact. Poison. Mr Carter had said that he had some in his shed. She could feed it poison, then when Mr Carter returned it would be dead. She could claim it had died of fright. She would do it during assembly, June Fuller could sit with the children, it was not unusual for a teacher to be absent occasionally if they wanted to assess a child or prepare something for the next lesson.

She felt better when the decision was made and started to put toys on the tables.

When all the children were safely in assembly, Cynthia made her way to the caretaker's shed. It was behind the main buildings of the school and was just that. A shed. It had a large padlock on the door. She had not predicted that. Guessing the key was probably kept in the office she went to ask Pauline Brookes. She said that yes, the key was on one of the high hooks just inside the door. She considered asking why Miss Mott needed it, decided she could do without the condescending answer and lowered her head back to the computer.

Cynthia carried the key back to the shed. She felt very excited, as she had on the night of her walk. It was so rare for her to do anything unusual and it made her feel strangely powerful. She was doing something unexpected and probably against the rules. Her heart was fast and pink spots of colour had appeared on her cheeks.

The lock was solid but well maintained and it slid open easily. Cynthia removed the key and put it in her pocket as she entered the shed. One did not grow up with George as a brother and leave a key in a door to a room that you entered. Not more than once.

The shed was full. Buckets, spades and tools littered the floor. There were shelves on both sides, completely full of cartons and boxes, nails and glue, and cleaning products. It seemed to Cynthia to be a very masculine place, she felt that as a woman she should not be there. This strengthened her resolve, she was on a mission. She began to search, beginning with the higher shelves as the most likely place for a dangerous substance. It did not take long to find. It was a box with a rat on the outside and several warning signs.

Inside were small sachets claiming to contain poisoned grain. Cynthia removed a single sachet, slipped it into her pocket, relocked the shed and returned the key. Pauline did not even look up as she hung it back on its hook.

In the classroom, Cynthia quickly pulled the chair away from the cupboard door and looked inside. The rat began to scream at her, jumping around and climbing the sides of the trap. Cynthia smiled. This was one bully who would not be surviving. She used some small scissors with pink plastic handles to open the sachet. Inside was grain dyed blue. It had a chemical smell. Cynthia wondered if the rat would be stupid enough to eat it. Not knowing how to put a receptacle into the trap, she poured the grain through the bars. The rat scampered to the far end and sat, muttering rat obscenities at her. The grain fell into the trap, some falling through the bars onto the shelf and the floor below. She took the dustpan and brush and swept them up, then put them into a carrier bag before placing it in the dustbin. She was careful. Children were so casual about chewing their fingers. Satisfied that there was nothing further she could do, she closed the cupboard door and replaced the chair that was blocking it. She then began to sort reading books.

Cynthia thought about the rat all through the next lesson. She wondered if it was eating the poison, if just running across it and then licking its paws would be sufficient. She wished she had thought to pour some actually onto the rat.

June noticed that she was distracted and looked exhausted. She thought that she had a slightly wild look in her eyes, but dismissed the thought as fanciful. Miss Mott could not ever be described as wild.

When all the children had left for lunch, Cynthia told June there was nothing she needed her to do. As soon as the classroom was empty, she checked the cupboard. The rat looked back at her. It seemed somewhat more subdued, it did not scream, but neither did it look ill. Cynthia wondered how long it took for the poison to work. She had assumed with so small an animal it would be fairly instantaneous. Was there a 'use by' date on poison? She had not thought to check. Perhaps it was ineffective after all these years. There was no way of knowing if it had actually eaten any of the grain, certainly not a sizeable amount. She closed the door and went to eat her lunch.

In the staffroom, Esther and Andrew were discussing the Art Week. Esther suggested that they have a general theme of flowers. Andrew looked unimpressed.

'Flowers? I can't say that seems very inspiring. Not sure the boys will want to paint flowers either. Isn't the idea of all picking an artist theme enough? Why do we need to link it even more?'

'We don't, it's just a suggestion,' said Esther. 'I thought it would make for a nice display.'

'I think flowers would be pleasant,' added Cynthia. 'If one might add a vote.' She did not actually care, but the thought of making it more difficult for Andrew was appealing. If one viewed this as a competition then someone had to lose and in her mind, he was the obvious choice. She wondered if Esther had chosen flowers for this very reason.

'I don't want to force it on you if you're not comfortable,' Esther continued, looking concerned. 'I'm hoping it's something we will all enjoy and will help to raise the profile of the school a bit. Did you have a different idea?'

'It will only serve to prolong the issue if we all input ideas,' asserted Cynthia. 'I think it was your suggestion Esther and if flowers are what you had envisioned then flowers are what we shall paint.'

'Let's think about it and discuss it tomorrow,' suggested Esther. 'Cynthia, how is the new little boy settling in?'

'He seems a sweet little chap,' began Cynthia and gave a brief description. He seemed a nice enough child but she felt there was more going on behind those innocent eyes than he was showing. Not that she shared this thought with her colleagues. They only needed to know that he was not crying every two minutes and seemed competent. She rose to make herself some tea. Her sandwiches seemed too strong and she wondered if she had applied more pickle than usual to the cheese. She was not really hungry anyway.

Cynthia sat and sipped her tea, listening to Esther and Andrew. It seemed he was learning to speak Mandarin. She failed to see how that would be useful in life, there were so few Chinese children in their town and they had never had one attend the school.

The afternoon session felt long. The children were restless and Cynthia had to repeatedly remind them that at school one worked quietly. Even when she was reading the story at the close of the day, Billy decided to get up and go to the play house. She realised that he had problems, suspected that he was on the autistic spectrum and was beginning the slow route to have him formally assessed. It was unusual for him to simply wander away though, especially during a story. He usually liked to see the pictures, even if he did have a tendency to hum sometimes. Lauren turned to watch him. Cynthia told her to face the front. He could come to no harm, she could see him, she would continue with the story while he sorted the plastic tea set. Perhaps it had been left in the wrong order and it was bothering him, easier to leave him than to try and persuade him to stay sitting with the rest of the class.

When the children and June had finally gone home for the day, Cynthia checked the cupboard. The rat looked squarely back at her. It did not move or make a sound and it looked unhappy. The paper lining the shelf was soiled with a heap of dark brown. Cynthia began to wonder how exactly the poison worked. It was certainly not as fast as she had anticipated. She felt a sense of accomplishment, she was winning.

There was a sound behind her and Mr Carter peered over her shoulder.

'Did we manage to catch anything? We did, splendid. Oh. Oh Miss Mott, what have you done?'

There was no hiding the lurid grain. If the creature had died as expected, she could have cleaned it all away and no one would have known. As it was it sat in the corner, accusing her of both theft and murder. She felt angry rather than guilty.

Mr Carter lifted the trap from the cupboard, scattering grains of poison and excrement.

'I had better go and finish this one off quickly. It's cruel to leave him to suffer. I'll come back and clean up shortly.' He sounded cross, disapproval in every polite word. Cynthia could think of no reply.

She began to sort her things while Mr Carter was gone. She had no rubber gloves and refused to tackle the mess in the cupboard with her bare hands. He was not gone long. When he returned he carried a steaming bucket and was wearing gloves. He emptied the cupboard and washed it thoroughly, not speaking until he had finished. Cynthia busied herself with her papers, pretending to not notice the silence. She wanted to ask if the rat was dead and how he had killed it. It would not have seemed appropriate so she did not but there was a gleam of triumph in her eyes. She had won and it made her feel powerful.

He turned to her. She sat at her desk, writing notes in the TA book ready for tomorrow. She was aware of his gaze but did not turn.

'It's a shame you took it into your head to use that poison,' he began. 'It's not a nice way to die. It's what they give people with blood clots you know, thins the blood. They basically bleed to death internally.'

Cynthia did not smile but she was glad it had suffered.

'I apologise if I have upset you. However, one was unaware of when you planned to return and felt it prudent to take matters into one's own hands.' She was not going to say she was sorry for killing it. She had read in its eyes that it hated her, thought all the same things that everyone who had laughed at her her whole life had thought. It was right for it to die and right that she should kill it. That was what justice was all about after all, getting what one deserved. She closed the book and placed the pen back in the pot on her desk.

'Come now, Miss Mott, I think you knew that I would be back by home time,' he said, unwilling to let this drop quite so quickly. 'I would've dealt with it for you. There was no need to trouble yourself.' He resisted saying 'interfere' but she knew what he was thinking.

Cynthia stood up. 'Thank you Mr Carter, as ever, you are most kind. Let us hope that we do not have a reoccurrence tomorrow. Perhaps it was the only one in the vicinity.' She collected her papers, stuffing them into her bag, picked up her coat and walked to the door. 'Good evening,' she said as she left.

When she was in the corridor, safely out of sight, she slowed. She found that she minded what Mr Carter thought of her, minded very much indeed. She did not care to be criticised by him. She felt that the rat was somehow wreaking revenge, that its power was stretching out to harm her relationship with the caretaker. No, she could not quite think of him as merely the caretaker. He was almost a friend. Had been, before that creature had arrived.

She walked through the school, feeling her bag heavy on her arm, the strap digging into her flesh. She had books to mark, but she did not feel inclined to sit in that room a minute longer. She would finish her work at home. She dug into the side pocket and retrieved her car keys. Her home seemed very attractive this evening. A place to hide.

When she arrived at the cottage she left her bag in the sitting room and went to write a note for Tommy Martin. He would come tomorrow while she was at school and she needed to leave clear instructions. Especially concerning the return of her crockery. She wrote some instructions, then paused. She would be unable to make him a drink, nor did she intend to leave him with access to the cottage. However, the shed had power. She could leave him the equipment to make himself some tea. It seemed hospitable. He might mention to Mr Carter that she had been kind.

There was a kettle in the bottom of her wardrobe. She went upstairs and pulled it out from its hiding place behind her shoes. Actually, it was new, had never been used. George had sent it to her years ago. He had visited and laughed at her kettle, whistling away on the hob. Told her she was old fashioned to the point of being prehistoric and life was too short to wait for such a thing to boil. Three days later this new kettle had arrived, sent straight from the supplier, no note attached. As with all gifts from her brother, Cynthia had felt the implied criticism more keenly than any gesture of friendship which may have been intended. She had never used the kettle, relegating it to the back of her wardrobe. Now it might prove useful. It seemed appropriate that the gardener should use it. Perhaps she would find the kettle too had been placed in a bush.

She carried a tray, laden with kettle, tea bags, mug and sugar. The sugar was in a cereal bowl. She was not going to trust him with her sugar bowl but neither did she want to give him a whole bag of sugar. He did not look an overly clean individual. She left them in the shed with a list of instructions and went back to her work. Not that she could concentrate. Her brain did not seem to function any more. Nothing did. She was so incredibly tired.

Chapter Twelve

ANDREW shared his disappointment about the 'flowers' theme with Trevor and Harry. Having a quick pint after their Mandarin lesson seemed a good tradition to follow, so they sat around a sticky table in The Bell, sipping warm beer and comparing inconsequential details about their week.

'Bit girly,' agreed Trevor, then looked worried. He was not entirely sure if the whole teaching primary children was not a bit girly in itself. Not that he could say that.

'I got given flowers once,' admitted Harry. The other two looked up, startled. 'Yeah, was a girlfriend, gave them to me for Easter one year. I didn't really know what to do with them, put them in an empty marmalade jar but it kept falling over.' He suddenly saw the funny side of his own story and let out a peal of laughter. It was surprisingly high pitched and loud. Several other people turned to look. Trevor and Andrew laughed, more at his piggy giggle than at what he had said.

'Well, how'd you find Mrs Wang this evening?' asked Harry, 'Any easier?'

'Ah, Wang *tai tai*,' said Trevor, in his best Chinese accent. 'Still didn't understand most of it. I'll give it a couple more weeks then pack it in I think. Harder than I was expecting, life's just too short.'

'It is hard,' agreed Andrew, 'but I felt like I was getting to grips with it a bit better this week. I've been watching lots of Chinese DVDs, think it helped to sort of tune in my ear. I could understand most of what she said this lesson. Well, the English bits anyway, but that's a start.' He told them about his lessons in the local restaurant. Trevor and Harry were slightly shocked, seemed a bit eccentric to do something like that. But then, he was a primary school teacher, what did you expect?

'You asked them if they're legal?' asked Harry. 'I bet they're not. They all come over you know, stay long after their visa has expired. Saw a programme about it once.'

'Could you get done for that?' said Trevor, 'Knowing that someone is an illegal? Do you have to report it?'

'What, like accepting stolen goods?' said Harry. 'No, doubt it. Everyone knows they're illegal. Make nice food though so no one's making a fuss about it.'

Andrew had no idea if his pupils had visas or not. He had not thought to ask. He was not even sure if between them they had enough vocabulary for him to be able to ask. He shrugged, not his concern.

'They want English names,' he told them. 'They asked me to give them some. Never named anyone before, what do you think?'

'Gupta,' said Trevor, 'call one of them Gupta.'

Andrew smiled, 'Not sure that's quite what they were expecting.'

'Yeah, be alright until one of them turns out to be a Triad, then you'll end up in the dumplings,' said Trevor.

'Do they have Triads over here?' asked Andrew, worried.

None of them knew. They did not actually know much at all it seemed. A few half-truths from old television programmes muddled in with rumour and speculation. Andrew thought again about what a closed society he was beginning to encounter. They lived right under everyone's nose, but no one actually knew them at all. They could not even chat in a supermarket queue. They were physically present but cut off from the rest of society, moving only in their own Chinese circles. He wondered what he might discover, as he strolled back to his car, rattling his keys in his pocket as he walked. He glanced at his watch. He needed to mark some stories when he got home, write some comments that the parents would read and draw some smiley faces that the children would understand. Make the books look like they were regularly monitored.

***

Thursday morning, Andrew was photocopying worksheets by eight o'clock. He wanted to try and get his planning ahead of schedule so that he could leave promptly on Friday. The machine in the corner of the office whirred, spitting maths sheets into a tidy pile on the paper tray. They were going to all have the same sheet today, sets of shapes. He figured he could differentiate easily enough between the ability levels without having to bother with different sheets. Then they would be less aware of being 'in the bottom set' if they were less able. The sheet had big circles drawn on it, each one containing pictures of shapes. The thick kids could put a cube on each shape, which was one to one correspondence: tick. They could then count them, which was counting to ten: tick. Then they could put all the cubes together, which was adding: tick. They could write the total, which was recording: tick.

The more able children could manage without cubes. They could also have a quick guess at how many were in each set before they counted them, which was estimation: tick.

He knew that it was important that the children all covered the basic concepts for mathematics. He did find working to a prescriptive manual to be restrictive though. He also felt that having to open his records file and give each child the relevant tick next to their name for the concept covered, to be an utter waste of his time. It would take him about an hour after school to update the information. No one would ever read it and he knew perfectly well who was thick as a brick and could not yet count reliably, and

190

who had been counting their way up the stairs with Mumsy since they were two and could probably multiply and divide without too much effort. This whole emphasis on record keeping seemed an utter waste of time.

While the machine spat out his worksheets, he looked through the textbook in his hand, deciding which page to copy. He had gone up to Chinatown at the weekend and found a bookshop. He had looked up the word before he went and practised asking random Chinese people where the *'shu dian'* was. He had been rather pleased when he did actually find both the shop and an English/Mandarin textbook. It was a fraction of the price quoted on the internet. He hoped it would help his restaurant teaching, save him wasting a lot of time translating all the instructions.

He heard a cough behind him and looked up to find Miss Mott waiting.

'Good morning Mr Smyth, you have beaten me to the photocopier. Will you be long may I ask?'

'Oh, hello Miss Mott, I wasn't sure if anyone else was in yet.' He checked the number on the top of the machine. 'Fifteen more. Then I just want to copy a couple of pages from this book and it's all yours.'

She pursed her lips and sighed. 'Most inconvenient,' she muttered.

He was irritated. He knew it was annoying to have to wait, especially if you had left copying until a bit late, he knew all about that. But to try and make him hurry was just rude. They all used the photocopier, there was no set schedule, if you were unlucky and arrived after someone else, that was just tough. He glowered at the textbook in his hand.

The sheets stopped arriving and the machine pinged. Andrew lifted the lid, replaced the master sheet with his book, changed the quantity to five, and pressed go. Cynthia watched the sheets as they spewed out. They seemed to have Chinese writing on them. She leaned forward and took one. This did not look like year one work.

'And what pray, is this?' she asked, raising her eyebrows. The door opened and Jane came in.

'Oh blow,' she said, seeing both teachers, 'is there a queue?'

'I'm afraid so,' said Cynthia, 'but I am not sure quite what Mr Smyth is copying. Is this for the school?'

'Yes,' he began, about to explain that the school would undoubtedly benefit from his linguistic abilities. He looked at the two women. Jane Lancaster was neat, as ever, in a trouser suit, hair loosely tied back with some complicated knotted thing. Miss Mott on the other hand looked like she had been dragged through a bush. She had weight issues anyway but honestly, she looked worse than ever today. He could not be sure she had even brushed her hair that morning. Maybe she had a lover. Now there was a thought to put you off your food.

Jane reached forward and took the sheet from Cynthia. She frowned, then remembered that he was learning Mandarin. She felt irritated with Cynthia, she was invariably rude and this did not really affect her.

'I believe that mine is the only permission he needs to ask, Cynthia,' she said. She turned to Andrew. 'Ask first next time. I think I'll do some work in my office while I'm waiting.' She left.

Andrew scooped up his papers and followed her out. He had no desire to continue his conversation with Miss Mott, what a witch. A scruffy witch. The papers were warm and smelled of ink. He hugged them as he walked. He would go to the library next, find a couple of art books for Art Week. He had decided to teach about Van Gogh, feeling he was the less prissy of the flower artists. He quite liked Monet, with his great splodgy waterlilies but Miss Mott had bagged that one. He thought it would be okay, he could talk to them about representing an idea and using colour to make a mood, not worrying about whether it was exactly realistic or not. Maybe they could all have a different lot of colours and paint a copy of the sunflowers but using different palettes. So some could be green, blue, purple, others could be yellow, gold, red. Yes, he liked that idea. They could produce a really good display, especially if he gave them premixed paint; he had noticed the children seemed to mix quite dingy shades. He could get them to think about using different sized brushes, that could be his teaching point. They could each produce something bright and a bit different. He could group them according to the colour groups, that would look impressive, draw the eye. He was actually beginning to feel quite enthusiastic.

He went into the little library area and scoured the shelves for relevant books. There was only one and that was not much good. Never mind, he could call in at the town library on the way home if he managed to leave by half past four. Then he could finish planning in the evening. He sighed; it was one of the many drawbacks of being a new teacher. He suspected Miss Mott had, over the years, stored up a good supply of decent books that she could use when she needed. His budget would not stretch to that at the moment. He would find some pictures on the internet too, so they all had an idea of what they were painting. It would be good if they could actually go up to London, see the real paintings. Were they even in London? He could check later. It was time now to get his room ready, some of them would start arriving any minute. He noticed a mark on his tie and scratched at it irritably. It must be from dinner last night. Oh well, unlikely any of the kids would notice.

***

Friday was sunny. As Andrew walked down to the restaurant the last weak rays of the day were shining down on him. He felt it was a good omen. He entered the restaurant, which felt gloomy as a cellar after the brightness of the sun. The manager took him to the table and began to clear it, Bai Yun, Cheng Zhi and Shao Ling emerging from the kitchen area. They were all still dressed in their work clothes, white shirts and black trousers. He asked where Lao was. They told him no, Lao was not coming today. There was no reason given and he felt slightly annoyed. He had gone to some effort to prepare a lesson, it would have been nice to have been kept informed.

They all sat and the manager came back, carrying a tray of tea and a large white form. She placed the form in front of Andrew and passed him a pen.

'You sign,' she directed.

Somewhat bemused, Andrew took the pen and read the form. In large letters at the top it announced 'Application for Permanent Residency'. He looked up. 'Who is this for?'

'It for cook. You want see him?' she asked.

Andrew read further. 'I can't sign this,' he said, putting down the pen. 'It says I have known him for at least five years.'

'It big problem,' she explained, 'need English person sign it. You only English person we know. You want see him? I get him.'

'No, no,' said Andrew. 'Even if I see him, I still can't sign it. Look,' he pointed at the relevant section, 'I verify I have known... for at least five years. I haven't known him. Even if I meet him now, I still can't sign it. I can sign it in five years' time.'

'Okay, okay, no problem,' she said, taking the form and folding it. 'You drink tea, teach them English.' Then she left.

Andrew had absolutely no idea if he had offended her or if they had been expecting this response. He could not read Chinese expressions yet. He looked around the table. Bai Yun was to his left and she reached out and poured his tea.

'Here, you drink tea,' she said, smiling shyly.

Andrew was beginning to notice differences between the Chinese faces on his DVDs and he realised he could see them now in the faces in the restaurant. Cheng Zhi had a big moon face, the sort of face that smiles a lot. He recognised that as a Northern face. Shao Ling's face was longer, with a straighter nose, what he thought of as a Han face. Bai Yun had a petite face. He did not know where the features originated from but it was very pretty. She had her hair loose today and it was thick and black and very long, and he wanted to touch it. Felt that would be inappropriate.

He reached into his bag and pulled out his worksheets, passing them around. He told them he had been to Chinatown and managed to ask where the 'Shu dian' was. They smiled at him and took the sheets.

There was a short section about opening a bank account and then some questions, not dissimilar to an English comprehension paper. They looked at them for a long time and there was much discussion. He asked Cheng Zhi to read the Chinese, so he could hear the Mandarin, then he would read the English. Maybe he would pick up a word or two. Cheng Zhi started to read, then stopped. Bai Yun told him the word. He read a little more, then stopped again. Andrew frowned, not sure of the problem. He was reading the Mandarin version, his own language, why was he so slow?

Bai Yun spoke very softly,

'Teacher, China not same as England. Not everyone go school. Leave when money gone. Not read so good.'

Realisation flooded through Andrew and he felt terrible. Cheng Zhi could not read Mandarin. Andrew had never before met an adult who could not read and write, though of course he knew that in some cities it was a problem. It had never occurred to him that they would not be able to read the Chinese version of the text.

Bai Yun took over. She read the Mandarin and then Andrew read the English version. They stumbled their way through the exercises. It was much too difficult. Andrew realised he would need to prepare something different for future lessons or plan another trip to London to buy a simpler book. Ah well, at least he knew where the shop was now.

He gave up on the lesson and they began to chat. They each used the dictionary on their mobiles, which showed the English word, the Chinese symbol and the pinyin – the word written in letters so they could see how to say it. It was surprisingly effective and with a little miming, they managed a pretty good conversation.

'So, you have family back in China? Do you have any brothers or sisters?' asked Andrew. He knew that older and younger siblings had different words, so he used a combination of them all, not sure which was correct. He knew that China had a one child policy, so asked, knowing they would say no, so that they could then discuss it. He was somewhat surprised when Shao Ling nodded.

'Yes. Have two sister, one brother.'

'Oh. Is that allowed? You can? I thought in China everyone had one child. Law.' The sentence was a muddle but it seemed to work better than using all the words that he would normally say. If he only used the important words, using his dictionary for many of them to show the Mandarin symbol, then they understood each other. He wondered if his pidgin English was going to be all he learned at these sessions. Never mind, it was still interesting. Plus he got dinner out of it.

Shao Ling smiled. 'In city, one child. In country, need boy. Girl born first, have second baby. Girl born second, have third baby. Stop when boy.'

'Oh, I see, so your brother is the youngest? *Di di*? Little brother?' She nodded and smiled.

He asked about the rest of the staff and discovered that some were married, their spouses living in China. That was a surprise, he had assumed they were all single. Strange to be married to someone who you hardly ever saw. Not really a proper marriage. He then learned that one of the staff also had a son living there.

'Son? She has a son?' This really was surprising, why would you have a son and not live in the same country? He would understand it if they were divorced, that happened a lot, though usually the kid stayed with the mother, but not if the couple were still married.

'In China, baby go to…' there was again a discussion about the best word to use. 'Husband mother. She raise baby.'

'The mother-in-law? This is normal? Why doesn't the mother bring up the child? Doesn't she mind?'

'Mother young. Mother work, no time. Husband mother have time, she raise baby.'

'Does the mother's mother never take the child? Always the husband's mother?' This was very unexpected, he had no idea their cultures were so different. They were telling him as though they were surprised he did not know. It was completely normal to them.

They shook their heads. 'Husband mother. When she very old, she live with son. When she young, she raise his children.'

'So, when you were young, who raised you?'

They confirmed it was their grandmothers, until they were fairly old. They seemed to think it strange that English people wanted to keep a young baby. Young babies cry a lot, they told him, why would a young woman want that? Better for someone old to care for it. They laughed at his surprise. He noticed that Bai Yun had very neat teeth. Her eyes danced when she laughed, she was very pretty.

He asked her why she had come to England. 'Don't you miss China?'

'I love China,' she confirmed. 'But no work. If I in China, just sit all day. Not find work. No job. China got many many people. Not got many many job. Better to have job. England have work. I come find work.' She seemed slightly wistful when she spoke of China and Andrew wondered how much she missed it. It must be very hard if you had no real option but to leave to find work.

She slid off her chair, told him to wait and disappeared. When she returned, she was carrying a photograph. She held it in both hands and passed it to him.

'My family,' she said.

Andrew took the photograph. He was not sure if he was also supposed to receive it with two hands. The two hands thing seemed significant. He would ask Mrs Wang.

The photograph showed Bai Yun, younger, standing with another girl. They stood together laughing at the camera. Behind them was a concrete building and plants, some in tubs, some growing over the building. On the step behind them was a broken chair, the sort his grandmother had used as a dining chair. It was clean and tidy but looked hot and shabby.

'Your sister?' he asked.

'*Wo de jie jie*, my old sister, yes.' She smiled and nodded. Andrew was pleased he had recognised the younger Bai Yun, he must be getting better.

Both girls in the picture wore cut-off jeans and blouses. It was a whole world away. She told him that her sister had finished school, staying until she was eighteen. Bai Yun had left when she was fourteen because the money had run out. She helped her parents on the farm but her sister had made her keep reading, had helped her to learn new words. Andrew could not imagine how difficult that must have been, to in effect teach yourself to read. The Chinese had a completely different symbol for every word, so their reading would not grow, building on a foundation of letters like in Europe. Every word would have to be learned separately. There was no way of decoding a new word, working out what the symbol represented, you simply had to learn it in isolation, symbol and meaning as separate entities. He felt Bai Yun must be incredibly clever to manage that on her own, with just her sister to help her.

He looked at her now, in her black and white uniform, shivering because the restaurant was not so warm. He wondered why she did not wear a cardigan. Then wondered if she had one.

'Are you cold?'

'No, always cold,' she replied. Andrew was not sure if she had muddled the words for yes and no or if she was telling him she was okay. Their conversations were based on almost understanding, getting the gist if not the specifics. He thought it probably a good basis for a relationship. He was aware that Shao Ling was watching them, assessing. Maybe he should back off a bit. Still was not sure if the Triad thing was just a rumour. She said something to Bai Yun, who laughed. He did not have any idea what she had said, though it sounded Mandarin. It was rare now for him to not recognise any words at all. Bai Yun turned to him.

'You not understand. She speak Fujian. Very rude not speak *Pu tong hua*, Mandarin.'

'Fu-ji-an? What's that? Another language?'

Shao Ling answered, 'We all live Fujian. Fujian speak own language.'

'So not Chinese?'

'Is Chinese. Is, is...' she fumbled with her phone, searching the dictionary. She passed it so he could read the screen.

'Dialect. So, Fujian has its own dialect? But you speak Mandarin too?'

'Everyone speak Mandarin. China very big. Very many people. Every place speak own language and Mandarin. School and television only Mandarin.'

'And newspapers? Is that written in Mandarin or Fujian?'

'No writing. Fujian people speak, not write.' She seemed slightly confused by the question, as if not quite sure of the answer.

'But at home? At home with your family, you speak Fujian?' asked Andrew, wanting to clarify. She nodded.

'Where is Fujian?' he asked, bringing a map up on his mobile screen. They looked confused, were unable to tell him even if it was South or North. They discussed it in their fast Chinese, words merging into one, sounding cross but he knew that they weren't, it was just how it sounded.

'China very big,' they kept saying, as if explained their lack of geographical knowledge. Andrew was surprised but maybe if you never expected to travel anywhere, maps were pretty redundant.

He asked if they ever went to Chinatown. They looked confused, so he found the Mandarin name in his dictionary. They smiled and nodded.

'Teacher, we go often. It place where doctor live. And some friends. Good places eat,' Cheng Zhi told him.

'Ah, what is your favourite food?' asked Andrew. They looked confused. 'Eat what?' he asked, trying again. They looked for the correct word and then showed him.

'Chicken's feet? You eat chicken's feet?' Andrew thought that sounded awful.

'Feet best bit,' said Cheng Zhi. 'Chicken breast worst bit. No flavour, very dry. English people eat very dry food, not much taste. We like bits that English people leave.'

'Do you cook?' asked Andrew. They all told him that no, only the cooks cooked. At home, their mothers had cooked but they had never learned. That seemed a missed opportunity to Andrew, who was rather fond of Chinese food.

As if on cue, the manager appeared. Andrew felt like Mr Benn, a cartoon he had watched as a child. When the shopkeeper appeared, Mr Benn was whisked off to another land or back home again. For an hour a week Andrew was in China, everything was foreign, even the way they thought about life was different to him.

Then the manager appeared and that signalled that it was time to be English again. He smiled, she was carrying a white plastic bag.

'Sweet sour chicken,' she told him. 'You like?'

'Yeah, great, I like all Chinese food,' he said. Then remembered the chicken feet. 'I like everything on your menu,' he clarified. 'Dumplings are my favourite.'

She nodded, handed him the bag and took him to the door. The restaurant was shut now so she unlocked the door for him and gave a slight bow.

'*Zai tian*, goodbye. You come next week.'

'Yes, see you next week,' said Andrew with a wave. As he walked back to the car he thought about Lao not coming. He should have given them all his mobile number, so they could let him know in future if they were not going to be there. Annoying if he turned up and no one else did. Maybe if Bai Yun had his number she would contact him. Or he could ask for her number, text her. Yes, next week he would give them all his number and ask them for theirs. Not look too obvious. She was pretty though. Perhaps she would go to Chinatown with him, show him things he didn't notice on his own. They could have dinner. Not chicken's feet though, that sounded revolting.

He reached his car and put his dinner down in the footwell, jammed between his bag and a heap of books he was taking home to mark. He thought about what they'd told him, as he pulled out of the parking space. That was a bit weird. They had such different ideas to him, to the English. Could a relationship work between a Chinese girl and an English boy? He grinned to himself as he approached the traffic lights. Might be fun to find out.

His previous girlfriend had been pleasant enough but a bit boring. His sister had worked hard to get them together and it had been fun while it lasted. But then she had tried to get serious, had kept telling him about friends who were getting engaged, people their age who were married already, asking him if he wanted to have kids. He got the hint and ended it. Wasn't fair to keep her hanging on if that's the route she was planning to go. He was too young to settle down, wanted to have some fun first. Had only just managed to escape from his parents, a bit too soon for being all heavy and committed to any one person. Of course, she hadn't been happy. Lots of tearful phone calls. And texts. He didn't know how someone managed to weep by text but she managed it. He felt bad, obviously, but better in the long run. Set her free to find someone else. Set himself free too.

He could see a lot of advantages to having a girlfriend who didn't understand everything you said. It would certainly add an interesting element. And she was very pretty. Very pretty indeed.

The light was red so he stopped and reached for his music, selecting something easy to relax to. Was it unethical for him as teacher to see one of his pupils? No, he thought it was safe enough, both adults, not taking advantage in any way. Not really abusing a position of trust because they were teaching him too, was more of a mutual sharing of languages than a formal teacher/pupil relationship.

He realised that he did not even know if she had a boyfriend. She could be engaged for all he knew. Or not find English men attractive. He didn't know if they were allowed to have relationships, they all lived above the restaurant, was it controlled, like a boarding school arrangement? Did the manager monitor their social lives? Did they even have a social life?

'Only one way to find out,' he told himself as the light turned green and he moved away. 'Only one way to find out.'

Chapter Thirteen

THREE weeks later, Saturday was bright but cold. Esther needed to shop, not an activity she enjoyed. Joseph needed new shoes, she needed some new clothes. Something attractive but modest, not expensive (like that was an option) but also not too cheap in appearance. People might not want to pay the minister a huge salary but neither did they want his wife to look like she visited jumble sales. They did not want her to wear clothes that showed cleavage, nor did they want her to look frumpy, out of date, she should look as if she read the same magazines they did. Esther knew all this, wondered what it might be like to choose clothes that she and Rob would like, perhaps a sexy top for the summer, something with straps and lace and not much else. Not an option.

Joseph was taking his time over breakfast, not doing a very good job of ignoring Samuel who was gloating because he did not have to come too. He was supposed to be doing homework but Esther knew that as soon as they were in the car the computer would spring into life and zombies would be slain.

Eventually they were ready to leave, coats found, shoes on, list in bag. Rob was in the study, finishing his sermon for the next day, preparing PowerPoint slides, choosing hymns. Mrs Beaton was going to play the organ, the 'band' were all away this week. Esther knew the organist would be cross that she was not given the hymns until the day before, annoyed that she could not practise. Esther also knew that the timing would make very little difference, that she would play most songs at the wrong speed and with no imagination or musical emotion whatsoever. Mrs Beaton would mention it to Esther over coffee. But not Rob, very few people complained to Rob, it was easier to drop dissatisfaction into conversations with Esther, to let her tell her husband.

It was one of the hardest things she had had to become accustomed to, people criticising her husband when she knew he was worn out, doing more than anyone else could possibly do. Most people only saw one aspect of his job, the bit they were present for. They forgot about all the midweek meetings, the school assemblies, the visiting. Even when their complaints were justified it was hard, no one likes to hear someone they love being criticised. Most people viewed it as their right, he was a public figure and therefore they had every right to give their opinion about how he was performing. Giving feedback. Of course, sometimes the opposite happened too, someone would start to hero worship him, spend a little too long chatting after church, inventing problems so they could come round and be 'counselled'. Esther had received her fair share of invitations to dinners and functions, not because people enjoyed her and Rob's company but because he was 'The Minister'.

Joseph started to fiddle with the car radio, listening to each station for a few seconds before moving it on.

'Can't we just listen to one station? They'll change the song in a minute anyway,' she suggested.

'Not this one, it's rubbish,' he said, flicking to the next station. 'Ugh, this one's awful, we can't listen to this. Oh wait, this one's okay.' He sat back, looking out the window, tapping his nail against the glass in time to the music.

'How's school been this week? Did you make the team?' The football team was a source of great stress to Joseph. He loved football, lived and died for which teams were moving up or down the tables but his own playing was only almost good enough for the school team. He was the man they called on when there was a flu bug or a clash with the swimming team.

'Next week I'm playing,' he told her happily, 'it's an away match with Redhill Boys. Can you come? Other mums do. You haven't watched me for ages.' He liked when someone was there to watch him, shouting when he did something well, someone to chat about the game to afterwards, so Sam heard, knew he had played well. Someone to take him straight home after he had changed so he did not have to wait ages for the teacher to finish and then go back to school in the minibus with all the other boys who had not had parents watching.

'I don't know if I can,' said Esther. She felt guilty, knew she hardly ever watched. It was just too hard to fit everything into the week. If she was at school she felt guilty because there was something with the family or at church that she was missing. If she was 'being a mum' she felt guilty because she really ought to be sorting out something for school. At the moment she had to prioritise school, she must not appear anything other than fully committed. It was not worth risking her job over a football match. She would ask Rob if he could go, though he'd been snowed under himself lately, it seemed like the whole town was dying and asking him to take the funerals. He had barely caught his breath after Christmas and now they were plummeting towards Easter.

She swung round the roundabout and joined the slow line of cars filtering into the car park. She hoped there would be spaces; it was later than she had hoped to arrive and parking could be tricky on a Saturday morning. She ran through her mental list of things to buy. Shoes first, they were the main reason they had come. Then she would pop into Debenhams, have a quick look for something suitable to wear on a Sunday for special occasions, a nice skirt for Easter Sunday. Then the supermarket. Joseph would complain but there was no time to come separately and he could help carry. She also wanted to buy some flowers, ready for the Art Week this week. She was rather excited about it, it seemed to be going well. Pauline had sent out invitations to all the governors and told the local newspapers. She had wanted to buy some flowers, have some big arrangements around the school. She had wondered about taking the flowers from church after the service on Sunday. They always had flowers at the front, bought and arranged by a volunteer from the rota. She even got as far as asking Rob what he thought, could she take it to school? After all, they often used their personal stuff for church events, it was only fair to be able to take something in return occasionally. Rob had pointed out that the flowers were always given to someone in the membership who was ill, that it was not really appropriate for the school to have them when someone had bought and donated them for the church use. He suggested she ask Jane for some money. She had asked Jane, which had caused much sighing and huffing but she had eventually been given a budget and told she could give in her receipts. A small budget. Not enough for anything flamboyant but hopefully she could find something bright.

They inched into the car park and followed the line of cars higher and higher up the ramps, searching for a free space. Joseph pointed out a couple of vacant places but they were small, parking would be difficult. Esther did not enjoy parking. Eventually they found two spaces next to each other. She swung the nose of the car round and glided in, shuffled backwards and forwards a couple of times into exactly the same position, then gave up and put on the brake.

'Is that it?' asked Joseph, looking at the space between their car and the one next to it. 'Should be ideal if a small triangular car comes looking for somewhere to park.'

She laughed, poked him and got out, threading her bag onto her shoulder.

'Come on, let's find you some shoes.'

The shop was crowded. There was a ticketed system in place so they pulled one from the dispenser and began to wait. She pointed out a few pairs of black school shoes to Joseph, who was looking at football boots. He said they were all fine. When the assistant finally called their number Esther asked if they had the cheapest pair in his size. He went off to have his feet measured. Esther wished she had thought to tell him to wear socks without holes in. His big toe stuck out. It was very pink. He tried on the first pair.

'Yep, they're fine,' he announced and began to take them off.

'I think you should walk in them,' said the assistant.

He stood and walked up and down the shop, the shoes obviously sliding up and down with each step. The assistant frowned and moved to feel his toes, which were some way back from the end of the shoe.

'They're much too big. Try these,' she said, handing him another pair.

He stood to push his feet into them, they were small and stiff. He curled his toes to stop the nail banging on the end.

'Yep, they're fine,' he said.

'Joseph, they are much too small,' said Esther. 'We are not going to be quicker if you just say yes to everything. We need to know whether or not they fit. Here, try this pair.' She passed him a third pair. He pushed his feet into them and began to walk the length of the shop. Esther called him back and told him he needed to tie the laces first. He did so, but loosely, so they flapped about. The assistant rolled her eyes and bent to tie them. Joseph looked uncomfortable, now he felt like a little child, having his shoes tied for him, it was just embarrassing. They would never be tied anyway; he just tucked in the laces when he was at school. Probably not something he should mention to his mum though.

This pair fitted and Esther went to pay. They were more expensive than the other pairs. She briefly thought about suggesting they looked in another shop first. Very briefly. She handed the box to Joseph to carry, then led him towards the supermarket. She was not sure she could face buying clothes with him there, maybe there would be time next weekend.

The supermarket had a large array of flowers just inside the door. They sat in metal containers of water, wrapped in cellophane sleeves, carefully colour co-ordinated. All were more expensive than Esther had anticipated. In her mind she had imagined great lilies, sunflowers, roses, in big displays of colour, brightening the school, adding a touch of luxury. Instead she could afford a few bunches of chrysanthemums. They sat dripping forlornly in the end section of her trolley, their heads faded and small. She sighed and pushed through the crowded shop in search of food for the week.

Joseph walked beside her, banging his shoe box against his leg, telling her about a complicated film he had watched with Samuel. It seemed to involve zombies, of course and she was only half listening. She was trying to find some meat for Sunday, something she could roast that did not cost too much. Everything cost too much. She picked out a large joint of pork. She could roast it for Sunday and fry the leftovers for Monday. It had not been wrapped properly and pink blood dripped onto the floor, and soaked her hand. She sent Joseph back to the vegetables section for a plastic bag and searched for a tissue. Shopping was always stressful, everything was too expensive. Joseph returned with the plastic bag but no shoes. He had put the carrier bag down to tear the perforated strip. She sent him back and he reappeared waving them at her and grinning. She suggested he put them into the trolley, she did not want to have to buy them a second time. Then she headed towards the cereals. Two boys ate a surprisingly large quantity of cereal in a week.

It was over an hour later that they arrived back at the car. They had seen three church members and four parents from school. Esther had stopped to speak to all of them. Joseph was now extremely stony faced and began to throw the bags into the back of the car. Esther stopped him, said she could manage herself and suggested he sat inside and waited for her. He sat glaring out the window, cross that so much of his Saturday had disappeared into a chasm of chatting grown-ups. Esther sighed. Sometimes she felt she was walking a tightrope and juggling all at the same time. There just was not enough time. She could not please everyone but sometimes she worried that actually she did not please anyone. Not even herself.

***

Sunday started slowly with a strong cup of tea and a long shower, then sped up with a start when Esther realised that Rob was leaving already and she was later than she thought. He kissed her cheek as she pulled the pork out to start preparing it, telling her he would see her later. The fridge was set too high and the meat had partly frozen. She frowned at it, realised she had not responded to Rob and shouted goodbye as the door slammed shut.

She considered serving a sandwich lunch and eating in the evening, knew that everyone would complain and Rob would be disappointed, then decided the joint was not completely solid, it would be fine, she would just cook it for a bit longer. Sunday lunch was always a half-hearted affair. They followed the British tradition of always having a roast dinner at lunchtime but no one was really hungry, being used to eating their main meal much later on other days. It was also tiresome to prepare because by the time she and Rob had finished talking to everyone it was fairly late and they really wanted to eat the second they walked in the door. She tried to combat this by preparing vegetables the day before, leaving potatoes soaking in salty saucepans of water and carrots peeled and cut in bags in the fridge.

She dumped the pork in a tin and squirted honey from a tube along its length, then smeared on mustard with a knife. Some of the honey got into the mustard pot, which would cause someone consternation when they came to use it. Nothing she could do now. She covered it with foil, set the oven to low and went to call the boys. It could cook slowly while they were at church, self marinading as it heated.

As she and the boys struggled through the wind towards church, they were passed by two motorbikes. The boys both stopped to watch as they roared past, feeling the vibrations deep inside, wishing it was themselves dressed in leather, free and fast. They were surprised to see them slow and then turn into the church car park.

'Do you think they're coming to church?' said Joseph, that would be cool, something unexpected.

'More likely coming to sell drugs or knife us as we go in,' muttered Samuel, wanting to appear aloof and superior but as keenly interested as his brother. They both hurried slightly, wanting to see what was happening.

As they turned into the car park, both bikes were there, parked in the corner under the elm by the broken fence. They went inside to find the riders had removed their helmets and were being greeted by Mr Wilkes. The boys watched as they walked stiffly in their leathers into the church, clutching their helmets under one arm, smoothing their long tangled hair with the other. Their trousers squeaked with each step. They walked confidently to the front row and sat in the middle, helmets on floor, black books stuck out in front. They managed to look confident in a slightly aggressive way, as though daring anyone to challenge their right to be there. The boys sat further back, watching them constantly. They wondered why they had come, if they would heckle their father, try to cause trouble.

A few people whispered about them as they came in, asked who they were. Old Jim Lidiard hobbled to the front, stuck out his hand for them to shake, welcomed them and asked where they were from. The boys strained to hear the answer but Mrs Beaton was playing too loudly. Then their father appeared and stood at the front. He welcomed everyone for coming, his gaze taking in the two new arrivals. He gave them an especially warm smile. Esther knew he would be pleased and interested to see them there, that it would give him a boost of adrenaline, help him to be especially entertaining today. He loved having new people at church, a chance to tell someone about his God, someone who may not have heard before. She wondered who they were. What a shame the band were away, it seemed they always had visitors on the Sundays when the church was not at its best, like a woman caught without her make-up on.

Rob announced the first hymn, the words appeared on the screen and Mrs Beaton began to play. Everyone stood. Everyone except for the two bikers who shared a look and decided they would remain seated. It made Samuel shiver, though he was not sure why. Was there going to be trouble? After a couple of songs, prayers that were, in Samuel's opinion, much too long and a long long list of notices about forthcoming events which no one would remember, Rob began his children's talk. He was talking about covenants, promises and gave several examples of promises that people make today. He held up different items, symbols of promises, like wedding rings, bank statements. He included an example of a hire purchase agreement to buy a Harley-Davidson. That made everyone smile. Esther had known that he would acknowledge the two men somehow. Then he talked about God's promises, that he said that anyone could come to him, no matter what they have done. He talked about being part of a family and what it meant to be included in God's family, to be loved and accepted. As he spoke the men leaned forward. One of them nodded. They were obviously listening, interested in what Rob was saying. Samuel felt deeply disappointed.

Towards the end of the service, there was communion. Wooden trays of tiny glasses containing a red liquid were passed around. It was meant to be wine but Baptists did not include alcohol in their services so it was a substitute, often blackcurrant squash. Esther took her glass and held it on her lap, waiting for the signal that they should all drink together. She noticed that the visitors had also taken a glass each. When Rob indicated the congregation should drink, the two men tapped their glasses on their knees and downed the contents quickly, as though drinking shots. Esther supposed the glasses did resemble shot glasses. She had never noticed that before.

At the end of the service, after what felt like a week to the boys, they escaped into the hall for some watery orange squash and tried to see who could collect the most biscuits from the plate before someone spotted them and sent them away. Joseph managed to get seven and stood in the corner of the hall eating them. They were chocolate ones, a rare treat. The pile in his hand was beginning to melt, leaving brown smears on his skin. The two bikers had been brought into the hall by Stacey and were helping themselves to coffee. They looked awkward with their helmets, out of place amongst all the hand knitted sweaters and sensible winter coats. Joseph felt they should be swigging beer rather than the cheap brand of coffee in a smoked glass mug. It was not right.

Rob came through to the hall and went to speak to the men. They had a very long conversation. Joseph finished his biscuits, licked his hand clean and went to find Esther, to ask if they could go home. He had just found her when Rob appeared and called her over. He introduced the men, Jonathan and Scott, told her he had invited them both for lunch, was that alright? Esther smiled, told the men they would be very welcome, did they both like pork? Good, then she would go ahead, get the vegetables boiling, perhaps Rob could bring them when he came.

Esther called Samuel away from the game he was having with a friend, told Joseph to collect his coat and they set off at a fast march.

'Did you know Dad was going to invite those men?' asked Joseph

'No, but that's okay, we've got a huge piece of meat. I just hope it's cooked. I need to peel some extra potatoes. I wonder how much they'll eat, they look like they'll eat lots.'

'Well, I think Dad should ask before he just invites people,' announced Samuel, 'there might not have been enough. Who are they anyway?'

'I don't know, I guess we'll find out over lunch,' said Esther calmly. She was thinking about lunch, deciding she had enough potatoes, especially if she made some stuffing too. She could heat up some frozen sweetcorn, that would make the carrots stretch. Maybe cook a chocolate pudding in the microwave, that was quick and she was sure she had all the ingredients. They had ice cream and she could open a tin of peaches. Yes, she thought it would be alright. She just hoped that joint was cooked through.

When the men arrived Samuel was told to offer to hang up their jackets. He took them in his arms, impressed by their weight, not sure a plastic hanger would be strong enough. He had grumpily helped his mother to set the table, filling the water jug (though he was sure bikers did not drink water) and distributing paper napkins. That also seemed grossly inappropriate. Joseph had been put to work tidying the sitting room. He had mainly just heaped everything in a pile on the landing, deciding they could put it all back later, when the visitors had gone. His mum was too busy to notice now and would be too tired to comment later.

The men were deep in conversation with Rob when they

arrived. They went straight into the study which the boys found rather disappointing, not emerging until Esther called them for dinner. They sat at the table, looking much too big for the small dining area. Joseph sat next to one, Scott, noticing that he smelled of cigarettes and oil. Their great hairy fingers were stained black around the nails and their hair seemed to frame their faces like lion's manes. He wondered if he could grow his hair that long.

Esther passed them plates of food, told them to help themselves to vegetables, asked where they were from, were they staying locally? It seemed they had been merely passing on their way to the coast, had come into the church for a dare, to see what it was like, having not been inside a church since they were toddlers. They had been interested by what Rob had said, wanted to know more. They told Esther that yes, they had family, one lived with his girlfriend and baby, one lived alone. Rob talked to them about bikes and music and whether they had jobs and where they had grown up. The boys listened. Neither parent asked if they took drugs, if they had ever killed anyone, how fast their bikes could go. They were interested when the men swore and neither of their parents reacted like it was anything unusual, surprised that they both drank lots of water, seemed to enjoy the meat (which was a bit tough in their opinion) and were deeply impressed when one went to use the downstairs toilet and could be heard peeing for a considerable length of time.

When the meal was over, Esther offered them coffee, which they both drank black. She cleared the plates while Rob took them both back into the study. She scraped the remains of the meat onto a plate. No way there would be enough for another meal. She would need to buy something on her way home from school, hoped there would be time after getting everything ready for the art sessions. Otherwise they would have to eat pizzas from the freezer, which would please the boys. Not much goodness though, just sugar and flavour.

She glanced at the clock. She would have liked to go over her plans for the week. She did not usually work on a Sunday, tried to keep it as a special day, a holy day that was different from the rest of the week. They tended to discourage the boys from doing homework on Sundays too, though that was increasingly difficult as Samuel always seemed to find something he had 'forgotten' until Sunday evening.

This week was different though. It was important that she was well planned, that nothing went wrong. She felt very much on show, needed this to go well, to be something she could use as evidence when pleading her case with the governors. She could really have done without guests for lunch. She knew it was part of Rob's job, something he felt was important. He felt that if they were hospitable then others in the church would be, that this was a principle set firmly in the Bible, a way of life they should all emulate. She agreed, in principle. It just rarely happened when it was convenient. Rob said life was like that, if they decided to follow God then they had to follow all the time, not only when it fitted in with their schedule. That was fine in theory, the trouble was, she had the school schedule to juggle too. Sometimes she felt completely drained, giving to the church, giving to the family, giving to school. She wondered when she would be filled up again herself. She could certainly use a top up of energy. Ah well, perhaps Rob would be able to help these men in some way, show them a little of what God was like. Perhaps she should be trusting that God would sort her job for her, try to worry a bit less.

She finished stacking the dishwasher, put the meat pan to soak in the sink and wiped the surfaces. Then she went upstairs to look through her files. There was a mound of magazines, books, dirty socks and sweet wrappers on the landing. Joseph. She would have a word later, too tired and busy now.

Chapter Fourteen

CYNTHIA Mott arrived at the school in a rush. She had again not slept well nor eaten breakfast. The morning traffic had been full of incompetent drivers, pulling out in front of her at junctions or driving much too slowly for the rush hour traffic. Twice she had used her horn. She felt late and hassled and swung the car into the last space. She misjudged the position and there was a crunch as the back wing hit a post. Braking hard, she flung open the driver's door and marched round the side of the car to examine the damage.

The post was short, much too low to be easily noticed. It was positioned to mark the end of the parking space, an attempt to stop people reversing into the fence behind. It was both unnecessary and dangerous in Miss Mott's view. The post now leaned over, the ground below it slightly raised where the force had started to lift it from the ground. The back of her car was moulded around it, the plastic bumper shattered at the point of impact. There was nothing she could do now, she would not even think about it.

She opened the back door, hauled her bags from the seat and walked into the school laden with books. She had some large volumes about Monet and had borrowed others from a teacher friend. She dumped them in her classroom (no sign of rodents today, thank goodness) before heading off to the stockroom. She needed to sort out her art paper before the other staff members took what she needed.

The room smelled dry, of dust and paper and powder paint that had escaped from the square tins that sat in a corner at one end.

She scanned the paper. Sugar paper, that was easiest, its absorbent surface would hold the paint nicely. Blue, that would complement the waterlilies and mean that the shoddy painters, those who rushed and left gaps, would not have glaring holes in their water. She counted out sheets of paper. If the whole school were to do the same artwork, she would need lots. It was heavy and she hugged it to her bosom as she walked to the paper cutter, anxious to not crease it.

She slid four sheets into place, knowing from experience that four pieces of sugar paper would, with effort, be cut by the guillotine but five would not, they would crumple in protest and be spoilt. When she pulled it free, she noticed that the end sheets were stained pink. Someone must have cut paintings and not wiped the cutter clean afterwards. It was not good enough. Selfish and sloppy. Probably Mr Smyth. She felt the annoyance rise up inside her. Really, it was too bad. It was going to be a busy week, they all had to do their best, he must have known it would colour the next paper, it was just selfish. She screwed the stained sheets into a ball and marched to the recycling bin. It was full of damp paper towels. The recycling bin was for dry waste only. They had repeatedly told the children that. It was the duty of the teacher to ensure they regularly reminded their class. Obviously someone had not. Probably Mr Smyth again.

Cynthia reached inside and pulled out handfuls of damp towels, shovelling them into the correct bin. It made her back ache to reach down and was a most unpleasant job. One she should not have to do. There was a noise behind her and she looked up to see Esther Pritchard approaching the paper cutter.

'Good morning Cynthia, how are you today?' smiled Esther.

'You can't use that,' stated Cynthia. 'I have not finished cutting my own paper. I was just sorting out wrongly placed waste paper.' She quickly moved back to position and began to chop the rest of her paper. She would be two pieces short now. If she went to fetch them the Pritchard woman would use the paper cutter and delay her. She glowered at the pile of paper. It would have to be done later.

Esther moved back and started to tidy some bookshelves while she waited. Poor Cynthia, she was obviously very stressed. She looked as though she may not have combed her hair this morning too. Esther thought it best to not mention it. Perhaps this art week was more of an ordeal for everyone than she had anticipated. She hoped not.

Cynthia finished cutting her paper, made it into a tidy stack, no need to hurry for Esther Pritchard, it was her fault they were doing this ridiculous performance anyway, heaved her bag onto her shoulder and returned to her classroom. She began to unfold sheets of newspaper, spreading it across the tables. There was a sound from the rat cupboard (she would always think of it as that now) and she stopped. There was silence. She lowered the newspaper and crossed to the cupboard. She heard no sound. Gingerly she opened the door. The trap was there, on the same shelf. It was empty. Disinfectant wafted towards her and she shut the door. She must be imagining things.

Heels clicked along the corridor and Jane Lancaster appeared in the doorway. She was wearing a smart navy suit for the occasion and very red lipstick. Cynthia thought she looked as if her mouth was bleeding. She equated make-up with clowns. Clowns and hookers. She forced herself to not frown at her head teacher.

'Ah Cynthia, nice to see that everyone is here nice and early. Are you under control, found everything you need? The governors should arrive at nine and I'll give them coffee before I bring them round. Then after school on Friday we have a man from the paper coming to take photos. The parents should all be here then, looking at the displays with the children, so there should be a nice busy atmosphere. Is everything okay?'

'Someone left the guillotine dirty. And the paper towels were deposited in the wrong receptacle. Perhaps it could be raised at the next staff meeting. One should not have to clear up after one's colleagues,' began Cynthia.

'Absolutely, I'll bear that in mind,' said Jane as she moved towards the door. Honestly, silly woman, that was hardly relevant. She looked back at Cynthia as she continued to spread newspaper on the tables. She was wearing an old pair of black woollen trousers. There was a light mark on the back, as if she had sat on something dirty. Her creased pink blouse was untucked at the back and her orange cardigan clashed loudly. Jane wondered if she had looked in a mirror that morning. Or even paused to consider which clothes to wear. It looked as if she had simply pulled them randomly from the cupboard and dressed in the dark. She considered if there was a way to mention it, to suggest that appearances this week mattered. No, she was not brave enough, could not even begin to think about how she would start such a conversation. She nodded and left.

She made her way to Cherry Class. Andrew Smyth stood at the sink unit, surrounded by boxes of paint and large plastic cups. He was spooning the powder into the cups, then adding water and a little soap to make it stick better. Each one had a fat brown brush stuck into it and it was placed in the circular paint holder. He had chosen the colours carefully, wanting the finished painting to be bright and unusual. He would not put out the colours the children would want to use, blue for sky, yellow for sunflowers, then they would be forced to use different colours, to think about the impact they were making. He looked up as Jane entered and gave her a crooked smile.

'This stuff plays havoc with my hands,' he said with a laugh, 'I'm going to have green fingernails for days.'

'You could always wear gloves,' suggested Jane. She smiled. 'Everything under control? Are you ready for our big week?'

'I think so.' He was not going to mention how worried he was about teaching other classes, about being watched while kids he didn't know ignored him in front of an audience. Just have to hope Maddy stopped things going too awry.

'Excellent, I'll leave you to get on with it then. Shout if you need any help. Oh, and you have purple on your face, there, just under your right eye. Yes, you've got it. See you later then.'

Jane clicked her way to Pear Class. Esther was sitting at her desk, writing. She looked up and smiled when she saw Jane. Her tables were bare, the Year Two children were old enough to put out the newspaper themselves and it was good for them to take some responsibility. She was feeling nervous, hoped this week would go smoothly, make everyone feel a bit more positive. Make her position a little less uncertain. She assured Jane that yes, everything was under control and she was looking forward to the week. Then she went back to her planning, wanting to leave very specific instructions for Judy Mann so that nothing went wrong.

***

When Oak Class were all settled on the carpet, the register taken to the office and everyone's 'News' told to the class, Miss Mott opened her first book. As she turned the pages, showing the children the paintings, she talked about the life of Claude Monet. She told them he had been born in Paris (they looked at where that was on a map) and talked about his family. She explained that as a boy he loved to draw caricatures, not always kind ones and that it was not until he was eighteen that he began to paint. Most of the children heard very little, but they were still and quiet, engrossed in watching the coloured pages turn, which was sufficient for Miss Mott. They looked at some of his early caricatures and she explained that he had looked at the people around him and chosen one aspect to enlarge, so that everyone could guess who the picture was of. The children were then all given a piece of white paper and sent to the tables to try to produce a drawing of someone in their family.

They sat at the tables, fat black pencils in hand, swinging their legs and drawing. Within seconds, some of them had finished and placed their picture on Miss Mott's desk before going to play with the puzzles she had set out on the side tables. She had known they would finish quickly, that most of the pictures would be indiscernible as people even. Hopefully the older children would produce something more interesting for the final display. It would show progression if nothing else.

Cynthia and June Fuller sat at opposite ends of the room, each with a pile of reading books. They called the children to come and read, sent them to find their picture and then wrote who it represented on the front and 'by'. The child was then directed to add their own name underneath before putting it on the finished pile and going to look through the art books. When they had looked at all the books, they were allowed to return to their puzzle. Having a list of instructions to follow was no problem for some children, a challenge for others and they did not even bother to try with Lauren, simply giving her each individual instruction as she was ready.

Cynthia called for James Buchan and he came over. His picture was almost finished and he brought it with him, passing it to her as he swung his bottom onto the blue plastic chair and tucked his legs beneath him.

'Have you finished your caricature?' she asked, taking the paper from him. The drawing resembled a snowman, a small circle with eyes and mouth above a larger circle.

'Yes. It's you. Do you like it?' said James.

Miss Mott did not like it. She did not like that he had not drawn a family member as instructed nor did she particularly like the representation of herself. She told him, rather sharply, that he was meant to be drawing someone in his family. Perhaps he could start again and draw his... She stopped. Perhaps he could draw someone in his family. She opened the book and gave it to him to hold. As he began to read, slowly but accurately, Miss Mott looked around the room. Most children had finished now. She would finish hearing James read and then put out the paints, call them all to the carpet and explain the second stage of their activity.

When they were all on the carpet, Miss Mott showed them how they could use the paints. She pinned a large piece of paper to the easel and used the paint to form the image of a tree, using just the primary colours, painting the general shape with dots and then filling in the background. She spoke while she painted, explaining how Mr Monet had worked, how he had liked to paint outside but they were going to do their pictures in the classroom. At one point the door opened and Jane Lancaster appeared with three governors. They hovered awkwardly in the doorway, watching. She did not invite them in, pretending to be engrossed in her teaching. They drifted into the room and began to look around, talking to June in loud whispers.

'Who are those people?' asked Mandy. The whole class shuffled round to look.

Miss Mott told them to sit properly, the visitors had come to see which children were listening nicely. The class turned their bodies back, folded their arms in an attempt to look tidy, but kept their heads firmly looking towards the strange adults who were wandering around their room. One of the women thanked Miss Mott, who nodded and they left. She continued with her explanation. They were now going to paint a picture using just red, white and blue, in tiny dabs. They would gradually build up an image. Just like Monet did when he painted waterlilies. It sounded so simple, relaxing almost. She knew that it would not be.

By the time the children went to assembly they had all completed both a caricature and a painting. The drying rack was full of pictures, the paint dripping slowly onto the floor. It was impossible to tell what some had attempted to paint, though many had repeated their caricature, with great fat arms in yellow and bold blue heads. None had used dots, despite Miss Mott showing them what she hoped they would do. Never mind, they were colourful and the older children would make better attempts.

Billy had managed a painting by himself and June had watched him carefully, removing it from him before he had chance to cover the entire picture with a wash of blue. He usually painted over his work before they could remove it so she felt rather pleased with herself. They had, in the past, displayed one of his 'blue square' paintings. If she was honest, they were not so very different from some of the work that was displayed in the Summer Exhibition at the Royal Academy each year. However, a child was meant to paint what they were all directed to paint. To have an actual picture painted by Billy was a prize. June took him to wash his hands; he was terribly worried that some yellow was on one of his fingers. He tried to wipe it on the wall as they walked to the sinks, so she held his hand firmly in hers. He hated that, was upset by the physical contact and started to whine, a high pitched hum like an alarm. She was relieved when they reached the sinks and she could let go and turn on the tap, letting him wash away the offending yellow.

Cynthia led her class to the hall and took her seat opposite the piano, leaning back with her arms firmly crossed. She looked at the wall, freshly covered in backing paper, waiting for each class's offering to be displayed. She would cut some green paper to use as a mount for her pictures. She must remember to collect it during playtime, before another staff member took it all. And she needed another sheet of blue, she mustn't forget that.

She was suddenly aware the school were all standing, waiting to sing their hymn. She stood quickly, knocking her chair. It slid across the shiny floor into the ankle of Mandy, who jumped, then squealed with pain. Miss Mott glared at her, letting her know that any sound during assembly was unacceptable. Mandy stood very still, deciding if the pain or Miss Mott was the bigger influence. She decided Miss Mott was and returned to the song. When assembly finished and they filed from the hall she had a pronounced limp.

Cynthia did not go to the staffroom at playtime. She did not want a drink and could not face making polite conversation in a confined space with the visiting governors. She collected what she needed from the stockroom, then looked through the children's work.

The drawings were interesting, one could tell a lot about a child's development from what they drew. All had drawn heads, bodies, eyes and mouths. Most had included arms and legs. A few had drawn noses and eyebrows and hands with spidery fingers all around the edges. The more detailed pictures tended to be done by the more able readers. She would save them after the display and use them as evidence at parents' evening. So few parents would accept that reading was often a case of child maturity, that some children were not yet ready to begin reading and therefore would not read fluently for a while, it was not a reflection on either their intelligence or her teaching skills. Perhaps if she showed them these drawings, which she could arrange in order of ability, anonymous but clearly marked with the child's reading level, they would see that maturity and reading were closely linked. Perhaps.

In the playground, Mandy was limping next to her friend, who had put her arm around her and was helping her to the bench. They sat side by side, swinging their legs and watching the boys play football. The ball was on a corner of the playground. It was not allowed on the playground, being a field game, permitted only when the grass was dry enough. Mandy considered whether she should go and point this out to the teacher on duty. She decided not to, she would have to limp or Jackie would know she was pretending and she couldn't really be bothered. She leaned towards her friend, her eyes very large and solemn.

'Miss Mott kicked me,' she whispered.

Jackie looked at her friend. That did not sound likely. People generally only kicked if you had something they wanted or you had spoiled their game, neither seemed to apply to Miss Mott. However, Miss Mott was rather grumpy today, had told her off for licking her finger to clean her shoes during register time and this was quite an interesting piece of news, one that she could tell lots of other people.

'Really? Did it hurt? Did you cry?' she asked.

'It hurt lots, I can't walk now,' admitted Mandy, looking pitiful. 'But I didn't cry, I was very brave.' Jackie put her arm around her shoulders, gave her a cuddle. Which was very pleasing. Jackie then bounced off the bench.

'You stay here and rest, I'll be back in a minute,' she said. This information was too exciting to save, she must share it at once. She skipped across to Lauren, who was trying to untangle a skipping rope. The wind caught at her hair, it tickled her face and she pushed it away so she could see the other girl, watch her face when she shared her news.

***

After playtime, Miss Mott took a group to the maths table. She wanted to continue with a repeated addition exercise. She had a tray of small plastic teddy bears, which would serve as counters but were much more interesting than cubes. The children were restless, had not settled well after their playtime, stirred up by the wind and excited by the sunshine. She would give them a moment to find their places, then call to them all and ask for silence. Her head ached and she was tired. She felt irritated, wanted them to concentrate, they had wasted enough time already with the silly art project. Tomorrow she would be teaching the same lesson but to Cherry Class. She really could not be bothered.

She sat at the table and put the tray of bears on the table. Jackie reached out a hand to take one. Instinctively, without thinking, Cynthia raised her hand to slap her wrist. Not really a smack, not strong enough to be a slap but definitely physical admonishment. Definitely beyond her remit as a teacher. Jackie screamed. It was a small scream, more of a whimper but was still grossly overreacted. The moment would probably have passed had it not been witnessed by Jane Lancaster, who had chosen that exact moment to put her head around the door of Oak Class.

Jane looked around the door, surprised by the general bubble of noise from what was usually an almost silent room and saw Cynthia hit a child's arm and that child cry out and clutch her arm as though in pain.

Jackie had been horrified that Miss Mott had attacked her. She knew that she should not touch the bears but thought she could probably take one to play with while Miss Mott talked. She had not expected to be hit. It had not really hurt, she hardly felt it actually, but she knew that this was a teacher who kicked, who obviously was dangerous and therefore she was frightened and felt it probably would have hurt, she was just very brave and so hadn't noticed the pain.

Jane Lancaster walked into the room. Cynthia looked up, registered what had just been witnessed and was horrified. She opened her mouth then closed it. What could she say? I didn't mean to do that? It didn't hurt her? It was an accident? None seemed appropriate.

'Miss Mott, I think perhaps you are not yourself today,' said Jane.

She spoke slowly, giving herself time to think, wanting to contain the situation but knowing she must deal with it. 'I think it might be best if you go and rest in my office for a while. Perhaps Mrs Fuller could look after the class for now? Could be in charge until lunchtime?'

June Fuller nodded. She had heard Jackie cry out, they all had, had seen her clutching her arm, but did not know why. She wondered if Miss Mott dropped something on her. The woman did not look well anyway, had not looked well for a few weeks now. She was irritable too, difficult to work with and short with the children. Perhaps she was ill, suffering from stress or something.

She left her seat at a table of children who were writing a sentence about Monet and went to the maths table. Cynthia rose unsteadily. This all seemed terribly extreme, a complete overreaction. She had hardly touched the girl. There was a glint of steel in Jane Lancaster's eye though, something she did not feel up to arguing with, not now, not today, she was too tired. She picked up her bag, thanked June Fuller, and left the room.

Cynthia walked to Jane Lancaster's office in something of a daze. This felt very unreal, as though she was dreaming. She opened the door and went to the large chair, sat on it, put her hands on the armrests, tried to gather her thoughts. She was not entirely sure what her position was. Obviously she was not allowed to strike a child, that would be an offence, she would be dismissed immediately. However, had she struck a child? Did a disciplinary tap on the wrist qualify as having hit her? She was not sure. It had all happened so fast. It seemed inconceivable that one tiny, thoughtless action, could end her career. Surely they would take into account her teaching record, her years of experience, the numerous children she had taught. She was not sure. She felt terribly insecure and suddenly very alone. It dawned on her that very few people would be sorry to see her go, she had no real friends on the staff and now they had been pitched against each other in this competitive manner, the other teachers would no doubt be relieved that she was going, she was the loser, the one who was making space for them.

She buried her face in her hands, afraid that she might cry. She could not even begin to think of a defence. She did not know what to say.

Jane Lancaster came in carrying two mugs of tea. She put one down next to Cynthia, saw her face and reached for a box of tissues, offered them, then sat in the chair next to her desk. She took a sip of her tea. It was hot and strong and whilst she would have preferred a gin, it was good enough for now. She watched Cynthia blow her nose, fight to control herself. She waited, not wanting to speak until the other woman was composed enough to listen. She did not like conflict but this was her job and she was good at it.

She had some sympathy for Cynthia. She could see that she was not coping at the moment, that her general appearance and tense manner were symptoms of something else. She was not a doctor but she thought she could recognise severe depression when she saw it. She also hoped to not lose Cynthia. She did not actually want to lose any of her staff but if she had to, Cynthia would be her last choice. She was an angular personality, difficult to work with and obviously had little respect for Jane. However, Jane considered herself above that, able to stand back and look at situations objectively. It was why she thought she was a good head teacher. She knew that Cynthia came with a wealth of experience, the parents respected her and she could teach. She might prefer books to computers, she might resist any new initiatives, but at the end of the day, she could take a five-year-old and teach them how to read better than any of the other staff. There was not much she had not seen, had not experienced in the small world of the reception class and she was a highly valuable asset. An asset that Jane wanted to keep. If she could.

Cynthia seemed calmer, so she began.

'Do you want to explain what happened Cynthia? It appeared that you hit Jackie, did you?'

'No, no, not really. It was a tap, a tap on her wrist, she was taking a bear and she knew that she was not allowed to.' She stopped, what could she say? That she was tired, that she was not sleeping or eating, that everything seemed so difficult. None of that seemed relevant. She took a deep breath. It came out as a shudder.

'Cynthia, I think you need to rest. I think you need to go and see a doctor and ask to be signed off with stress for a few weeks. You need to have some time to sort yourself out, to get well again.

'I'm not sure what will happen with Jackie. I expect we can contain the situation, her mother is a sensible woman, she will understand that children exaggerate. I looked at her arm, there is no mark, I think we can argue that you didn't strike her, if we need to.

'However, this should never have happened. You know that we do not ever do more than restrain the children if their safety is at risk, that we never physically discipline them. Even if sometimes we would sorely love to. What you did was wrong. I believe it happened because you are ill. I am hoping this need go no further, though I cannot guarantee that if the mother decides to pursue it. It may have to come before the governors but I hope not. I shall certainly not raise it. On the condition that you take some time out and see a doctor.'

'I'm not sure that is possible,' began Cynthia. The steel in Jane's eyes glinted, the hardness spreading. Cynthia realised arguing would be futile. 'Who would teach my class? Do we have money for supply staff?'

'That is not your problem, but yes, we can sort out something. If you are signed off for a certain period the insurance will cover a supply teacher. In the meantime I can take your class. It is not so long ago that I had a class,' she added, seeing the scepticism in Cynthia's face.

'Now, I suggest that you remain in here until lunchtime, then collect your things and go home. I will explain to the children that you are unwell. Perhaps you could let me know by tomorrow when you will be seeing the doctor and what they say?' She stood, smoothing her skirt. She did not want to discuss this, to argue. She knew she was right and the decision was made. She smiled, collected the empty mugs and left.

Cynthia watched the door close. She leaned back on the chair, closed her eyes. This was beyond belief. It had happened so quickly, was such a small thing really. She did not want to go home. If she stayed in her cottage, her mind would be restless, she needed the routine of planning, teaching, to keep her thoughts steady. She did not want to spend hours alone in her cottage, with nothing to think about except the possibility of losing it. Yet she was too tired to think of a plan, something to say in her defence. She would have to accept this. For now.

When she heard the children go onto the playground, released for the lunch break, she picked up her bag and went back to her classroom. The work had been tidied away. She did not look at what had been accomplished in her absence, how much time had been wasted. She stuffed her planning book into her school bag, she would need to tell Jane what to do tomorrow. Perhaps she could return on Thursday, help to display the art work, show that her lessons had been innovative and sound. She did not want the display to make her teaching appear less good than the others.

She glanced around the room, wondering if anyone would miss her. Her eyes rested briefly on the rat cupboard. It was silent but she felt that somehow that rat was to blame, it was a sort of karma for her having caused its death. Her eyes narrowed. She would kill it again given the chance, despite what Mr Carter thought. Ah, Mr

Carter. She would now have no opportunity to see him, to have a pleasant chat, to share something of her day. She would miss seeing him. She wanted to be able to explain that this was not her fault, it had all been escalated to ridiculous proportions. But how could she? It was hardly appropriate for her to go and find him now, she had clearly been given her marching orders by that woman. Nor could she contact him... that would appear odd.

Perhaps she could ensure though that he contacted her. She slid the heavy bag from her arm and moved it to the corner of the classroom, to a place where it was not obviously noticeable but where someone cleaning would be sure to see it. She delved into the depths and pulled out her lunch box. That was something personal, something that should not be left in school for several days to go mouldy. She balanced it on top of the papers and files so it could be clearly seen. There, a forgotten bag with something that needed attention. Surely someone would feel it was appropriate to at least telephone her, to let her know it had been found, to remind her she should return to school and collect it. Maybe he would suggest that she came when the children were not present, when he alone was in the building. The thought was rather thrilling. Of course, someone else might phone. Or nobody. But it was worth a try, nothing ventured, nothing gained, as her mother used to say.

She pulled on her coat, moved a chair to better obscure the bag from general view and left.

***

Mr Carter did not telephone Miss Mott, he delivered the bag in person. He had found it, mentioned it to Jane Lancaster, who told him Cynthia had gone home ill and was not expected back before the end of half term. He decided he would call in on his way home, give her the bag and check that she was alright. He had never known her to take sick leave, so was concerned it might be something serious. He was also uneasy that their last conversation had not been overly friendly, he had been cross with her.

He knocked loudly on the cottage door then stepped back onto the path. Cynthia heard the knock and rushed to open the door. He saw that her eyes were red, her hair was messy and her clothes looked as if they may have been worn for several days. He was worried. This was not the fastidious Miss Mott he knew. He held the bag out.

'Good afternoon Miss Mott. I found your bag at school and Jane Lancaster told me you were ill so I brought it round. Are you alright?'

Cynthia smiled, her plan had worked even better than she had hoped. It made her feel powerful, that she could influence things, make them happen. She opened the door wider.

'That is terribly kind of you. Would you care to come inside? Partake of some tea perhaps?'

David Carter stepped into the cottage. He was surprised at the state of disarray. The curtains were closed, the fireplace was full of ash, dust lay on every surface and it smelled musty, as if it was some time since the windows had been opened. Two china cups sat on top of a book and there was a magazine on the floor. He looked at Miss Mott. She looked terribly tired, her skin having lost its shine and looking almost grey. The dim light did not help.

'Miss Mott, are you alright? Have you seen a doctor?'

'Of course not,' she snapped. 'One cannot obtain an appointment the day that one calls the surgery. I am being seen tomorrow, at eleven o'clock.

'Now,' she said, keen to move the conversation away from her health, which was perfectly adequate, she was just tired, 'would you care for tea?'

'I don't really have time, but thank you. I just wanted to bring you your bag, check that you were alright.' He paused, not really sure what to say. He knew this woman, with all her funny corners and anxieties and strangely formal way of speaking. Something was wrong, she was behaving very oddly but he was unsure what he should do, unsure what his role was. He decided that returning the bag was sufficient, the doctor would probably sort her out. 'Is there anything you need? Are you alright?' he asked again.

'Yes, completely, thank you,' she said. She was cross now. She wanted him to stay, to talk to her. But she did not wish to discuss her health, could not understand why everyone was suddenly obsessed with it. She opened the door again. 'Thank you so much, very kind of you.'

Cynthia stood behind the closed door for a long time after Mr Carter had left. She had so wanted him to stay, so needed some company. Never mind, she would cope. She went upstairs and lay on her bed. So tired. If only she could sleep.

Chapter Fifteen

ANDREW was pleased with the results of his first lesson of Art Week. He had left Maddy to mount all the work on a contrasting border and felt that his display board would look suitably colourful. He was more worried about tomorrow. Tomorrow was Oak Class.

Andrew had never taught a Reception Class before, having managed to sidestep that particular delight during his training. He had watched them walking into assembly, seen how when they first started school they had a tendency to talk loudly during the prayer or stand up unexpectedly if they wanted to go somewhere. They were, he thought, more like puppies than children. However, Miss Mott would have trained them a bit, they wouldn't be completely random. He hoped. No, it was more Billy that worried him. Billy was, they all thought, autistic. He had heard discussions about getting him assessed, Maddy and June had lots of conversations about his latest exploits, his shouting and humming and refusal to remove his socks for P.E. Andrew was not quite sure just how you were meant to teach a child like that. A child who feared any change in routine, who was being put into a new classroom with a new teacher and a new classroom assistant.

Originally, the plan had been for June Fuller to travel with him. That was before Miss Mott had decided to be ill. Andrew was not quite sure what was wrong with her, it all seemed very sudden and very peculiar. Maddy said she had heard there was some kind of row between her and Jane Lancaster and she had been sent home in disgrace. Sounded unlikely. Why would Lancaster put herself forward to have to teach a class at short notice on a week when governors were in? Why would Mott agree to go, come to that? No, he was suspicious that there was something else going on. The woman had been a wreck for weeks now, anyone could see that. He wondered if she had been hitting the bottle. Not that any of this helped with the Billy problem.

As soon as he was home, had taken off his jacket and opened a beer, he pulled his laptop onto the bed and did a Google search. There were probably research reports and massive tomes he could read but Google was the quickest, fairly reliable and would give him some idea of what to expect.

He scrolled down the screen, past all the adverts for expensive books on the subject. He found a useful article and began to read. It seemed to focus a lot on potty training, he was hoping that wouldn't be a problem, hadn't heard the classroom assistants talk about that. Talking seemed to be different too. He knew that Billy *did* talk, so maybe he was more Asperger's than autistic. Andrew assumed that was better. There were a few helpful suggestions but most articles seemed to repeat the same advice and most were about how to diagnose autism, or were medical reports. He felt himself begin to do slow blinks, his eyes unfocussed, he began to drift off to sleep. He shut the laptop and went in search of food. He would play it by ear, usually worked.

***

The following morning Cherry Class seemed extra noisy. Andrew had to shout at them three times before he had even taken the register. They were going to Mrs Pritchard for the lesson. This, it appeared, was wildly exciting, on a par with an outing. Andrew feared they would be disappointed. A child came 'with a message', letting him know that it was time to swap classes. He sent his children off to Pear Class, warning them to walk and not run, then listened to their high pitched chatter disappear along the corridor. He and Maddy went to Oak Class. The little ones could not be relied upon to walk unaccompanied to the new room. Maddy came because he wanted back-up. It would be a bad start if he lost one.

Jane Lancaster was standing tensely with the children, waiting at the door for him to arrive. She told him that all were present, forced a smile and returned to sorting paper ready for the stream of Pear Class who were approaching.

Andrew led the children to his own room and settled them on the carpet. This took some time as two wandered off to inspect various corners. Billy, he assumed it was Billy, stood uncertainly on the edge of the carpet. He did not intend to sit. The carpet was green. He did not like green. He gazed out of the window, refusing to look at the man and woman who had ushered him there.

Maddy went over and rested a hand on Billy's shoulder. Andrew knew this was a bad move, realised he should have imparted some of his new found knowledge to his assistant but it was too late. Billy began to hum. It was not a good sound. Maddy removed her hand but the humming continued.

'Right, Oak Class,' began Mr Smyth, deciding the best tactic was to ignore the humming. He didn't actually know any alternatives. 'We are going to learn about an artist called Van Gogh.'

A girl laughed. 'Van Cough? That's a funny name! Did he have a cough?'

'No, he was a lorry,' said a boy next to her. Several children began to laugh, overly loudly, seeking attention from this new teacher. They had seen him in assembly, knew his name, but none of them had actually spoken to him.

Billy stopped humming. Someone had mentioned lorries. He did not know about lorries but he knew about cars. He knew a lot about cars.

'Did you know that Mercedes have brought out a new GCL?' he asked Mr Smyth. 'It is like their C-class but it's a four by four. It's a bit like the BMW X3.'

Andrew frowned. Okay, so he knew that having a passion in a subject was one of the autistic 'signs'. He had read this. He had not read how exactly he was supposed to handle it. Was there an 'off' button? Billy was now reciting colour options for the interior. He seemed to have memorised the seller's manual.

'Yes, Billy, thank you,' he said, 'I'm sure we would all like to hear about that later. But first we are going to look at some paintings.'

He quickly turned on his PowerPoint presentation, started to flick through the images. As he had hoped, the class quietened, their interest captured by the colours and pictures. He began to explain what the paintings were, careful to keep the sentences simple, to try and help them see the use of colour, to notice how each painting made them feel.

He then stood, leaving the last slide on the screen and walked over to one of the prepared tables.

'Now, if you come over here I'll show you what you're all going to paint,' he instructed. The children stood. One wandered over to the window and gazed outside. Most arrived at the table and began to touch the paper, put their fingers into the paint pots, push the child in front so they could get a better view. Billy realised they had stopped looking at paintings. This meant he was allowed to speak again. He moved around the children, stood next to Mr Smyth.

'It is quite like the Audi Q5 too,' he continued, 'but it is twelve millimetres longer.'

Andrew wondered what he was talking about, realised he was back on his car monologue. He seemed to have picked up exactly where he had broken off, like a CD on pause. Impressive really. Though he suspected that the child had no idea what a millimetre actually was.

The whole class was pushing forwards, wanting to be at the front. Andrew thought again that they were like puppies. They seemed very small to him, almost knee height. He would have to avoid stepping on them, that would look bad. Maddy had collected the stragglers and led them to the table.

'Now,' he instructed, 'I want you all to take one big step backwards.'

The children all stepped back, some taking an exaggerated giant step and almost falling over. The circle of children was bigger and everyone could see. Billy was talking about 'over five hundred litres of boot space'. Andrew suggested that he should wait until playtime, he would be able to listen then, now was the time for Billy to watch. Then he would do a painting.

He saw the children with paint on their hands begin to wipe them on their sweatshirts. He hadn't told them to put on aprons yet. He quickly instructed them all to go to the sinks and wash their hands, the last thing he needed was complaints from parents about stained clothing. He had intended for only the painty children to go but the whole class streamed over to the sink in the corner. There was more pushing as Maddy tried to get them into a line, helped each one wash their fingers, sent the clean children back to the table.

Andrew glanced at the clock. It seemed to be moving very slowly. This was a nightmare. Any wrong word and the children moved as a mass, had a mind of their own and were completely unpredictable. He felt a movement and looked down.

A small boy was wiping yellow paint on Andrew's trousers. He froze when Andrew looked at him, gazed up with huge eyes and his lip started to quiver. Was Mr Smyth going to shout at him? Before he could say anything, the boy had dissolved into tears. Great streams of water ran down his face and he gulped breath through his dribbling mouth, shaking with fear. Maddy abandoned the tap and came over. She put an arm around the boy, told him to stop crying and wiped his face. Andrew watched helplessly. What had just happened? The children at the sink were now all soaked, someone had put their hand too close to the flow of water and it had shot out, drenching the group. Another child, a girl this time, began to cry. Her socks were wet. It was cold and uncomfortable.

'Okay,' said Andrew over the general bubble of noise. 'Everyone go back and sit on the carpet, I think we need to start this again.'

The children hurried back, shuffling to be near the front. This was most unexpected and rather fun. Miss Mott's lessons were never like this. A few took a detour on their way to the carpet, managing to walk in the flood on the floor and leave pleasing footprints as they walked.

The damp children all went to Maddy, keen to show her their wet socks and trousers. Some of them were so wet that the water seeped out of their socks, over their shoes and puddled on the floor. Maddy deftly removed the socks and hung them, dripping, on the fat white radiator under the window. The children shuffled onto the carpet, uncomfortable in bare feet pushed hurriedly into plimsolls. She settled both of the weepers, blew their noses, took them to the carpet. The door opened and Pauline Brookes walked in with two governors. Andrew smiled, glad they had not been two minutes earlier. He turned back to the class, making his voice very deep, speaking very slowly, leaning forward so they would listen.

'Now, we are going to go and put on aprons. No, not yet, sit back down. That's better. I will touch your head and when I do, you will go and get an apron. The rest of you will sit very still. When you have got an apron...' he paused. He had been about to tell them to take paper and go to a table. No, it would be better to do this in stages. Very simple stages. 'When you have got an apron, put it on and come back to the carpet.'

He began to move amongst the class, touching heads lightly with one finger. They felt germ-ridden and he was very aware that several had the tell-tale white specks of head lice. The children went to where the aprons hung next to the door and Maddy helped them to struggle into one. The plastic sleeves were stiff and too long, so she rolled them up. Tomorrow she would suggest that each class took an apron with them, was surprised Esther had not thought of that herself.

Andrew waited on the carpet, flicking through his slides again so the waiting children had something to watch. It took longer than he had expected. But that was okay. The governors were now looking at the work from yesterday, noticing his PowerPoint slides, muttering quietly. The general atmosphere in the room was calm and controlled. Finally they left, nodding their thanks, going to the next room. Andrew sighed with relief. Now he just had to survive the rest of the period.

The painting activity went mostly to plan. He had simplified his instructions, giving one direction at a time so the children could follow them. They painted with enthusiasm. And great speed. He had been rather shocked by how quickly they finished and how unpersuadable they were to add more detail. He grabbed some paper from the 'rough paper' drawer and asked them to do a second one. Then a third.

There was a minor incident with Billy, who completely refused to use anything other than the 'correct' colours for the flowers. Daisies were not blue or purple. He was adamant that only white and yellow could be used. With green for the stalks. After some discussion (actually, not really a discussion as Billy hummed loudly while Andrew tried to reason with him) he was given the appropriate coloured pencils and allowed to continue. He then drew a beautifully detailed picture. Very slowly. Andrew peered over his shoulder, admired it and told him he needed to get a move on or they would be late. Billy picked up his paper and colours and moved up into the next place. Andrew watched, confused for a moment, then realised the 'get a move on' comment had been taken literally.

There was one other mishap. Quite a major one. A girl, Natalie, arrived at Andrew's side looking worried. She held up a finger covered in thick brown. He frowned, thinking that Maddy must have decided to mix some brown paint. He told Natalie to go and wash her hands, then continued to suggest ideas that the children could add to their paintings.

'But it smells,' said Natalie. She looked extremely perturbed.

A sudden horrible realisation dawned on Andrew. The brown was not paint. He had no idea how it had got on the child's finger. Nor did he want to know.

'Mrs Brown!' he said. She looked up, surprised by the volume and tone, not used to commands from him.

'I think this child might have,' he paused, decided 'shit herself' might not be an expression he wanted repeated in multiple households at tea time, said, 'had an accident.'

Maddy came over.

'Oh,' she said as she saw the situation. 'Thanks,' she muttered as she took the girl, firmly holding her by the wrist, to the staff toilets to clean her up. She would phone the mother and ask her to collect her. This was so not her job.

***

By Friday, Andrew was rather pleased with how his Art Week had gone. Although Oak Class had been something of a steep learning curve, it had provided lots of fodder for a good laugh in the pub afterwards. Maddy did not find it quite so funny, having informed him that the 'brown' had fallen out onto the floor during the clean-up and next time she would teach the class and he could do the manual work.

They stood in the hall waiting for the other staff to arrive, watching as parents were dragged by their children to look at various pictures. He was pleased to see how much the children themselves valued the work, which was unexpected. They even liked seeing what the other classes had done, comparing the work with their own, all agreeing that Penny in Pear Class had done the best paintings. Esther had put together a little programme, a bit of fun really. It had listed the children's work, with a title and each child had chosen a price, as if they were for sale. Most were hoping to raise millions of pounds for their work.

There was a small board near the doorway and Esther had covered this with explanations about the week and a few photographs of the children working. This had caused more discussion than expected due to their child protection policy which did not allow images of the children to be used on the internet or for advertising purposes. Jane Lancaster worried that this might fit into the 'advertising' box as they were trying to promote the school. Esther was keen to use them, Andrew thought the whole discussion ridiculous, Cynthia was not present so her view was mute. The photographs had been used.

Andrew glanced at the time. He had told the restaurant that he might be late but he still hoped to get there fairly soon. He would try to switch mobile numbers with Bai Yun today, see if he could take that a bit further. He was not sure how long he would be expected to stay for.

Esther and Judy arrived. They had released their class, tidied the room and now joined Andrew in the corner next to a table of unappetising drinks. A grumpy Melissa Dodds, one of the dinner staff, was pouring something pink from a jug into plastic cups and scowling at everyone. A few children had taken one and were walking around, oblivious to how much was slopping onto the floor as they pointed at pictures and showed their parents their own. And their friend's. And Tommy's, who pushed people. Esther looked nervous.

'Do you think this is okay? Should I open a window? I'm not sure if the lighting in here is really good enough for this.'

'It's fine,' Andrew said. He understood that this was her big event but at the end of the day, they were powder paint pictures by a bunch of kids. Only their own parents would really look at them. It was a nice idea but probably not worth the amount of fuss.

Jane Lancaster and a man carrying two cameras arrived. He was stout with a lot of dark facial hair and a very large red nose covered in pimples. The sort of person who looks like they have bad body odour, even if they don't. Jane looked exhausted. She had not enjoyed her few days of teaching. Each day had begun early and ended late and she was still behind with her own work. She hoped it would not be for too much longer. She frowned as she walked across the hall. The floor seemed very sticky.

She greeted the staff and introduced Mr Hodge, from the local paper. Andrew recognised him from his picture, which was placed prominently on the back page each week. 'News and Views From Your Locality.' He stepped forwards, shook Andrew's hand, started to look around the hall.

'Well, this all looks interesting,' he said. 'Do you have anything particular you want me to get or shall I just get a few shots of general scenes? The parents can buy the prints, I'll give you the website address for your newsletter. I'll include a couple with the article in next week's edition. Unless something big comes up of course. Can't promise anything.' He gave a guffaw. Several children turned around to look, surprised by the noise. Jane gave a thin smile. Andrew wondered what big scoop he was expecting, Marksbridge was hardly the sort of place where aliens would choose to land. He glanced at Mr Hodge. Then again...

The two classroom assistants were discussing the parents in loud whispers, Maddy pointing out certain people to Judy. Andrew hoped no one could hear them. Their comments were not the most polite, especially about those who had raised particularly rude children. They were moaning about the parents who had 'phoned in with sick children' today, the last Friday before half term. Very suspicious. Esther crossed to Jane.

'How is Cynthia? Have you spoken to her since she went home?' Jane had been largely invisible this week, rushing from classroom to office, not welcoming disturbances. Esther had heard that Cynthia had gone home ill at short notice but nothing else. She hoped it was nothing serious.

'Yes, I spoke to her again yesterday. She had been to see her doctor, had got some pills,' Jane paused. The conversation had been an awkward one. She had genuinely been concerned, keen to know what the doctor had said. Cynthia had been vague, saying only that nothing was wrong, she was perfectly fit to return to school but yes, her GP had prescribed her some medication, had given her a certificate for sick leave for a week. She hoped to return after the half term holiday. Jane had felt this might be too soon but had not known how to suggest this. She was also very torn as her own work load was fairly untenable for the long term and there seemed to be a shortage of supply cover in the area. Winter was always difficult. Too many coughs and colds.

As if on cue, the door opened and Cynthia walked in. Even from the other side of the hall, Andrew could see that her hair was wild, matted, uncombed, her clothes in disarray. She began to walk around the hall, peering closely at the boards, standing before her own class's work and leaning forwards.

'Oh no,' breathed Jane. 'I did not foresee this.' She joined Cynthia at the Oak Class board. Andrew watched with interest, feeling he was missing something, wondering if perhaps his theory had been correct after all. He could tell by the way Miss Mott stiffened that the conversation was not going well. She flung out an arm and gestured towards the paintings, her head nodding frantically as she spoke to Jane. He could not hear what they were saying but both women seemed very tense.

With a loud exclamation, 'Well, really!' Miss Mott turned briskly away and marched from the hall. All heads turned to see what the noise was as the door banged shut behind her furious back.

Jane Lancaster stood for a moment, then returned to the staff. She looked shaken.

'Are you alright?' asked Andrew. He had absolutely no idea what was happening, but even he had detected some kind of muted aggression in the exchange.

'Yes, yes, of course. I believe that Cynthia might be more ill than she realises.' She stopped, unwilling to say more, not wishing to compromise another member of staff.

She would wait, tell Bill about it later over a large glass of something strong. She did not trust Cynthia to appear normal, to not say something untoward to a parent or worse, a governor. She had suggested that she should leave, that the art display was part of her job and she was on sick leave, should be resting. It had not gone well but at least she had left. Her eyes had been full of threat, she had told Jane that she could not do this, could not exclude Cynthia from her rightful place, that she would regret this ludicrous decision. But she had left. A scene had been diverted. Jane was confident she had done the right thing.

Andrew wondered again how long he was expected to stay for. Jane was now deep in conversation with a governor, Esther was chatting to a parent. He turned to Maddy.

'How long do you think we have to stay?'

'Well, I'm leaving right now; I need to get to the shops. I would think it's up to you when you leave,' said Maddy.

Andrew decided he would talk to a couple of governors, make

his presence felt. Then he would sidle off, hope nobody noticed for a while. It wasn't as if he was needed, he was just standing there like a lemon, watching parents look at paintings. Most of them had left now, it wasn't exactly a full gallery. The only remaining parents were the social ones, sipping the indiscriminate pink liquid, wishing it was wine, making animated conversation, laughing loudly. He was definitely surplus to requirements. Next week was half term. He had nothing planned, could pop into school one day, get things sorted then. No need to do it today.

***

When Andrew arrived at the restaurant he had to bang on the door for a while before he was noticed. The manager came and unlocked for him, showed him to the table, then disappeared. He assumed she was collecting his students. Nothing was ever explained. He unloaded some papers from his bag and waited. He waited for a while. Bai Yun and Lao appeared, smiled, sat down. After a few minutes the others arrived. Andrew felt the lessons were low on their list of priorities, that perhaps they were less keen to learn English than their manager had been for them to learn. They seemed reluctant to be there. It was not encouraging.

He began by telling them about his week, about the art display, the artists the children had studied. He showed them some of the pictures on his phone, asked them what they thought. They had passed it around, told him they were 'good' or 'not good'. Not quite the extensive vocabulary he had hoped for. Bai Yun asked him where they were. He looked up *mei shu guan* in his dictionary. Confirmed that yes, they were in an 'art gallery'. He wondered if now was the moment he could invite her to go and see some, to maybe visit the National Gallery with him. No, he was not quite brave enough. Not in front of all the others anyway. Better by text, when he could use his dictionary, make sure his rubbish pronunciation didn't get in the way. Less embarrassing if she refused too. He had not yet exchanged phone numbers, there never seemed to be an opportunity. He would do it today, he decided, silly to keep putting it off. Next week was half term, ideal time to suggest they met somewhere.

'If I am ill – *ru guo wo bing, wo gei nimen dian hua* – I'll phone you. Give you a phone call?' he said.

They nodded, yes, that was what they expected him to do. That was good, always a relief when they understood each other.

He wrote his own number onto some paper, then passed around another piece. They all wrote their numbers and handed them back. Bai Yun and Lao did not refer to their phones, simply wrote them from memory. That was impressive. He knew his had '300' in it but always needed to check the rest.

They had written their names in Chinese script next to their numbers. It looked like scribble. Andrew could recognise many symbols but these were impossible, did not resemble any writing he was used to. He explained his problem and they laughed. He felt like a small child, those who could only read printed text, tended to be thrown by cursive writing, were unable to read it unless the letters were exactly like the printed material they were used to. He was the same. These hand written names were an enigma.

Bai Yun took the pen from him. She wrote her name again, slowly this time, each stroke carefully written. That was better, now he could see the word he recognised as '*bai* – white'. She laughed at him, showing those straight white teeth, her dark eyes sparkling, teasing.

He would text her later. See if she replied, if she would meet him.

He looked up. Lao was watching closely, a half smile on his face. Andrew could not read the expression, had no idea what he was thinking. He wondered if Bai Yun had a boyfriend. It would be good to know before he made an idiot of himself. Hard to know how to broach the subject though, he could hardly just come straight out with it, much too obvious. Especially with Lao giving him appraising looks with that mocking smile. He decided to steer the conversation in that direction, see what happened.

'I have to go to a wedding soon,' he said, 'my cousin is getting married. *Biao ge*, cousin. *Jie hun*, married.'

They smiled, nodded, letting him know they were following.

'In England, the bride wears white dress. Same in China?' he said. Easier to speak in pidgin English, to only say the essential words. They still got stuck, gave him that blank look so he found a few words in the dictionary and showed them.

They told him that no, most women in China got married wearing red. Red was a lucky colour.

'My wife wear red tee shirt,' said Lao. 'No money for special dress.'

'You have a wife? Here? Or in China?' asked Andrew, surprised. This had never been mentioned before. Maybe they all had spouses tucked away in China. Perhaps he was getting his hopes up for nothing with Bai Yun.

Lao shook his head. 'Not China, wife in England. Huang Tai Yang, Yellow Sun. She work in London, I work here. Sundays she come here. When she pregnant, we live together. When baby born, we take to my mother in China, then Huang Tai Yang go back to her job. Is usual.'

Andrew was silent. This was unexpected. They had told him previously about being raised by grandmothers and he knew the manager lived separately to her husband but he had not realised how common this was, that this was an accepted way to live. He could not think how to react, so simply nodded. Now he needed to check about the girls, couldn't risk putting his foot in it.

'What about the rest of you? You married too?'

They giggled, shook their heads. Shao Ling whispered something to Bai Yun, there was more giggling, they told him something about Shao Ling and a cook but he didn't catch it. Didn't care. The important thing was Bai Yun was unattached, the way was clear for him to give it a try.

The manager appeared with some tea and a piece of paper. His heart sank, another residency request? No, this was a letter. It was from an electrician. The manager wanted to know why he was asking for money, told Andrew they had not had any work done, wanted Andrew to please sort out. Andrew read the letter but nothing was terribly clear. He decided to phone the number printed at the bottom.

A woman answered. Andrew explained he was calling on behalf of the restaurant, wanted to query a bill, please could she explain it to him. She took the reference number from the letter, checked, then informed him that actually it was not a bill. It was an estimate. Their engineer had been asked to call and quote for some work. He had not yet done the work, they owed nothing, this was just to let them know what it would cost if they went ahead.

Andrew thanked her, said he would let them know, finished the call.

He sat for a moment. This was quite complicated vocabulary. He wondered how these people coped, living in a world where they understood so little of the language. No wonder that they often appeared suspicious, were worried they would be taken advantage of, cheated. What would they have done if he had not been there? Who else could they ask? He was not sure if they were incredibly brave or incredibly foolhardy to leave China and set up life here. It was certainly not easy.

The rest of the 'lesson' was taken up with Andrew trying to translate what he had learned. It would have been impossible without a dictionary.

As he walked to his car, bag of food in hand, Andrew felt exhausted. The day had been interesting, he had to admit that. He liked teaching in the restaurant, even when it involved more advising about life than actual teaching. It made him feel significant, that he was doing something worthwhile.

That evening, lying in bed, he decided to text Bai Yun. He had been thinking about it for weeks, had finally got her number. If he didn't do it now, chances were he never would. He wrote what he wanted to say on a scrap of paper, adding the English letters, the pinyin, underneath, so he would remember how to type it into his phone. He was asking her if she would like to go to London with him on her day off. Nothing else, no plans, they could decide that later. If he invited her for a meal or to the cinema she might refuse because she didn't fancy the activity rather than didn't fancy him. Keeping things simple was a lesson he had learned well that week.

He typed the message into his phone, checked it, pressed send.

At half past midnight, when the restaurant had shut for the night, her reply came through.

'I say yes. Day off Friday. What time you want meet? Bai Yun.'

Andrew smiled, rolled over, went to sleep. The phone slid off the bed and fell amongst a pile of papers on the floor.

Chapter Sixteen

IT was fairly late before Esther managed to leave school and it felt even later, the black sky cold and starless. She felt pleased with her week, satisfied that it had been good for the school, would be thought of in a positive light and this would reflect well on her.

She was tired though, talking to the parents was always draining. You could never be completely relaxed, knew that the slightest thing might be exaggerated, repeated time and again. She always tried to appear calm and accepting, even if slightly bland. Sometimes she longed to be honest, to tell a parent that actually their child was completely thick which was no surprise really, they just needed to look at the mother to understand why. Or to answer back when a parent was rude, to tell them something was none of their business or that what they were saying was atrocious and they should know better. But she never did, of course. Being able to keep quiet was one of her strengths.

Today, most had wanted to talk about their half term plans anyway. It was ski season and the talk had been about possible snow on the mountains and which were the good runs. Esther couldn't have joined in even if she had wanted to. She had never been skiing. It was unlikely that she ever would, not while she was married to the minister. Churches did not pay enough for holidays like that. It wasn't something she resented, it was a known part of the job, something that you accepted if you went into the ministry. Sometimes though it made her feel lonely, a bit left out. She and Rob had good brains, they were both graduates, both enjoyed a good discussion, were well educated. The people who they enjoyed being with, those who were naturally friends, those of a similar intellect, all had much higher salaries. It made it hard to have enough in common with them to feel equal, like real friends. Even if they did socialise with them, go out for dinner or invite them to the house, Esther was ever aware of the budget, of how much the evening was costing them. Some of their best friends knew this and tended to pick up the bill, but she felt awkward about that too. It made her feel that they weren't the same, were seen as a charity. Rob told her not to be silly, that if they were doing God's work then friends paying for them was part of that, she should let them pay, it was just money, just another resource that God had given to them. Rob being able to preach was a gift as much as their friends' money, both were supposed to be used and she shouldn't be so hung up on it. 'It's just money,' he would say. Just money.

She had learned too that having parents as friends was not a good idea. When she was younger she had socialised with some mothers, feeling they were all in the 'mums together' club. She had thought, hoped, that it would be different to having friends in the congregation, would be trouble free. It wasn't. It had caused problems. Sometimes her friends had been annoyed with her because she had refused to break professional confidences. They felt that as they were friends, she should not withhold information, whatever she knew was fair game for them all to know. When she had resisted, told them that actually she couldn't discuss the latest governors' edict or what was said in the staff meeting concerning a particular child, they were cross, felt slighted, stopped inviting her to things. Even when friends respected her position it had not always been easy. They would mention things about her to other parents, those with whom she wanted to keep a strictly professional facade. No, friendships with parents were as fraught with problems as friendships within the congregation. Which made for a potentially lonely life.

She opened the boot of the car and heaved her bags inside. Her classroom was clear, all ready for after half term, so she could spend as much time at home as possible. She would pop into the shop on the way home, pick up something for dinner. She was so late already, a bit longer would make no difference, Rob knew today was the big day. She would cook something nice for dinner, meals had been a bit scratchy this week, all her energy going on school, trying to make it perfect.

Esther started the engine and pulled away from the school, passing Jane's car parked in the corner. Poor Jane, she had not enjoyed the week. Oak Class were never an easy class to cover anyway and she had not taught for a few years. Esther had never seen her look so tired. Not that she had appeared any less professional, of course. She was good at that, at presenting an image to the parents and governors. She had not made any sort of speech at the gallery, but she had spent time talking to each of the governors and had found time at the end to thank Esther, to tell her it had been a good idea, was worth the extra effort, nice to have a focus for the term.

Their little gallery had been well attended, nearly every child had a parent who popped in, even if just briefly. They had 'opened' the gallery half an hour before pick-up time, to try and stagger the visitors a little. This hadn't really worked of course, it never did. Most of the parents wanted to go in after they had collected their child, so they knew which paintings to look at and could be seen to be interested. No point in being a good parent if your child wasn't there to witness it. The few parents who did go to the gallery first had not allowed any extra time, had left home at the same time, which meant they were simply later collecting their children, leaving them in the care of the staff for longer. This was inconvenient when the staff all wanted to hand over their classes quickly and go to the gallery themselves. Organising the parents was always the hardest bit, Esther felt. They could never be relied upon to behave as you hoped.

Esther drove slowly, she was tired. She planned her shopping list, hoped she wouldn't forget anything. As she passed the roundabout at the end of the High Street, the turning to Cynthia's lane, she wondered how she was. Her sudden absence had been a bit strange, though anyone could see how stressed she had been lately, so Esther was not completely surprised. She had though, been surprised by the terse exchange when Cynthia had arrived in the school gallery that afternoon. When Esther had first seen her, she had thought how nice it was, that even on sick leave she had wanted to be part of the event, to see what the children had produced. Then, when she had seen her expression, that wildness in her eyes as she talked to Jane, Esther had been slightly shocked. There was something unbalanced there, as if that tightly controlled personality was beginning to come apart at the seams. Poor Cynthia. Esther doubted she had many friends. Perhaps she should buy her some flowers or a little plant, take it round on her way home, let her know that she was being thought of. Yes, she decided as she guided her car into a parking space, glad no one was present to comment on her driving, yes, that was a good idea. The supermarket was bound to have something bright but not too expensive.

The shopping was quickly sorted and within the hour Esther was back at the car, stowing a faded pink plant in the rear footwell. She glanced at her watch and decided she had time to take the plant now, it would be quicker than making a special visit over the weekend. She could legitimately say she had no time to stay. She felt slightly guilty at this, knowing deep down that Cynthia probably needed a visit, someone who would sit and listen to her. But Esther just could not face it, not today. The plant was better than nothing she reasoned.

There was a space in the road just beyond Cynthia's cottage and Esther walked back to the front door. She had never been inside the cottage, though had a couple of time dropped off things for Cynthia on her way past. She stood on the step, reaching up to knock. The plant pot touched her coat, leaving mud specks. She was brushing them off when the door opened.

Cynthia looked at Esther with suspicion.

'Hello Cynthia, I was just passing on my way home and thought I would pop in with a plant for you. How are you feeling? I was sorry to hear you are ill.' She held out the plant and smiled.

Cynthia took the plant and looked at it. It seemed even more faded now. Esther wished she had taken the trouble to buy some wrapping paper for the pot, made it look less like an afterthought.

'That is most kind of you, I shall place it on my window sill,' she looked up, stared Esther in the eye, added, 'I am quite well thank you, I am unclear as to why Mrs Lancaster felt it necessary to ban me from school, to send me home in such a manner.'

Cynthia paused. She was consumed with anger when she thought of how she was being treated, the unfairness of the situation. She felt rather emotional and did not want to break down in front of the Pritchard woman, that would never do. Never show weakness to the enemy. Esther Pritchard was most certainly the enemy, her main competitor for the teaching position. She resisted the urge to scowl.

'Well, I'm sure the children missed you for their Art Week,' continued Esther, wondering if she was going to be invited in, realising that she was not. 'They did some lovely displays. Did you have a chance to see them before you left?'

'I did not leave,' corrected Miss Mott, 'I was forced from the premises. I know what you're all up to, you know, I am not an idiot.' She leaned forwards towards Esther, her eyes unnaturally bright, her breath sour as it wafted towards Esther's face.

'You will all be sorry you know,' she whispered, 'you will live to regret this.'

Then, as if they had been having a perfectly normal conversation, she straightened, smiled, looked at the plant.

'Thank you kindly for this. It was a lovely thought. Nice to see you, bye bye.' The door closed before Esther could reply.

For a moment she stood where she was, too surprised to move. Then an overwhelming urge to giggle beset her. The day had been too long, had too many pressures, she was unable to react calmly. A small laugh escaped and she returned to her car, sat for a moment and laughed properly, loudly, letting all the tensions evaporate. What a surprise that had been. It was so weird it was funny, hilarious even.

She stopped. Actually, it was not funny. If anything it was slightly alarming, that someone could become so unhinged so quickly. Or perhaps she had misunderstood, perhaps that had not been a threat. The thought of Cynthia Mott coming after her for a fight was too funny and she began to laugh again. Then she took a deep breath, forced herself to take control, and drove away.

She did not see Cynthia watching her from the upstairs window. Nor did she know that the faded pink plant now rested in the dustbin.

Esther arrived home to find Rob was out, Joseph was locked in the bathroom and Samuel was screaming through the door at him. This was so not what she needed.

'Open the door,' shouted Samuel, 'you little shit. Open the door so I can punch you.'

Esther felt sure that now was not the time to give feedback on the wisdom of that comment or the likelihood of it being successful. She sighed, not sure she had the energy for teenage angst today. She wondered where Rob was, felt let down that he had allowed her to come home to this, sent up a quick prayer, knowing she needed help to diffuse this little delight. When she spoke it was with the quiet, controlled, slightly deeper voice that she used to settle classes and uptight parents.

'Samuel, stop banging on the door, you will damage it. Come and help me put the shopping away and tell me what the problem is. And where is your father?'

Samuel gave a last kick to the bathroom door and stomped down the stairs. He followed her into the kitchen and slumped in a chair. He was not going to help her. Not if she was going to give him a lecture. She always sided with Joseph, it wasn't fair. He was blamed for everything. He glowered at her, refusing to speak.

Esther pulled shopping from the bag, screwed up the carrier bags and stuffed them under the sink. She delved into the heap of food, found a bag of chocolate biscuits and threw them at her son. He caught them, looked surprised, started to open them. He still did not speak but his expression softened. Esther did not know what the problem was but she doubted it was either serious or unsolvable with chocolate. Boys never grew up, they just got bigger. She reached over him, putting tins and packets into cupboards, taking others out, making a pile of the food she needed for dinner on the worktop.

'My day went well,' she said, determined to break the silence, to not let him break her mood. 'We displayed the children's work and the parents came to see them. And a photographer came from the local paper, so it might be in next week's edition. I hope so. I was pleased with it, it looked really good and the children enjoyed it. I'm hoping I'll get some credit for it when they come to decide who has to be made redundant.'

Samuel took out a biscuit and began to lick the chocolate from the top. He knew this irritated her. Something inside of him needed her to shout at him, so he could shout back. He knew what she was doing, trying to appear all calm and unbothered, to trap him into talking. It wouldn't work though. He took a bite of biscuit, crumbs falling onto his school jumper.

'I thought I would make a lasagne for dinner, a sort of celebration for half term,' continued Esther, pretending she had not noticed his silence, the sullen expression. She rarely made lasagne, even though it was a favourite. It was too much effort, like making three different meals and only getting one dish out of it.

She tipped the beef mince into a saucepan and put it on the hob to fry, looked for the onion.

'How was your day?' she asked.

Samuel considered for a moment. He liked lasagne, knew that if he pushed this too far she would send him to his room and he might miss it. Decided it was not worth the risk, he would be polite.

'It was alright till I got home,' he offered, 'then the little shit started going through my bag, looking for stuff to steal. You should tell him off, not me.'

'Don't swear,' said Esther, but mildly, with no real anger. Anger would make him worse, unleash a torrent. She was not sure she could cope with a torrent today. 'Where's Dad?' She pulled out a knife and began to peel the onion, slicing it into slippery half moons, then threw them into the pan. They sizzled as they hit the fat.

Samuel's eyes began to sting. He decided he would try to leave, see if she stopped him. He thought the door bashing was probably her main worry, she seemed remarkably in control considering. Probably he wasn't going to get the lecture. Not that she would say anything to Joseph-the-shit either, which he definitely deserved. He held the biscuits low, hoping she wouldn't notice he still had them.

'He went out. Some sort of emergency. The Tylers. Said he should be home for supper.' He began to sidle from the room.

Esther reached out, took the biscuits, let him go. She opened a tin of tomatoes, stirred the beef and onion mixture, which was already beginning to stick to the pan.

In the bathroom, Joseph wondered what was happening. He

heard them go into the kitchen, did not hear shouting, wondered if it was safe to emerge. He did not altogether trust Samuel when he was angry, had received a few knocks in the past, knew he could hit to hurt when he was angry. And he had certainly been angry.

The trouble had started when they got home from school. Their father had been on the telephone, as usual, so they had gone into the kitchen looking for food. They were both eating cereal when Rob had opened the door, said he needed to go out, would they be okay until Mum got home? Of course they would, they told him, they weren't babies. They raised their eyebrows at how stupid parents could be sometimes and took the cereal into the lounge, switching on the television. All was going fine until Joseph remembered he had lost his calculator. He knew that Sam had one the same, figured he could take it from his school bag, claim it was his own, let Sam get into trouble for needing a new one. He had gone into the hall and started to search Sam's bag. That was when he had seen the pictures. Lots of them. Breasts of all sizes, drawn in great detail in the back of his rough book. Some of them were quite good, Joseph was impressed. Samuel appeared in the hall, saw what he was doing. Joseph's mistake was in mentioning the name, Clare Beackon, which was written in the margin. It acted like a catalyst, driving his brother into a rage greater than he had ever seen before. He rushed upstairs, into the safety of the bathroom, hooting loudly to let Samuel know that he wasn't scared, it was all wildly funny. Samuel chased him, grabbing at his heels, shouting that he was a sneak, had no right to go through his bag, he was going to kill him. The door had been locked seconds before the weight of his brother had banged against it. Then Samuel stayed there, shouting abuse, thumping and kicking the door, until their mother had arrived home.

Now Joseph was bored. He had drunk some water from the tap, told himself he was not bothered, checked out the stuff in the medicine cabinet. He noticed some was out of date. He would mention that, let his mother know she too made mistakes. That might make her feel less inclined to shout at him, make them more balanced on the 'wrong' scales.

He pressed his ear against the door. Sounds from the television floated up the stairs. He could smell cooking too. He was hungry. He slowly inched the bolt back from the door and opened it a crack. Samuel was nowhere to be seen. He decided he was probably safe enough, now his mother was home, and went down the stairs, quickly so his brother could not suddenly leap out and land a punch, into the relative sanctuary of the kitchen.

Esther glanced up. She was shrouded in steam. Vast amounts of fat had melted out of the mince so she had strained it into a bowl. It sat there looking brown and evil, congealing at the edges. She had dumped the tomatoes in the pan and was now melting butter for the sauce. She did not really want to sort out the boys. She gestured towards the saucepan.

'Come in and stir that,' she said. 'Don't let it stick. It might need water added. I'm making lasagne, you can help me until your brother has calmed down a bit.'

This seemed like a good option to Joseph so he obliged, stirring the wooden spoon round the pan, enjoying the smell and the wet heat that covered his hand. He hoped she wouldn't ask him any questions. There was no way he could tell her what the argument had been about, way too embarrassing. Plus she might find out about the calculator.

The telephone rang. Esther turned off the heat under the sauce and hurried to the study. She picked up on the eighth ring. It was Sue Keier, a young woman from the church.

'Hello, is that Esther? It's Sue here. I did try Rob's number but his phone is off. As you know, me and James got engaged a couple of weeks ago and we wondered if we could get a date in the church diary for the wedding? Then we can start booking stuff. We only want something small, so were wondering about September. Is that too soon do you think? Will the church be booked up already?'

Esther congratulated her and said how lovely it all was while reaching for the computer and pulling the online church calendar onto the screen. She scrolled through the months.

'Okay, I have the calendar now. Which date were you thinking of?'

'Well, really we'd like the nineteenth. Is it free? We thought we'd better book the church first, then we can start to organise everything else. If too much stuff is booked up already, especially the reception venue, then we might have to change it.'

The day looked empty but Esther knew that Rob did not always remember to add dates to the calendar as efficiently as everyone assumed. He tended to scribble things into his pocket diary and sometimes forgot to transfer them.

'It looks okay, but there might be something that hasn't been put in yet. If I were you, I wouldn't book anything definitely until you've spoken to Rob. Or Charles, he would know.' Charles was the church secretary. He was slightly more organised than Rob. Slightly.

'I'll leave a note for Rob so he knows,' said Esther. She did not say he would return the call. He might, but not necessarily promptly. She had learned to manage people's expectations, it avoided some criticism. She repeated her congratulations, asked if they wanted Rob to lead the service and said goodbye.

She frowned as she returned to the kitchen. As she had expected, they did want Rob to lead the service. He would be pleased, considered it a great privilege to lead the wedding and funeral services of his congregation. But Esther knew that it was a lot of work and very time consuming. He would need to plan the sermon, lead the rehearsal and the day itself would be a whole Saturday. As

Sue was a church member, the wedding would be included as part of Rob's regular work. He would not receive any extra pay for the extra work. Esther knew this was normal, taking weddings and funerals was part of his job. But often people forgot that it was all extra work. He would not stop leading the Bible study or miss a deacons' meeting just because he had a wedding and a funeral in a week. If people from outside the membership asked to be married at the church, then Rob would be paid an additional amount. Sometimes quite a nice amount. It still diverted his time but at least Esther felt there was some compensation.

The time was another whole issue. Rob had his day off on Saturdays. They had decided that although it would clash with weddings, it would mean that most weeks he would be at home when Esther and the boys were there. She found that she now resented weddings, seeing them as stolen family time. She knew rationally that it was part of his job, that he could have chosen any day for his day off and they had known from the outset that weddings tended to be on Saturdays. However, as he spent more and more time at work, ministering to the growing congregation, Esther found the part of him reserved for family was getting smaller and smaller.

Ironically, most people thought weddings were a 'perk', that he was lucky to be able to go to so many weddings, he was often invited to the reception afterwards, so had a whole dinner and party 'for free'. They had no idea that actually he had little in common with many of the guests, he was there in his official capacity of 'minister', was not able to properly relax. It was not a restful experience, did not in Esther's mind qualify as a day off.

She returned to an empty kitchen. The mince was sticking to the base of the pan and turning black. Joseph, bored, had decided to take his chances with Samuel. They now sat in stony silence staring at the same television screen, each waiting for the other to speak or move so they could make a sarcastic remark and reopen the argument.

Esther tipped the meat into a clean saucepan and ran water into the burned edges of the original. The water hissed and spat as it touched the burned base. It suited her mood perfectly. She added some more liquid to the meat and returned to her sauce.

She had just added flour to the melted butter when the telephone rang again. Sighing, she turned off the heat under both pans and went to answer it. She wondered why the church had never paid for a phone extension in the kitchen. They probably considered it unnecessary as everyone used mobile phones now. They tended to forget that ministers often need to turn off theirs.

She listened as the answerphone clicked in. It was Roselyn. Esther returned to her cooking. She did not have time for Roselyn today. The good thing about answer machines was they had limited space, after a few minutes she would be cut off.

Rob returned home just as Esther was serving the lasagne. He came straight into the kitchen and kissed the back of her head as she spooned squares of pasta and sauce onto plates. Some sauce dribbled onto the work surface and she frowned at him.

'I'm busy,' she said.

'Yes, sorry, I'll go and check the answerphone and come back when it's ready,' he said, walking from the kitchen.

'No, don't leave,' she shouted after his departing back, 'it's ready now.' He had gone. She frowned at the salad and dumped it on the table, calling to the boys. They loped from the lounge, tall and lean and hungry. Usually she liked to see them come for food, that eager light in their eyes. It was pleasing to feed your children, whatever their ages. But not today. Today had been too long and she had received too many knock-backs. Her happy mood had evaporated with the burned mince. The family were wary.

Esther had to call Rob from the study. Although he knew she

263

was serving the food, he had become distracted with something in the study and never returned. She and the boys waited until he arrived at the table. He sat and said grace, thanking God for the food and for his wife. It did nothing to improve Esther's mood.

She had worked hard this week and had wanted him to be her backup at home. Especially today. He had known she would be late, had needed him to keep an eye on the boys. Plus she just wanted to get home and tell him about it, to share her success, bask a little in knowing her idea had gone well. For once, Esther had wanted her work to dominate. It had not.

'So, where were you? I thought you would be at home while I finished off at school?' she said.

Rob took a mouthful, knowing from her tone she was spoiling for a fight, hoping to give himself time to choose his words carefully. The food was hot. It burned his tongue and he spat it back onto the plate.

'Good one Dad,' said Samuel.

'Sorry, that was hotter than I was expecting,' apologised Rob, reaching for his water glass. 'I had to go out, the boys said they would be okay. The Tylers needed some help, I'll tell you about it later.

'So, how was your day? Did the display look good? Did lots of people come?'

Esther chewed her food. It was hot but it was easy enough to take small mouthfuls and blow on it first. His table manners were appalling. Especially in front of the boys. How could she begin to hope they would learn from her when they had Rob as a role model? She frowned at him.

'It was fine thanks,' she said. She found she did not want to talk about it. Not now. She had been bursting with it when she got home, desperate to tell someone. But the boys weren't interested and he hadn't been here, again. It seemed he was rarely here these days when she needed him. She had to fit in the cracks left by his job. Well, she wasn't a machine, she could not turn her needs on and off to suit the demands of the congregation.

They ate in silence.

After the meal, when the dishwasher was glugging through the dirty crockery and the surfaces had been wiped, Rob tried again. He found Esther tying up the bin bag ready for the dustbin and offered to take it for her. He returned and put his arms around her waist. Esther was aware he had not washed his hands after returning from the dustbin.

'Hey you,' he whispered into her hair, 'I'm sorry I was out. Are you still cross or can you tell me about your day? I want to know. I've been hoping it went well for you.' He kissed the top of her hair, feeling her tense body in his arms, knowing he was going to have to work a little harder before she would relent.

'Yes, like I said, it was fine.' Then the desire to tell him won. Esther slumped into a chair and turned to him, began to tell him about the display, about the photographer, the governors. She told him about Cynthia arriving and the strange conversation with Jane, then about delivering the plant and how aggressive Cynthia had seemed.

Rob listened. He listened for twenty minutes, watching her face, smiling at her expression as her eyes shone with success as she talked about the gallery.

Then he told her that the Tylers were having marriage problems, had called in something of a crisis, had asked him to go at once. It had all been very emotional, Brian Tyler threatening to leave, Jenny in floods of tears. He did not give any details, just enough for Esther to understand that it had been important, he had needed to go.

It had been chaos when he arrived, summoned by a tearful Jenny who sounded on the point of hysteria. The couple seemed to have spent the afternoon shouting at each other, accusations flying back and forth, control and energy seeping away in equal measure. When Rob arrived at their large modern semi, he had found them both in the lounge. He could tell at once they were both exhausted, physically and emotionally. They just needed someone to step in, to intervene for a moment so the escalating emotions did not completely take over. Before they did something they would regret, got to a point they might never be able to return from. Rob was that person. He did not need to say much, his mere presence helping to calm things down, to bring a modicum of normality, a reason for them both to hold back a little, keep their behaviour in check.

He had no idea what the final outcome would be. Broken marriages could nearly always be repaired but only if both sides wanted to, were willing to put in the work. And it would be hard work, over a long time, he knew that, had seen it many times before. For now though, they just needed a barrier, his being there had been enough. They had been calm when he left. They would meet again, he would give them regular counselling sessions until they either were equipped to continue the work without him or he felt the need to refer them to someone with more expertise. It was draining work. Satisfying, but now he too was exhausted. He was also aware he had once more failed his own wife. There was nothing else he could say, not for now anyway.

He stood, kissed her head again, told her he was just going into the study. He wanted to check his diary, get back to the Tylers with some possible dates. It would also give him an excuse to speak to them again, check that everything had remained calm in his absence.

Esther watched his back as he left the kitchen. She loved this man. She loved sharing her life with him, wanted him to know about her day. And she was proud of him, really she was. She was proud of how good he was with people, how he would always give time to those who needed it, good advice to those in trouble, would listen at length to those who had problems.

'But sometimes,' she thought as she rinsed the cloth she was holding, 'sometimes I wish he would remember that I am part of his congregation too. Our marriage needs as much of his care as everyone else's.' She threw the cloth into the sink and went upstairs to find a load of washing for the machine. She was aware that yet again, her husband's job, the value of what he did, had eclipsed her own.

Chapter Seventeen

THE fire warmed her cheeks, a warmth like a kiss. Then her neck, chest, arms enfolded into the heat. The heat began to be uncomfortable, reddening her skin. She lifted her hands, shielding her face. It became too hot for comfort and she stepped back, enjoying the searing flames, the cleansing hotness. She watched the flames reach higher, striving to join the black smoke as it furled towards the night sky, blending with the clouds, obliterating the stars. Hungry, devouring, destroying. The noise was immense, a great rush of air and crackles, pops, the occasional boom as something exploded. Something ceased to exist, consumed by the cleansing fire.

It was justice on a grand scale. No one could fail to notice that the old was being wiped out, punished in the eternal way, the Biblical solution. There would be no ignoring of her now, no denying her power, her rights.

She could see very little of the inside of the building, the odd glimpse of books curling in submission, a desk dancing with tiny flames that danced along its edge, licking the varnish, waiting to consume the thick wood. A picture board alive with light and colour, the flames mimicking the colours of the paper, green, blue, red, disappearing in seconds as the fire whooshed along its length, gaining momentum as it rolled towards the cupboard and settled to heating the contents, wisps of smoke growing in intensity as the heat built.

A window shattered with a pop, the blackened glass falling like raindrops onto the withered grass in front of her. The smoke billowed out, glad of the freedom to swell outwards and upwards, the air thick with it, filling her sight, her nose, rushing into her throat, making it hard to breathe. A harsh, acrid smoke, full of chemicals and poisons. She coughed.

The cough woke her. She was in her chair, the flames in the grate warming her cheeks. Her head had dropped onto her shoulder and she straightened it, feeling the tendons in her neck scream in protest as she moved from the strange angle. She wiped a line of dribble from her chin and raised her shoulders, wanting to ease the ache. Her mind was numb as she fought to sort reality from dream, to decipher what was real and what was imagined. Imagined or predestined.

It had been a good dream. A dream of revenge. Cynthia felt a strange bubble inside her, as though she now had a mission to accomplish. She rose unsteadily from her chair, she needed a cup of tea before she thought about this. A cushion fell from her lap and knocked the packet of pills from the table. They lay on the floor, unopened, ignored.

Making tea was a settling activity. There was calm in the bubble of water in the kettle, the clink of cup against saucer, the softness of teabag lying in the cup. It gave her time to think, to readjust to wakefulness.

To have slept in the chair was uncomfortable but hardly surprising. She had not slept at all last night. For several nights in fact. It barely seemed worth the ritual of washing and changing into night clothes when one just lay on the covers, watching the ceiling, counting the long hours until the light began to seep around the curtains. So last night she had decided to not even bother. She had read her books and walked to the stream and emptied her cupboards, wiping the surfaces before replacing everything. Then in the cold grey of dawn she had lit a fire and sat in her chair with a magazine.

She looked at the clock. It was still early, not even lunchtime. The actual name of the day was less certain but she did not waste effort trying to sort that out. Days were an irrelevance now, she saw no one and did nothing of value. They were long and fruitless. It felt an age since she had seen anyone, had needed to even speak.

She carried her tea back into the sitting room. Some of it slopped into the saucer as she sat but she failed to notice. As she settled into her chair, her foot touched the pill box. She frowned at it for a second, then kicked it out of sight.

The doctor had been unhelpful. That had been an annoyingly long morning, her thoughts full of school, how the children would be faring without her, which traitor would be teaching her lessons, would their paintings for the display be of a good standard.

She had arrived at the surgery a good five minutes before her allotted time. A bored receptionist was standing behind the counter and the telephone had rung just as Cynthia arrived. Instead of ignoring it, or even acknowledging her presence in any way, the woman answered it, leaving Cynthia standing in front of her, waiting. She waited for long minutes. The receptionist had checked her computer, pulled out a file, written some notes, all the while speaking in a clipped sharp voice. All the while ignoring Cynthia, who stood awkwardly waiting. When the call finally ended she glanced up at Cynthia with a frown, as if cross to find her still standing there.

'Yes?'

'Cynthia Mott. I have an appointment. I believe it was five minutes ago. I was here on time.'

'Number five. Take a seat.' No apology, no smile, no humanity.

Cynthia sat. She watched the board in front of her, waiting for her number to be called. She had no idea how long she would be waiting, if the doctor was running to time, if indeed she had missed her own slot whilst standing before the receptionist like an animal.

It was rude. Cynthia felt the whole world was rude. Rude and unkind. She did not need to be here anyway, had only come because that infuriating woman had insisted. Cynthia knew that when Jane Lancaster phoned her she would ask, would check that Cynthia had obeyed her instructions. Given that she was the individual who now decided Cynthia's fate, could turn the governing body, ensure that she either kept or lost her job, she had not felt able to ignore her. So she was here. Sitting on a plastic seat, inhaling goodness knows how many germs, waiting for an indeterminate amount of time while the rude receptionist sorted papers and chatted to colleagues. Cynthia's eyes narrowed. She deserved better than this.

The doctor, when eventually seen, had been brisk. She examined Cynthia, asked about her eating and sleeping, which Cynthia told her were all completely fine. She then asked how she could help, listened carefully while Cynthia explained about the misunderstanding at school. She followed up with some seemingly unrelated questions. There had then been a pause while she checked Cynthia's records. She prescribed some pills and told Cynthia she would like her to make another appointment for two weeks' time. Said something about seeing a counsellor. Completely unnecessary. She had written a certificate, saying that she should remain off work for that time, smiled, stood, shaken her hand and dismissed her.

Cynthia had collected the pills. They were in a flat white box. She did not know the colour of the pills themselves as she had not taken any. Did not intend to ever take any. They were not required. They would remain enclosed in their white plastic capsules. She was not going to risk muddling her thoughts, being less astute than normal, due to one silly incident at school. The doctor had said they were for depression. Well, Cynthia was not depressed. She was angry, wronged, worried, but not depressed. She had heard about people who took antidepressants, how they became dependent on them, couldn't function properly. She wondered if it was a ploy, if Jane Lancaster had asked the doctor to prescribe them so that Cynthia would never be well enough to return to school, to keep her job. To keep her cottage, her life. But that was probably silly, probably the doctor had decided on her own. It was important to keep track of reality. Though that was becoming increasingly difficult, especially as the days blurred together.

She took a sip of the tea. It was very hot and burned her lip, reminding her of the dream. She smiled. It had been a good dream. The school had been burning, destroyed completely. That seemed immensely fair. If she had to endure having her job, her classroom, her security, wrenched from her so abruptly, then surely no one should have it. There had been no casualties in her dream, her mind was not the warped mind of a lunatic. No, simply the building had burned. While Cynthia watched. It felt very real. She was good at fires.

Could it become a reality? Was there a way to cause the school to burn down? Perhaps a lightning strike. She did not know very much about lightning, whether it was possible to encourage a strike. She knew it was attracted to metal. But how would one place something of the right attraction onto the roof of the school? No, even if she knew when a storm was due, that was hardly possible, one could not scrabble about on the roof unseen. She would need a better idea than that.

Her tea was finished and she placed the cup and saucer carefully onto the heap of books on the table next to her. Then she adjusted her cushion and sat back, watching the flames in her grate, waiting for inspiration. It was not real, of course, she would not really destroy the school. But if she were going to, what would be the best method? It was an amusing thought, something to occupy her mind.

The hardest part of making a fire was keeping it alight. The initial kindling would be no problem, the school was full of paper, all of which would catch light easily. She would need an initial spark though. A match was no good. She knew from watching the occasional crime show on television that the fire brigade were terribly clever at finding how fires had been started. No, better to have some sort of electric fault. She pictured her classroom, walked around it in her mind, looked in cupboards, searching for something to use.

Ah, the broken heater. In the back of the stockroom was an old electrical heater. Several years ago, she couldn't remember how many, she had worked there for so long, they had used that heater. On snowy days, when it was too cold to work because the old pipes were inadequate, they would use an electric heater. It could be plugged in, standing in the corner, and it helped to take the chill off the air. It should have been removed long ago, was dangerous, they had been told that however cold their rooms might be in the winter, it was no longer considered safe to use a free standing electric heater. She didn't know where it came from originally. The important thing was that anyone could have placed it in a room, turned it on, caused a fire. It was not hidden, was in the back of the cupboard but plainly in sight. The sort of thing that vandals, youths from the local estate, might well find and use to cause damage.

If it were placed in the middle of the room, perhaps facing down, as if knocked over, then it would be sure to overheat, start a fire. She could surround it with a circle of newspaper from the painting cupboard, give the initial sparks some fuel. Then place some thicker paper further back, for when the fire started to get really hot. She wouldn't use any kind of liquid fuel, that was sure to be detected, possibly traceable. But paper, anyone could use paper.

She wondered if glue was flammable. They used a non-poisonous, white glue. Would it burn? It was a shame she wasn't still teaching and could check during a lunchtime. They did have some varnish though. It wasn't used very often, being rather expensive. However, she had bought it to varnish some loaves of bread. If one varnished bread it sealed it, stopping it from going mouldy. It was then very durable and could be used in the 'Home Corner'. It was cheaper than buying plastic toy loaves and looked better. The remaining varnish had been placed on a shelf. There was probably half a tin left. She was sure that would burn well, it could be used near the initial spark point, to ensure the fire spread onto the paper. Perhaps the tin could be placed under a wooden chair. They had some miniature chairs, they were painted, they would probably burn easily. And the cushions of course, big bags of foam they used for the children to lean against when reading. Or was the foam fire retardant? It might be. Laws had become so picky these days. Everything had rules. Lots of furniture was made to not be flammable. It was annoying. Perhaps the older furniture though, the objects bought by the school many years ago, before all the new policies, that might burn well. It seemed appropriate to Cynthia that the older objects, the things that had been there when she first began teaching, would now conspire to help her. Not that she intended to actually do it, of course. It was just a daydream, something to pass the time.

She wondered how she could ensure she was undetected. Entry to the school was easy, she could simply use her key to access her classroom. All the staff had a key to their own outside door, enabling them to work during the holidays and weekends. She, of course, was not meant to be working at present. She pursed her lips at this thought, a stone of cold rage in her stomach. But she still had her key. Perhaps she should make a copy, hand back the original. Then if it were ascertained that someone had gained access through an unlocked door, she would not be a suspect. She smiled, yes, that was a good idea. She could travel to Tunbridge Wells, that was a big town within easy reach. She could be anonymous there, get a key cut, hand the original back to the school so the supply teacher could have access. Or perhaps one of the London suburbs would be better, somewhere that lots of commuters passed through. Somewhere she would never be remembered.

Her own fire was beginning to die back, so she reached forwards and added a log. That would not be necessary in a burning school, she thought, lots of available fuel there, it could spread undeterred, leaving a wake of destruction as it went from one source of fuel to the next. The walls would remain of course, they were solid stone, been there for centuries, a fire would not touch them. But everything inside, everything that made a school a living vibrant place, would be destroyed. There would be nothing of worth left. Nothing that her successor would enjoy.

She could go to the school at night. She toyed with the idea of taking a taxi so that her car wouldn't be spotted, realised that was ridiculous and thought about where was best to park. Somewhere secluded would mean her car was less likely to be seen. However, if it was seen, it would be remembered. There was a public house within walking distance. She could perhaps park there and hope the number of cars ensured that hers was not remembered. But then she might be seen, worst of all seen by someone who knew her. No, probably the lane behind the school was best. She could wear dark clothes, blend into the night. Perhaps she could hide her number plate somehow. Or park under a coloured light so the colour of her car looked different. She had read that in a detective book once, when she was younger, when she was still influenced by what her friends were reading rather than what was to her own taste.

She picked up her magazine and began to flick through the pages, enjoying the shiny colours, the hint of a smell from a perfume sample. She couldn't read any of it though, her mind was too unsettled to concentrate. Closing the pages she stood. She would get a key cut. She absolutely did not intend to burn down the school, however having a key, retaining something which should rightfully be hers, was appropriate. She would do it today, now, before someone requested that she return her key. It would be most unlucky if the Lancaster woman should turn up at her door unannounced and demand the return of the original before she had had a chance to make a copy.

The thought of a teacher arriving at her door made her scowl. She thought of the Pritchard woman, simpering on her step, pretending to show concern. But Cynthia had seen her, had watched while she laughed at her. She clearly found Cynthia a huge joke. Probably shared a joke with the Smyth boy about how they were well rid of her. Well, they weren't. She had gone nowhere. She would fight them to the end. She had her plan. Not that she intended to enact it, she told herself as she climbed the stairs to her room. It was only pretend.

Cynthia pulled open her cupboard and gazed at her clothes. There were so many. For a moment the effort of making a decision was too much for her and she sank onto the bed. She was so tired. Did it really matter what she wore? Then she thought of someone arriving, demanding that she hand over her key. Yes, it mattered. It mattered very much. She peeled off her trousers and sweater. They smelled. Perhaps she should bathe. No, better to do that when she returned, she would feel better then. She rolled up the dirty clothes and left them on the floor, then crossed to her cupboard.

She would wear something plain, something that would make her blend into the crowd. She would travel to Croydon, find a cobbler there who could cut her a key. There was one at the station, she had noticed him in the past, had heard the screech of his machines as he worked, smelled that acrid metallic smell mingling with the stench of chemicals, the aroma of shoe menders everywhere. A station. Yes, that was a good place to be unobtrusive. She would wear travelling clothes, nice shoes, a smart coat. Perhaps a hat, she had a comfortable one from Marks and Spencer, she could pull it down a little, keep her face in shadow. She could carry a case too. Or perhaps take her little pull-along bag. People would assume she was just passing through, was travelling a distance.

She pulled what she needed from the cupboard and hauled her case from its place under her bed. It felt much too light, she was sure people would guess it was empty. She opened the zip and threw in her dirty clothes, and a book from her bedside table. That would add a little weight. Then, feeling better than she had for days, she left the cottage and drove to the station. She felt almost happy. She had a purpose, she was on a mission.

There was no one who she recognised at the station and she sat next to a window on the train, watching the scenery pass, seeing nothing. She chose a seat in the middle of the carriage, feeling it less likely that someone would walk down and disturb her when there were other empty seats nearer to the doors. As it was half term, there were several families on the train. She had forgotten about that, realised that the chances of meeting someone she had taught were high. However, she was lucky, recognised no one. She took it as an omen.

When she reached Croydon she lifted her case from the train, such a big gap to the platform and no one offered to help her of course, then headed off towards the exit ramp. The station had changed since she had last been there. They had built a lift and a whole new set of stairs so people could reach other platforms easily. But the ramps at the front were still there and she pulled her case up towards the ticket office, walking quickly, hoping the cobbler still had his little stand in the entrance.

The automatic gate ate her ticket and she walked towards the exit. There were a few tiny shops selling magazines and cards, a flower seller and a couple of ubiquitous coffee shops. There was also, nestled between them, the cobbler. Cynthia wondered how many commuters found it necessary to mend their shoes on the way to work. Clearly enough for it to be worth his rent. He was perched on a high stool, reading a newspaper. Cynthia looked at his thin grey hair for a moment, then went over and asked him if he could cut her a copy of her key. She feigned a Scottish accent, hoping to add to her disguise. The man gave her a sharp look and she wondered if perhaps he was Scottish himself, would know she was pretending.

'Let's 'ave a butcher's,' he said.

Cockney accent, that was good. She passed him the key. He nodded, turned around, selected a template and began to cut. Cynthia held her breath, not wanting to inhale the metal dust, feeling the smell of chemicals was already beginning to give her a headache. He handed back the key and the copy, she paid and left, hurrying back to the platform. The man watched her go. He wondered why she had used a funny accent and why she would be wearing a thick coat and a hat on such a warm day. Ah well, you see some funny people in this job, he thought and went back to his paper.

Cynthia returned to the main ticket office and squinted up at the train times. She wished she had thought to bring her glasses, not that they would have fitted with her disguise. She moved closer, standing right in front of another passenger who frowned at her hat, moved to the side so he could still see. The large red numbers came into focus and she saw that she had about twenty minutes to wait until her train arrived. She would have rather liked a cup of tea but felt this was both a waste of money and slightly risky as someone might remember her. Better to wait on the platform she decided. She fed her return ticket into the machine and pulled her case towards the ramp.

Returning home was mostly uneventful. There had been a family who Cynthia recognised waiting on the platform so she had hurried into the Ladies' and waited there until just before the train arrived. It was smelly and her case had been a struggle to fit into the cubicle, she had been forced to wedge it above the toilet seat. Most unsatisfactory. When the train arrived she had crept out, ensuring the family were safely stowed in a carriage near the front then she hurried towards the back of the train, catching someone's ankles with the case as she ran and earning herself a raised finger and a harsh shout of abuse. She settled into her carriage and hoped she had managed to infect them with AIDS from the toilet seat. When she alighted at her station another passenger had attempted to help her with her case. Cynthia had told him very curtly, 'thank you kindly but I can manage', snatching the case away from him. He wondered what treasures were being carried and returned to his seat.

Tommy Martin was in the garden when Cynthia reached the cottage. She saw his thin body stretched over a spade, digging her vegetable patch, from the kitchen window. She returned the case to under the bed, first putting it into a large black sack, very aware it was now contaminated with toilet germs. She had planned to have a bath but felt uneasy with Tommy there. The cottage windows were quite low and she did not know if he would be able to see her silhouette through the frosted glass. She decided his presence was fate, he could be her accomplice. She placed the original key into an envelope and wrote Jane Lancaster's address on it. Better to post it to her home, then it would be received quickly, be out of Cynthia's keeping within a couple of days. She added a short note, explaining that the key to her classroom was enclosed in case it could be of use to the supply teacher. She would collect it on her return to school when she was well again.

She went into the garden.

'Good afternoon Tommy, I wonder if you might do me a service?'
Tommy looked up and grinned.

'I wonder if I might trouble you to go to the post office for me? I am taking medication and unable to drive for the time being. Would you be terribly kind and post this letter? It's quite heavy so you will need to ask them to weigh it and then I need it to be sent first class. If you could be sure to ask them for a "proof of postage" receipt, that would be lovely. Shall I write it down for you?'

'No, that's okay, I'll remember.'

'Thank you so much. Could you go now? I will of course pay you for the whole afternoon. I am rather anxious that it should go, you see. Would that be alright?'

Tommy straightened. This was unexpected. He had only been digging for about half an hour. Going to the post office was a hassle but a lot less time than a whole afternoon's work. He took the envelope from her, noting the weight.

'This might be expensive,' he told her. 'Are you sure you want first class? Second class is almost as quick and would be cheaper.'

'No,' she said sharply. She did not like to be questioned. 'First class. I will give you twenty pounds. Here, give me the receipt and the change when you come next week.' She passed him the money. It was neatly folded in half.

Tommy took it in his muddy fingers and slid it into his back pocket. He took his anorak from the shed and left, leaving the spade standing in the earth, like a sentry on duty. This was a nice piece of luck. He glanced at his watch, decided he would go straight to the pub, he could do with a drink after that digging. Miss Mott would never know if he went to the post office tomorrow, she would blame the postal service for being slow, not him. He slid the envelope into his pocket and wheeled his bike down the footpath, avoiding the thorns from the overhanging bushes. Yes, he could definitely use a pint. His mum might be going to the shops tomorrow, she would take the envelope for him if he asked. He wondered if a 'proof of postage' had the class of postage written on it. If not he may as well send it second class and pocket the extra money. It was going to arrive late now anyway, he reasoned, no harm done, he may as well make a little profit.

When he had gone, Cynthia ran herself a hot bath. She felt better than she had for weeks, as if she had accomplished something of worth. She added some bath salts, a present from a child at Christmas, slid into the warm water. The heavy perfume enfolded her, the steam caressing her skin, easing her tension. She absolutely had no intention of setting fire to the school. That would be an act of lunacy. However, the knowledge that she could, that it was within her means to destroy what they were trying to take from her, was exhilarating.

Reaching for a sponge, she allowed her mind to wander over further possibilities, what she would wear, dark clothes obviously. She should take some matches, just in case the heater plan failed; there was no way to test it beforehand. She wondered about taking some 'false evidence', something to make the police think someone else had started the blaze. Then dismissed the idea as too risky. Better that they should just flounder in the dark with no suspects at all. She squeezed the water over her shoulder, enjoying the tickle. Of course, she should resist the urge to linger once the deed was done. It would be delightful to stay and watch but she would be sure to be seen. Better to leave at once, to hurry to her car parked in the dark lane and to drive straight home. She could read about it in the newspaper afterwards. It would be rather fun. She rose from the water with a great whoosh and pulled a towel from the rail. As she dried herself vigorously she began to plan her lunch.

***

It was the Thursday of half term, when other families were tiring of bored children and Esther had braved a trip to the zoo with her boys, that Cynthia decided to take her plan one step further. Not that it was real of course. But every tiny action towards the end goal confirmed to her that it was possible. That the power was hers if she chose to use it. Not that she would, she was not insane. But owning the ability to wreak havoc was very pleasing.

It was nearing midnight and Cynthia was suffering another sleepless night. She had emptied and tidied her wardrobe and sorted out the heap of magazines that littered the corner of her sitting room. Now she was tired, bored and restless. She considered lighting a fire in the grate, then smiled as she imagined lighting a fire in her classroom instead. She began to wonder if that electric heater was actually still in the stockroom. It had been there for years but she could not be sure if she had seen it recently. It was nagging at her. She was also anxious in case the key she had cut was wrong, perhaps not cut quite true, if when she came to use it, if she ever did, then it would not turn, she would be locked out.

Rather than spend the remainder of the night fretting, she decided to go and find out. She would feel better doing something useful and it would be good to leave the confines of her cottage without the fear of meeting anyone. Plus she still found it exciting to be outside during the night. It would be an adventure.

She pulled on her coat, collected her handbag from the table and set off.

The roads were deserted, the town was asleep. It was a cool clear night. She felt as if she were the only person alive. She passed the school and continued to the junction with the little lane that ran behind the common. She parked as close to a bush as she could, the branches scratching against the side of the car. She hoped they wouldn't leave a mark, a clue for the police, she would have to check that in the morning, perhaps buy one of those little tubes of touch up paint from Halfords.

It was very dark, she wished she had brought a torch. The ground was hard underfoot, probably there would be a frost tomorrow. She felt very exposed walking across the common. An owl hooted and something rustled in the bush behind her. There was a light wind, it pulled at her hair and tugged at her coat as she hurried towards the school. It looked very different in the night, the big windows blank and staring, like a monster waiting to devour her. A car drove along the road, the headlights great eyes, reflecting patterns across the black windows of the school.

When she reached her door she felt in her bag for the key. It sat at the bottom, next to her tissue and comb. Her fingers shook as she fitted it into the lock, took a breath and turned it. The lock was stiff but it slid open. Cynthia smiled.

She opened the door and stepped inside. The room was empty, unfamiliar. She felt very unsafe, watched even and she turned, locking the door behind her, shutting out anyone who might have followed her. She then walked to the light switch and pressed it. The light flooded the room, banishing darkness, monsters and shadows. There was safety in the light, comfort. The room looked as familiar as her cottage, the smells of children and paper and feet mingled to welcome her. This belonged to her.

She decided to check the stockroom, see if the heater still existed. Then she could return home, knowing that her plan, which would never be more than a plan, was truly viable. The corridor was a black tunnel but the light from her room allowed her to see the switch, next to Pear Class and she hurried to press it. She walked quickly to the stockroom, lighting her way as she went, telling herself it was sensible lest she trip on some abandoned object, knowing that the dark unnerved her, made her feel exposed.

When the light in the stockroom was safely illuminated, she

pulled the door shut behind her and went to the far corner. There were two large cardboard boxes, she couldn't lift them but was able to drag them slightly to one side. There, in the corner like a sleeping snake, was the black and white flex that she had hoped to see. Reaching down she felt for the metal back of the heater, found it with her finger, improved her grip and pulled. It was tight, but she managed to haul it over the edges of the boxes and put it in front of her. It sat there, looking at her. It was low, with a curved shiny back to improve radiation and three bars safely placed behind a grill. There was a socket in the stockroom, goodness knows what its purpose was, useful for tonight though. Cynthia lifted the heater so the flex would reach and inserted the plug into the socket. Just to check, to see if it still worked. It did. With a fizzle the bars behind the grill began to glow, to gradually turn from black to red as the heat inched along them. She began to smile, feeling her mission was accomplished when a movement caught her eye. She turned in horror as the stockroom door burst open. With a scream she stepped back, banging her leg against a stack of paper which began a slow steady slide onto the floor.

There, in the doorway, feet apart, ready for battle, stood Mr Carter.

'Cynthia !'

There was a moment. Neither spoke. Both horrified.

Seeing the heater, hearing the hiss and pop as the metal expanded, he stepped forwards, reached for the plug, removed it from the socket.

'Why are you here?' asked Cynthia, suddenly angry. He should not be in the school at this hour, it should have been empty. There was no reason for him to be present.

'I was passing, saw the lights,' he spoke slowly, trying to sort this in his mind. 'Cynthia, what are you doing?' He crossed to her, put an arm on her shoulder, ready to comfort or restrain, whichever was necessary. His police training automatic, keeping him calm, watchful, ready to react. First to secure the area. He needed to move them to a more public area, somewhere that could be overlooked, though who would be looking at this hour was anyone's guess. But remaining in a hidden stockroom was foolish, even during the day. There could be allegations. He needed her somewhere more public, where she was less likely to behave violently. He did not know what he was dealing with here but it looked terribly like she was trying to start a fire in the stockroom.

The warmth of his hand was very real. It woke Cynthia as though from a dream. She saw the scene through his eyes, realised what it looked like, began to explain. But what could she say? She burst into tears. Loud, heaving sobs, water running down her face, a stream from her nose. The crying of a child.

David Carter firmly led her from the room. He left the lights on, took her arm and walked to her classroom. Perhaps she would settle there, calm down, give him some kind of explanation. He wondered if she was mad, if the balance of her mind had completely gone. As a serving officer he had had the power to section someone in this situation, to remove them instantly from the streets and into the care of a professional. He was not sure if he had the same rights as a retired officer, nor whether they were needed but if he felt it necessary he would bluff his way, convince her that she had no option but to accompany him to the station. He needed to make sure she was safe and no danger to anyone.

For the first time in a very long while, David felt a sense of purpose. When his wife had died, leaving him alone and aimless, he had been unable to muster any enthusiasm for anything, especially his job. Taking early retirement, leaving the force, had seemed a sensible decision. It was not a job you could do half-heartedly. He was relatively young and fit, so staying at home, doing the 'normal' retirement activities, golf, sailing, were too old for him. He was not ready for that. Taking a job as a caretaker had seemed ideal. It had filled a gap, given him a reason to get up in the mornings. But he was aware that much of his capacity was under utilised. Most of his skill and talent were never used. He had added boredom to his loneliness. Now, here tonight, he was needed. All his skill as a wise negotiator, the ability to contain a situation and stop it escalating, had woken up. He was himself again.

Cynthia walked to her desk, sat in her chair. David Carter pulled up a table, perched on it, watching her, waiting for her to calm down and speak. There was a box of tissues on the desk and she pulled out several, mopped her face, fought for some control. Her voice was hoarse when she spoke and very quiet. He leaned forward so he could hear.

'I was simply checking the heater. I wanted to know if it worked. It was just a daydream, I never planned to do it. I couldn't sleep you see. I never sleep now. Sometimes I walk at night, it's rather exciting. And I wanted to see if the heater was still there. I was just checking it. But I wouldn't have done it. Not really. I'm not completely insane.'

The words were a torrent, a quiet muttering. She stopped, raised her head, looked at him. It was hugely important that he should believe her. She was not entirely sure herself what would have happened if he had not arrived but she was certain, almost certain, that she would simply have unplugged the heater and left. That was, after all, what she had come to do. It was a fantasy, an imagined adventure. Now it looked horribly like some of it was coming true.

David Carter sat for a moment, deciding. Her intentions seemed somewhat muddled. There was no doubt in his mind that the chances of her doing serious damage had been a distinct likelihood. However, she seemed calmer now and he thought the risk to herself and the school were minimal. That she was under great stress, clinically depressed, was clear.

'Cynthia, since you became ill, have you seen a doctor?'

She was interested that he used her first name. Perhaps now she was no longer deemed fit to teach she did not merit the same respect. She stiffened.

'I am not ill. But yes. Jane Lancaster insisted. I have been prescribed some medication and given leave of absence. I intend to return to my post after half term.'

He stood up.

'Right, I am going to drive you home. You can show me what you have been given.' That would give him a clue as to how astute the doctor had been, if she was receiving the correct care. 'We can decide what to do after that.'

Cynthia opened her mouth to protest. Something in his tone stopped her. He was not behaving like a caretaker; she decided to do as he said.

'I have my own car,' she said.

'We can sort that out in the morning. Where is it parked? The lane? It's safe enough there for now. You shouldn't be driving, not in this state. Come along, let's get you home. Now, which door did you come in by?'

He checked the door was locked and then led her through the school, using his own keys to lock the main entrance behind them. He left the lights on. He did not want to be in a dark school alone with her. She might be frightened. He could return tomorrow and turn them off.

He escorted her to the passenger door of his car and stood close as she got in and put on her seat belt. Memories of accompanying felons flooded back. Not that he thought she was a criminal, just someone who was losing touch with reality a bit.

There was something comforting about being driven. The motion of the car helped to calm Cynthia. She tried to explain that there was nothing wrong, she had intended no harm. She had just needed to check that the key worked because sometimes a new key was cut incorrectly, they could be stiff and not turn. David listened. He did not ask her why she had cut a new key nor what she had intended to do. He wanted to keep her calm, to check her medication, to allow her some rest. Everything else would come later.

When Cynthia pushed open her front door, she felt she had been away for days. It was cold in her sitting room. David led her to a chair and she sat. It reminded her of that day before, when he had been so kind to her. She showed him the pills.

David took the box. He didn't recognise the name but figured they would help a bit. He noted that the packet was unopened and raised his eyebrows at her.

'I am not ill, you see,' she said, keen to defend herself. 'I do not need to take them. They will muddle me. I remember my mother took pills, she was terribly fragile, everyone knew that she couldn't cope, was no use to my father at all. But the pills didn't help. She always said that. They just made her sleep all the time.' She stopped. Sleep seemed terribly attractive right now.

'Cynthia, I think you are ill. I think some chemical in your mind has got itself out of balance, you are not yourself. You must see that you're not. This not sleeping, wandering around at night. That's not you, is it? You are a very sensible person.'

'Yes, I am,' she agreed. Her eyes, very round, shone with fresh tears. 'I am sensible. I seem to have got myself into bit of a mess though. It's because I am so tired.'

David pushed two pills through the foil. They were very tiny and very pink. He held them on the palm of his hand.

'I think these will help you to sleep. I will fetch some water.'

She sat very still, heard him run the tap, fill a glass. His heavy steps returned. He handed her the glass, watched her swallow the pills.

'Now, you are going to go upstairs and sleep. I am going to stay here, in this chair.' He lifted a hand when she started to protest. 'We're not arguing about this. You are not staying on your own and I need to decide what to do. But that can wait until tomorrow. For now you need to sleep. In the morning I will be here and we can have a proper talk, but it's too late now.

'Do you have a spare blanket? Good, I'll come and get it, then I will rest here in this chair. I will not come upstairs, I won't disturb you. But nor will I leave you on your own. Not yet.'

She obeyed. She had no choice really. As she lay in her bed, staring at the ceiling, wondering what the pills would do to her mind, she decided she didn't really mind him being there. It was quite comforting to know he was in her sitting room, in the chair. Would still be there in the morning. She yawned. She closed her eyes, swollen from all that upset and breathed a ragged breath. Then she slept.

Chapter Eighteen

THE day after Cynthia's adventure, Andrew was showering ready for a trip to London with Bai Yun. They had agreed to meet at the station and he planned to take her to the National Gallery, show her Trafalgar Square, then get something to eat. There was an Italian cafe that would be good, not too expensive and they would be sure to have places. He hadn't booked, better to keep their options open, see how it went.

The water rained down on him, not as hot as he might have hoped but good enough for a quick hair wash. The Lynx hair gel foamed nicely, trickling in fat globs down his back as he rinsed off. He would at least smell nice. Did Chinese girls like the same smells as English ones? He wasn't sure. He had his sister to thank for his scrupulous hygiene, the slightest whiff of an armpit when they were growing up and she had treated him like a dustbin. He had soon learned that girls like clean. He stepped out into the cold bathroom and reached for a towel. Sometimes he felt his landlady was slightly mean over electricity bills, could maybe stretch to allowing her lodgers a bit more heat.

He dressed with care, casual but neat – clean jeans, a bit tight from the wash but they would loosen up – combed his hair so the fringe flopped attractively over one eye; checked his wallet, mobile battery, keys. He felt excited as he left the house. Usually first dates were a bit daunting, something to be endured and you just hoped to not mess up too badly. But this one promised to be fun. If he analysed it, he supposed he felt slightly superior to Bai Yun, that if she didn't like something it would be down to her being foreign, not a failing on his part. That took some of the pressure away, made the date a bit less worrisome and a lot more fun. He wondered why he hadn't thought of finding foreign girls before.

Bai Yun was waiting on the platform. So were half the school. Crap, he hadn't thought of that as a possibility. It was half term; the station was full of mothers trying to talk to each other while their kids wandered up and down kicking things and chewing packets of sweets. He did a quick scan, realised he knew at least six of the children, decided he would go to the far end of the platform and do his best to not be noticed.

He approached Bai Yun, smiled, probably still a bit soon to try a kiss, nodded towards the end of the platform and led the way. A couple of mums caught his eye so he gave them a, 'hello, I'm not on duty so don't speak to me' nod. They took the hint, though he guessed he might be the topic of conversation for a few minutes. It was hard to be anonymous when you taught in the town where you lived.

The train was on time and they sat in the first seats in a carriage full of excited children. He didn't think he knew any though. Bai Yun sat next to him. The train was very full and her leg touched his. He could feel the warmth of her through his jeans. He didn't move away. Nor did she, which was definitely a good sign.

She leaned towards him, '*Wei shen me... why...*' she beckoned towards the full coach. He grinned, explained that it was a school holiday. Lots of bored children being taken to London for the day.

The train arrived and they filed out, following the line of passengers towards the ticket barrier, then out onto the street. There was something exciting about London, the noise, the people, the red buses and black cabs, the pollution stained buildings that had stood for centuries. They left the station, turning left towards Trafalgar Square, weaving their way through hurrying people, knocking the occasional shoulder, muttering an apology. The wind was cold and the noise from the traffic made talking difficult. He asked Bai Yun if she had been there before. She nodded, yes, lots of times. They were very near Chinatown.

He had forgotten that. He asked about the gallery, was relieved to hear that no, she had never been inside before, had only stood on the steps to take photos. They climbed up to the entrance hall, then stood for a moment, enjoying the quiet after the bustle of the square outside. Official looking curators with serious faces stood behind desks, people spoke in hushed tones.

Bai Yun took out her purse, ready to pay. Andrew told her that no, it was free, no charge. He knew how to say that, it was a useful phrase when dealing with Chinese people who were often wary of hidden charges. He would have paid for her anyway, his sister had trained him well, he knew that girls liked to be paid for, treated like a lady. Did Chinese girls though? He had no idea. Was not sure he knew how to say that anyway.

Andrew opened a map and asked her which paintings she would like to see. She smiled. He loved that smile.

'I don't mind. All of them?'

He laughed, 'Not all of them. Too many. Okay, let's just wander.' He led the way into the first gallery.

They went up to the second floor and started to wander past Degas, Van Gogh, Cezanne. Bai Yun recognised some of the pictures but not the names of the artists. Andrew was surprised, he thought that the whole world knew about art. They looked at Pissarro, Seurat then onto the Impressionists. He was pleased to see Monet's *Water Lily Pond* still hanging, though it always looked much smaller than he anticipated. He pointed at it, asked Bai Yun if she knew the painting. She looked at the colours, the great swirls of blue, yellows and white, smiled and said yes. But her eyes were shaded, her face said no. He worried that she might be seeing this as some sort of test of knowledge. He would stop asking. He didn't care what paintings she knew or didn't know. He just wanted to kiss her at some point.

They went through into the Great Britain room. There in the centre was Turner's *The Fighting Temeraire*. The mood of the painting always struck him, the browns and dingy yellows, the sadness of the event reflected in the dying sunset. He wondered if he had enough language to convey this to Bai Yun. No, not nearly enough. He settled for 'sad' and 'boat very old'. But she then looked confused and checked were not *all* the paintings old? He tried to explain that yes, they were, but this was an old painting of an old boat. The word for old, the only one he knew, was '*Lao*'. His sentence was a mass of '*Lao*' this and '*Lao*' that. They were both confused.

He gestured towards the leather chair in the middle of the gallery and they sat, absorbing the mood of the painting. He reached out an arm, slid it along the back of the chair. She noticed, didn't move away, smiled up at him. When they stood, he took hold of her hand and they walked through the rest of the gallery holding hands, a couple. A couple who didn't understand much of what was said. Her hand was tiny and fragile, it disappeared almost completely in his. Holding it made him feel very strong, protective.

They wandered through some more rooms, pausing at the paintings they liked. Mostly he was aware that he was holding her hand, that she didn't seem nervous and that people would know they were a couple. This was good. He suggested lunch. She nodded, asked where. He named a few restaurants but she wrinkled her nose.

'You like Chinese food. We go Chinatown. I show you good food.'

'Well, we could. But I'm not eating chicken's feet.' He might as well clarify that straight off. He was willing to try some new food, he liked most Chinese food, but there were limits.

Bai Yun led the way, she knew the streets well. They left Trafalgar Square and strolled up Charing Cross Road. They passed old record shops, book stores, small patisseries. He held her hand and watched their reflection in the windows, decided that they looked a good couple. Then they turned left, into a different world. There were a few tourists but most people were Asian – Chinese or Japanese, he couldn't tell which. He liked walking with a Chinese girl, it made him feel like he belonged.

They went into a tiny restaurant, up some narrow stairs and into a dining area above the street. It was fairly poorly lit but seemed clean. The smells of fried garlic and onions wafted around them, impregnating their hair and clothes, unmistakably Chinese. Bai Yun spoke to the waitress. Andrew listened hard but only understood a couple of words. They were shown to a table and slid into a booth, sat opposite each other. The menu was in English but they brought one in Chinese for Bai Yun. The waitress hovered, did Andrew want a Chinese one too? He waved her away. He would rather know what he was ordering than risk eating something dodgy.

They had a slip of paper and a pencil. The dishes were listed in Chinese and they needed to mark which ones they wanted. Bai Yun took charge. He was surprised by that, had only ever seen her being submissive, shy. She was on her own territory here and was different, more assertive. He liked it.

She asked Andrew what he liked to eat and he picked a few dishes. She added her own choices and gave the order to the waitress, who returned with a beer for Andrew and tea for Bai Yun. He suggested that she could have beer or wine but she giggled, told him her 'jiu liang', her alcohol tolerance, was 'not very big'. This sounded to him like an excellent reason to drink some but thought that maybe it wouldn't be polite to suggest it. Not on their first date. Worth remembering though.

When the food arrived Andrew picked up his chopsticks and

attempted to use them. Bai Yun laughed and showed him how to hold them properly. She took his hand in hers, positioned the chopsticks, showed him how to manipulate them. She then gestured for him to try the food she had ordered. It included a dish of chicken's feet. He made a fuss and she giggled. It didn't look like chicken's feet, it was just skin. It had somehow been slid off the bone. It looked anaemic and greasy. He refused her kind offer and settled for dumplings.

Conversation was still difficult but they managed. They were both relaxed now, she was in her own culture and he had drunk a couple of beers. He asked about her childhood, what school was like. It sounded very rigid, not very 'child centred'. She told him that every day she took a boiled duck egg for lunch. Even from a very young age she had to peel it herself at lunchtime. She told him that she learned to do it very quickly or else she would have eaten a lot of shell. She ate as she talked, often speaking with her mouth full. It was slightly off-putting but he knew that it was just another cultural difference. One he could ask her to change if they got that far. Otherwise he would never suggest they had lunch with his parents.

As they ate, Bai Yun kept his dish full, using her chopsticks to add a constant supply of meat to his bowl. At one point she lifted some chicken's foot, teasing him, waving it towards his mouth as though she would feed him some. He wondered if this was polite, should he also add food to her bowl? He lifted a dumpling, carried it precariously to her bowl with chopsticks, dropped it in. She gave him that smile again, said thank you. Clearly giving food was part of the culture, it was quite nice actually. As long as she didn't try to actually share food, he wasn't so keen on that. His sister would eat his half-finished meals, which was revolting.

They also touched on politics and Chinese history. He asked Bai Yun what her view of Chairman Mao was. He had read several articles that claimed he had been a cruel leader, been responsible for the deaths of thousands of Chinese people, that he had 'invented' a famine to assert control. He also knew that in many places he was still honoured, that in Beijing people still visited his mausoleum.

Bai Yun told him that it was 'complicated'. She said that in many ways he was like Hitler, partly good and partly bad. That was a surprise, Andrew had never heard Hitler described as 'partly good' before, except in *The History Boys* film, when they were trying to be clever. He asked her what she meant, hoped he wasn't starting a relationship with a Nazi sympathiser. She told him that for the country, many of Mao's rulings had been good, he had unified the country and increased their recognition as a world power. For that he should be honoured. But many of his policies were bad, had caused a lot of suffering, for that he should be judged. She took a sip of her tea, slurping loudly. There was a difference of opinion depending on your generation, she told him. The older people, like her grandmother, thought Mao was good. The younger people, her own generation, mostly thought he had been bad. She frowned and narrowed her eyes. It was not an easy question, she told Andrew, she wasn't too sure which side she was on.

They finished the meal with more tea. Andrew sat and sipped from the white china bowl. It was very hot, almost too hot to hold. He slid down slightly in his seat so his knees touched hers. Again, she didn't move away, just looked up at him and smiled. He wanted to move the conversation to something more personal but was unsure how, felt the distance of their cultures. What was appropriate? For a while they just sat, not speaking, watching people pass beneath them on the street.

'Are they Chinese people or Japanese?' he asked her.

'Pob'ly Chinese' she said, 'this Chinatown.'

'But can't you tell? If you see someone in the street? Do Chinese people look different? I know that us Brits all look the same,' he teased. 'But can you tell who's Japanese?'

She turned and looked at his face.

'You not look same. I know your face.'

That was pleasing and he grinned.

'I know Japan people if they speak. Sometimes from their hair or clothes. But not really, faces same as us,' she explained.

He leaned forward, so did she. Their faces were almost touching.

'And are English blokes attractive then? Or do Chinese people only like each other?' He held his breath. That had sounded so corny, real cringe factor. But he was off territory himself here, couldn't read her like he could English girls. He wanted to be sure before he made his move, didn't want to get this wrong.

She smiled up at him and blushed, whispered, 'I think your nose too big but yes, you can be boyfriend, have nice face.'

He let the nose comment pass, leaned even closer, kissed her very gently. This was going exceptionally well.

She screwed up her face, said, 'Smoke.' Kissed him again.

He took her to a park next, somewhere they could find a bench, have a proper kiss without being noticed. Then they walked, looking at the ducks and geese on the lake, enjoying the sensation of walking together. Andrew had his arm around her and she fitted snugly under his shoulder, the top of her glossy head close to his chin. They talked very little, not wanting to stop and use dictionaries, finding it was easier to just point at things as they passed, to talk about the immediate, things that didn't matter if they weren't understood.

Then, at one point, as they stood on a bridge watching the branches of a willow brush the water, he asked about her visa. How long was she able to stay in the country?

He felt her stiffen beside him, pull away slightly. There was a long pause. Then she said, so quietly that he had to dip his head to hear, 'I not have visa.'

At first he thought he had misheard. How could she not have a visa? You wouldn't get into the country without one. Or perhaps she had one and it had expired? 'What do you mean?' he asked, 'Has it expired, run out? Have you been here too long?'

She shook her head, moved away but kept hold of his hand.

'We sit,' she said.

They walked to a bench. It was chilly and he put his arm around her, shielding her from the cold. She seemed embarrassed, unsure of what to say. He wanted to reassure her.

'It's okay,' he said. Though he didn't know if it was okay or not. 'I'm not going to tell anyone, you can trust me.'

'Yes,' she agreed. 'You boyfriend.'

He smiled. He liked her saying that.

'I not have visa. I not have passport. Big problem. But I work hard, not take from country, not be lazy person.'

That was a shock. How could it even be possible? Andrew began to wonder what he had got himself into.

'No passport? Then how did you get into England in the first place? By boat?' Was she one of those people who he saw on the news, crammed into the back of a lorry, smuggled into the country? It didn't fit with the pretty girl who giggled at his jokes, who worked hard to send money home to her parents each week.

'No, I fly. I get plane from China to England. When I arrive they stop me, say I need passport. They take me to room, get translator, explain that no papers, no stay. I sign form to say I un'erstand. They say I have to stay in locked place, tomorrow they fly me back to China. Then man go out room, leave door not locked. So I leave. I have address of restaurant, I go there. They not find me.'

'Which restaurant? The one in town?'

'No, different one. My father, he pay cousin, get address. Tell me to go there, can earn money, have better life.'

Andrew sat, watching the ducks squabble on the bank. This was big. He felt way out of his depth. He'd never been in any sort of trouble with the police, had never wanted to. Did he believe her? He thought he did. There was an innocence about her, a naivety that he found very attractive. It was that child-like quality that made him believe her, to think it possible that she might set out from China with no papers, no money, trusting that the address from her father was all that she needed. Then the determination to leave the airport, to simply walk out from the immigration room, to disappear into an underworld of restaurants. That was brave, something he could admire.

The duck on the bank was cleaning its plumage, digging into its wings with its beak, pulling at the feathers. Some were plucked out and lay ignored on the mud. A treasure for a child to find later. Andrew watched, glad of the distraction. He was aware that Bai Yun had moved from under his arm, was watching him, assessing his reaction.

'You tell police? You not want be boyfriend now?'

'No, no, of course not. And yes, I do.' He pulled her close again, held her protectively. He could feel her through his coat, very small, very strong. She was like a bird herself, tiny and independent.

'I just don't know how that was possible, didn't know people could get in that easily,' he said. 'Which airport? Heathrow?'

'No, was in North. Lot of people come with no passport. All my friends at restaurant, they not have visa, they just arrive. In China, people know this. Just need address, need restaurant in England, place to work.'

'So, what happens if you need help? If you need to go to hospital or to the police?' he asked.

'We not go. We go Chinatown for doctor, very expensive. Not

need hospital. If go to police, they send me back. I not want go back, no work in China. In England I work hard, send money to my mother, have good life...' she paused. 'Have you now,' she added, very quietly.

Andrew sat very still, holding her close. This was all a bit heavy. He liked her, fancied her, wanted a girlfriend. But he wasn't sure if he was ready for this. Was he committing a crime just by knowing? Did the law demand that he should go to the police? And what about her? She was terribly vulnerable, living below the sight of normal life. If the restaurant owner chose to abuse her, to hurt her, to take advantage of her sexually, what could she do? Where could she run to?

On the other hand, he really liked her. His life was, frankly, boring. He was stuck in a job he couldn't afford to leave, dealing with stressy women and little kids. Here was a beautiful, intriguing woman who seemed to like him. She made him feel capable, clever, strong, things he hadn't felt for years. Should he just dump her because she came with some problems? Quite big problems though.

He needed a bit of time to think about this, get some advice. He had a friend from uni who worked at the Home Office, he would know some law, know if he could get into trouble for knowing her. He liked her but he wasn't exactly going to throw away his life for her. At least she had told him early on, before he got too involved. He didn't want to walk away but he could. If he had to, he could. He pulled her to her feet.

'Come on, you'll get cold. Let's walk for a bit.'

When they arrived back in town, they said goodbye at the station. Andrew didn't want to walk to the restaurant with her. He was not quite ready for their relationship to be that public, especially before he had decided what to do. He promised to text her. He could tell from her face, her subdued expression and quiet voice, that she knew he was unhappy, preoccupied. Knew that he didn't know what to do.

He kicked a can as he walked. This was so not what he had planned. In many ways the day had been brilliant, just what he'd hoped. Then she had ruined it. Not that he blamed her, he was glad she had told him, given him the chance to back away before he was in too deep. He just wasn't sure that he wanted to. Ah shit, why was life always so complicated?

As soon as he was home he pulled out his mobile, phoned his friend.

'Hi, Nigel, it's Andrew here, Andrew Smyth. Yeah, long time. How're you doing? Good, good. Listen, sorry to phone out of the blue like this but I've got something I want to ask you about. Have you got a minute? Can I ask some questions?'

They talked. When Andrew finished the call he realised he was still standing in the hall, had been for some time. He went up to his room and flung himself onto the bed, stared at the ceiling. It needed painting, there was a smudge of brown where the roof had leaked years ago. It looked like smoke. It blended well with the beige stains from his own smoke. He reached out and grabbed his cigarettes, inhaled deeply, feeling his lungs relax.

Nigel had been useful. He said that the number of illegals entering via restaurants was well known and largely ignored. They were impossible to trace once they were in the restaurant system, moving freely from job to job, impossible to track. They often used false names and unless they were arrested and fingerprinted, they remained unfound. He said that mostly no one in authority cared too much. They worked hard, provided a service to the community and other than not paying tax were pretty much law abiding. The amount of money needed to find them, detain them, deport them, just wasn't worth the tax payer's money.

What usually happened was they stayed in the country, working hard and staying out of trouble, under the radar, until they had lived in the country for long enough. After you had lived here, self-sufficient, for a certain amount of time, then you could apply to stay permanently. The amount of time was changing all the time. It used to be seven years, then went up to eleven. He wasn't sure now exactly how long it was, could check if Andrew wanted to know. It wasn't a fact the Home Office tended to advertise, obviously. Either that or they married an English citizen. Or, if they were female, they got pregnant. It didn't matter if they were pregnant by an English man or not, the fact of having a baby on UK soil was usually enough to ensure they could apply for permanent residency.

As for Andrew himself, he was safe enough as long as he didn't try to smuggle anyone into the country. Or employ someone who was illegal, there were big penalties now for doing that. Not knowing was no defence, an employer was expected to check, to know that everyone on the payroll was allowed to be in the country. Probably a bit dodgy if he offered a place for someone to stay too, being a landlord for illegals wasn't a good idea.

Then he asked why Andrew was asking, was he planning to drive some truckloads over to supplement the lousy teacher pay? He had laughed, explained that he was teaching in the restaurant, wasn't sure what his position was if any of his students were illegal. Thanked him, finished the call. Now he needed to think.

For the first time, he began to wonder what Bai Yun herself had sought to get from the relationship. Had she seen him as a route to residency? Was he a convenient male who might be able to father a child or offer marriage? Had she had a plan all along? He didn't think so, preferred to think she was innocent, liked him, was as keen to try out a relationship as he was. But he was no fool, it was a distinct possibility that she had an ulterior motive. Did he care? Yes, he did. That was a deal breaker as far as he was concerned. He was nobody's meal ticket.

But what if she hadn't? She had offered the information freely, he hadn't found out from one of the others. What if she sincerely liked him, wanted to have an honest relationship and so had decided to tell him early, knowing she would risk losing him. Did he want to throw away something that could turn out to be really special?

He sighed and ran his fingers through his hair, leaving it mussed and unruly. He would like another cigarette but was trying to cut down, was a bit concerned he had a cough developing that he didn't like, thought he would quit before he did any major damage. He glanced at the time. Six o'clock. He would allow himself another smoke at seven, then that would be it for the day.

He tried to imagine how he would feel if he didn't know she was illegal. Had he enjoyed the date anyway? Yes, mostly he had. He still got a thrill from looking at her, feeling the silk of that long hair on his arm, kissing her. All very nice. And he admired her, thought she was brave and strong and interesting. But the language was bit of a pain, if he was honest. They could communicate but not really chat. The few proper conversations had been hard work, lots of checking things on his phone, a bit stilted. That would get easier, obviously, but it was a factor, something to consider. He wasn't going to be having any heartfelt dialogues any time soon. He liked what he knew of the culture, liked that women seemed to be happy to let the man lead, that wives still tended to cook for their men and look after them a bit. But was it worth the other stuff? Could he cope with all the problems? Did he want to? If he kept the relationship going, would a bit of him always wonder how much she liked him and how much he was just an available English man?

He groaned and rolled off the bed. This was too hard, too much effort. He would get something to eat and think about it tomorrow. His mum always told him to sleep on a big decision, he decided it was good advice. Plus his head was beginning to ache with it all now. He went downstairs and started to search through the fridge for something easy to eat.

***

The next morning, after a sleepless night, he was still no nearer deciding. He stood in the kitchen making tea, his feet cold on the hard flooring. The thought of keeping the relationship going for a bit longer, enjoying her physically while knowing he was never going to commit to anything, was very attractive. But he also knew that would be wrong, his upbringing had instilled a certain respect towards women that he couldn't ignore, much as he would like to. He was too old to muck around now, he had to behave like a grown-up. He thought he would try and delay things a bit, put her on hold. Let her know that he was worried; though he was pretty sure she had picked that one up already, but not end anything yet. Not that there was much to end, they had barely got started he thought wryly, adding milk to his tea.

He knew that such a conversation should be had in person. He also knew that the vocabulary was beyond both of them. Plus her next day off was a week away and he would see her at the restaurant on Friday when he went to do his lesson. Better to sort it now, send a text, not keep her hanging on wondering if he was going to write.

He took his tea upstairs and balanced it on a book. Pulled some paper from a folder, an old lesson plan, that would do, began to write. He copied the characters from his phone dictionary, tried to think about the grammar, planned what he wanted to say. Then he wrote it into a text.

He said he had enjoyed the day and that he really liked her. He was very busy for the next few weeks so probably it would be best if they stayed as just friends for a while. He hoped that was okay.

He looked at what he had written. He had included both the English words and the Chinese characters, hoping that between the two she would work out what he wanted to say. He wasn't sure if the word for 'friend' and the word for 'boyfriend' were the same, wasn't sure if it was clear. He hoped so. It was the best he could do. He pressed send and reached for his tea.

Before he had finished drinking, while he was still holding the warm cup and deciding whether to make toast or have a shower first, a reply came.

He read, 'That is okay. I understand. Thank you.'

He stared at it for a long time. What did she mean? Did she really understand? He swore and threw the phone onto the bed. Then he went for an almost hot shower.

Chapter Nineteen

Esther made her decision three weeks into the second half of term. It was not difficult; she did not agonise over it or have sleepless nights. She knew that something had to change, the idea presented itself to her and she instantly knew it was the right thing to do. She decided to tell Jane this morning, to start the ball rolling as it were. She drove to school carefully, her day planned, her decision made. She had told Rob, asked him what he thought. Not that she needed his opinion, she had known at once that it was the right thing to do. Had known the moment she thought about it and the uncomfortable ball of stress that had lodged in her stomach dissipated, leaving a warm calm peace, confirming that this was right.

She turned into the school grounds and parked next to Jane's car. Good, she was already here, Esther could pop in to see her straight away, make an appointment to see her later. Or tomorrow. There was no hurry other than politeness. It was rare that a personal decision should affect others so deeply but Esther knew that this was one of those occasions. She pulled her bags from the boot and slammed it shut with a satisfying thump.

As she walked to her classroom, she noticed that Cynthia's door was open. She put her head round and called hello. Cynthia looked like she was trying to climb into a cupboard. She straightened and waved.

'I am attempting to reorganise some of this mess,' she told Esther. 'It seems to have got away from me rather.'

Esther smiled in acknowledgement. She certainly knew how that felt. She went to her room. Cynthia was so much better now, the break had obviously done her good. She had returned a week ago, was more tired than before perhaps, left a little earlier than she had in the past. There seemed to be some kind of agreement with Jane, Cynthia taught her class but did not attend assemblies or staff meetings. Her work load was reduced. But she seemed more in control, had sorted out her appearance, was back to the Cynthia they all knew. It was as if her body had been present for a few months but her mind and personality had disappeared and become someone else. Esther was glad she was back. She realised she had missed her.

Cynthia struggled to pull the last few folders from the back of the cupboard. They escaped from her grasp and slid to the floor, their slippery covers sliding over each other, spreading out, shedding loose pages as they went. She sighed. Her room was in such a muddle. She was disappointed with herself for not noticing sooner, for letting things get so muddled. But that was all part of the illness. It was an illness, she knew that now.

After that terrible night, the stuff of nightmares, things had begun to improve. David, she thought of him as David now, had, as promised, been sitting in her chair when she woke. He was a strangely assertive David, taking charge and not allowing her choices. First he had given her tea. Rather weak tea but it was hot so she had drunk it without comment. Then he had informed her that he was going home to shower and change and that she should do the same. He would return in forty minutes and drive her to the surgery. They were going, together, to see a doctor. He would be present at the beginning, he wanted to give some information to the doctor, be sure they knew the situation. Then Cynthia would have her consultation. They would decide, by this she was aware that he meant he would decide, what needed to be done after that. She had informed him that getting an appointment within a week of requesting one was quite impossible, that she did not require medical help and it was a gross waste of resources, that she was grateful for his help, but he had clearly misunderstood the situation last night and she was completely able to make decisions about her day by herself. He ignored her and left, saying he would return in forty minutes.

They had gone to the surgery. Her own doctor had been unavailable so they saw someone else, a man whom Cynthia did not know. She wondered how David had managed that, what he must have told them. Perhaps being an ex-policeman still held some sway. She didn't know.

The doctor had listened, made many notes. He had kept his face expressionless but had asked a lot of questions, especially irrelevant ones about her mother's health. Had Cynthia known what medication she took? She did not. Did she know the nature of her problem? She did not. She only knew that her mother was weak, flighty, lived in her own world much of the time, was no help to her father. That had been Cynthia's job, to fill the void, to be his support. Her mother was a lazy woman, sleeping for much of the day, unwilling to change her schedules for anything, even if there was an emergency. 'Not now,' she would tell Cynthia, 'I can't do that until I have had my rest.'

The doctor had written her a new prescription, told her, 'you might not notice any effect for a couple of weeks', but she could return to school after another week at home if she felt well enough. Then Cynthia had left and sat in the waiting room, like a child waiting for a parent talking to a teacher, while David and the doctor had a discussion. She was not sure if this was legal, didn't break some doctor/patient confidentiality. Perhaps the policeman thing was a factor. She had given her permission of course, when the doctor asked her view. She was still uneasy about last night, about the possible consequences.

She had then spent another week at home. David had visited regularly and she had taken her pills. She slept a lot at first.

Being back at school was like a tonic. She found she was worrying less, things seemed less important. There were also fewer omens, she no longer received subliminal messages, took things at face value. She was waiting for an appointment to see a specialist, some kind of mental health expert. Not that she thought that was necessary now but David had made it a condition for not going to the police, not telling them what he had found that evening in the stockroom. She had complied.

***

Andrew had not had a good few days following his trip to London. He had attended his lesson with Mrs Wang but not understood very much. They were studying shopping, how to ask to try on new clothes. It didn't interest him and the new vocabulary washed over him. He had thought constantly of Bai Yun, wondering if he had made a huge mistake, let something that could have been good, special even, escape. He had not felt better after he had sent his text. It had nagged at him, like a child beggar tugging at his clothes. He found he could think about little else.

When he did his usual pub visit with Trevor and Harry he found he didn't want to talk about Bai Yun. Usually he had a funny story for them, something from school or the restaurant. But not that day. Talking about the restaurant, mentioning Bai Yun even in passing, was too close, too uncomfortable. Instead he talked about school, told them about the possible redundancy. He knew he shouldn't, was breaching professional confidentiality. But you had to talk to someone, didn't you and these were his mates, unconnected with the school.

He had told them about Miss Mott, wondered if he could assume his job was safe now, now that she was off on sick leave for something weird. He didn't say she was drinking too much, left it vague, just in case he was wrong about that. Not that he thought he was.

Trevor said it was more complicated than that. They had had some redundancies at the bank a couple of years back and the law was pretty tight. He talked a lot about 'fair process', having to show that everyone had been treated equally, had the same chance to keep their job. It depended on the criteria the governors decided on for who should go, if it was purely financial or would be based on experience, what someone would bring to the school. If Mott was ill then unless the illness impacted her job, meant she couldn't do it any more, then it couldn't be taken into account, was irrelevant. Andrew was pretty sure that drinking too much would impact her job, she would be declared unfit to teach. If that was what was wrong of course. He finished his own drink, his second, considered a third. Decided he was probably drinking too much himself. Drinking too much and smoking too much. He would cut down on both. Start next week. He ordered a third round but didn't suggest shots.

As the hours had passed, Andrew had begun to feel more and more uncomfortable about the decision he had made. Sitting there in that pub, his back pressed against the hard wooden back of the chair, he watched a group of girls. They were probably on their way to a night out, all dressed up in heels they couldn't walk in and sparkly tops that showed more flesh than they hid, faces made up with dark eyes and red mouths. Quite pretty a couple of them, all looked English, all looked boring. They kept gazing round the pub, laughing a bit too loudly, looking to see who had noticed them, who might come over and join their group. Not Andrew. He realised they held no interest for him, it was like looking at painted plastic when he had seen a real jewel, something a bit different, something of value.

He had finished his drink and told his mates he was heading off. He walked back to his car, aware of a heaviness, the feeling he had made a big mistake. He would text her again, try to change things back to where they were. Yes, he had decided, he wouldn't wait until Friday, he would send her a text as soon as he got home. Tell her he'd been thinking, the day had been fun, maybe they could do it again. He would worry about the visa thing later on, after he knew whether they had a good thing together or not. When he knew for sure if she would be worth the hassle of getting it sorted.

He had sent the text but received no reply. That worried him. Then, on the Friday he had found out why. He had turned up at the restaurant as usual, perhaps a bit earlier, perhaps a bit more eager. He had wanted to see Bai Yun, to ask if she had got his text. He would watch her face, see if she looked pleased to see him or not. Except, he hadn't. He hadn't even seen her.

When he arrived at the restaurant, the manager had let him in as usual, gone to fetch his students, brought him tea. There was something about her manner, a sort of hidden excitement that Andrew had picked up on, wondered what it meant. Then the others had arrived, Lao, Cheng Zhi, Shao Ling. But no Bai Yun. He had asked, where was she, was she ill? Not coming today? He wondered if she was too embarrassed to see him, if he had upset her by the first text and perhaps she had never seen the second. He thought it was good that he was here, he could ask them to get her, would try to explain even though it would be embarrassing with an audience. But he would try, try to put it right.

But he had not had the chance. It was Lao who told him, had seemed pleased to tell him, his mouth curved like it was a huge joke. He had said that Bai Yun had left. She was missing China too much so had gone home. She wouldn't be there any more.

Andrew had looked into his smiling face and known he was lying. Bai Yun had no passport. She couldn't just decide to go home and catch a flight, even if she had had the money. He was lying but Andrew didn't know what the truth was. Was she there and hiding? Had she left? Was she in some sort of trouble? He had nodded, played along, acted like he believed Lao and it was no big deal. Then he had done his lesson, automatically going through the worksheets he had planned, helping them to learn English while resenting the time, wanting to leave this place where they all smiled and lied so easily. This place where he didn't really belong.

He had been glad to go back to school after the weekend, to have something else to think about. The children had distracted him, helped him to not spend every minute thinking about Bai Yun, wondering if he ought to do something, should try to find her. Maddy had noticed he was tense; the half term break had done nothing to refresh him. He was short with her a couple of times, snapped at the children. She wondered what was wrong, decided it was probably girl trouble, would pass soon enough.

Andrew told Esther about it. He hadn't meant to, wasn't really the sort of thing you did talk about. Unless you were female. Females talked about everything, the more personal the better it seemed. But he was a bloke, not much given to 'sharing'. Private meant private. You talked about things, what was happening, maybe the odd discussion about footie or politics. But not your private life, stuff that was worrying you. Who wanted to hear about that?

They had been in the staffroom. Jane had swept in and rushed out again, muttering about prospective parents and budgets and she hadn't forgotten Esther, would wait for her after school. Cynthia Mott had not appeared. She had started going for a walk at lunchtimes, sometimes with Mr Carter. Andrew wondered if that was a 'thing', if she was making moves on him. He hoped not, Carter was a nice bloke, why would he want to get saddled with that old trout? He had decided to ask Esther, see if she had noticed anything. She confirmed that yes, she had seen them together but she assumed they were just friends. They had, after all, worked in the same school for years now and they were a similar age. She thought it was rather nice. Then she asked if Andrew was seeing anyone special.

He'd said no, of course, keen to move the conversation on. Then he'd admitted that there was a bit of a problem actually, things weren't going as well as he'd hoped. Esther had listened. She was good at that, sort of neutral, non-judgemental, a bit removed. It was like she was in a different emotional place to the rest of them, saw things differently. Perhaps having kids did that to you, changed your priorities. Anyway, whatever the reason, she was easy to talk to and he was stuck for ideas, so he talked. He told her about the lessons, about getting to know Bai Yun and deciding to take it further. He told Esther they had been to London during half term and got on really well. Then how Bai Yun had told him about the visa and he had chickened out, felt that he couldn't handle it. Then afterwards he'd got to thinking a bit more clearly and realised he'd made a mistake, been a bit hasty. Tried to change back again. But they'd told him she had gone and she wasn't answering her mobile and he was worried. Worried and pissed off at himself for being an idiot.

Esther hadn't spoken for a while. She thought about what he was telling her. Then she asked why he was so sure that Lao was lying to him, was it possible that Bai Yun had been deported? Andrew said no, he thought it was a bit quick for that. Well, agreed Esther, it did seem to be a bit of a dead end. But he shouldn't give up hope just yet. Maybe the girl had been upset, felt rejected. Perhaps in a couple of weeks, when she had recovered a bit, she would feel better and contact him. There was no reason to think she hadn't got the text. Esther also said she thought he shouldn't judge the rest of his students so harshly. She understood that he could tell Lao was laughing at him and maybe he was. But that didn't mean they all were. Chinese people were as different as English people. If she worked with someone a bit nasty, a bit quick to lie, that wouldn't mean that she was like that too. Why didn't he try and talk to one of the other girls? See if they could help him at all.

He thought that might work, he would give it a go. He thanked her, told Esther she was good at listening and giving advice. He supposed that came from being married to a vicar. He would have to be careful not to say too much in future, he laughed, now they were supposed to be on different sides, competing for the same jobs.

Esther had paused. 'That's nice of you to say so,' she said. 'Actually, I've been thinking about that a lot lately, about being married to Rob and the job and everything.' She stopped. She didn't know how much to say. She hadn't even talked to Jane yet. She brushed some crumbs from her lap and pulled her bag onto her knee. Best to not say too much, not yet.

***

Esther found Jane in her office after work. The children had all been returned to their mothers and carers, rushing from the school in a mass of coats and lunch boxes, bursting with things to say. They left a trail of lost plimsolls, forgotten paintings, broken pencils. They always did. The teachers had returned to their rooms collecting lost items as they went, it was like fruit picking Esther sometimes thought. She had tidied her room and filled out her records book. Then she had gone to find Jane, she could think about her plans for tomorrow later, she wanted to get this over with.

As she pushed open the office door, Esther noticed her stomach was churning, she was nervous. She smiled at Jane, who scooped her papers into a heap and beckoned for her to take a chair. Esther sat on the low green sofa next to the desk. The 'naughty chair' she always thought, reserved for misbehaving children and teachers who needed to be spoken to. Jane smiled, her eyes tired.

'Would you like some tea?'

'No, thank you,' said Esther. She just wanted to get this done. She was sure that her decision was the right one but now that she was actually telling Jane about it, making it definite, limiting her choices, it felt a little scary. 'I wanted to talk to you about our jobs, about the redundancy.'

Jane nodded. She wondered where this was going. She certainly had no new information to give if this was a fishing trip.

'Well, I love my job,' began Esther, 'and it's actually been really important to me, helped to give me something outside of the home, away from Rob's job.' She stopped. A rush of emotion flooded her mind and her eyes filled with tears. Goodness, she did hope she wasn't going to cry. That wouldn't help at all. Perhaps she should have accepted the tea. She coughed, trying to give a reason for her pause. 'The thing is, it's got more difficult lately. Rob would like me to do more in the church...'

'No', she thought, that sounded wrong.

'I would like to be able to do more in the church,' she corrected. 'But there is never enough time. You know how that is.'

Jane smiled. She certainly did. If she had forgotten the demands of a class during her time as a head teacher she had certainly remembered them again during her weeks covering Cynthia's class. Not that she'd hated it. In fact, once she had got used to it, had organised some sort of routine, she had enjoyed it. She had realised how much she missed, stuck away in her office, juggling meetings and paperwork. But doing both had been near to impossible. Like Esther said, there was never enough time.

'There's also the boys,' continued Esther. 'I thought when they were older they would be less work but actually that's not true. They need less of me physically, I can leave them in the house on their own, but emotionally I worry that I'm short-changing them. I seem to be stretched in all directions.' Again those tears, threatening to spill, her throat tightening with emotion. 'I love my boys,' she wanted to cry, 'I love my family, I love them and I'm failing them all. I don't have enough energy to give to them.' She breathed, took a minute. It was getting dark outside already, she was ready for spring now. Ready for a change.

'Anyway, I've been thinking. I was wondering if there's any way that I could work part-time. Could my job be a job share? Would that save enough money, if you employed someone cheap, so there wouldn't have to be a redundancy? At least not yet, you would have a bit longer before the governors had to decide?' She stopped.

Jane was frowning now. This was moving beyond Esther's role, was not necessarily linked to what she decided about her own job. The governors and Jane would decide what happened, that wasn't for the staff to think about. However, she did have a point. Esther being part-time would not save much money. Unless the other part of the job share was Jane herself. Could she do it? She liked being in the classroom, maybe this was a solution. She picked up her pen and fiddled with it, drew some circles on the paper in front of her. This was certainly worth some thought. She added some shading to the circles, then looked back to Esther.

'Is this definite? Are you formally telling me that you want to be part-time? I obviously can't give you an answer now, I would have to take it to the governors. But if it's not a viable option, you might be throwing away your chances of staying. They might decide that you should be the one to go. You realise that, don't you? I think you're great, would be sorry to lose you. But they won't understand really, they'll just think you're less keen than the other two.'

Esther nodded, she understood that. She knew that even having this conversation would be a catalyst, would cause a change that she might not be able to stop. 'Yes, I know,' she said. She thought for a moment about the money, about the things the boys would have to forgo, the fuss they would make. Then she reminded herself that they were older now, they could get paper rounds or garden work soon, earn their own spending money. And it was like Rob said, it was just money.

For too long she had felt that she was fighting for her right to be independent, her right to have a life that was separate from the church, from Rob's job. But that was beginning to mean that she was also separate from Rob, that her time and energy were so wound up in what she did at work that she resented the bit of her that needed to support Rob. She had never wanted that. She could see that in fact the church did get 'two for the price of one', that if she was going to be a 'proper' wife, to give Rob and the boys what they needed, what they deserved, then she needed to let that resentment go. She needed to give more of herself to the family. She wanted to stop fighting.

Jane told her she would take it to the governors and see what they said. She thanked Esther for her candidness, hoped they could work out something that pleased everyone. Esther got up, thanked Jane for her time, went back to her classroom. She would miss the money of course, it had been nice to afford little treats. Not enough for anything big, but it had meant the boys could have most of the same things their friends had. She would have to let go of that, hope they coped with being a bit more 'different', having the oldest model of mobile, the cheapest brand of clothes. She began to stuff folders and books into her bag. 'Just money', she said to herself. 'Just money.'

She lifted the bag. It was made from some sort of sacking, probably came from a charity catalogue. The stitching began to stretch alarmingly, the load too heavy. Esther sighed and lowered it back onto the table. She bent her knees, hooked her hands under the bag and lifted it, hugging it to her like a baby. A lumpy heavy baby with sharp corners that dug into her chest.

'I never wanted to marry the minister', she reminded herself, 'I fell in love with the man, not the job.' But Rob was the minister, being his wife meant she was the minister's wife. She had played her part well, acting out the role she found herself in but never really becoming it, never really letting herself lose the resentment every time it infringed on what she saw as her real life. Well, she was letting go now, she thought as she carried her load into the corridor. She was going to stop pretending and start being. She was going to embrace this job as willingly as she had embraced the man. Fifteen years late, maybe, but hopefully not too late.

In the corridor, she nearly collided with Andrew Smyth who bounced out of his classroom. His smile was huge.

'Esther. Glad I caught you. You were right. I texted Shao Ling, the other girl. She told me Bai Yun changed her number, the last one was a work phone, she had to give it back when she left. I've got her new number, already sent her my text.' His hair flopped over his eye and his grin was all consuming. He looked very young.

'He looks like one of my boys,' thought Esther, a wave of affection catching her. She repositioned the bag, earning herself a new bruise in her ribs.

'That's marvellous Andrew. Did she say where Bai Yun is? Is she still in the country?'

'She certainly is. London. Apparently moving suddenly is normal, might not be my fault.' He hoped not, hoped that his nerves hadn't caused her to flee. Even if it was his fault, he had a chance now to put it right.

'Well done,' said Esther, beginning to walk away. 'Let me know if she replies,' she called over her shoulder, wanting to leave. The day had been emotionally draining. She needed that cup of tea now. Tea and her boys. They would take anyone's mind off anything.

She smiled as she thought of them, the bag rough against her skin, heavy in her arms. She was glad to reach the car and lower it into the boot. The lid slammed shut with a bang and she climbed into her seat. Home now.

***

Jane was still sitting in her office, phone in hand. It was warm against her cheek and she sat for a moment, letting thoughts wash through her mind, her body immobile. She had spoken to James Bird, the chairman, put her plan to him. Esther could teach part time, maybe three fifths. Jane would cover the rest. Her pay would remain the same but she didn't mind that. The money saved by Esther's reduced hours would possibly be enough. The numbers were beginning to pick up for the following year, they might be able to delay a redundancy for a year. Perhaps indefinitely. They could keep three classes though. It would mean more work for her but she liked the idea of some regular teaching and Esther could do all the boring bits, the parents' evenings, the reports, the records. It would be easier for her, she was used to it. She moved her hand, put the receiver back on the telephone. It dinged.

Yes, she thought it was a good plan, hoped the governors would accept it. James Bird had hummed and hah-ed a bit, but that was just him, he was always like that, never liked to commit. But she thought the numbers added up, she looked again at her jottings on the pad in front of her. She would push them, get them to agree. Then she would tell the staff. Poor things, they'd been under enough tension this year, it would be nice to relieve some of that stress. She dropped her pen into the carved wooden pot on her desk.

'Competition,' she thought, 'was not always a good thing.'

***

Andrew was the last teacher to leave that day. His classroom was tidy and his paper for the next day sat in a colourful heap on his desk. He had forgotten to turn off the lights but David Carter would do that, sighing at the wasted electricity.

As he drove home, he felt his phone vibrate. He slid it from his pocket at the traffic lights. It was from Bai Yun. She would like to meet him. Day off Wednesday. He grinned and turned the CD volume up. Some things were just meant to be, he thought, just meant to be.

More books by Anne E Thompson

See the website: anneethompson.com
for details of publishing dates.

Counting Stars

THE guest house had three stories. She knew this, just as she knew they were connected by both the wide main stairs and the narrow hidden steps originally used by the servants. She chose the wide stairs, her hand skimming the smooth oak bannister as she climbed.

She wanted the third floor. The first two floors were the regular rooms, often used by families who booked two or three at a time. There were standard doubles, large twin bedded and tiny single rooms. Each one boasted a sink but the guests had to leave the safety of their room if they needed the bathroom. There was a selection of bathrooms with over bath showers and single cubicle toilets placed conveniently along both floors.

But the third floor was special. The third floor was where the en suite rooms lived. Each room had a double bed, matching furnishings and a small private bathroom, for guests who could afford the en suite tax, who could afford a little luxury. They were at the top of the house (if one does not include the attics, which had been renovated for the staff to use) and they enjoyed a view of the sea. A tiny view. A glimpse really, between the tree tops.

However, it was not to one of these rooms she went. It was to the rather unnecessary extra bathroom. It sat between two rooms, tucked back in an alcove. The wood slatted door was painted to match the other doors and would have been easy to miss, angled as it was away from the landing, almost as if trying to hide. A shy door. But she knew it was there and cautiously opened it.

Inside was what one might expect to see in an upstairs

convenience. Behind the door as you entered, on the left, was a white china toilet with high water closet and old fashioned chain for flushing. Opposite it, on your right as you entered, was a white sink. It had been tastefully littered with miniature soaps and scrubbed sea shells.

None of this interested her. It was as she remembered. She went straight to the cupboard. It was set in the wall to the left of the toilet, opposite the door. It was raised a good four feet from the floor and reached nearly to the ceiling. The door was tongue and groove, painted white to match the chinaware. There was a small lock on the right and she was relieved to see the key was still in it. They had always kept the key there for fear it would be lost, some traditions never change. It seemed unlikely that a guest would bother to open the door even if they ventured in to use the toilet.

She reached up and turned the key. It was small and stiff but it ground its way round and the door swung open.

Inside there were no tidy piles of linen or spare toilet rolls. There were steps. Great stone steps which led up and away.

Smiling, she closed and locked the door, putting the key safely in her jeans' pocket. She could feel it there, digging into her hip. She would come back later with the family.

***

It was dark when she returned and very late. She first woke the mother who seemed to be expecting her. They spoke little as they gathered some warm clothes, pushing them into a small backpack. Then they woke the children together, the mother going first into the room, hushing them, telling them it was an adventure, they needed to be quiet. She had worried they would speak in their high child voices, voices that seem to penetrate so clearly, and wake someone. But they were older than expected, the boy almost as tall as his mother, at that lanky thin stage that so often precedes manhood. They seemed to catch the mood of the adults and compliant with sleepiness they allowed themselves to be dressed and guided up the stairs.

She could tell the mother was surprised to be taken into the small washroom. She held her children close to her and watched silently as she first locked the door and found the key to the cupboard. They all peered in, stared at the steps, wondered if their legs were long enough to climb those big slabs of stone. Would the girl manage? The mother spoke a single word,

'Up?'

She nodded, understanding the question, knowing the answer.

And so they climbed. First onto the lowered lid of the toilet, using it as a first giant step, then into the cupboard. She went last, helping the mother, passing her the girl, helping the boy. She squeezed in behind them, twisting to pull the door shut, turning the key, delaying anyone who might follow. They went up and round.

The steps, which you might have assumed, as the mother did, would descend, first went up. They climbed steeply, turning as they went, following the line of the chimney breast. Then a straight section, long and thin with a slight draught that made them shiver. The floor was different here; weathered floorboards and they knew they were crossing a section of the attic, hidden from view behind the thick stone walls. Then at last, down. The steps were built into the ancient walls, unseen, long forgotten by all but a few.

It was very narrow. The boy caught his elbow on the rough stone wall and cried out, angry with the wall, angry with himself. His sister's eyes grew very large as red blood oozed from the cut and they wondered if she might cry. The mother touched her hair, comforting and warning in one smooth stroke. Then she bent, sucked the wound clean, her eyes telling the boy to be brave, he was a man now. Then they continued, down, down. The girl almost jumping, the steps were so tall, clinging onto the back of her mother for support. Down, down. Below the second floor, then the first, then the ground. Into the earth.

The steps finished and they faced a tunnel. Long and dark. A passage with no end. Where monsters might live. She snapped on a torch and the monsters retreated, back into the gloom beyond the beam. They walked on.

The floor was earth, hard and dry. Then stones, then rock, carved by men long ago, deep under the ground. The rock was shiny in places, she worried they might slip and they all took a hand, turning slightly to walk in pairs along the narrow tunnel. On and on where once they had walked down. Not stopping, not speaking, though she knew they now could. For they were under the sea and no one would hear but mermaids and crabs. But what would they say? Words would only stir emotions and they needed to be locked away until there was room to set them free. Later, much later.

The girl started to slow, for the walk was a long one. She thought of her bed, of the dreams she had left and began to whine, to make tiny whimpering sounds. The boy was silent, just looked at her, his eyes unreadable.

Still they went on. The air was stale and chill but they were moving and not cold. It smelled of sea and salt, and mermaids' hair. Still holding hands, almost dragging now, wondering if they could make it, wondering how long to go, how far to return.

Finally, they arrived. The passage widened, began to slope upwards, then four rough steps hewn from the rock and then sand, soft and damp, clinging to their shoes, creeping into their socks. They came up, out of a cave and she saw they had arrived. The sky was black and starless when she turned off the torch. Their faces were very white.

Still silent she turned. First she hugged the mother, pushing hope and strength into her. Then the girl, lightly and with affection. Then she hugged the boy, roughly, willing him to be brave, to take his father's place. Then she left them, turning swiftly away and dipping back into the cave. They were on their own now.

Counting Stars is now available from Amazon as a Kindle book.

Joanna

I FIRST saw them on the bus. They got on after me, the mother helping the toddler up the big step, holding the baby on her hip while she juggled change, paid the driver. I wondered why she hadn't bought a card or paid by phone, something quick so we didn't all have to wait. I watched as she swung her way to a seat, leaning against the post for support, heaving the toddler onto the chair by his shoulder.

Then they sat, a happy family unit, the boy chattering in his high pitched voice, the mother barely listening, watching the town speed past the window, smiling every so often so he knew he had her attention. Knew he was loved. Cared for. They had everything I didn't have but I didn't hate them. That would have involved feelings and I tended to not be bothered by those. No, I just watched, knew that those children had all the things, all the mothering, that had passed me by. Knew that they were happy. Decided to change things a little. Even up the score, make society a little fairer, more equal.

Following them was easy. The mother made a great deal about collecting up their bags, warning the boy that theirs was the next stop. She grasped the baby in one hand, bus pole in the other and stood, swaying as we lurched from side to side. She let the boy press the bell button, his chubby fingers reaching up. Almost too high for him. Old ladies in the adjoining seats smiled. Such a cosy scene, a little family returning from a trip to the town. They waited until the bus had swung into the stop, was stationary, before they made their way to the door. I was already standing, waiting behind them.

The mother glanced behind and I twisted my mouth into a smile, showed my teeth to the boy who hid his face in his mother's jeans, pressing against her as if scared. That was rude. Nothing to be frightened of. Not yet.

The family jumped from the bus and I stepped down. As the bus left I turned away, walked the opposite direction from the family. In case someone was watching, noticing, would remember later. Not that that was a possibility but it didn't do to take chances. I strode to the corner, turned it, then made as if I had forgotten something. Searched pockets, glanced at phone, then turned and hurried back. The family were still in sight, further down the road but not too far. She had spent time unfolding the buggy, securing the baby, arranging her shopping. All the time in the world.

I walked behind, gazing into shop windows, keeping a distance between us. They left the main street and began to walk along a road lined with houses, smart semi-detached homes with neat square gardens. Some had extended, built ugly extra bedrooms that loomed above the house, changing the face, destroying the symmetry. There were some smaller houses stuffed by greedy builders into empty plots, a short terrace in red brick. It was just after this that the family stopped.

The mother scrabbled in her bag, retrieved her key. The boy had already skipped down the path, was standing by the door. The mother began to follow but I was already turning away. I would remember the house, could come back later, when it was dark. I would only do it if it was easy, if there was no risk. If she was foolish enough to leave the back door unlocked. No point in going to any effort, it wasn't as if they meant anything to me. There would be easier options if it didn't work out. But I thought it probably would. There was something casual about her, about the way she looked so relaxed, unfussy. I thought locking the back door would be low on her priorities until she went to bed herself. People were so complacent, assumed the world was made up of clones of themselves. Which was convenient, often worked to my advantage. As I walked back, towards the bus stop, I realised I was smiling.